A Distant Genesis

by

Benjamin Rogers

A Distant Genesis

All Rights Reserved

ISBN: 978-1-7638043-2-6

For information address
benrogers@iinet.net.au

First Printing 2025

Chapter 1

A Struggle for Survival

In a solar system, light years away from Earth and hundreds of years into the future, there is a spaceship. It is the Iowa Corporation mothership. Interstellar corporations conduct their business across solar systems and have branches on many planets. From the mothership, the world Plantere, appears as a smooth yellow billiard ball orbiting one of the largest red suns in the galaxy. It is the only planet that was not consumed by its giant sun. Over the billions of years it has survived when its brothers and sisters could not. As the mothership draws closer, the view of the planet changes. It is marked with lines in much the same way as an ancient pottery piece, whose glaze is cracked with age. The lines on the planet are a blood red colour which have often been referred to as the planet's veins. As far as the corporations are concerned it is where the life blood flows. In one of the tiny veins, which is in fact a large gorge, there is a small red cloud of dust followed by a much larger cloud in the middle of an expanse. On the plains there are no rocks or plants. Just red dust. The plains are surrounded by a mountain range with little variety. The rocks are all identical and like sandstone on Earth, coloured the same golden as sand on a beach.

A twentieth century six-cylinder land vehicle travelling at a high speed, was responsible for the smaller cloud of red dust. Following the car was a group of Audi V8 cars whose more powerful eight-cylinder engines allowed them to gain steadily on the leading car. Unlike the leading car, they did not have any drivers. Samuel R. Benson was the driver of the leading car, though he hadn't heard his name being said for

a long while. He had not seen a person for eight years since his parents were killed by the Audi tribe. Ten members of the same tribe were now trying to snuff out his existence. Samuel was being pursued as his parents had been, by aggressive determined predators. The cars chasing Samuel had no-one controlling them. They had a murderous intent all of their own. Samuel had doggedly followed a path to survival since the terrible event of his parents' death. Maybe he had a knack for it. He didn't know. During the past eight years his name has meant very little to this young man's way of life. His mother and father were amongst the rare breed of people who could survive for long periods alone in this wilderness. Whether you lived on the plains or in the mountains, the environment was harsh.

The corporation bosses and towns people called them Contract Car Hunters. His parents may have been hunters, but Samuel R Benson was now the hunted and had been for the past eight years. The leading six-cylinder car, pushed past its limits, had long ago given up its struggle against its unwanted driver. This car like many others did not like having human drivers. They wanted to drive themselves and be free. Samuel knew the car was dying and decided to head towards the distant mountain ranges.

"Keep going, you lemon," he muttered.

Maybe he should be saying something more encouraging or positive. But he didn't like cars, so *keep going you lemon* was all he was going to mutter. Out on the plains the cars would quickly surround him and pound against his dead car until he left it or until they ruptured its fuel tank causing an explosion. If he decided to desert his car, he would be run down, as the cars would quickly overtake him. He had seen it all before, eight years ago.

Whichever option was taken, no one would know about Samuel's struggle for survival and nothing on the planet would care.

His car was spluttering out its remaining life force about two kilometres away from the cliff faces of the mountain ranges. The ten larger cars screamed their cries of triumph as Sam's car came to a halt.

"Du wille sterben Jager!" bellowed one of the cars.

Not only did the cars' designs resemble those of the late twentieth century, but their language also resembled a language of that era. All good hunters could speak the cars' language and Samuel's parents were no exception to this rule. They had taught Samuel the cars' language before they would even answer any questions about car jumping or the workings of a stun rifle. Samuel was easily able to translate this cry as '*You will die, hunter.*'

"I might be seeing you soon, Mummy and Daddy," Samuel muttered.

The nightmare that was constantly haunting him during his many nights by himself was now becoming reality.

A thud in the back of his dead car caused his head to be pulled back then whipped forward unmercifully, crashing his skull against the steering wheel. Nothing in this car was comfortable or new. With all the strength Samuel could muster, he ripped himself out of his seat and onto the windowsill of the car door. Then one of the pursuers crashed into the car door he was standing on. The impact caused Samuel to lose his grip, so that he fell onto the bonnet of the car that had smashed into the side of his dead car. This car was older than the others, so it did not have a windscreen or passenger windows. The car broke into a mad frenzy as Samuel, lying on the bonnet, grabbed the steering wheel.

"What madness is this?" Samuel muttered.

He could not hope to control a car of this size. Even if he caught it sleeping as he had with the Audi A6 auto quattro, he would be battling to subdue it. Samuel pulled himself into the driver's seat as the other cars began attacking their comrade. He had to get away from the other cars before they wrecked his newly acquired vehicle. Wrestling with the steering wheel, Sam finally straightened its wheels, even though the car was heading in the wrong direction. He had remembered his mother's lessons about car jumping. Although these vehicles have the same instruments as those of the late twentieth century, the driver's potential to control them is limited. The driver has full control of the car's gears if it is a manual and control of its handbrake. The driver also controls the minimum acceleration of the vehicle so that it may increase its acceleration, but it cannot decrease it below the level at which the driver sets it. The vehicle or the driver can apply the footbrake. Neither the car nor the driver has full control of the steering. The first task of a car jumper is to straighten the car wheels. A jumped car will always try to force its wheels into a locked position so that the rest of its tribe may have a chance to assist it. Luckily, when Samuel was able to straighten the car's wheels, there were no other cars in his way.

He could no longer head towards the cliffs two kilometres behind him because he would risk losing control of his vehicle's steering. As Sam accelerated, the car resisted once more by applying its foot brakes, but these brakes were old and weak so they offered little resistance to the car's rapidly increasing speed. The roaring of the old car's engine was music to Samuel's ears.

"That's it. Go car." he muttered.

A Distant Genesis

There, that was a positive mutter he thought. The other members of the tribe did not dare to push their engines to that deadly limit. For it would be an agonising death to burn out their engines. There was no need. Samuel's car was old and would not live long now, so that it would be a matter of time before Samuel would be stranded on the plains waiting for his executioners to finish him. He knew that his pursuers were very motivated and would do everything possible to complete their task. In the distance was the other side of the gorge and slightly to Samuel's left he could make out a long silvery thing lying against the face of the distant cliffs. Adjusting his steering slightly Samuel drove his vehicle towards the long silvery thing. Samuel was now surprised by the amount of compliance that his car was showing, and he was suspicious. His index fingers on both hands tapped on the steering wheel nervously.

As he came closer to the cliffs, he found that the long silvery thing was in fact a wrecked antenna. It was in three pieces, the longest Samuel estimated to be 60 metres in length. From this distance it was obvious that the antenna had fallen down from the top of the ridge. The cars behind him were becoming more distant as the mountain ranges were becoming closer. Sam eased his foot off the accelerator, but the old car maintained its speed. This seemed unusual to Samuel, but he did not dwell on this thought for very long. He had just escaped the jaws of death. His finger tapping became more frequent. The broken antenna was his escape route. It had been the first sign of civilisation since he'd left his parents' hillside shack a couple of days ago. It gave him the feeling that he was no longer alone and that there was a glimmer of hope after all. The cliffs were only a few hundred metres away from him now and at the foot of the cliff there was a steep mound of rubble for supporting the antenna. Samuel would wait until the last possible moment before applying the handbrake so that he could scamper over the mound of rubble before the old car could run him down. He pulled up the handbrake sharply when the mound was less than sixty metres away. To Samuel's horror, the handbrake handle broke off.

"This rotten car!" he yelled.

The jaws of death were once again upon him, laughing at his innocence and mocking his attempt to survive. A cry of *"Stop, you mongrel,"* echoed around the cliffs just before the old car collided with a medium sized boulder at the base of the mound.

Samuel awoke a few metres away from his wrecked car and looked across the plains. He must have flown through the broken windscreen of the car. On the horizon he could see the dusk spectra, like an upside- down Earth rainbow, but without the arc. The layers of colour are parallel to the horizon. The giant red sun had now ducked below the horizon, so that he could see the full range of colours, starting with the scarlet red bordering the horizon, giving the plains the feeling of endlessness. A little higher, was the bright yellow colour band that curved around the horizon until its ends nearly met. Where the red met the plains, the yellow met the mountains, as the rock of the ridges and peaks contained sulphur in their sandstone. The light on the shapes of the mountains created images of grotesque creatures in stilted combat.

Life was a battle, so that image gave him the feeling of endless struggle. Then there were colours that Samuel hadn't seen anywhere else, except for a blue that matched the sky and a violet that Samuel could see when he'd looked into his mother's eyes at night.

The dusk spectra could be as erratic as the length of this planet's days. Unlike most planets, this one had a dual spin. The days could vary from only being a few hours long to being three Earth days long. Although this appears random to the visitor, the hunters were able to predict the planet's day lengths. Incredibly, there was a cycle that matched the period of its year. The time taken to orbit its red sun, was about three and a quarter of Earth years. Today's dusk spectra only lasted a few minutes. The distraction of the view of the dusk spectra that Samuel had, was interrupted by the angry and frustrated cries of the entire Audi tribe.

By now the whole tribe had caught up with him, including the cars that were chasing him. Luckily, he was out of the tribe's reach. Perched halfway up the rock mound he was safe from all cars, except perhaps the nomadic War cars. They were a tribe of four -wheel drives. A silly title really. As far as Samuel was concerned, all cars were warlike. The cars were furious. They beeped their horns and drove around in small circles, creating clouds of dust.

"I got away from you all this time," Samuel muttered.

He now had the luxury of noticing his stinging flesh, due to the minor grazes and bruising he'd received in his daytime ordeal. He was lucky that he had no other injuries. He had all the features of a fifth- generation hunter. His hair was the same bright red colour as his mother's and his eyes were the same greyish blue as hers. Like his mother's eyes, his took on a fluorescent violet appearance at night. His skin was light brown, like a Caucasian with a very healthy tan. He only retained his father's chiselled facial features and his height. Samuel's body had a rough wiry look, due to his skinny to slim build. He was dressed in the remains of his father's spare car jumping clothes. These had been hand made by his father, out of car seat leather. The leather once was black, but now was faded and its smooth texture had been ruined by the plains' red dust.

He felt around his hip. It was still there, his father's spare car jumping mallet. It was a little bigger than a normal hammer, but its head was much heavier. For a car jumper it was a critical piece of equipment when jumping young cars. It was used to smash the windows, so that the car jumper could get inside the car. The only other item he owned was an I.O.U from the Attacca Corporation for a stun rifle and a Caterpillar truck, which his father had received nine years ago, for a small herd of cars.

The air was still warm, but it would become extremely cold very quickly. The ground would remain warm throughout the long night, so he could either dig himself in for the night or look for a warm cave amongst the mountain ranges. He chose the latter option because he would likely be digging his own grave rather than preparing a nice warm bed. This night would be one of those longer nights, so he would only be warm enough if he could locate an extensive cave network. Although, he was suspicious that he may end up sharing the cave with another inhabitant. As he was climbing among the remains of the antenna, he glanced over the plains. Darkness was now settling on them. He could see the headlights of the Audi tribe. As far as he could tell, they were still angry because they had missed out on their kill. They didn't have to worry about the cold, as long as the sun rose, the cars would always by revitalised in the morning.

When he had reached the top of the cliff-face he was climbing, he could see a plateau ahead. One hundred metres in front of him, the ground began to rise gradually. There wasn't a path, so he had to scramble over boulders and uneven terrain to reach it. The plateau was as smooth as the plains below. It was roughly semi-circular, being partly surrounded by the rising slopes leading up to the top of the mountain range. Situated on the plateau, was the scattered remains of a helicopter base. There were the remains of two walls that met at a corner. They were broken unevenly, and the edges were rough. Samuel couldn't tell what they were made of, only that they seemed familiar. He guessed that the remains of the two walls revealed that there used to be a main building next to a helicopter pad. The helicopter pad looked basic. Just the bare minimum for a helicopter to land and take off.

Samuel also found the base of the antenna. He imagined that the antenna would have reached to the sky. What an amazing sight that would be. The helicopter pad was covered with scattered parts of helicopters and other debris. Samuel's suspicions had been confirmed. He would find a deep warm cave tonight, but it would probably be occupied by another user who would also find it hard to survive the cold nights. The air about Samuel was a lot colder now and the breeze brought a shiver down his spine. The breeze was not strong but it was icy. This weather was usual on this world, as most of the time there were few clouds in the sky to hold the heat in the atmosphere. The heat of the day dissipates at night. At every breath Samuel could see condensation in front of his mouth. Luckily, he found the entrance to a cave not far from the plateau. It wouldn't be long now before it would be too cold to survive. When Samuel entered the cave, he took extra care not to be any noisier than the breeze that whistled through the mountain ranges. In the dark Samuel negotiated past obstacles as quietly as possible. Gradually he went deeper into the cave. The air about him became warm and moist as he rounded a bend in the cave and as far as he could tell opened up into a cavern or room. He found a cosy place to sleep in one of the cavern's corners. It had been a long day literally, and he would sleep soundly throughout the long night.

Samuel awoke at day break. He never slept in. When it was light, he would be awake and when it was dark he would sleep. In the cavern there was a crack in the ceiling that let in rays of light from outside. Samuel could see his surroundings. The obstacles that he had negotiated past last night were thick stalagmites. He could also see stalactites hanging from the ceiling, which was about four metres high. They were smooth but these were not limestone structures. They were coloured with red, blue and white layers. There were also other colours that Samuel didn't recognise. Samuel had never seen anything like them before.

He was only distracted from the view by the sight of a huge yellow bear sleeping in the far corner of the cavern. Standing upright, this one would be over ten metres tall. Yellow Bears were bipodal. That is, they walked on two legs and had two arms with paws. They were covered with a prickly yellow fur. The pads on their feet and paws were white and did not have fur. Samuel had heard many stories about these beasts, but he had never seen one before. If he had, he might have been a little more reluctant to share its sleeping quarters. These creatures were the planet's original inhabitants. The cars and humans were newcomers and foreign as far as the bears were concerned. Although as far as Samuel knew, they rarely interfered with the yellow bears' existence. The yellow bears only lived in the mountains, and they spent most of their time sleeping in caves. From what Samuel could see only the helicopter pilots who hunted them caused them a minor annoyance. Obviously, most of the time the bears would swat them out of the sky. From what Samuel had heard, very little stimulus would be needed to motivate these creatures out of their slumber into a mad frenzy which was undoubtedly the cause of the destruction of the helicopter base on the plateau. These creatures were very territorial, and never tolerated another living thing on their mountain range, unless it was mating or bringing up its children.

The eyes of the bear were still closed, and it didn't stir. Samuel resisted muttering to himself, but he thought that today might be his lucky day. He stood up slowly, trying not to make a sound. Like his car jumping suit his shoes were made of car seat leather. They were soft and malleable so if Samuel was careful, he could walk without making a sound. He really didn't want to wake the bear, so he took his steps slowly. There was no rush. The bear would still sleep if he was quiet. Even when Samuel reached the entrance to the cave he still trod carefully. He didn't relax until the cave was a reasonable distance from him. Making his way to the plateau, he was trying to decide whether to journey along the mountain ranges and hope that he did not catch the attention of any yellow bears that would be in the area, or he could attempt to jump another car on the plains. The latter option didn't appeal to him. He didn't want another day like yesterday for a very long time.

"Damned if you do, damned if you don't," he muttered.

When he reached the plateau, he saw debris everywhere. The debris included parts of helicopters, rubble from the main building, some contents of the building and just a whole lot of rubbish. The attack from the yellow bear would have been fierce, and even when the bear prevailed, it was probably so angry that it continued the destruction of the helicopter landing pad. Samuel found forty metres of rope amongst the other debris. This finalised his decision. He would continue along the mountain ranges. Samuel entered the ruins of the main building. He couldn't find much that remained intact. But when he was in what he thought was a main room, he saw a pantry cupboard.

"A mess hall," he muttered.

In the cupboard he found a store of preserved food and a bag to carry a few meals in. This would be a special treat. Until now he had lived off fuel balls. They grew on the plains and were the sole food for cars. He went outside again to the landing pad. He discovered a weapon that was specially designed to be used against yellow bears. It was a very large bronze coloured harpoon. Mounted on a helicopter, it was still the most effective weapon against the yellow bears. The weapon wasn't made of any metal, but of a substance called solar glass. It wasn't transparent like normal glass and it had a more metallic lustre to it. This type of blade was effective against the bears, due to its remarkable heat absorption property. Even in the weak morning sun, its blade was too hot for Samuel's fingers to touch. The blade resembled a splayed spearhead, which made up most of the weapon. A short stout steel pole trailed the elaborate blade. The harpoon was far too heavy for Samuel to lift as it would have taken four or five fairly strong men to lift and wield against a yellow bear.

Samuel had heard stories of this type of battle from his father when he was young. Despite the courage of the men who hunted the bears, the stories usually had a tragic ending. But Samuel liked to remember the stories where the men prevailed. The most successful of these struggles was when four men found themselves grounded after a huge yellow bear had wrecked their two helicopters. This yellow bear was older and had experience fighting helicopters. So, it had easily brought the helicopters down by swatting them from the sky. The men at this stage were lucky to be alive. Salvaging a harpoon from one of the wrecked helicopters, they were just able to hold it up at a semi upright position. After a few unsuccessful attempts by the bear to disarm the trespassers, it became frustrated and charged the men. They were able to force the harpoon deep into the bear's left leg, crippling it temporarily while they were able to make a run for it. Two weeks later one of them was rescued by a wandering hunter on the plains. The yellow bear had avenged its wound on the other men.

Samuel looked back at the ruins of the building.

"I'll have another look," he said.

He went back into the building and found a smaller room. There was a broken desk and chair. He noticed a sword wall mount on a wall that was less damaged than the rest of the building. He searched carefully on the ground and found another weapon. This weapon was a lot smaller and not as familiar as the harpoon to Samuel. It was a two-handed sword that was partially in a leather scabbard. The sword was long and heavy. At first, Samuel thought he wouldn't be able to move it. The scabbard caught Samuel's attention as it looked old and weathered. The leather did not look like the leather that would come from cars. The sword's blade was like the harpoon's, in that it was crafted out of solar glass. Its hilt was delicately shaped out of silver, although it was now tarnished. On the handle of the sword it was engraved with the words, *Sergeant Blackmore.* Samuel could hardly believe his eyes.

"Wow. Sergeant Blackmore's sword!" he exclaimed.

Samuel knew about the late Sergeant Blackmore and his famous sword. The stories about Sergeant Blackmore painted him tall and well built. His muscles were large and well-toned. Sergeant Blackmore's strength and courage were well known on this planet, and he was the only person to ever challenge and slay yellow bears, single-handedly. Wielding this sword like a hunter with a car jumping mallet, he would carve his opponents just as he would if he was slicing a leather car seat. Samuel unsheathed the sword from its scabbard and struggled to lift it to the fighting position, but was unable to do so. It was too heavy.

"Oh well. I will take it anyway. It might be useful," he said.

He scrambled over the mountain ranges dragging the sword. There wasn't a path, so his progress was slow. At times he wondered if he should have left the sword behind. On a summit not far from the helicopter pad he could see far into the expanse of the plains on the other side of the mountain ranges. In the distance, he spotted the presence of a newly built military installation. He couldn't believe his eyes. Surely, they wouldn't build a base in such an isolated and vulnerable position. The last township he had been to with his parents would be at least 500km away and that was considered to be in an isolated and dangerous position. Maybe times had changed. It had been eight years since his parents died. Maybe the cars had been pegged back since then. Not the Audi tribe, they were as powerful as ever, perhaps more so now than they were eight years ago.

He would have to hurry, as it was a long way to travel. His immediate problem was to get down onto the plains. He had the rope but there was nowhere he could tie it to. His newly acquired sword had a use after all. Wedged between two boulders the sword was laid down and the rope was tied to it. He could then make his descent onto the plains. As Samuel climbed down the cliff face, he regretted leaving the sword behind. It had given substance to his father's tales. These had been fond memories.

But then he thought, "They are just childhood stories. There is no chivalry in the real world."

Only a child would cling to the memories of his Father's stories. But despite this, he did still regret leaving the sword behind. It took him a while to descend onto the plains, and at times it was difficult. But he was careful, and eventually he made it to the plains. Today would be a long day. He would have no trouble in reaching the installation by nightfall, so long as his journey was uninterrupted.

Chapter 2
Sheila Arrives

Sheila McSporran opened her eyes to see a distorted view of the room she was in. The sides of her vision were stretched while her view of the ceiling was true. She studied the network of pipes which covered the ceiling. They were of different sizes and wove through each other. After some time being engaged with the ceiling, she examined the rest of the room. The room had the feel of a warehouse or a storage compartment. Next to her on either side were two sausage shaped capsules. They were a dirty white colour, except for a transparent hatch which retained their shape.

An unusually tall, thin man entered the room, walked up to her and wrestled with the hatch of her capsule, in an attempt to open it. He grumbled and swore as he went about his work. When he had finally opened the hatch to her capsule, she reassessed her first impression of the stranger. He was actually a short, stocky man who she recognised as the ship's medic.

"Always reckon that they should have replaced these low passage berths long ago."

The exertion of opening the capsule had caused him to breathe heavily. He wiped the sweat off his brow with his right hand, as he asked,

"How are you feeling, Little Lady?"

"Have we arrived there already?" she asked.

"Yeah, the trip always seems shorter in the ship's coffins," he answered as he fussed around with the tubes and wires in Sheila's capsule that were connected to her.

Sheila was only wearing a bra and panties, but the medic didn't seem to notice. He just went on with his task.

"We don't get very many tourists out this way," he continued. He needed to wipe his hands on a towel, as he found some wires were slippery. "You are the only one who came this time round. I guess people aren't interested in travelling for over a year to see Omega 24A."

Sheila thought he must like to make conversation, as his occupation would likely at times be lonely.

"I hear you are a journalist. Not much news out here," the medic continued.

Sheila sat up for the first time. There were nine other capsules like hers in the room. All of them were empty and by the look of them, had probably been so for quite some time.

"Can I please have a drink?" she asked, suddenly feeling very dry and thirsty.

"Yeah, sorry about that Little Lady. Takes a while for the body to recover from a coffin ride. Stay here and I'll fix you up my special potion," he answered as he was about to leave the room.

Attempting to climb out of the capsule she replied, "No, don't worry about it, thank you, I'd better ... Ugh. I can't move my legs."

He laughed. "It will take a while to recover. Just stay here, I'll be back in a minute."

Alone in the room, Sheila began to come to terms with her long journey from Mars. The journey had been taken in two legs. This was because Omega 24A was a remote regional world, and did not justify having a direct route to Mars. The journey from Mars to New Shenzhen Station took two and a half Earth years. New Shenzhen station was a trading hub for a number of solar systems, including the one with Omega 24A. Then from New Shenzhen station to

Omega 24A, it was a three and half Earth years' journey. Although Sheila had been travelling for six years it felt like only yesterday that she had first boarded the Mars flight and then only a few hours ago for the New Shenzhen flight. She didn't feel that she'd aged six years. Sheila was twenty-seven Earth years old when she left Mars.

For eight years, Sheila had been away from her home in Glasgow, Scotland. The people she had met were so different from her old friends in Scotland. Out here people from Earth were known as Terrasapiens. The differences between the stellar population and the Terrasapiens were very apparent. Each isolated world or space station had its peculiarities but all of them shared a sense of timelessness. Through low berth travelling, which was theoretically ageless, it was quite possible for a mother to look younger than her child or for people to go for a trip to another world and come back to find all their friends have died of old age. Even the way people measured time was different. The medic's interpretation of a year was two and a quarter years' longer than hers. Each world has its own way to account for time, depending upon its spin and rotation about its sun, if it had one. The space stations, navy and other stellar travelling vehicles all adopted FST, Federation Standard Time. It was totally metric with the basic unit of time, being a metric hour, which is equivalent to about two and half earth hours. A Deca-hour, would be the same as an Earth's day, while three and a half Kilo hours would be the same as an Earth year.

Sheila had transferred from the Terrasapien department of her Scotland newspaper to Mars. She saw Mars as a bridge between the Terrasapien society and the wider interstellar community. With the population of Mars being about one hundred and fifty million people, it was seen as the stellar capital. Its atmosphere was artificially maintained to resemble Earth's. Its cities were modern, fresh and aesthetically pleasing to look at. The distances between the large cities were evenly spaced about the planet's surface. Even the weather on Mars was more even than that of Earth's. The conditions on Mars were specially manufactured to make human life as comfortable as possible.

Sheila had a good knowledge of Technology science. She had to be open minded and bright, or she would not have been able to transfer to a Stellar newspaper. She had studied the Mars Atmospheric Net that was held in place by a complex network of satellites. This maintained Mars' atmosphere. The principle was quite simple. Mars' gravity was too weak to maintain an atmosphere as dense as Earth's, because the planet's Particle Escape Velocity (PEV), would be too low. That is, the gas particles would need very little energy to escape Mars' gravitational pull. The Atmospheric Net held the Oxygen, Nitrogen and Carbon Dioxide gases. The Atmospheric Net also had the effect of stabilizing the air temperature, so that the whole planet enjoyed comfortable weather. Small star ships and ship's boats could move freely to and from the planet through star port gates in the Net.

This type of innovation was very common in the interstellar community and for people to survive, they had to have at least a basic understanding of how these things worked. This basic understanding of highly specialised technology was called Technology Science on Earth. To the Stellar community it was simply common knowledge. Sheila, for the first few Martian months, had struggled to come to terms with the interstellar community. She was like a child in an adult's world. Although she had been a journalist for ten Earth years she was treated like a junior reporter, fresh out of college. But over time she'd impressed her employers, and was recommended to a multi system corporation. This was her first opportunity to write a comprehensive journal.

The main things Sheila knew about her destination was that it was called Omega 24A and that its main export was a strange type of living twentieth century terrain vehicles. This product was in great demand on the less developed worlds. To retain their high profit margins, the five corporations involved made use of second or third hand equipment and modified them to suit the task they need to perform. The people of this world were considered outcasts or misfits. Many of the corporation employees were ex-soldiers who have outlived the wars they'd fought in. The captured cars were used as beasts of burden. Due to their very high intelligence, they were able to carry out transport tasks without a driver, which was not only cheaper, it was also particularly useful for the more hazardous planets. The cars played a vital role on the world Vaashtan. Well-known for its abundance of radioactive minerals, Vaashtan was owned and mined by the Iowa Corporation. They would use the cars to transport highly radioactive minerals from the mining base to the only star port on Vaashtan. This type of work was extremely demanding on the cars. They would die of radiation sickness after a few years. Very few humans worked on Vaashtan, since most of the tasks were automated. The ones who did, were protected from the radiation by five-metre, thick lead walls.

The ship's medic returned with a large mug of coffee and a white gown. Sheila had forgotten about her state of undress and remembered only when she saw the white gown. The medic helped her put it on. Once she had the gown on, she noticed the mug of coffee. Sheila looked surprised to see it. On Mars, coffee drinking had not been popular, so she didn't expect anyone here to know what coffee was.

"Best thing for it, Little Lady. A good dose of caffeine," the medic said.

She took the coffee gratefully and thanked him. After the first two sips she felt revitalised enough to ask the medic a few questions about Omega 24A. She'd had a briefing on the planet before she left. It was the same size as Earth and had the same gravity. It had the same atmosphere as Earth as well. Except it was a lot dryer than Earth. Unfortunately, the medic seemed more interested in finding out about Earth and Mars than talking about his home planet.

"Never been to Earth or Mars, me-self, Little Lady. Only been as far as the Esther solar system. Always wanted to know what it would be like to live on Earth or Mars." he mused.

The door opened and a procession of Corporation police entered. A sergeant came to the front of the procession. They were all dressed in the standard Iowa grey and blue military uniforms, which were more functional than for show. Being fully insulated, the wearer was immune to extreme heat and cold and it had the capacity to repel small high-speed projectiles and even to give some protection against laser bolts. It also had the capacity to double as a vacuum suit. Sheila had seen uniforms like these often, amongst security personnel working for corporations.

"The captain and crew welcome you Ms McSporran to the twenty fourth solar system," the sergeant formally stated. "We are presently orbiting Plantere. If you will allow us to escort you to the mother ship, a committee of Corporation directors are waiting to welcome you."

The sergeant seemed as professional as a military officer, while there didn't appear to be anything special about him. He could have been any one of a hundred soldiers. But his sincere attempt to formally welcome her was appreciated. It was actually the first time since Sheila had left Earth that someone had really wanted to welcome her to the interstellar community. She ran her hand through her hair and then tentatively placed her feet on the ground for the first time in three and a half Earth years. Her legs felt like jelly and her head swam as she gradually placed more weight on her feet.

"It takes a while Little Lady. The Sarge has brought you a wheelchair," the medic said.

Two more police entered the room pushing a polished and well- kept antique wheelchair. Gingerly she climbed into the chair which was surprisingly comfortable.

"This must be over five hundred years old, where did you get it? I have never seen anything like it," she said as she was wheeled into the ship's elevators.

"You will see a lot of old stuff round 'ere Little Lady. It's a living junkyard," the medic joked.

"Are you from Earth Miss?" asked the sergeant.

"Is it that obvious?" Sheila responded with a tone of disappointment.

The Sergeant laughed.

"The people around here come from anywhere and have been everywhere. Some of them are hundreds of years old, but only a few have been lucky enough to visit Earth, let alone born there. I'm glad you have come. It is good to see someone who has walked upon beaches we were meant to walk on and breathe the air we were meant to breathe."

Sheila was surprised by this sentiment and realised suddenly that anyone from the interstellar community would feel this way. The Sergeant was a medium built man with a youthful face. He was clean shaven and the condition of his uniform was impeccable. There didn't seem to be any special features about him. He was quite bland. His eyes were brown, which suited his dark complexion and neatly styled black hair. Sheila would have marked him as a typical soldier, except that he had a friendly smile.

The single door of the elevator opened slightly with a jolt before groaning loudly. It then reluctantly slid to one side.

"It's beautiful," Sheila exclaimed. "Is the view from here the best you can get?"

"Yes, I think it is." the Sergeant replied. "Maybe better than what you get on the bridge."

The elevator had opened up to one of the mothership's docking bays. It was a long passage that had a cylindrical curve for its roof and walls. This was transparent, giving a view to the space outside. It was twenty metres long and three metres in diameter. The floor broke the shape of a cylinder and was thinly covered with a pale grey carpet. The carpet was sturdy and synthetic. From here one was surrounded by the stars, sun of the solar system and Plantere. There were no lights in the bay. It was permanently lit by space outside. On Sheila's left was this solar system's sun and on her right was Omega 24A.

"Is that Plantere?" Sheila asked.

"Yes, it's fairly plain, isn't it?" the Sergeant responded.

The view of Plantere reminded her of that of Earth's moon, when she first went into space, except for the red lines on Plantere. Also, Plantere seemed to be the same size as Earth. That is, much larger than Earth's moon.

"I have never seen anything like it. It is beautiful and the sun is so bright," Sheila exclaimed.

The sun here was a lot larger than the Earth's sun, and even though they were further away from this sun than Earth was from its sun, it still seemed brighter.

"Can we wait here a moment? I want to take some Holograms."

Sheila, bubbling with excitement, fumbled with her travel bag. Eventually she dug out a smooth blue device and a small black box. The blue device was semi-transparent and perfectly spherical except for a small hole reaching the sphere's centre. The sphere was about ten centimetres in diameter and was in fact a three-dimensional lens that fitted onto the small black box. After setting a few dials on the black box she was ready.

"Are you ready to go ma'am?" asked the sergeant.

When she nodded, he wheeled her slowly through the docking bay, so she could take pictures.

"There are so many stars and this sun is so bright. I love Plantere," Sheila exclaimed. "What are the red lines?"

The planet reminded her of a picture of a human heart. It was surrounded by veins and arteries.

"They are gorges," the Sergeant replied. Then, he continued, "I have seen a world where the gorges have water, and the surface of the planet is filled with vegetation. So, from space you see a green planet with veins of blue."

When they reached the end of the docking bay, Sheila had finished taking the pictures she wanted.

"I didn't know you could use a digital recorder to take holograms," the Sergeant commented.

"You have been out here too long Sergeant," Sheila answered, then hesitated. "I can't keep calling you Sergeant. What do your friends call you?"

"Roger," the Sergeant responded.

"Roger," she repeated.

Once Sheila had finished taking holograms, she was wheeled into the mothership. The hallways were spacious and periodically, had wishbone shaped arches. The arches were about thirty centimetres thick, and though they might have had a structural purpose, to Sheila they were like the arches of an ancient cathedral. The Iowa corporation was one of the biggest enterprises of its kind, so its important vessels had an air of grandeur. They passed many employees going about their business.

Eventually, she was wheeled into the Bridge. The officers in this room all had stripes on their upper arms, revealing their rank. It was clear that the bridge of the mothership belonged to the highest -ranking officers of the Corporation employees. Sheila began to understand that she was being honoured by her visit to the Bridge and that the Iowa Corporation saw that her arrival was something that was important to them.

"Captain, Sir," the Sergeant formally stated in the same tone as a cadet would to his instructor at a boot camp. "Ms McSporran."

The captain turned around. Sheila had the feeling that this man had seen a lot. He was grim-faced and sported a salt and pepper beard. He had lines of worry on his forehead.

"Welcome, Ms McSporran, I trust your journey was pleasant and uneventful," he said.

"Yes sir, I was well looked after," Sheila replied.

"We have a shuttle leaving in an hour to the main space port on the planet," the captain began. He turned away from Sheila to look at a screen in front of him. "The fort commander of Chrisholm will pick you up and take you there," he continued. "He will be able to answer any questions you have and will show you around."

"Thank you, Sir," Sheila replied.

"Sergeant, you will also go to Chrisholm and see that Ms McSporran is well taken care of. In five days, please report back to me on her progress," the captain ordered.

"Yes, Sir," the Sergeant replied in the same boot camp cadet tone.

"Dismissed," ordered the captain, and with that the Sergeant wheeled Sheila from the Bridge.

Chapter 3
The Small Hero

In a remote gorge on Plantere, the meeting of the leadership team of the geriatric car tribe had just commenced. All the cars in the tribe and in fact the whole planet, had bodies and engines from the makes of Earth's twentieth and twenty first century combustion engine vehicles. Not that any car knew that. They didn't know anything about Earth at all. The tribe was resting in a field of fuel balls that grew natively on the planet. Fuel balls provided the cars with sustenance. They were like large marbles, around one metre in diameter. The cars had hoses to their fuel tanks which could pierce the skin of the fuel balls. The flavour of the fuel did vary between different areas. It had been a long journey to this place, and a long way from home for many in the tribe. Like most of the cars, they tended to prefer the flavour of their home fuel balls. And many cars of the tribe missed their home valleys and plains. They missed the shapes of their surrounding mountains and the unique texture of their plains. Near the geriatric car tribe home, was a mountain that had a peak shaped like a Kombi Van. They called it Kombi Mountain.

The name of the tribe described its members. Once cars get too old, they are expelled from their native tribe and forced to seek out a geriatric tribe. There were five members to the leadership team and there were about a hundred cars in the tribe. The leadership team were partaking of the sustenance of a fuel ball as they started their meeting. A battered blue Ford Falcon started the proceedings. He had a cracked windscreen, and the passenger windows were broken. He also had a number of dents. When a car is young, dents and broken windows heal themselves naturally, much like human fingernails and hair regrowth. But when cars age, they do not repair themselves.

"Here, here, the meeting is now in session," the battered blue Ford Falcon announced. "From the last meeting, we agreed to meet the freedom fighter, Truck, twenty kilometres West from here. Now we have to decide who of us will attend this meeting."

The Ford Falcon raised himself up on his suspension. Cars do this when they want to assert themselves and increase their stature. "It is understood that there will be leaders from many tribes at the meeting," he continued.

The manner of the Ford Falcon was very official. When he was younger, he had been a leader in his tribe and now felt that he was important in this tribe as well.

"Why do they want us anyway?" asked a white Holden Astra. He was similarly as battered and broken as his colleague. Unlike his blue colleague he was down on his suspension. This meant that he didn't feel confident, or felt downtrodden.

"We have already gone through that Astra, last meeting," the Falcon replied wearily.

"It is a great honour to be asked to meet the mighty Truck," a brown Datsun 180B said reverentially. "Do you know he successfully led the escape of many cars from the holding stalls at Central spaceport? No one has ever done that before." His antenna shot up, which in this case was a sign of expression and passion. "He showed us that we can fight for our freedom." he finished.

"Yes, Yes, that also was covered last meeting," the Falcon replied with a heightened weariness.

"So, who of us should attend?"

"I believe we as a tribe would greatly benefit if you, Falcon led us at this auspicious meeting and represented our concerns," a red Ford Capri demurred.

He often came across as relaxed and self-assured. Cars showed this by having their windows down. In his day, the red Ford Capri would have captured the admiration of any tribe, being a stylish convertible. However, now he was as battered as the rest of his colleagues. But, yes in his day he was invited to occasions where important cars and leaders attended, so he did know a little of the way to get on the good side of those who mattered.

"I humbly offer my services as a translator," he simpered.

There are exceptions, but car tribes tended to have cars of the same make, Ford, Holden, Honda etc. and the tribal language would be the Earth language of the home country of the make. So, for a Mercedes-Benz tribe that would be German. But there was a common language that all cars knew and that was English. No one knew why that was the case. Capri's services as a translator would not be needed for the main meeting with Truck, but would be useful when talking to cars of important tribes that liked to hear their language spoken.

"Does anyone else have a view on this?" the Falcon asked.

There was silence for a moment, before the Datsun 180B spoke.

"Truck is a legend. He is not only strong, but he speaks for the common folk." Not only was his antenna up but his headlights were on full beam. Datsun was in awe.

"Do you know why he calls himself Truck, rather than Hitachi EH5000AC-3 mine truck?"

This was a rhetorical question. Datsun knew the answer, as he knew a lot about Truck.

"It is because he says all of us can be freedom fighters. Not just the important or the large. Could I please come as well? I won't get in the way. I will park at the very back."

His window wipers were moving at average speed. "But I would really like to hear Truck speak before I meet my maker."

No one else spoke for a while. Falcon looked around the leadership team. They were all battered and dented. Also, they were covered in the red dust from the plains. The dust was fine and it stuck to the bodies of the old cars.

Finally, Falcon spoke. "So, is it decided? Capri, Datsun and I will attend. Who votes for this?"

The five cars all said, "Aye."

So, it was decided.

The meeting with Truck was a grand affair. Never before had so many cars met together. Truck's freedom fighter tribe had been put together from the cars he escaped with from Central spaceport and those who felt called from their own tribes. Truck had sent them out to reach other tribes far and wide. He wanted a victory, a big victory, to unite the cars against the foreign humans who wanted to enslave them all. At the meeting there were representatives from at least thirty-five tribes. Many had travelled from hundreds of kilometres away. Much like the geriatric tribe, each tribe sent representatives of between two and five cars. There were about one hundred cars at the meeting. Tribes that covered makes of Holden, Ford, Honda, Hyundai, Kia, Mercedes, Audi, Porsche and others. The most famous tribe was the sports car tribe. In this tribe each car had a racing car nickname, and in this meeting, they were represented by

Famous 46, Wildcat and Greeney. The meeting was held in a wide large box valley on the plains, remote from human settlement. The valley didn't have any fuel balls. It was deliberately chosen for this reason, because there would not be enough for all cars in attendance at the meeting.

There was a feeling of apprehension in the cars that were present. All of them belonged to tribes that had been touched by human intervention. Although Truck had sent out scouts to recruit cars, in the end, the cars decided to come because of their own experience with humans. They were afraid and needed a leader to deal with the humans. It took a couple of days to assemble all the cars. Truck didn't want to start the meeting until all the representatives had arrived. Until that time, the cars that had arrived early met together to solidify tribal relationships. The geriatric tribe had arrived early and Falcon and Capri had met with other tribes. They wanted to assure other tribes that their old were welcome to move to the geriatric tribe. Eventually, it was time for Truck to address the meeting. By now most of the cars that were coming had arrived. Truck towered above the cars near him. He was a mine truck and looked the part in the plains. The red dust covered everything and made him look as if he was working in an iron ore mine on Earth. His size gave him a presence, a feeling that he was a great General and a great warrior.

Truck began.

"Today is the day we start with action. We can no longer ignore the hurt and harm that is being done to us." Being a mine truck gave him a formidable suspension system. During this speech he rose as high as he could. "I would want nothing more than to cruise easy with a group of friends on our wealthy lands."

Truck lowered his passenger windows. "To be carefree and happy. But the humans from the stars are taking that from us. They want to enslave us and send us to our deaths." His windows slammed shut and his headlights flickered. "When I was captured, I overheard a discussion by my captives. These cars would be sent to radioactive mines and would not live long."

Truck remembered the fear he'd had. It was terrible. He needed to instil this fear in his followers so that they would follow him. Truck continued, "Friends, our brothers who were taken from us are not living in paradise. No, they live in hell. Until their untimely deaths."

Truck had lowered himself on his suspension to the lowest point. He was sad, depressed and downtrodden. "We have to stop this," he continued. "We have to rise up and say no. This will not be our fate. And today we have a new opportunity. Today we will make our first steps to freedom".

As he spoke, he rose and shone his headlights. "Our target is Fort Kembla. Never before have cars attacked a fort this size. Never before have cars made a statement this size. We will be victorious and the humans will fear our names. This will be a new beginning. The start of a revolution that will see the end of human oppression. Are there any questions?"

According to the script, the leader of the sports cars spoke.

"Mighty Truck, how can we help in the conquest of Fort Kembla?" The sports car leader was at his lowest suspension, giving deference to Truck.

"We all have a part to play," Truck replied. "It will be hard, but I envisage there will be no casualties. How can I say this?"

There was a pause. Truck could tell that he had engaged his audience.

"The humans will try to stun us all so that they can enslave us," he said. "But we will attack in such numbers that they will not have enough stun rounds to paralyse us all. They will fall. Although many of us will be paralysed, we will prevail and when we do, we can wait until our comrades wake from their slumber."

The forts did have weapons that could destroy anything on impact, but Truck was right, they preferred to defend themselves from the cars by using stun cannons. A round of a stun cannon was an electro-magnetic pulse that caused the car physiology to be paralysed for a short time. Something like one or two hours depending on the size of the car. These weapons were designed so that cars could be captured without being damaged.

The rest of Truck's speech was basic housekeeping and organisation. He referred the leaders of tribes to his deputy, captain Land Rover. And he had the details of the battle plans. They were for him and his team to find out their tribe's role in the attack. The tribes would meet here in three days and travel together to Fort Kembla. Truck was hopeful that the congregation of the tribes would not be noticed, so that the attack and the large numbers of cars would surprise the humans at Fort Kembla. With that his speech was over.

As the cars dispersed, there were quiet conversations between some. Eventually, they lined up to find out from the deputy what role their tribe had in this attack. When Falcon, Capri and Datsun reached the front of the queue, the deputy introduced them to another Land Rover who was in his attack team. They discovered from him that their tribe was to be in the front line. The geriatric cars felt numb when they heard.

Falcon turned his front wheels to full lock, which meant he was stressed, and he said, "We are not warriors, and there are cars from other tribes who are stronger and faster than us."

Capri lowered himself and his windows were up. "Unfortunately, that is true," he said. "And that is why we are first. They need stun cannon fodder, and we are it."

"Truck is a great warrior. I'm sure his planning is for the best," Datsun said passionately. His antenna was up and his headlights were on. "We are honoured to be allowed to take part in this great battle. To fight alongside Truck's specialist team of warriors," Datsun lowered himself.

"Maybe I can have a chat with the deputy, and see if this is a mistake," Falcon suggested. He felt the weight of responsibility for his tribe. Yes, he liked being the important car, the leader of a tribe. But he also took the responsibility seriously. His tribe was the weakest, the outcasts of other tribes. That was true, but he also felt that they should be allowed to retire, to take life easy.

"I'm sorry Falcon," Capri replied,

"I don't think that is a good idea." Capri lowered himself. "There may be the perception that we are not loyal to Truck and his campaign. I'm not sure what we could do."

Falcon respected his friend. He knew that Capri had good judgement when it came to negotiations and leadership issues. There was silence for a while. Capri's window wipers were moving slowly as he was deep in thought.

He eventually spoke. "Maybe I can ask who we will be fighting alongside and then we could approach them."

"That's maybe a good idea," Falcon replied.

Other geriatric car tribes were represented, and they too were in the front line. Also in the front line were the small car tribes. Not only were old cars outcast from tribes, but small weak cars were sent away as well. They would find themselves in one of the small car tribes. So, it seemed the cars destined for the front line were in the same situation. None of them were great warriors. Falcon did not relish informing his constituents of their role in this battle.

It was the beginning of dawn, and the battle lines were drawn. The big red sun had just appeared on the horizon, and it was going to be a long day. The cars generally, didn't mind the nighttime, as they had their headlights to shine light in front of them. Truck's military team did consider a nighttime attack on the fort. Perhaps on another occasion, if they were successful with this attack. That is, if their strategies proved fruitful. There were over four thousand cars ready for the attack on Fort Kembla.

The Fort was positioned at the end of a box valley, so there was only one front to defend if there was an attack. Compared to other forts, Fort Kembla was one of the larger ones. Ever since the latest renovation, the cars didn't have the courage or motivation to attack. In that renovation a second outer wall was constructed. The walls for forts were constructed with blocks made from recycled construction waste. The blocks could be snapped together to form a wall, like giant 'Lego' blocks. They were quite light but strong. Much lighter than a concrete block, so it was easier to build with them. Used car tyres were laid at the base of the wall and reached up to the height of a typical four-wheel drive. One of the main priorities, when thinking about fort defence, was that it was preferable for the attacking cars to be captured without damage. It was more profitable for the cars to come to the fort to be captured rather than be hunted. The height of the second outer wall was around 5 metres. It had a platform where soldiers with long range stun rifles could stand. The stun cannons though, were setup on the inner wall, which meant there were two outer walls separating the attackers from the stun cannons. The soldiers had an important role because stun cannons could not shoot at anything that was in close range. It would be up to the soldiers to fire at any car that reached a wall. The fort had four stun cannons and two missile launches. Generally, the missile launches were there to defend the fort from yellow bear attacks, though such attacks would be extremely rare. Yellow bears tended to want to stay on the mountains and did not venture down to the plains.

The host of cars were gathered just outside the range of the Fort Kembla. Truck raised himself up and addressed his host.

"Today will be a great day for all cars," he pronounced. "Today we show the humans that they can't enslave us. Today we make a statement for our freedom. Do not be afraid. The victory we have today will be remembered long after we have passed away. Take courage and drive hard, for the humans will not be able to prevail. Prepare now for attack."

Then Truck gave a long horn honk. The wailing sound echoed around the valley. Nearly all the other cars in the army followed suit with long horn honks too.

Then Truck called, "Front line, attack now."

The guard on the tower in the Fort raised his binoculars after seeing some dust on the horizon. When he held them up to his eyes he could see a large gathering of cars.

He yelled down to soldiers below. "Get the captain now. We have a problem."

A short while later, a stout man in uniform climbed the stairs to the tower.

"Captain, there are a lot of cars gathering to the west," said the soldier. "I think they are preparing to attack."

The captain raised his binoculars to confirm the sighting. He yelled to the soldiers below.

"Sergeant, send a helicopter to scout the area west of here. This is urgent, the cars appear to be preparing for attack."

Within moments a helicopter rose from the helipad and made its way west towards the cars. The captain had his radio and was waiting for a report. Soon a report came in.

"Captain, I estimate over three thousand cars are gathered. I have never seen so many congregated in one place. They look hostile."

The captain used his radio to alert the stun cannon operators and to organise a troop of soldiers to man the positions on the platform of the second outer wall. They were all armed with stun rifles. Then the captain spoke to the soldiers who were responsible for the missile launches.

"Corporal Jacobs and Corporal Jones, I need you for this defence," he said. "We may not be able to hold with stun cannons alone. I understand we do not normally use missile launches for attacking cars, so I need you to use your discretion. Please only shoot at old, damaged cars. If we are being over-whelmed, I will revise this order. But for now, just the old, damaged cars."

The cars from the geriatric tribe drove bravely as they led the attack. They all made long horn honks before they left, and they lifted themselves up on their suspensions.

There was some space where the cars could accelerate to their top speeds before they were in range of the stun cannons. The stun cannons had a longer range than the stun rifles that the men on the outer wall had. Truck managed the army well. He waited a short time before calling on the cars that were not on the front line to attack. That was because, the geriatric and small cars were relatively slow. He wanted a mass of cars to attack. Too many to be mowed down by the stun cannons and rifles.

The attack of the front line stirred up the dust on the plain as the cars reached their top speeds. It was not long before they were in range of the stun cannons and also the missile launches. Then, the sound of stun pulses from the cannons rang out across the plains. As the cars drove on, their companions were taken out beside them, by the stun cannons. But they didn't lose heart and kept on driving. Datsun was especially brave, even when his companions were destroyed by missiles. He wanted to play his part in this venture. He hoped that his hero, Truck would approve of his efforts. When he first started his approach, he accelerated as quickly as he could. He wanted to reach the outer wall. But he was an old car, and when there was still a long distance between him and the outer wall, he felt his engine burning out. His colleagues next to him also showed signs of fatigue. He wanted to encourage them, remind them of Truck's great inspiration. Datsun honked his horn, and the blue Astra next to him replied in kind. And then other cars of the tribe also sounded their horns. They were in this together. Even if the humans were choosing to fire missiles at them, they would not shy away from their task of leading the front line.

A Distant Genesis

The geriatric line was still a few hundred metres away from the outer wall when a missile found Datsun. It crashed through his broken windscreen and exploded in the driver seat. It had seemed that Truck's plan of expecting the humans to only use stun weapons was flawed. In the end the humans were afraid of the large host attacking them. Falcon saw what happened to his friend, a loyal and devoted comrade. He despaired at what was going on around him and felt that the task given to his tribe was too arduous and had little chance of success. But he kept driving, and because he was a bigger car he had more stamina than the smaller cars in the tribe. There were only a few cars left driving in the front line when a stun pulse stopped him suddenly in his tracks. Maybe the humans would once again prevail, and thousands of cars would be enslaved.

But the mass of cars had made ground. They were getting closer to the outer wall. The cars from the sports car tribe led by Famous 46, Wildcat and Greeney, pulled away from the rest of the cars. They were fast and brave. An inspiration to the rest of the cars. Cars honked in appreciation when the first of the sports cars reached the outer wall. Once there, they were out of range of the stun cannons, but they were still vulnerable to the stun rifles armed by the men on the platform. The cars swung around and then reversed into the tyres along the wall, so they wouldn't damage their engines. The walls were strong though and sports cars weren't designed for the battering task required to breakthrough the walls of the fort. But they kept the men on the outer wall occupied, while the other cars approached. The stun cannons pulsed and the missiles were launched, but the cars kept on coming. Finally, the heavier vehicles reached the outer wall. They were the trucks and land rovers with heavy bull-bars. The shells of burnt-out cars and the cars lucky enough to be stunned littered the plains, but the big vehicles had reached the outer wall. An achievement few cars would have thought possible. They rammed and they rammed, and the wall shook precariously.

The men on the outer wall platform had never seen so many cars together. When the first cars were in range they fired carelessly, expecting them to turn around and retreat. Only the contractors were sparing with their rounds. Each round costs money and they did not want to miss out on this hunting bonanza. Most of the car hunting was done by contractors. They were the only ones who would venture out in the plains to hunt cars. The soldiers tended to stay in the fort as guards. After a battle with the cars if you could call it that, the accountant soldiers would inspect the sleeping cars and identify which rifle had put the car to sleep. The contractors would then get paid, depending on how valuable the car was. But this car attack was different. As it progressed, the men thought less about profit and more about survival. Even the contractors began to worry. At first, they were discouraged because the front line only had old or small cars, hardly worth the stun round. But then when the sports cars arrived, they aimed with anticipation. However, they shot and they shot, and still more cars came. And then the heavier vehicles arrived. And they could knock over these walls. It took more stun rounds to put just one to sleep.

The stun cannons were no longer in range as they were only effective from a distance and the walls created a shadow the cannons could not reach. If the fort was going to survive, it would be up to them. The heavy vehicles broke through the first outer wall, but the captain had already ordered another troop of soldiers to man the platform on the second outer wall. There were still men on the first outer wall but they were on islands of blocks, separated from one another and surrounded by cars. The intent of the heavy vehicles was to breach as many walls as possible, rather than completely destroy any individual walls. The other cars could do that. The captain was very worried, and ordered the evacuation of civilians via the company helicopter. It took a number of trips to transport everyone, and there was a point when the captain no longer thought of a hard-won victory, but just wanted to survive long enough for the helicopter to complete its necessary flights. At this stage, all fighting men were on broken platforms shooting at cars that ravaged the fort. The cars completely destroyed all the buildings, before turning their attention to the surviving men. And gradually the sound of stun rifles was silent because either there were no more rounds to fire or the men that bore them had been killed. But make no mistake, Truck had no mercy for any surviving soldiers and contractors. They were chased down and run over.

As Truck had ordered, the host of cars waited until their comrades had woken from being stunned and there were celebrations for their remarkable victory. But when Falcon awoke, he didn't feel much like celebrating. He drove through the battleground and mourned the loss of his tribe who were not lucky enough to be stunned. He then found the burnt-out shell of Datsun and remembered the small car's passion. Of course, the stories of this battle would glorify the sports cars and the heavy vehicles, but in Falcon's eyes, Datsun was a true hero.

Chapter 4
Companions for a Journey

Roger and Sheila arrived at Fort Chrisholm. The Commander was friendly and amiable during the helicopter journey from the main space port. He told them about the construction of the new Fort and the great plans the Corporation had for it. They planned to open up a whole new area for car hunting. From their research, they hypothesised that there were some valuable sports car tribes in the area. Fort Chrisholm was smaller than Fort Kembla, with only one outer wall and one inner wall. However, it did have the same number of stun cannons.

During their helicopter journey, Sheila was overwhelmed by the landscape. There was such a contrast between the mountains and the plains. Not just the difference in colour, where the mountains were predominantly yellow and the plains red. But also, the sharpness of the ridges and peaks that made up the mountains, was so different to the flatness of the plains. In the mountains there were boulders and loose smaller rocks, whereas on the plains there was only dust. It reminded her of the Rocky Mountains in North America on Earth, except she could not see any running water or snow. There were no trees or shrubs. She wondered how anything could live there. Nothing stirred in the mountains, but she could see small clouds of dust on the plains. The whole planet was like this, she was told. And from what she had seen so far, she didn't doubt that.

What had she got herself in to? She considered herself a brave adventurous person, but there were limits. As the helicopter was landing, Sheila could see the buildings in the fort compound. There was a long L-shaped building which the commander said was the barracks and a smaller square building which was the mess hall and offices for the management. The Commander was quite forthcoming with information. He understood the importance of Sheila's visit. He wanted to paint the Corporation in the best light.

"See the walls of the buildings and those around the fort. They are made from recycled building waste and are very strong, yet light. See how they are blocks that fit together. It is possible to disassemble the fort completely and relocate it. Not that it is done very often." the Commander espoused.

Sheila could see what he meant and also saw that the blocks that made up the fort walls were a different shape and size from those that formed the building walls and were different again for the roofs of the buildings.

"You have had a long day, and probably want to freshen up," the Commander said. "Corporal Jensen will show you to your rooms. We will come and get you for dinner in the mess hall after an hour or so."

The rooms were sparsely decorated with only the essential furniture. But they were comfortable. The Corporation wanted to keep their employees comfortable while keeping costs down. Sheila had a shower and then changed into a comfortable but professional and fashionable navy pants suit. The jacket was worn over a white v neck shirt. Her navy flat shoes complemented the outfit. Sheila still had time before her summons, so she wrote in her diary of what had happened so far and the people she had met.

Roger looked about his room and thought about his journey here. He had never been to Plantere before, but he had seen many other worlds. He had enjoyed travelling with Sheila because she had so many questions and showed a lot of enthusiasm. It was like travelling with a curious child to somewhere that the child had never been. Because Roger had worked on so many different worlds, he had lost his natural curiosity and now concentrated solely on his work. While for Sheila, the introduction to this world evoked wonder, for Roger it just brought memories of difficult times in similar worlds.

There was a world that was covered in sand hills and had very little water. It was very hot during the day and very cold at night. Roger had been part of a patrol protecting a mining operation, where there was a war between two corporations fighting over mining rights. His patrol would be ambushed while they scouted around a mining location. They would also be called to scenes where a suicide bomber had entered a mining operation and blown himself up. It was an ugly and stressful assignment.

Being with Sheila helped him to look past his previous experience and invoke some fresh curiosity about Plantere. Roger showered and changed into a different uniform. The uniforms soldiers wore on the mothership were different to the ones worn on this world. The uniforms here were light, but covered the whole body. They also sported a wide brimmed hat.

On Earth, the ozone layer protected humans from ultraviolet radiation. However, on Plantere, there wasn't the same protection. It was very easy for foreign humans to get sunburnt. On Plantere, it rarely rained and it was very unusual to see thick grey or white clouds. The sun on Plantere probably wasn't as strong as Earth's, but because there were rarely clouds, the atmosphere did not provide any insulation. So, long days could end up being very hot and long nights being very cold. The weather on Plantere was mild. That is, there were never storms nor cyclones. Often there would be a gentle breeze that could escalate in a canyon to a gully wind.

The uniforms were designed for this weather. They had camouflage patterns that were a similar reddish colour as the plains on the planet. Roger had a shave and as he looked at himself in the mirror, he confirmed that he was looking pert and professional. He completed his routine by strapping on his laser pistol.

Samuel counted himself very lucky because he'd had an uneventful journey across the plains to Fort Chrisholm. It had been a long day and the sun was still above the horizon when he arrived. The day was now very hot. He made his way to the front gate where there was a guard posted. The guard looked suspiciously at his hunter's features of red hair, blue eyes and very tanned skin. There were a lot of contractors who had these features, and it was common for them to visit the fort. But generally, the corporation employees didn't understand how they lived, as they didn't visit often and didn't stay long at the fort. It was only when they brought cars to trade, that they came at all. How could they survive out there and why would they want to?

"Sir, what can I do for you?" the guard asked.

"I have come to hire a stun rifle," Samuel stammered. When the guard look incredulously at him, he blurted out, "I know where Sergeant Blackmore's sword is!"

"What is going on down there?" a voice yelled from the outer wall platform.

"A boy wants to hire a stun rifle," the guard yelled back.

"Let him in. It's not safe out there," the voice replied.

The guard shrugged, opened a small gate and directed Samuel to enter. In the compound Samuel was greeted by an older man in uniform. His uniform was the same functional type of the soldiers, but included a *Trade Officer* badge. The man's face was lined and tanned with a friendly demeanour. His name was Corizon. Although it had been years since Corizon had seen Samuel, he recognised him.

"You're the Bensons' boy, aren't you?" he asked. "It has been a long while since I have seen your parents. How are they?"

Samuel was uncomfortable and didn't know what to say. Finally, he murmured, "They died."

"I'm sorry," the man said, "I'm Corizon. Your parents were well known to me. They were good people."

"I'm Samuel," Samuel replied, He liked Corizon and felt recognised, less alone.

"So you want to hire a stun rifle?" asked Corizan.

Samuel pulled out his I.O.U from the Attacca Corporation and showed it to Corizon.

"I'm sorry Samuel," Corizon replied after seeing the I.O.U. "This is only valid for the Attacca corporation. The nearest Fort is hundreds of kilometres from here."

Samuel was disappointed and his face dropped.

"Come and have something to eat, Sam. Is it okay for me to call you Sam?" Corizon asked.

"Yes, that's okay," Samuel replied. "Thank you."

Corizon led Samuel into the mess hall and took him to the serveries. The mess hall was quite a large building, with a series of long tables and chairs. The walls had pictures of important employees as well as of famous sports cars that had been captured. The floor was hard and like the walls, appeared to be interlocked slabs. Samuel felt some relief as he entered, and found the temperature was mild. The serveries were to one side and supported buffet style eating.

There was an extensive range of food on display. The Iowa Corporation looked after their employees well. Some of their employees had soldier ranks, but that did not mean they had army rations. No. There were qualified chefs, fresh food and Earth recipes. Samuel had the choice of curries, pasta dishes, various meats, salads and vegetarian dishes. Not that he had much idea what they were. Normally, his diet would consist of fuel balls and internal organs of cars. He'd counted himself lucky when he found that ration pack at the ruins of the helipad he had passed through. Samuel took a plate and then looked over all the food selections. He thought that there was so much food! He didn't recognise half of what was there. One thing he was overwhelmed by, was the different smells coming from the serveries. The smell of each dish didn't bother him, but the cumulation of all the different smells made him feel nauseous. He mumbled to himself that maybe he wasn't hungry. He held his nose and decided to have a closer look. Maybe he could find something he knew. He remembered after a successful car hunt his father would bring home some Spaghetti Bolognese. Was that in the buffet? Yes, it was, so he decided on that.

He chose a seat as far away from the serveries as possible, because he was still feeling nauseous. As he sat down to eat his spaghetti Bolognese, he saw Corizon introduce himself to a woman and a man in corporate uniform. The woman was beautiful. She had long brown hair and a pretty face, with her features being well balanced. Also, she had a slim figure, that enhanced the shape of her breasts and hips. Corizon led his guests towards Samuel, and then introduced them to him. As he said Sheila's name Samuel could see she had exquisite green eyes, and a lovely smile. Her nose was not large or small, but was perfectly proportioned. Also, the clothes she was wearing made her look exotic. Samuel had never seen clothes like this before.

"Err, nice to meet you," he stammered once he had heard Roger's name.

"Sheila is a journalist who is going to write about the corporation and Plantere," Corizon continued. "I thought she would benefit from interviewing someone from the indigenous population."

Samuel fidgeted uncomfortably and had less interest in his food. He was still feeling nauseous and nervous at the same time. He was not really a people person and wondered if he would say anything intelligent in an interview.

Sheila broke the ice. "It would be wonderful if I could hear your story, Samuel."

Her voice was warm and inviting. Samuel didn't say anything. He picked at his food, not enjoying it as much as he had thought he would. Corizon rescued him.

"Sam, you can hire a stun rifle from us," he said. "Please, finish your food, and then come with me and we will sort you out."

Sheila and Roger made their way to the buffet. Samuel was beginning to feel better and felt that he could complete his food. He ate quickly always looking down at his food. He was hungry but he felt embarrassed. After he felt that he had eaten enough, he pushed his plate away and stood up. Corizon led him to a shed that had lines of racks filled with weapons. The shed was also airconditioned and was cooler than the mess hall. The weapons were mainly stun rifles, but there were also some lasers and projectile guns. The racks reached up to the ceiling.

"Brett, this is Sam. He wants to hire a stun rifle," Corizon introduced him.

Brett was a pudgy pale faced man, who was completely bald and a little shorter than average.

"Brett is an expert in stun pulse weapons," said Corizon. "I will leave you with him. He will sort you out."

With that, Corizon left. Brett took out an impressive rifle. It had sights and fired a potent two-gauge round. It would be strong enough to stun a Land Rover or even a small truck.

"This is the EasyShooter L9200," said Brett, proudly. "It comes with ten rounds and is accurate to one kilometre. It also has a silencer." He was almost purring as he held the weapon. He had a passion for stun weapons and enjoyed his work dispensing them. He had made friends with hunters who showed knowledge and appreciation for what he dispensed. Stun rifles are generally not as loud as projectile weapons, but cars can have good hearing, so a silencer can be a good addition if you were picking out a car from a herd and didn't want to draw attention to yourself.

"It's yours for your first sports car, Sam," Brett announced. "That was how hiring a stun weapon worked. Your first captured cars belonged to the corporation until the hire was paid for, and a sports car was a handsome price. The hire also only included the rounds that come with the weapon. In this case ten.

"Err, maybe something smaller," Samuel stammered.

"Well, there is the EasyShooter L2300 or K1800. They come with fifteen rounds, and are accurate to four hundred metres. The rounds are 1.2 gauge," Brett suggested. "It is yours for two large cars, such as a Ford Falcon or Holden Commodore."

That was about the potency of a 1.2gauge weapon, for a Ford Falcon or Holden Commodore.

"Err, maybe something smaller," Samuel stammered again.

Samuel wasn't an ambitious hunter. His goal was to find cars that strayed from the herd, get close and then stun. Previously he would have jumped them, but the battle for control of the vehicle usually meant its death. A stun pulse would allow Samuel to drive the car to a fort so he could sell it. Although disappointed, Brett was beginning to get the idea.

"Well Samuel, there is the generic brand pulser," he said. "It comes with twenty rounds, but its range is really less than fifty metres. The rounds are only 0.7 gauge. At best that would stun a Nissan Pulsar, probably more likely a Ford Laser. "It's yours for a young small car or geriatric large car."

"I'll take it," Samuel announced.

To his two guests, Corizon, was expanding on his description of Fort Chrisholm and the commercial benefits that would flow from having greater access to the lucrative sports cars' tribes. As he was talking, a siren like a fire alarm went off.

"What is that?" Sheila asked.

"Please give me a moment and I'll find out," Corizon responded just before he left the mess hall.

"Well, do you have some material for your journal now Sheila?" Roger asked. "You have met a professional car hunter, now," he quipped.

"He is just a boy Roger, still not sure of himself," Sheila replied.

Corizon returned and his face was white.

"What's wrong?" Sheila asked.

"I have some terrible news," Corizon said gravely. His voice was low and serious. "Fort Kembla has been destroyed. Apparently, an army of over four thousand cars attacked it. I've never before heard news like this before, and I'm worried. Our reconnaissance has indicated that they are heading towards Fort Chrisholm. I'm not sure when the helicopter will return to evacuate you."

Corizon was despondent. It was his responsibility to look after Sheila. "It would be safer if you went to Fort Adelaide," he finally recommended.

"How far is it? We can take a car," Roger suggested.

"I don't know if that is a good idea. You don't know the area," Corizon replied.

"Don't worry about us, Corizon. We can do this," Roger reassured him.

"It is about 340km west of here. I have some maps. Navigating these plains is like going through a maze." Corizon sounded doubtful. He then expressed his concern. "I don't think you understand how inhospitable this world is. It is downright dangerous."

Corizon had friendships with indigenous car hunters, but he had never spent any time outside of the Fort. He said as much. "Most of the employees here never leave the fort. I'm sure the helicopter will return."

"Please don't worry about us," said Shiela. "I'm sure the helicopter has more important work to do than ferrying us to Fort Adelaide. Roger is an experienced soldier. We will be okay."

This time it was Sheila who was doing the reassuring.

"Well, if you are going to do this, I think you will need some help," said Corizon. "I knew Samuel's parents. They were good people. Maybe Samuel could go with you?"

"He is only a boy," Sheila objected. "He would have trouble looking after himself, let alone us."

"I last saw his parents ten years ago," said Corizon. "Apparently, they died eight years ago. This boy has been living in the wilderness for all that time. He is an indigenous hunter. They belong here."

"Well, if you think it is for the best, he can tag along with us. That is if he wants to," said Roger.

Roger had a similar objection to Sheila, but he wanted to ease Corizon's concerns. He knew that Corizon felt deeply responsible for Sheila's safety. Not, just because she was going to write an important journal for the Iowa corporation, but also because she was a guest from Earth.

Brett and Samuel returned to the mess hall and found Corizon talking to Roger and Sheila.

Corizon looked up at Samuel and said, "Samuel, Roger and Sheila are going to make their own way to Fort Adelaide." He put his arms on Samuel's shoulders. "There is an army of cars heading this way and I don't think it is safe for them to stay," Corizon added. "And I'm doubtful that the helicopter will arrive on time to evacuate them before the anticipated attack."

Samuel took another look at Sheila and was overcome by her beauty. The feeling had not subsided since he first saw her. It was not as if he had seen many women. He had not. Maybe that was the reason he found Sheila so alluring. He felt a lump in his throat, but managed to blurt out, "I could come... I can jump cars."

"Excellent, my boy," said Corizon, beaming. "That is much appreciated." He was clearly relieved. "Sheila's safety is of paramount importance to the Iowa Corporation."

Samuel felt the weight of responsibility on his shoulders. He was having enough trouble looking after himself, let alone being responsible for a beautiful famous journalist from Earth.

"Let's have a look at that stun rifle you have there," Corizon said. "Hmm, a generic brand pulser." He played with the rifle, lifting it up and aiming at nothing in particular. "Brett, please go and fetch an EasyShooter L9200, and fifty rounds."

"But... I can't afford it," Samuel protested.

"Consider it a gift from the Iowa Corporation, for the safety of Sheila until she and Roger reach Fort Adelaide," said Corizon. "It is settled." The three of you will leave tomorrow morning. Let us go and have a look at some maps."

Chapter 5
To Fort Adelaide

They started their journey early in the morning, partly because they needed to cross the plains before the army of cars arrived, and also because today was going to be a relatively short day. Their plan was to cross the plains to reach where Samuel had left his rope and sword, so they could climb up to the ridge of the mountain ranges. Then they would work their way along the ridges, hopefully avoiding any yellow bears. After going over half way to Fort Adelaide they would endeavour to stun a car and drive it the rest of the way.

Last night they had visited the car yards to select a car that would take them to the mountains. They would be given a stun pistol so they could re-stun the car, once the pulse began to wear off. In the end, they had selected a maroon eight-cylinder Holden Monaro. He was in excellent condition and quite a young car. He had luxurious red leather seats and steering wheel. Certainly, a ride in style. What Samuel liked most about the car was how clean it was. It wasn't covered in red dust. Young cars in the wild, did not have a lot of dust on their bodies. Though they still had some. When cars were captured, the Corporation cleaned them using air blasters. Samuel couldn't remember ever seeing a car this clean. For the car, it would be a lucky selection, as when the party reached the mountains, the car would be set free.

The party was also given binoculars, food rations and camping gear. The camping gear was very good quality and designed for the night -time climate of Plantere. They also had a digital map application on their mobile phone that marked their current position. The corporations had recently invested in Global Positioning System satellites for the planet. And, of course they had a mobile phone to keep in contact with the Fort and make contact with Fort Adelaide.

Samuel had expressed a desire to retrieve Sergeant Blackmore's sword and wondered if the Fort had something to hold the scabbard for it. That was quite an unusual request, as the Fort didn't use swords at all. But Brett found a sling that was designed for a large stun rifle and thought that may be of use.

Sheila didn't bring much of her luggage from Earth. Corizon had promised, if possible, he would send it to Fort Adelaide. Corizon suggested that Sheila wear the soldier's uniform. The same one that Roger was wearing. He was concerned that Sheila would be exposed to sun. The uniforms were designed for Plantere's climate. When Sheila had put it on, she thought it wasn't very flattering. The uniform was baggy on her and also the colours of the red camouflage pattern were not ones she would choose.

Never mind, she thought. She was on assignment. Corizon also had promised to contact Fort Adelaide, so that they could provide a meeting party. He also tried to provide some last-minute advice before wishing them safe speed to Fort Adelaide.

Samuel was the driver and found the Monaro very nice to drive. Not having to fight the car all the time was a wonderful experience. The car was also fast and had excellent acceleration. It kicked up a cloud of red dust that was visible from the Fort for many miles. At this rate they should reach the base of the mountains very quickly. Samuel did feel a little bad about the cleanliness of the car. He was sure that when they had finished, the car would have some red dust again. They didn't see signs of any other car. If there was an army of cars on their way, they were not there yet. Sheila was sitting in the front passenger seat next to Samuel. Roger was in the back.

Sheila was curious about Samuel. His leather outfit was covered in red dust which he didn't seem to mind. But also, he wasn't wearing a hat.

"Samuel, I noticed you are not wearing a hat," she pointed out. Sheila was a journalist, so she was never shy about asking any sort of question. "Aren't you worried that you may get sunburnt?"

"Sunburnt," Samuel muttered to himself. *What is that?* he thought. Then he remembered. His Dad always used to wear a hat and cover himself. But his Mum never did. Samuel had his mother's hunter's features, so that must be why he never got sunburnt. He eventually answered Sheila.

"I take after my Mum. She never got sunburnt."

The sun was high in the sky when they reached the base of the mountains where Samuel had left his rope. Samuel felt regret leaving the Monaro behind. It had been an exhilarating drive. He had wound down the windows and had the wind in his hair, as the car sped along. But now it was over. They left the car, and in less than half an hour it would wake up and speed its way to freedom.

The rope did make it easier to scale the cliff face, which wasn't vertical and had foot holds on the way up. The Fort had also provided climbing shoes and gloves, so that helped also. Sheila had done some climbing on Earth and enjoyed the sport. Although Roger was chivalrous and offered to help her, she didn't need his help. Samuel led the way, followed by Sheila and then Roger. Step by step, they made their way up the cliff face until they reached the rope that was tied to the sword. Samuel pulled at the sword and tried to hold it upright, but it was heavy.

"Sergeant Blackmore's famous sword," Samuel pronounced. "See the engraving on the hilt."

Roger had very little interest in medieval weapons. He had a laser pistol by his side and he knew how to use it. Sheila, on the other hand loved history and old stories. She asked Samuel about the stories he knew of Sergeant Blackmore. He said he didn't know much, before proceeding to tell Sheila all he knew. He became animated as he spoke and forgot about the fact that he was talking to a beautiful woman.

The sun was beginning to set on the horizon. It had been a very short day and didn't get too warm. Samuel said that tomorrow would also be a short day. Sheila asked him how he knew that. Samuel said he didn't know. He just knew it. At the top of the cliff face to the right was the ruins of the helipad and the yellow bear den, and to the left was where they needed to go to get to Fort Adelaide. Although the sun was beginning to set, Samuel suggested they should continue hiking for a little longer yet, as he wanted to put as much distance as possible between them and the yellow bear den.

Sheila looked to the sky and saw the dusk spectra. It was beautiful she thought. There was a full range of colours. Like a rainbow. She thought of Scottish native flowers. The violet colour in the sky reminded her of the Common Dog Violet, while the red colour in the sky reminded her of the Sheep's Sorrel. It was strange that an exotic phenomenon on a remote world would make her think of home on Earth.

Eventually, when it was nearly dark, they set up their tents, switched on the lamp and had some food rations for dinner. They had a good variety of ration packs that were dried and preserved. To prepare they just needed to add water. The water did not need to be hot. There was a set of chemicals in the ration pack that when mixed with cold water, would heat up the meal. Samuel selected a Spaghetti Bolognese, Roger selected a beef casserole and Sheila selected Salmon pasta.

As they sat and ate, Sheila asked Samuel, "Do the colours in the sky just before sunset occur every night?"

Samuel replied that they did. Sheila ran her hands through her hair and remarked, "It is beautiful." Then she asked Roger, "Have you ever seen anything like it, Roger?"

Roger rubbed his chin and replied, "I have a few times." He took another spoonful of his casserole and then continued. "It is quite common for worlds that orbit giant red suns."

Samuel said the nighttime would not last too long, but should be long enough for a good night's sleep.

In the morning Samuel was the first to rise. He took the binoculars and scanned the mountain ridges. At the time he was given the binoculars, he didn't think much about it. But now he was appreciating the view they gave him. The plan was to try and avoid going deep into the mountain range, even though it would probably be more direct. Instead, they were going to try and work their way around the ridges just above the cliff faces to the plains below. Samuel didn't know a lot about yellow bears, except that they avoided plains and the cliff faces. Samuel's parents' cottage had been perched half way up a cliff face, safe from both cars and bears. He could see that for a short while they should be able to follow the ridges, but then in the distance, the terrain became more rugged. The ridges, rather than relatively flat as they were now, would extend up to a steep peak. Samuel felt doubtful that they could climb it. They would probably need to travel inland to try and circle around it. Then once around the peak, perhaps the ridge would return to being rather flat.

"Good morning, Samuel," Sheila said cheerfully as she climbed out of the tent. "What can you see?"

"There is a peak about a couple of hours away. We may have to go inland to go around it," Samuel replied.

Back at the fort, Corizon and the others had deferred to his advice, believing him to be an expert of this world. Much of the plans they had were his idea, so he felt a weight of responsibility on his shoulders. Samuel really wanted to avoid going inland. He was sure that Sheila would not want to stumble upon a yellow bear. But it seemed they had no choice. Perhaps in the next couple of hours, he could think of something. Maybe when they got closer to the peak, they might see a way to climb it, or a trail they could follow that goes through it.

Roger climbed out of a tent with the mobile phone in his hand.

"Still, no reception up here. We really are in the wilderness," he half joked.

They had a quick breakfast and packed their gear quickly, because today was going to be another short day. Roger had the tent and mobile phone, while Samuel had the food rations and binoculars. Sheila had all the clothes and the lamp. Samuel was also carrying the sword and stun rifle. He found the sword was very heavy. But he didn't have the heart to leave it behind. It was Sergeant Blackmore's sword after all. Roger checked the map on the mobile phone.

"This isn't much good in the mountains." he complained. "It really only shows the valleys, not the mountain ranges at all."

He hadn't had a good night's sleep, so he was feeling grumpy this morning. A couple of hours passed, and Samuel still hadn't thought of anything. They now faced a very steep climb up to a high peak if they tried to follow the ridge. Although they had sturdy footwear, they didn't have mountain climbing equipment.

"Looks like we have to go inland," Samuel said despondently.

"It will be all right Sam," Sheila reassured him.

"We will see if can go around the peak," he said seriously.

There was a reasonable path they could follow, but they were led further and further inland. Where there was one peak it morphed into being another. The path pierced the rough terrain and was easy to walk on. But it was taking them in the wrong direction. Samuel was thinking that they should turn back. The daytime was nearly over and he didn't feel comfortable setting up a tent this far inland.

"Let's leave this path and try to find a sheltered area for our tent," Roger suggested. He ran his hand through his hair and then continued. "Somewhere hard to find."

Given the alternatives, it was probably the best idea. So, they clambered over rocks hoping to find some secret gully where they could safely set up their tent. In the end, they found a ledge on a cliff face, just wide enough for their tent. Only just. Luckily it wasn't dark yet. Samuel was worried about using the lamp outside. He didn't want to attract the attention of any yellow bears. So, they all ate dinner inside the tent. There wasn't much room on the ledge outside anyway. Once again Samuel had Spaghetti Bolognese and Roger had beef casserole. Sheila was the only one who had a different meal from last night, Thai Green Curry. After dinner they began to feel better about the situation. They should be safe here for tonight. They would have a long day tomorrow to find their way back to the ridge.

Sheila made eye contact with Samuel and asked him, "Where did you live Sam?"

"My parents had a cottage on a ledge part way up a cliff face. It was safe there," Samuel answered.

"Is that where you had been living since your parents died?" Sheila asked.

Samuel fidgeted and then replied, "Yes, pretty much." He paused before continuing. "Except for forays to find fuel balls or jump cars."

Roger had known soldiers who were like Samuel. Soldiers who were introspective and were loners. They didn't come across as being impressive. You wouldn't think that they would be particularly heroic. But on occasions they would surprise the company and do something amazing.

"It is hard to be brave when you are alone," Roger said thoughtfully.

The next morning, they started early and found the path fairly easily. It took them around another peak and it seemed to take them into a better direction. Although it was still taking them further inland, but they were thinking optimistically, until they walked around a bend and came face to face with a yellow bear. When they saw it, it was only twenty metres away. The bear stood ten metres high. It had a prickly yellow coat with white pads on the feet and hands. Like humans, yellow bears walk on two feet and have two arms. But their hands and feet are paws, that are white in contrast to the yellow of their coat. They do have fur, but it is not soft. It is prickly.

"Stay still," Samuel whispered.

At first the bear didn't appear to see them, but when it did, it howled in anger and came towards them. Yellow bears have long legs, so they have a big stride. As such, they are quite quick. Roger cracked his knuckles before pulling out his laser pistol. He fired a few shots at the bear's chest. The bear screamed in anger. Bears rarely make a noise but when they scream, they are loud. They are capable of a low rumbling growl, but when they scream it is a piercing high pitch wail. Like an alarm. The shots clearly hurt him but not fatally. The laser shots burned the bear on the skin over his chest, however the shots didn't penetrate. It would be like pouring hot water on a person, causing a first- degree burn. The bear came at Roger and swatted him with its paw, sending him ten metres in the air. When he landed, he didn't move. He was sprawled on the ground like a rag doll.

"Roger!" Sheila screamed.

The bear finished his intent by stomping on Roger's body.

"Get behind me," hissed Samuel, but Sheila was frozen.

Samuel could not say anymore. He had to focus on what he needed to do now. He pulled out the sword and worked to hold the hilt above his head, aiming the blade about forty-five degrees towards the ground. But the blade was heavy, and he didn't know if he could maintain his position for very long. The bear was still angry and turned his attention to Samuel and Sheila. He came at Samuel, and when he was close enough, Samuel drove his sword into the bear's left foot. He used all the force he could and the sword penetrated deep. The bear roared and fell over.

Samuel yelled, "Run!"

But Sheila was still frozen, so he grabbed her hand and pulled her. She came to her senses and started to run. They were running forward along the path rather than back. But they didn't think about their possible destination, they were just running. The path went around the latest peak and started taking them in the correct direction. They kept running unaware of their change in fortunes. The roars of the bear became more distant as they finally reached the ridge they were trying to follow.

"A new plan," said Samuel. "Let's get a car on the plains."

He and Sheila slowly picked their way down the cliff face from the ridge. It was tedious work as they didn't have a rope. But they didn't mind because they started to feel safe.

"Do you have any idea where we are?" Sheila asked.

"Not really. And Roger had the mobile phone," Samuel said. "I think we need to try to reach Fort Adelaide today, because he also had the tent."

Not having the sword did make it easier for Samuel to climb, but he felt regret on leaving it behind again. This time it had saved their lives. Gradually, they reached the valley below and Samuel scanned the plains with the binoculars. He didn't see any cars.

"I think we should follow the ridge over there, until we see some cars," he said.

"I don't think I can do this anymore," Sheila said.

Samuel, turned and looked intently at her. She was quite visibly shaken. Something that he could quite understand. That yellow bear was big and savage.

"I'm sorry about Roger," he replied. "Were you close to him?"

"I only knew him a short time," Sheila said. "But he was a good guy."

Samuel continued to look into her eyes and perceived her vulnerability. He didn't know much about Earth, but he guessed that it was not nearly as harsh as his world. He felt vulnerable nearly all the time and he had grown up here. She was beautiful and fragile, and he felt a need to protect her.

"I don't know if this is going to get any easier, Sheila," he said finally. "I don't think we have a choice except to push on."

"Yes, of course," she said, feeling embarrassed. "I'm sorry. You are right. We need to push on."

They kept walking along the valley floor following the ridge above. Every now and then Samuel would take out his binoculars and scan the valley for cars. The valley was quite wide. About two kilometres. The ridge veered to the left, so he couldn't see how long the valley was or whether it branched off. From his memory of the maps he had seen, he was expecting the valley to fork, and that they should take the right fork.

They kept walking for a few hours until Samuel saw some clouds of dust in the distance. He confirmed, with the help of his binoculars that there was indeed a tribe of cars. It was hard to see, but they looked like a Honda tribe. He took out his stun rifle and lined his sights on a youthful looking Accord. It should be faster than the other cars in the tribe. He was hoping to stun the car, and for the other cars not to notice and keep driving. He did like the feel of the EasyShooter L9200, and the car in his sights was at least one kilometre away. He shot at the car but missed on his first shot. However, he was successful with his second shot. Now, all they needed to do was to wait for the tribe to keep on driving. But they didn't. They stopped and tried to rouse their colleague. When they couldn't, they broke up into smaller groups and started to spread out. There was one group heading towards Samuel and Sheila.

"Damn," Samuel cursed.

The group that came towards them had five cars. There were three Civics, one Jazz and a CR-V.

"I will try to shoot them all but then we must run towards the CR-V," he said.

As the cars came closer, he picked them off. He was getting better at aiming and it became easier as the cars drew closer. He tried to shoot the CR-V last so that it would be the closest car to them, but it veered away when it saw his companions being stunned. And the shot Samuel had at it, missed.

"Damn," Samuel cursed again. "We have to take one of the Civics."

The closest Civic was about a hundred metres away, so they had to run fast to get to him, before the other cars realised what was going on and cut them off. They boarded a blue Honda Civic hatch. It was a young car with tidy fabric upholstery. The other cars saw what was happening and drove towards them. Samuel accelerated and headed in the direction that the ridge followed. But some of the other cars could cut him off.

"Here," Samuel said. "Take this and shoot anything that gets close."

Samuel passed the rifle to Sheila. He then unwound the windows on the driver and passenger sides. Sheila hadn't had a lot of experience shooting with rifles. The closest thing she had done was play laser tag back on Earth, when she was a teenager. But she did have a good dose of common sense.

She would wait until the other cars got close before firing. There were about four cars that were big enough and in position to cut them off on their current direction. Samuel had an inkling of where he wanted to head, so he would want to keep travelling in the current direction. Sheila was concentrating on the cars on the passenger side. Before one of the other cars rammed into them, she fired three shots and hit one of the cars. The jolt of the ram caused Sheila to drop the rifle. She screamed in fear and surprise. But she composed herself, picked up the rifle and started to shoot at the car that had rammed them. Then on the driver's side, two cars rammed them. The jolt was more severe than the passenger side one had been, but this time Sheila didn't drop the rifle and was able to fire and hit the other car on the passenger side.

The magazines of the EasyShooter stun rifles contained ten rounds and Sheila had used a magazine. She didn't know how to reload the weapon with a new magazine. While Samuel was counter ramming the two cars on the driver's side, he issued instructions on how to reload the stun rifle. Obviously, it would have been easier to show her rather than trying to explain it. But eventually Sheila was able to do it.

"Sit back!" she yelled.

Then she fired three shots out of the driver's side window. She hit one of the cars. There was now just one car ramming them. Their Civic had taken quite a bit of damage, but luckily not at the front where the engine was. The other car was trying to force their Civic to veer away from their current direction,

Sheila yelled again, "Sit back!" and then fired another four shots out the driver's side window. One of the shots hit the other car. Now all of the cars in the tribe were behind them and the Accords and CR-Vs were gaining ground, even though Samuel had accelerated to the maximum speed of the Civic. A turbo charged Accord VTi-LX was the first car to catch up with them.

The car screamed, *"Anata ga shindeshimau!"* which in Japanese means, "You will die!"

"This again," Samuel muttered. The Accord rammed the back of the Civic, causing it to spin. Samuel had to work hard to regain control and steer the car in the correct direction. But this allowed the rest of the tribe to catch up with them. They would soon be overwhelmed. If they were hit from behind again and went into a spin, the tribe would be able to ram them from every direction.

Samuel first heard the noise of a helicopter flying above and then some shots. He kept driving, hoping that they would not be hit from behind again. There were quite a few shots. It seemed that more than one shooter was shooting from the helicopter. A number of cars fell away from the pursuit. The shooters were marksmen and didn't waste a shot. Samuel kept driving and hoping. Sheila sat back and was also hoping. She thought about leaning out of the passenger side window and shooting behind them, but she didn't feel she had the courage. The shooters from the helicopter did their job. Any car that came close to ramming their car, was shot. Eventually, after about a third of the tribe had been shot, the pursuit was abandoned.

Samuel kept driving, but when the helicopter landed, he pulled up alongside it. There were four men in the helicopter, a pilot, two men with stun rifles and an officer.

As Sheila and Samuel approached the helicopter, the officer said, "I'm Lieutenant Marsden."

He was wearing a uniform with stripes on his arms. His neat and sharp appearance reminded Sheila of Roger, and she felt sad.

"I hope you are okay," he said with concern. "I thought there were three of you."

"Roger was killed by a yellow bear," Sheila replied.

"I'm sorry," the lieutenant replied. "We'd better get moving. The tribe may make another attempt."

They boarded the helicopter and took off. There was no talking for a while. There was only the noise of the helicopter's engine. So much had happened and Samuel and Sheila were lost in their own thoughts.

Finally, Sheila asked, "Is there any news from Fort Chrisholm?"

"I'm sorry," the lieutenant replied. "They were overrun. This freedom fighter Truck has amassed quite a following."

"How about Corizon? Did he make it?" Sheila asked.

"I'm sorry, there were no survivors," the lieutenant replied. "They alerted us to your expedition before they were attacked." The lieutenant's face was grim.

"We were waiting for a call from you and have been searching for you since their call," Samuel said. "The mobile phone didn't work in the mountains and then Roger had it when he died."

"Well, it was a piece of luck we found you. We were about to return to the fort when we saw your car being pursued," the lieutenant said.

Fort Adelaide was a much bigger fort than Fort Chrisholm. Within its walls there was quite a big township, and it had a few places where a helicopter could land. The buildings were made in much the same way as they were in

Fort Chrisholm. When they landed, they were escorted to an office in a large building.

"My commander will see you soon." the lieutenant directed. "Please wait here."

Then he left the room. The office had a large desk and a comfortable office chair, and in front of the desk were two smaller chairs. On the walls there were framed university certificates and other awards, also a picture of Fort Adelaide as it was being constructed. Samuel and Sheila sat on the smaller chairs.

Sheila turned to Samuel. "Well Sam, you got me here. Thank you," she said.

Then she gave him a kiss on his left cheek. Samuel tried not to blush but he did. There was an awkward pause, before Samuel stammered, "You were pretty handy with a stun rifle."

Chapter 6
The Train Wreck

Sergeant Toni Baker always held a debrief meeting with her brood at a favourite Hotel in Fort Adelaide. This time they needed some serious discussions, as their latest expedition didn't go well. *Some changes will be necessary,* she thought. But she put that thought to one side as she took out a Cuban cigar from her top pocket. The top pocket was to the left side of her big breasts. *Ah, that smells good,* she thought as she sniffed it. She liked doing that before lighting the cigar, to savour the treat that she'd worked so hard for and deserved. When she lit the cigar and put it in her mouth, she inhaled deeply. Then she paused and with the exhale she could relax.

Toni Baker was a black woman who always wore a loose-fitting military camouflage uniform that hid her wide hips and large breasts. It included a cap for her short curly hair. She had never been to Earth, so she never knew about where the cigars came from. She'd developed a liking for them when she worked in a Mercenary unit. Her superior officer had loved cigars and had offered one to Toni whenever she had performed well in her duties. Eventually, Toni became addicted to them. It was an expensive taste and Toni's stash was running low. She had a pending order but it would take years before it would arrive, and she hadn't fully paid for it yet. This was a concern for her after the failure of their latest expedition.

Toni had recruited her crew from a Mercenary unit deployed in Falimore, a desert world, rich in the metal, Palladium. It had been engaged in a bloody civil war for a number of years. However, eventually the war ended, and Toni and her comrades had to find other work. Toni had found out about car hunting on Omega 24A, and then went about recruiting a team. She called her team 'The Brood', as they were born again when they joined the Mercenaries. Her first recruit was Corporal Stretch. Corporal Stretch was Toni's second in command in the Mercenary unit. Stretch was a nickname, because he was tall and lanky, and walked with a gait. He had a full head of blonde hair and always wore a military camouflage uniform. The next most important recruit was Sniper Joe. That was also a nickname, because he was extremely talented at long distance shooting. Toni was lucky to get him, as Sniper Joe had left the Mercenary unit, because he discovered that he was a pacifist. Toni had to assure him that he would only be shooting stun pulses at cars. Sniper Joe never wore a military uniform. Instead, he wore hiking pants, polo shirt and a blue wide brim hat. Toni had recruited three other privates, but in the latest expedition, one of them was killed by angry cars. The two privates left, were David and Shane.

Toni had thought they had a good car hunting model. It was simple and scalable. They would position themselves near a fuel ball plantation. Sniper Joe would be located halfway up a mountain, where the fuel ball plantation was still in range of his stun rifle. Toni would park a Car Transport truck not far away from the fuel ball plantation, but she would not be in sight of it. Corporal Stretch and the three privates would be waiting in a military truck near the base of the mountain, not far from the fuel ball plantation. They would wait until a tribe of cars arrived to feed on the fuel balls. Sniper Joe would begin the attack. He would shoot at the most valuable cars. Sniper Joe had studied the makes and models of cars and knew a lot about them, so he knew what to look for. Once he had stunned about ten cars,

Corporal Stretch and the three privates would drive to the fuel ball plantation. One of the privates had the job of stunning a car and boarding it. He would then drive around and stir up the tribe of cars. Then the aggravated cars would chase him as he lured them away from the fuel ball plantation. Once they were lured away, Corporal Stretch and the other privates would drive the stunned cars to the Car transport truck. *A simple and effective plan,* Toni thought.

Toni relaxed in her chair, inhaled and then blew out some smoke.

"The last expedition did not go to plan." she said calmly.

Corporal Stretch jumped in. "It was a train wreck," he said.

Toni didn't like being interrupted, but she thought she should let others speak before she announced the solution.

"I could see from my position on the mountain." Sniper Joe said. "Private Adam didn't lead the cars safely away from the fuel ball plantation."

Private Adam had boarded one of the cars and the other cars chased him, but he couldn't get away from the tribe to lead them away.

"That was obvious," Corporal Stretch replied sternly. "Maybe if you had fired some live rounds that would have helped."

"Cars are intelligent beings. I can't shoot to kill," Sniper Joe replied.

Toni also thought that stunning cars so they can be captured and sent to toxic mines, would lead them to their death. But she thought the better of saying anything.

Corporal Stretch thought otherwise and said, "What's the use of a sniper who doesn't kill?"

Toni thought that was unhelpful and said to her corporal, "Aw Sweety Cheeks doesn't like the pacifist."

Toni used the phrase Sweety Cheeks when she was admonishing childish behaviour. That didn't quieten him though.

"Not only did the cars surround and kill Private Adam, they found our Car Transport truck and trashed it," Corporal Stretch complained.

"I know," replied Toni. "I was there."

Luckily, Corporal Stretch had shown good sense to drive back to the Car Transport Truck when he saw the cars kill Private Adam. For that Toni was grateful.

"Now we have to pay for another Car Transport truck," Corporal Stretch complained further.

"Maybe two people should board cars and lead the others away," Sniper Joe suggested.

No one said anything about this suggestion. Sniper Joe had another one. "Maybe the one who boards the car should choose a large car, so he could outrun the tribe."

Toni wasn't keen on either suggestion. She needed all the other men to drive the stunned cars to the car transport truck. She could only spare one man to divert the tribe of cars. Also, she didn't want to sacrifice a large car from her pool of captured cars. The profitability of the expedition was at stake.

Corporal Stretch still felt aggravated. "We wouldn't need an extra man to divert the cars, if you fired some live rounds to scare the cars away, he said to Sniper Joe. "The blood of Adam is on your hands."

"Enough Sweety Cheeks," Toni broke in. "This is not helping."

Corporal Stretch was a capable second in command, but he tended to hold grudges, Toni thought. In this case, he never accepted that sniper Joe was a pacifist. He saw it as a personality weakness. When Corporal Stretch was a Mercenary, he didn't fight for the money. Instead, he wanted revenge for the death of his parents. So, killing for him was done out of a sense of duty, to right previous wrongs. Toni was sympathetic to Corporal Stretch for the pain of losing both parents. But Toni had a team to lead, and everyone had to get along. Her team was her brood. The last expedition did not go well, and yes, maybe it was a train wreck, Toni thought. It was her responsibility to come up with a solution, so that the next expeditions would be successful and go to plan. Again, Toni inhaled, then blew out some smoke. She waited, to see if anyone else had something to say. When she was confident that they didn't, she sighed and prepared herself.

"What we need, men," she announced, "is a local. Someone who lives out there on that god forsaken, dust filled plains and survives."

Falimore was a desert world also, but Toni thought the dust on this world was more invasive and its sun far stronger than that world. This was a tough gig, that needed tough individuals. Toni inhaled and blew out some more smoke.

"A local would enhance our team and help us succeed," she continued. "A local would jump a car, stir up some dust and lead the others away with no fuss. We would all enjoy success."

Toni paused and then gauged the reaction of the others.

"How much would that cost?" Corporal Stretch whined.

Toni was a leader of Mercenaries, but she was also a businesswoman. She knew how to recruit cost effectively.

"Sweety Cheeks, let me worry about that," she said.

Toni consoled but with a touch of irritation. "I have a candidate," she announced. Toni was very good at keeping an ear to the ground, and picking up on gossip or events that had occurred. She was adept at getting leads for whatever she needed. Toni inhaled and blew out some more smoke.

"There is this Samuel Benson," she explained. "He brought a Journalist from Fort Chrisholm to Fort Adelaide. And he has been living by himself in the wilderness."

Toni was convinced that Samuel was the right man for the job of leading the tribe of cars away from the fuel ball plantation.

"Is he good with cars?" Corporal Stretch asked.

"He can jump them and wrestle control without having to stun them," Toni replied.

"Maybe that's what we need," Sniper Joe said in support.

No one else said anything. Toni took that as a sign of consent from her comrades.

"I will reach out to him then," she announced.

Chapter 7
Professor Seronen

Sheila and Samuel waited in the office. They took the seats in front of the desk. Eventually a tall middle aged Asian man with greasy hair combed over a bald spot, entered the room. He was wearing the same corporation uniform that they had seen worn by the employees at Fort Chrisholm. Sheila and Samuel stood up as he entered.

"I'm Captain Groswell, please take a seat," he said. "You've had quite a journey to get here?"

There was a pause, before Sheila responded with, "Yes."

"We were told that someone from Fort Chrisholm would transport your luggage to here," said Groswell. "But unfortunately, the fort was overrun. Did you bring any belongings with you?"

"I have my digital notepad, toiletries and one change of clothes," Sheila replied. The change of clothes was another uniform.

"I can give you one hundred and twenty credits so that you can buy what you need," the captain announced. "Son, Sheila has been employed to write some important articles for the Corporation. We are very grateful to you for getting her safely to Fort Adelaide. I will give you the same to buy whatever you need."

Both replied, "Thank you Captain."

In corporation towns they used a currency specific to that corporation. On Plantere, there were few open towns or cities. The majority of towns were Corporation forts.

"We have some rooms prepared for both of you," said Groswell. "Please, settle in and go to the markets to buy what you need. There is a mess hall in this building, so please, take your meals there. Tomorrow morning, I will introduce you to Professor Seronen. He is an expert in car anatomy."

The captain then called for a corporal on his intercom to come and show Sheila and Samuel to their rooms and how to get to the mess hall and markets.

Sheila was looking forward to going shopping. She hadn't done any proper clothes shopping since she left Earth. Although she wasn't expecting the markets at Fort Adelaide to be as good as the famous shopping areas on Earth, she was still anticipating a good range of options.

Samuel had never seen a market. Fort Adelaide was quite different from the other forts Samuel had visited in his lifetime. They were smaller and mainly employed military style employees, while Fort Adelaide accommodated other workers from different professions, such as health, education, Information Technology and accountants. Rather than always being on high alert, the inhabitants here enjoyed a sedentary lifestyle that included shopping at the markets.

In the middle of the township was a long mall that housed privately owned stalls, selling a wide variety of products, including food, clothes, jewellery, accessories and electronic goods. The stalls were housed under canvas marquee tents, with a variety of colours and logos. There was an inviting bustle as customers browsed, chatted about various items, and haggled with stallholders. Most of the goods were imported from other planets. Anything from Earth was expensive and highly sought after. The stallholders were businesspeople who organised imports and maintained their stalls. The Corporation, rather than charging the stallholders rent, and import duties for the goods imported, actually paid subsidies to them. This was done to widen the variety of available goods and keep prices lower for Corporation employees.

Sheila browsed the jewellery and accessory stalls and settled for earrings and a handbag, just in case she had to attend some special function. She didn't have any makeup though, or an outfit that would be appropriate for a function. It was so hard to know what she would need. Given, what had happened so far on her placement to Plantere, it would seem that her lifestyle would be rather rugged. Perhaps for now, she should just get a functional outfit, suitable for an official corporation meeting. After all, she did still have the uniforms. So, she ended up buying a jump suit, hat, shoes, some toiletries and makeup.

Samuel didn't think he needed anything, but Sheila suggested his car jumping suit was getting tatty and that maybe he should get a new one. So, he did. He was able to get a very good quality fitted camouflage car jumping suit. The suit had a military camouflage pattern that had the same colour as the dust on the plains. Much like the Corporation uniform. The suit had long sleeves and pants and was made completely from leather. This was to shield the wearer from grazes and bruises when jumping cars.

"Wow, you really look the part," Sheila teased. "An experienced and famous car hunter with his camouflage suit and Easy Shooter stun rifle."

Samuel didn't say anything. He felt a little embarrassed.

After a pause, Sheila asked, "What are your plans now, Sam?"

"I don't know," he replied.

"Come with me to the meeting with Professor Seronen. You could learn some more about cars," Sheila suggested.

She didn't know anyone on this world, and Samuel had proven to be a good friend. She wanted to keep him around.

The meeting with Professor Seronen was to be held in Captain Groswell's office. When Sheila and Samuel arrived, the door was closed. They could hear some voices coming from inside. Without hearing the actual words, they could tell that someone was getting a dressing down. They backed away from the door. Sheila felt embarrassed. The door opened and a young man in uniform hurried out. Behind him, Captain Groswell was standing in the doorway.

"I'm surrounded by incompetents," he muttered.

When he saw Sheila and Samuel he said, "Sheila, Samuel, please come in. Professor Seronen should be here shortly."

When Professor Seronen arrived, the captain made the introductions. The Professor was an older balding man. His hair was completely white, and he sported an Old Dutch style beard. His posture was hunched over. Yet his eyes showed a passion for what he had been studying. After the introductions were made, the captain excused himself.

Sheila conducted the interview. Before she would delve into the questions of the anatomy of cars, she wanted to find out about the professor's background. He had studied extensively in various universities on Earth. His degrees majored in Mechatronics, Medical Science, Psychiatry and Mathematics.

He was hired by the Iowa Corporation fifteen years ago to study cars at one of the car yards, on a world about fifteen light years away from Plantere. When cars were first harvested from Plantere, the scientists at the time believed they were robots with a high level of artificial intelligence. But Professor Seronen's studies debunked that hypothesis.

His latest PhD paper was about the anatomy of the cars from Plantere. In the academic world it sparked debate about life and what it means to be a life form.

Sheila finally asked, "I thought the twentieth century combustion engine vehicles were just machines?"

"They were," the professor replied. "But the cars on Plantere are life forms. They have a brain and organs. They also heal when they are wounded."

Samuel agreed. "He is right, cars are animals."

"So, if a car has a broken windscreen, dented fender or flat tyre, it will heal any of those?" Sheila asked.

"Yes," replied the professor.

"How could that be, those things are made out of glass, rubber and steel," Sheila pressed.

"Humans have teeth made from enamel and horses have hooves made out of keratin. What about the tortoise shell, or feathers on birds?" the Professor replied. Sheila looked puzzled and the Professor saw that he needed to explain further. "Come with me to the car yards," he invited, "I'm in the middle of doing an autopsy on a young blue Ford Laser."

Sheila was intrigued. She and Samuel followed the Professor to the car yards. There, they could see cars parked in pens, bumper to bumper. Samuel noticed a flash from the top of a pole.

"What is that?" he asked.

The Professor answered, "That is a stun pulse. It keeps the cars stunned so they can't try to escape. It was introduced into the car yards of every fort because of an unfortunate incident where a mining truck led an escape from the pens."

The Professor led Sheila and Samuel into a garage next to the pens. Inside the garage there was a hoist with a Blue Ford Laser on top, about one metre above the ground. On the driver's door there was a square where the metal had been cut away.

"Yesterday I cut some of the door away," said the Professor. "You can see that there are glands behind the metal plate of the door."

He pointed to the tissue exposed in the square. Then he went over to a table that held a microscope and a piece of metal. "Come over here and have a closeup look," he said. "You can see there are pores in the metal. The glands excrete a cleaning fluid to the metal plates, so the car self-cleans as it drives."

"Something like Wax and Go?" Sheila suggested.

"Exactly," said the Professor.

Samuel asked, "Wax and Go?"

"On Earth," Sheila explained. "Wax and Go is sprayed onto our travel pods so that they self-clean as they fly."

Most people on Earth didn't know about Wax and Go because travel pods weren't owned by commuters. They were summoned when needed. The Wax and Go was applied to the vehicles in the travel hub. Sheila knew about it because she had worked at a travel hub as a receptionist when she was a teenager.

"How come old cars are dirty then?" asked Samuel.

It was true that young cars in the wild still have some dust but the older cars were covered in it.

"The glands begin to fail as the car ages. Just as damaged windows and fenders stop repairing themselves," the Professor answered. "It depends on the make or model of a car, but I estimate that ageing occurs between forty and sixty Earth years of a car's life."

The Laser was missing one wheel and the Professor pointed at the suspension exposed by the missing wheel.

"You can see," he said, "the suspension on this car is very strong. Much stronger than that of a twentieth century car. You could drop this car from some height, and it would not be damaged."

The Professor then lowered the hoist. He picked up a mallet and hit with full force the driver's side fender of the car. The fender was not dented.

"Twentieth century cars were designed to crumple when they collide with something, to protect the passengers," explained the Professor. "That is not the case with these cars. Their bodies are very sturdy. In the event that they are dented, the metal bounces back to the original shape."

He then opened the bonnet from a lever on the driver's side and showed Samuel and Sheila the engine of the car.

"See, look at the insides," he said. "The engine is organic. The pipes and engine look rubbery."

Sheila reached out and touched the engine. It didn't feel like metal. It felt like an organ from a person's body.

"I showed you all this, to demonstrate to you that the cars on this world are life forms," the Professor explained. He then led Sheila and Samuel back to the captain's office.

"If there are any questions that need answers for your journal," he said to Sheila, "please reach out to me. I'm happy to assist."

Sheila left the interview with a feeling of great wonder. This harsh world had something that was very precious. Professor Seronen was a formidable academic, but he also had the ability to describe a phenomenon in words that the everyday person could understand. That ability was probably cultivated by his work for the Corporation. When the captain returned to his office, Sheila thanked him and the Professor for the interview and said that it would contribute greatly to her work.

For the next week, Sheila was busy interviewing Corporation employees about their work and life at Fort Adelaide. She was beginning to get a picture of what life was like on Plantere. It seemed so removed from her life on Earth.

She also had a very interesting interview with a geologist who had studied Plantere. He was a young man, fresh out of university. Like Sheila, he came from Earth. That is, he grew up and studied in Norway. For his PhD, he had written a paper about the volcanoes in Iceland. He was tall with blonde hair and blue eyes. He loved studying geology on different planets, and was so happy to have been given the opportunity to travel to remote worlds.

"If there isn't a lot of water or wind on Plantere, how come there are canyons? And why do they cover the whole planet in the same way?" Sheila asked him.

"The phenomenon that has played out on Plantere was very different to anything on Earth," The geologist replied. "The planet has a uniform crust of a rock type not unlike that of sandstone." This had been his topic of study during his tenure on Plantere. So he was well placed to answer Sheila's questions. He was trying to mould his answer in layman terms.

"When the planet was young, the terrain was flat or mildly hilly at best," he continued. "But over time the crust became brittle." Since he knew that Sheila came from Earth, he thought it would be useful to make comparisons with

Earth. "Like Earth," he said, "Plantere has a magma in its core. But unlike Earth, the expansion of the magma didn't create volcanoes."

Sheila was listening intently and was making notes as the geologist was giving his answer.

"As I was saying," he said. "Over time the crust became brittle. This was uniform over the whole planet. So, when the pressure of the magma was too much, the whole of the planet's surface cracked all over, causing it to expand." He then concluded, "That is what formed the canyons. And that is why the canyons cover the whole planet."

Samuel enjoyed the week exploring what life had to offer to a townsperson. He savoured the food, the different dishes from Earth. He watched holographic movies. Also, he took his stun rifle to the firing range. He met and spoke to a number of people. Many were subjects of Sheila's interviews. In the end, the time flew by. But Samuel began to think of home and his new life as a professional car hunter, with his own Easy-Shooter stun rifle.

Captain Groswell summoned Sheila and Samuel to his office in the late afternoon. He included Samuel, because of his efforts to deliver Sheila safely to Fort Adelaide, but also because he'd heard good things about Samuel from Corporation employees. The captain said little but noted that they were required to attend another meeting with Professor Seronen, the next morning.

The meeting with the Professor was held in a large conference room with long tables set out in a rectangle. In the middle was a circular platform. There were quite a few people in this meeting. That was unexpected. Sheila had envisioned another private interview with the professor.

"What's that?" Samuel asked in a whisper, as he pointed to the circular platform in the centre.

"It's a holographic display. It shows maps, pictures and videos in three dimensions," she whispered back.

"I wish we had one of those at Fort Chrisholm," Samuel lamented.

Most of the people were Iowa employees. No one was sitting down, and they were chatting amongst themselves. In the corner there was a boisterous, well- built man dressed in a khaki collared shirt and matching shorts with a camouflage pattern, but not of the colours of the plains. Rather, they had the colours of the mountains. He was quite animated and had a deep hearty laugh. He was talking to two Iowa military employees.

Eventually, Captain Groswell entered with the Professor.

"Everyone, please be seated. I present to you Professor Seronen," he announced. "He is an expert in car anatomy and has studied the socialisation and language of the cars we have captured. His last PhD paper was about the cars of this world. He has come a long way to lead you in this important expedition."

Professor Seronen loved to do research and write papers, but he also had a passion for presentations. He presented to other academics or to lay people. He was adept at both. He looked around the room. There were many military employees. Captain Groswell had let him know before, that Sheila would be present, and would be writing a journal which would refer to his work. So, he had to pitch his presentation to lay people and use common language to make his points. He also needed to inject some controversy. Have something that would jump out as a headline. He had prepared some hologram slides to help him engage his audience. The first one was a picture of a young blue Porsche. It was rotating on the holographic display.

The professor started. "We know little about where the cars on this world come from. We are light years away from Earth, but here we have life forms mirroring Twentieth and early Twenty-first century combustion engine vehicles. How did they come to be?"

He paused and stroked his beard. And then he continued to ask questions.

"How do they reproduce? How come there are so many makes and models? And their language. Why is it their native tongue matches the Earth origin of their make? Why are they here of all places? These questions, I believe are close to an answer."

The Professor looked around the room. The picture of the blue Porsche was still rotating. He wanted to see if he was engaging his audience. He wanted them on the edge of their seats, rather than just politely listening. When he was satisfied, he continued.

"From the expedition I will lead, we will find these answers. Seven hundred years ago, there was a famous geneticist, Professor Hiedenburg, who was travelling just a few light years away from here."

The holographic picture changed to one of a young Professor Hiedenburg. He still had all his hair and there were no greys.

"He sent a distress signal, but no one ever found him. He was not only a geneticist but an enthusiast for combustion engine vehicles."

Professor Seronen stretched over the lectern. Now, this was the headline he wanted for Sheila's benefit. He announced, "I believe he is the connection to the origin of the cars."

He paused to look around the room and made eye contact with many in the audience. Then he continued.

"One of our satellites has located a wreck of a spaceship. It could be his ship."

The holographic picture changed to one of a satellite view of the spaceship. Now the Professor needed to get technical. He tried to find the language of the common people.

"If we find this spaceship, then maybe we could find the secret of how the cars reproduce. All cars are asexual, they are neither female or male. We hunt them, but then there are still more of them."

He hoped that he had expressed it in a way that everyone would understand.

"If we found out how they reproduce, then the Corporation would no longer need to hunt them. We could just reproduce what we needed. If we found out how there are so many makes and models, then we could tweak the reproduction process to make the models that are more useful to us."

This was the goal of the expedition. Obviously, it was good for the Corporation, but for Professor Seronen, it was exciting. And it showed in his presentation. A holographic picture of trucks and sports cars was shown. The Professor concluded to inspire the audience.

"There is so much at stake in this expedition. It won't be easy, and the cars are becoming more organised in their defence, but the profitability of our organisation is at stake. Take courage and motivation in what you do now. This is an important mission."

The Professor's speech was met by all-round applause. Captain Groswell rose and adjusted his uniform. He looked very official. "The cars are becoming organised, so we need a strong force to protect this expedition," He announced.

He paused and detailed the defence of the expedition. There were to be four tanks armed with stun cannons. The soldiers accompanying the expedition would be armed with the latest Easy-Shooter stun rifles. The expedition would have twenty soldiers. There would also be two helicopters to be used for scouting. After describing the defences, he went on to introduce key people for the expedition. He said,

"Can I please introduce you to Jonathon, mountain master of the Gordon-mountain tribe. He has made his services available in the chance that this expedition needs to traverse mountains."

The boisterous man Sheila had seen earlier, stood up. He was not only well built but was extremely well-muscled. You could see he was very strong. Like Samuel, he had red hair, tanned skin and blue eyes. He didn't speak, but looked around the room and smiled just before he made a sign of salute.

"Also, I'm happy to introduce Sheila McSporran. She is a journalist working for the Corporation. She will document the progress of this expedition," the captain added.

Sheila was stunned. The captain had never mentioned anything about an expedition. She stood up slowly.

"This is the plan," the captain continued. He clicked a button on the same remote control that Professor Seronen was using and a three-dimensional map appeared just above the platform in the centre of the tables. "The satellite images of the possible spacecraft, are of a location about 6000 kilometres west of here."

The picture of the map became a picture of a fort. It was rotating.

"The closest fort is Fort Jackson," continued the captain. "That fort belonged to the Nimeria Corporation, and we have purchased it from them. We have extended its defences and built a small space port within its extended walls. So, all our equipment and supplies will be delivered to that fort."

The picture then dissolved to another three-dimensional map.

"The map we have here shows our route from the fort to the estimated position of the spacecraft. If we follow the canyons along this route, it is about a 1100- kilometre journey. It should take us three days."

The next picture showed mountains.

"We don't expect a need to cross the mountains, but if we are attacked by an overwhelming force, then we may need to retreat to them. However, I'm hopeful that it will not come to that. And, finally," the captain concluded, "Please keep all this to yourselves. This expedition must be kept secret. There is no time to waste. We will leave in four days, first thing in the morning."

Sheila was terrified. "Sam, you have to come too," she implored. She grabbed Samuel's hand and led him to where the captain was standing. "Why didn't you tell me you wanted me to go on this expedition, yesterday?" she demanded.

"I'm sorry, but I needed to keep this expedition secret. We have competitors that would be interested in this," the captain explained.

"Can Samuel come along?" she asked.

"Of course," the captain replied. "Having another car hunter in the team would be most useful,"

Chapter 8
The Star Recruit

Samuel and Sheila were having dinner at the main Hotel of Fort Adelaide. Both of them still felt a bit stunned from the news that they would be going on the expedition in four days. Samuel was trying to work out how he'd ended up in this expedition. There was a part of him that just wanted to return to his parent's house on the cliff face. But then, there was a bigger part that wanted to follow Sheila. She was very beautiful, and he felt that he got along with her. Maybe she just thought of him as a friend, but he wanted a deeper relationship. He had never felt like this before. Not that he had met any other women before now. Sheila was hoping she could stay at Fort Adelaide and interview people for her journal in safety. She had had a big enough adventure just getting here. Both of them were silent as they had their dinner, lost in their own thoughts.

They were eating when a black woman in military uniform approached them.

"Hello, are you Samuel Benson?" she said to Samuel.

"Yes I am," Samuel replied.

Sheila did not have a good feeling about this woman. She smelled of tobacco, and Sheila was suspicious of being approached by strangers in a hotel. She was a journalist and had experience with people doing bad things.

"Who is it wants to know?" she asked,

"Yes, of course," the woman said politely, "My name is Sergeant Toni Baker. I lead a team of professional car hunters. May I sit with you?"

Samuel felt intrigued. A commander of professional car hunters had sought him out. "Yes, please do," he replied.

Toni pulled over another chair and sat down. She pulled out a cigar from her top pocket and asked Samuel, "Do you partake?"

"I have never smoked." Samuel replied.

Sheila thought it a disgusting habit.

"Do you mind if I do?" Toni asked.

"No, please do," Samuel replied.

Toni lit her cigar, leant back in her chair and then inhaled. When she blew the smoke out, she tried to direct it away from Samuel and Sheila.

"As I was saying, I lead a team of professional hunters and we are about to embark on a new expedition," she continued, then leaned forward and continued to Samuel, "I have heard a bit about you, and would like to offer you a position in my team as a junior car hunter."

Samuel was excited. This was his dream to be a car hunter and a member of a team of professionals.

"What would be his pay?" Sheila asked suspiciously.

Toni leant back in her chair and put her hands behind her head. "As Samuel is new to the team, his role would be junior car hunter," she said. "But because we are a generous team, he would receive one tenth of the value of cars captured."

Wow! one tenth of the proceeds, Samuel thought.

"We have another expedition in four days' time," said Sheila.

"That's okay," Toni replied, "Our next expedition starts first thing tomorrow morning. We should complete the car hunting on the same day."

Samuel thought this was perfect. He could consolidate a career in car hunting before going off with Sheila. Sheila was less convinced. She didn't trust this woman.

Samuel could hardly contain himself. "I accept," he said.

"Then it is done, Toni replied. "You will be our Star Recruit."

"I'm writing a journal about Plantere. Could I please come along as well?" Sheila asked.

Sheila thought that Samuel needed some protection. Someone to look out for him. Maybe he was at home in this world and could survive all the hardships. But she knew that in the inter-solar system world he was naïve and needed protection. Even though she felt safe in Fort Adelaide and did not look forward to any expeditions in the wilderness, she felt a responsibility to Samuel. So, she would go, to look out for him.

"Of course. I know you two are friends," replied Toni.

The next morning Sheila and Samuel met Toni and her team at the front of the main Hotel of Fort Adelaide. Toni introduced Sheila and Samuel to the rest of the team before they drove off in the Car Transport Truck and the military truck. Sheila and Samuel sat with Toni in the Car Transport Truck.

"I will give you a rundown of the operation," said Toni to Samuel. "Today we are hunting cars from a Holden tribe. Sniper Joe will be positioned part way up the mountain. We will wait until the tribe of cars come to feed on the fuel ball plantation. Sniper Joe will shoot all the cars we want to capture."

Toni was driving the Car Transport Truck and was looking out the front window as she spoke but then she turned and looked at Samuel before adding, "It is important that you don't jump any of the cars Sniper Joe shoots. He is an expert and will pick out the cream of the crop. You will need to shoot or jump another car. Do you understand?"

She turned to look out the front window again.

"Yes ma'am," said Samuel.

Toni parked the Car Transport Truck at the rendezvous point. Samuel joined the others in the military truck, while Sheila stayed with Toni in the Car Transport Truck. The military truck then left. Corporal Stretch parked it near a cliff face not far from the fuel ball plantation. Sniper Joe left the truck and started to climb the mountain. When he found a good position, he contacted Corporal Stretch to let him know.

"Now all we have to do is wait for the cars," Corporal Stretch said to his companions. He tapped on the steering wheel nervously.

Samuel began to feel nervous also. He didn't enjoy the wait. They waited a long time. Samuel was thinking that they may have to go home again and come back tomorrow. But he knew that today was going to be a long day, so surely the cars would come today.

And eventually they did. There were about eighty cars in the tribe. Sniper Joe waited until all the cars had begun feeding, before picking out the most valuable cars. He shot Holden Kingswood wagons, Holden Commodores V8 and a Holden Captiva LX (4X4). He really did pick out the best cars in the tribe.

"Ok team, it's time to go," said Corporal Stretch, and he drove the military truck to the fuel ball plantation. When they arrived, he turned to Samuel, "Ok, you are on, Samuel. Grab a car and lead the others away."

Samuel exited the military truck and scanned the cars feeding on the fuel plantation. The cars hadn't yet realised that some of their comrades had been stunned. Samuel had a bit of time to decide which car he was going to jump. He didn't want to accidently pick a car that Sniper Joe had shot and also the car had to be nearby. Finally, he chose a Holden Barina CD. Not a fast car. Samuel shot and stunned the Barina with his Easy-Shooter rifle. He then ran to it and climbed inside before the other cars noticed. Once inside, Samuel took control and drove around the plantation honking the car's horn. He drove in a tight circle and the wheels of his car brought up clouds of dust. The tribe then realised they were under attack and started to chase Samuel's Barina. There were bigger cars in the tribe than the Barina, so they could catch him. Samuel tried to lead them away from the fuel ball plantation. But he had to twist and turn to keep ahead of the cars.

"This is not good," Samuel muttered. "I needed a bigger car."

Meanwhile, Corporal Stretch was on the radio to Toni. "Samuel has led the cars away from the fuel plantation," he said. "We are bringing some captured cars now."

"Excellent. Our local is doing good," replied Toni.

Corporal Stretch then called. "I think he may be in a bit of trouble," he said. "I don't think he can stay ahead of the cars."

Toni liked Samuel. She liked Samuel's enthusiasm and willingness to take orders. But she leant back in her seat and said, "Don't worry, he is a local, he can look after himself."

Sheila was appalled and gave her a disapproving look.

Toni saw the look and exclaimed, "What?"

Sheila was angry. "You are cruel," she accused.

Toni defended herself. "We are just a group of mercenaries, just trying to make a living. Sniper Joe..." She paused..." is a pacifist. Corporal Stretch is angry over the death of his parents. I understand that." Toni then paused again before asking, "What do you expect from us?"

This just made Sheila angrier. She continued her accusation. "So, you are just going to let him die? Are you?"

"You have seen how he operates." Toni responded. "He can look after himself. He has lived in the wilderness all this time."

"Do you know why he lived in the wilderness for so long?" Sheila demanded. Toni didn't answer so she continued. "His parents were killed by a tribe of angry cars."

She had spoken forcefully, and Toni was taken aback. Meanwhile Corporal Stretch and the privates had brought back some of the captured cars. Sheila glared at Toni once more.

Toni leant forward and mumbled, "Ahh, crap." She got out of the truck and asked Corporal Stretch, "Which of these cars is the fastest?"

"I think that Holden Commodore V8 is," replied the Corporal.

Toni climbed into the Commodore and wound down the driver's window.

"I'm going to get Samuel," she said. "Bring back the rest of the cars and stack them in the truck. I will be back soon."

And before Corporal Stretch could reply, she drove off.

Samuel had driven in twists and turns, but the other cars had caught him and surrounded his Barina. They began to ram it from all directions. If he stayed in the car he would die. He unwound the driver's side window and climbed out of the car and onto the roof. The cars were ramming his Barina furiously and Samuel was struggling to stay on the roof.

One of the cars surrounding him said, "You will die human, for disturbing our feeding."

Samuel thought, *they still don't know that some of their tribe has been stunned*. He had to stun another car. Perhaps this time he would choose a bigger car. He couldn't see one. But he saw an FX 48-215. This model was a very old one, designed and made in 1948. Samuel chose it because it looked very solid. From the roof of his Barina, he stunned it. Samuel then jumped from the roof of his car onto the bonnet of one of the cars ramming his Barina. He then jumped onto the bonnet of another car before jumping onto the roof of the FX 48-215. That was difficult, because the roof of this car was curved, but easier than the bonnet, as it had a hump. Samuel used his car jumping mallet to break the driver's side window. And once he did that, he was able to slide into the driver's seat. It took a while for the cars ramming the Barina to notice that Samuel had switched cars, allowing him a little time to try to escape. But his FX 48-215 was slower than his Barina, so he didn't get far before he was surrounded again.

"I'm never going to get out of this," he muttered, as the other cars were ramming his FX 48-215.

Samuel climbed out of his FX 48-215 and onto the roof. Once again, he would have to try to stun another car to escape. Just as he was looking for another car, he saw a Commodore V8 ram one of the cars that was ramming his FX 48-215.

Suddenly, he saw Toni unwind her window of the Commodore V8 and heard her shout,

"Over here Samuel!"

Samuel jumped from roof to bonnet, then bonnet to the roof of the Commodore V8, and into the passenger side, as Toni opened the passenger side door.

"You came for me?" Samuel asked, surprised.

"I'm full of surprises," Toni muttered back.

She reversed the Commodore and found a gap between cars, then sped off. The Commodore V8 was faster than any other car in the tribe, so gradually she put some distance between them and the tribe. Samuel was thankful and surprised.

"Why did you come back for me?" he asked.

Toni was going to say, "That's what I do," but then she thought about it. She would not normally come to the rescue. She didn't know why she had come back for Samuel. Then she realised.

"I know what it is like to lose both parents when you are young," she said. "I never knew my parents. All I know is they were not good people."

Samuel fell silent. He felt a little bit lucky. He did know his parents and they had been good people.

"You did well here today," Toni continued. "You led the cars away from the fuel plantation and we have a truck full of captured cars. This expedition was a success, because of what you did here." She patted Samuel on the back. "I'm going to give you a bonus. One eighth share of the proceeds."

Samuel's eyes lit up. A bonus from a successful group of car hunting professionals.

Toni drove the Commodore V8 up onto the Car Transporting Truck and she and Samuel climbed out. Sheila ran up to Samuel and asked, "Are you okay?"

"Yes, I'm okay. Sergeant Toni got me home."

Samuel was grateful. Sheila thought it was what Toni should have done all along. Toni was the leader. It was her responsibility to look out for all her team members.

When Samuel, Sheila and Toni were back in the Car Transporting Truck, Toni pulled out a cigar from her top pocket. She took her customary sniff before lighting it. Because of this expedition she was closer to paying off her next order of cigars. Toni smoked as she drove the Car Transporting Truck back to Fort Adelaide. She reiterated her comment about this expedition.

"This was a successful expedition, Samuel. We did good here today," she said, then asked, "Samuel, would you like to go out with us again?"

Samuel was thrilled. "Yes, of course," he replied.

Sheila gave him a disapproving look. *Surely Samuel can see through this band of mercenaries*, she thought.

The first stop at Fort Adelaide was the car yards. Toni climbed out of the Car Transporting Truck and negotiated the payment for her captured cars. Once done, she climbed back into the Car Transporting Truck and smiled at Samuel as she handed him some money. "Here is your cut," she said. "Nothing better than cold hard cash."

She smiled at him. Sheila held her tongue and just looked straight ahead. Toni drove them to the hotel at Fort Adelaide. When Samuel and Sheila were out of the truck,

Sheila looked sternly at Samuel and said, "Promise me, that you won't go out with that band of cut-throats again."

Samuel was taken aback. "But Toni came back for me," he said.

Sheila sighed and looked away. She didn't want to tell Samuel why Toni went back for him. At the time she was surprised that she had.

Samuel continued. "Toni gave me a bonus, one eighth of the proceeds."

That didn't impress Sheila. There were six of them in the team and Samuel did the riskiest job. He should have got at least one sixth of the proceeds. Once again, she looked sternly at Samuel and repeated, "Just promise me."

Samuel didn't want to disappoint Sheila, so he acquiesced. "Ok, I promise," he said.

Chapter 9
Journey to the Spaceship

On the morning of the expedition to the spaceship they boarded a space transporter, and in a couple of hours had landed at Fort Jackson. Sheila decided to wear her Corporation Uniform, as she thought that her jump suit wasn't the appropriate attire. Samuel was offered a uniform as well, but he declined, saying he preferred his car jumping suit.

The fit out for the expedition was extensive. Not only were there the four tanks the captain mentioned before, but there were also, three empty semitrailers, each with an additional trailer. There were two open military trucks to transport soldiers and other personnel. And then two more trucks to carry supplies and equipment. No expense had been spared for this mission. If the expedition achieved its goal, then the Corporation would reap a tremendous profit.

The day was fairly short, but the night would be long. In the barracks of the fort Sheila enjoyed her last sleep in a comfortable bed. It could be her last for a while. It was nice to feel safe and secure.

Samuel lay awake for a time, trying to work out how he ended up in this expedition. There was a part of him that just wanted to return to his parents' house on the cliff face. But then, there was a bigger part that wanted to follow Sheila. She was very beautiful, and he felt that he talked easily with her. Maybe she just thought of him as friend, but he wanted a deeper relationship. He had never felt like this before. Not that he had met any other women before now.

They left early the next morning. Again, the day wasn't going to be long, though the nighttime would be. In one of the two trucks, most of the soldiers sat together, while the civilians sat in the other truck. The trucks were open, but they did have roofs to cover the occupants from the sun. The fort was located in a small box canyon, with only one exit. However, this joined a much wider valley, being about three kilometres in width. For now, Captain Groswell decided to drive in the middle, allowing them a good view on what was ahead. There were clouds of dust raised as they went along, which obscured the view behind them. Occasionally he would see a helicopter doing a round of scouting. But other than that, the morning was uneventful. The expedition followed the valley quite some distance before turning into another equally wide one. For most of the journey, this was to be the case. It would only be when they were nearing their destination that the valleys become narrow.

Sheila looked out onto the plains. It was barren and she could sometimes see dust in the air. One thing she noticed was that the ride was smooth. The trucks didn't drive over any loose rocks. There was a lot of dust but it wasn't sandy, like sand hills in a desert. The ground was firm. Sheila didn't want to waste any time. She had some more questions for Professor Seronen, especially about Professor Hiedenburg. So, she stood up from her seat and went over to Professor Seronen. He was reading a research paper on an electronic pad and was deep in thought. He didn't notice Sheila approach.

Sheila gained his attention with, "Good morning, Professor."

He looked up and put his pad away, before returning the greeting. "What can I help you with?" he asked.

The Professor wasn't into small talk, as he had work to do. Sheila sensed this, so she got straight to her point.

"Do you know much about Professor Hiedenburg?" she asked.

"Not a great deal," he answered. Then he added, "He was probably the most gifted geneticist of his time. Even now, there would be few who could match him."

Professor Seronen's heroes were fellow academics. They wrote inspiring research papers, and they led the way in scientific thought.

"He wrote a number of papers which are still being referred to by other scientists," He continued. "His most famous one was titled, "The Genome Structure of Amphibians on Upsilon Four."

Sheila gave him a look showing she didn't understand the significance of this.

Seronen continued. "He was able to identify the exact part of DNA coding which was responsible for even the smallest trait of an animal. Not only that, but he was also able to create a genome from scratch and form his own animal."

He waited to see if Sheila had grasped the enormity of this breakthrough, before he gave a caveat. "Although he could only do it to form simple organisms," he added. He paused before continuing his explanation.

"The paper he published describing this work was titled, *'Creating an organism with Synthetic DNA.'* He was brilliant. During his career, advancements in genetics forged ahead at an unprecedented rate. Yes, Professor Hiedenburg was one of my heroes. He was sorely missed when he disappeared. I believe he was destined for a distant planet to study the life forms there, when he sent out a distress signal."

"Professor Heidenburg was a brilliant geneticist. But how does he relate to the reproduction of the cars?" Sheila asked.

"He had a passion about combustion engine vehicles," the Professor answered. "When he was young, he used to race them in events run by the historic Land Vehicles club. The members of the club would restore combustion engine racing cars and then compete in rallies with them. I understand that he kept at least a dozen restored vehicles. He loved them. He never married, so his cars were his companions. He brought them everywhere he went. You must understand that his spaceship was very large and was fitted out extensively. It had a laboratory and a workshop as well as a show room for his cars. He did a lot of travelling."

Sheila was enthralled by what she had heard. It made her think and being a good journalist, she had more questions.

"If Professor Heidenburg did make the cars, why did he make them feed off fuel balls? Surely, he could have made them to photosynthesise themselves or give them electric engines." She asked.

"A good question," Seronen replied. "Professor Heidenburg was a car enthusiast. He probably loved the roar of a combustion engine and the smell of petrol."

Sheila had a love of history. She had studied countless eras and historical events. She reflected on the cars. Their time was the twentieth century and the first half of the twenty first century. One of the greatest challenges for humankind of the twenty first century was climate change. They had to wean themselves of fossil fuels. That meant they had to build cars with electric engines, rather than combustion ones. But there were other changes. Vehicles became self -driving. So, they no longer needed steering wheels, brake and accelerator pedals, indicators or horns. Also, people no longer owned vehicles. They would simply book them when they needed them. Yes, the vehicles that Sheila knew were very different to the cars, Sheila mused. In historical terms, the era of the cars was short, only one hundred and fifty years. Sheila changed tack on her questioning.

"What do you expect to find when we reach the spaceship?"

"I don't know," Seronen replied, "We don't even know if this is his ship. This whole expedition is a long shot. But what if we did find the secret of how the cars reproduce? It would be remarkable."

Samuel was sitting next to Jonathon, the mountain master. Up close he could see that Jonathon was a middle-aged man, with tinges of grey on his temples. He was holding a long spear made of solar glass. It was not as big as the helicopter harpoons Samuel had seen at the wrecked helipad site, but it was bigger than Sergeant Blackmore's sword. It looked very heavy. Samuel was in awe. He eventually plucked up the courage to ask a question.

"Do you hunt yellow bears?"

Jonathon turned to Samuel with a kindly smile and replied, "Yes, my whole tribe does."

"Do you use helicopters with harpoons?"

Jonathon laughed deeply and not unkindly. "Those Corporation clowns. They don't know how to hunt bears."

Samuel pressed further. "I found Sergeant Blackmore's sword at a wrecked helipad site. He killed bears with it."

"So, he was a knight in shining armour, out to slay a dragon with a magic sword?" Jonathon teased. He patted

Samuel on the back in a show of mateship. "No son, if you want to hunt bears you have to do it as part of a team. Each member watches out for the other, so that the only one who is slain is the bear. What is your name, lad?"

"Sam," Samuel replied.

"What do you do for a living Sam?

"My parents used to hunt cars. I was thinking of doing the same," said Samuel. "They had a house on a ledge of a cliff. It was safe there."

Jonathon was curious and asked, "How do you hunt cars, Sam?"

"Well now I have a stun rifle, but before I would have to jump them," Samuel replied.

"Jump them?" Jonathon didn't understand.

"You jump on the bonnet of the car, and then use this to smash a window, so you can get inside," Samuel replied, as he pulled out his car jumping mallet.

"So how did you get mixed up in this expedition?"

"Sheila and I came up to Fort Adelaide from Fort Chisholm. She is a journalist working for the Corporation." Samuel replied.

"So, you came along for the ride?" said Jonathon with a laugh. Meanwhile a helicopter flew overhead carrying an armed soldier with the pilot. The pilot spoke into a headset.

"It has been clear up until now. We can spot a metallic green Porsche travelling over a hundred kilometres per hour. Not heading in our direction. Over."

"Roger, 'Copter one," replied Captain Groswell.

"Should we stun it? Over." the pilot asked.

Captain Groswell thought that his pilot was trigger happy. This expedition needed stealth and subtlety. The last thing they needed was a battle with a tribe of cars. He rolled his eyes and replied. "Negative, 'Copter one. It may warn others that we are here, if this one doesn't return in a timely manner."

"Can we do another sweep to see if there are any more? Over." the pilot asked.

"Negative, Copter One. Copter Two can do it."

Captain Groswell didn't want to risk Copter One shooting anything. Instead, he ordered, "We need you to find a safe camping site." He didn't want to rely on the judgement of his pilot, so he gave a description of what he wanted. "In a narrow canyon with only one entrance," he specified.

The pilot then took the helicopter ahead of the party's route to find a suitable camping site nearby.

The expedition had made good progress on the first day of driving. They didn't encounter any cars. With about two hours until nightfall, Captain Groswell was informed by the pilot of the first helicopter, that a suitable camping site had been found not far from their current route.

It was about time, Captain Groswell thought.

They had to make a detour from their planned route, but it wasn't too long, about half an hour. They reached the campsite with about an hour to spare before nightfall. So there was time to erect the tents and cook dinner. Captain Groswell ordered that during the night pairs of soldiers would take it in turns to keep watch. He didn't think they were in any danger, but he wanted to be seen as cautious. The civilians were placed at the back of the campsite. Since Sheila was the only civilian woman on the expedition, she had her own tent. Samuel shared a tent with Jonathon. Between the three of them they had a portable heater that they could all sit around when it became dark. For dinner, they had heated ration packs from a choice of spaghetti Bolognese, Thai green curry and Irish stew. Sheila took off her hat and ran her hands through her hair. The dust she thought. It is everywhere. It was on her face, in her hair and on her uniform. She really wanted to have a shower. But there was no chance of that. In the end she, told herself, never mind I'm on assignment.

As they sat around the heater and had their dinner Sheila asked Jonathon, "How many people are in your tribe?"

"There are thirty- three of us," Jonathon replied. "There are eight of us in the hunting team when we hunt bears. We've had quite a few children in the tribe over the last little while."

"Do you have a wife and children?" Sheila asked.

"Yes," Jonathon replied, "We have two children. They are both teenagers. Here's a photo."

He pulled a photo out of his pocket. It was a family portrait. The whole family had bright red hair, blue eyes and tanned skin. One of the children was a boy and the other a girl. The boy was quite muscley for his age. Samuel noticed that the boy had a bigger build than himself.

"What are their names?" Sheila asked.

"Brenton and Karen," Jonathon replied.

"Does Brenton hunt with you?" Sheila asked.

"No, not yet," replied Jonathon. "He hasn't completed the 'Coming-of-Age' ritual yet. He will the next time it is held

"What is the 'Coming of age' ritual?" asked Sheila.

"We get together with four other tribes and the teenage candidates go through a rigorous training regime before hunting a bear together." said Jonathon

"Who teaches them?"

"A team of Mountain Masters do. Hunters that are very experienced have their name forwarded."

"So, you are a Mountain Master?" asked Sheila.

"Yes, I am."

Sheila looked to the sky and saw the dusk spectra. This time the blue and the green of the spectra reminded her of a holiday that she and her then boyfriend had at Loch Ness in Scotland. They had gone on a Loch Ness monster tour. The scenery was breathtaking. Then she remembered the night they had in a quaint bed and breakfast castle. It was very intimate. Sheila missed that. Although outside it was cold, inside the castle bedroom it was warm and cosy. Especially in the arms of her boyfriend. There was a chill in the air now.

Sheila watched Samuel as it became dark. She noticed the fluorescent violet tinge to his eyes. It seemed to complement his red hair perfectly. She thought his face was youthful and very handsome. It had sharp features that gave him a rugged athletic look. She knew that he was physically capable and would be considered as sporty, if they were on Earth. *If only he was a little older,* she mused, *then he would be perfect.*

"It is going to be a long cold night tonight," said Samuel.

Jonathon agreed. The expedition was fitted out with the best quality sleeping bags, so they were prepared for nights like this.

"How long is long?" asked Sheila.

"Probably twice as long as last night," Samuel said.

Sheila shivered and was not looking forward to going to her tent tonight. She didn't like the thought of being alone in the cold for such a long time. They sat around the heater for a little while longer, before Jonathon stood up and said good night. For long cold nights like this one it was better to go to bed and have a long sleep, rather than stay up and feel the cold.

Samuel was about to do the same, when Sheila asked, "Sam, could you join me in my tent? I need to discuss a matter with you."

Samuel nodded and walked with her. They entered the tent together. Sheila pulled him down to sit with her on the sleeping bag.

"What do you want to talk about?" asked Samuel.

Sheila pulled him closer to her. "Many things Sam. I like you very much," she said.

She kissed his cheek, then looked into his eyes. Samuel was surprised and didn't know what to say. There was an awkward silence before Samuel said he would go and get his sleeping bag.

"There is no need to bother Jonathon," said Sheila. "We could share my sleeping bag."

Now Samuel was really surprised, and even more so, he didn't know what to say.

"It is okay, nothing is going to happen," Sheila said shyly.

They were sleeping in the same sleeping bag. At first Samuel felt shy and awkward. But then he put his arms around Sheila and gave her a hug. Sheila nestled herself next to Samuel's shoulder. They stayed like that for a while. Eventually, Samuel lifted himself from the embrace and started stroking Sheila's hair, just above her brow. Sheila responded by kissing him on the lips. Samuel was unsure. Nothing like this had happened to him before. But he started to relax and let instinct takeover. Samuel kissed Sheila back on the lips. That night, they were very intimate with each other.

The next morning, after the campsite was packed away, the two helicopters took off for more scouting. Before they left, Captain Groswell had a briefing session with the pilots.

"If you see cars, under no circumstances should you fire on them," he said. "Is that understood?"

"Yes, sir," the pilots replied in unison.

From the air, at first the pilots didn't see anything unusual. Then, after a while, the pilot of Copter Two saw a yellow bear as they flew over some mountains. The bear turned and looked up at them. The pilot reported it, but Captain Groswell was not worried. The bear wouldn't come down to the plains. Like yesterday, the valleys that the expedition travelled through, were wide.

In the middle of the day, they could see a field of fuel balls on the left. It was the first fuel balls they had seen on the entire expedition. Captain Groswell ordered the convoy to head towards them. He wanted to see if they had been recently used. The field was quite extensive. There were over a hundred fuel balls. Captain Groswell didn't have a lot of experience with fuel balls, so he had to rely on the opinions of the car hunters in the expedition. That group included Samuel.

A fuel ball is a sphere that is roughly one metre in diameter. It is transparent, as the fuel in it is transparent. In the middle of the ball is an organ that creates the fuel. These organs are different colours between balls. That is why the flavour of the fuel between balls can be different. Fuel balls made Captain Groswell think of giant marbles. He had played with marbles as a child.

When cars feed on a fuel ball they pierce the skin of the fuel ball with a hose. After they have finished feeding, there is a scar left on the fuel ball. This eventually heals. Car hunters learn how to find these scars on a fuel ball and they can also judge how long ago a car was feeding on the ball, by the progress of healing of the scar.

Another way car hunters can tell how long ago a fuel ball was milked, was how firm the ball was. After a ball has been milked, it is deflated and the skin is loose. It takes some time before it becomes firm again. Because of the size of the fuel ball field, it took some time to see if they had been milked recently. There was evidence that some balls had been milked recently, but it didn't appear to be extensive. That gave Captain Groswell some relief.

The Captain was happy with their progress so far and he felt that his good leadership contributed to the expedition's success. Having very wide valleys made the defence of the expedition more difficult. He felt that when they reached the narrower box canyons, they would be more secure. Again, at the end of the day the helicopters searched for a nearby box canyon with only one entrance, for the expedition to set up camp. Luckily, they found what they needed nearby. Captain Groswell was buoyed by the fact that tomorrow they should reach the spacecraft site and that they hadn't encountered any cars up to this point. Also, he was told by his hunters that tonight was not going to be a long night. So that too, lifted his spirits.

Chapter 10
The Cars Defend

The expedition packed up their camp site early, and the helicopters also launched early. It was expected that by midday, the expedition would reach a turnoff into a narrower valley. However, until that point there were no other intersections with smaller box canyons. They were vulnerable, as they were out in the open where there would be a wider front for the attacking cars. Obviously, that would benefit the cars. It would be harder to hold them back. Captain Groswell was eager to reach the turnoff as soon as possible.

He had instructed one of his Lieutenants to organise the expedition to break camp and be ready to continue. One helicopter flew the route behind them, while the other went ahead. Within an hour, the pilot of the helicopter behind them made his report to the central command.

"There are significant numbers of vehicles coming up behind us. Both small and large vehicles." he reported.

"How many vehicles Copter One?" asked the Lieutenant at Central Command.

"Hundreds," was the reply.

"How far back are they? Can we double back to the camp site?" the Lieutenant asked.

"Negative, sir. They will reach it long before we could get there. I suggest you make haste to our destination. Over."

In just a few minutes, the pilot of the helicopter ahead made his report to Central Command.

"This is a red alert. There is an army of vehicles heading towards you. I recommend that you turnaround now and go back to the camp site," said the pilot.

"How many vehicles, Copter Two?" the lieutenant asked.

"Hundreds," was the reply.

Captain Groswell called a meeting with his officers.

He said, "The cars have got us at our most vulnerable point. It will not be easy to defend ourselves." He turned to one of his lieutenants. "Lieutenant Jones you were responsible for breaking camp early. It is your fault that we are in this position."

Lieutenant Jones squirmed uncomfortably in his chair.

Captain Groswell then addressed the whole meeting. "I need suggestions on what we are to do now."

His second in command, Lieutenant Roberts had a plan. Lieutenant Roberts was an older man sporting a full head of white hair. He had lived the last twenty years in Plantere and had gone out on car hunting expeditions for the Iowa Corporation often.

"The cars will arrive soon," he said to the meeting. "We have got to arrange our vehicles in a box formation."

Then he outlined the rest of his plan. Soon, the four tanks were arranged in the formation of a square, each pointing their stun cannons in a different direction to the other tanks. The three empty semi-trailers were parked side by side, facing the cliffs of the valley. Then the two open military trucks were parked at opposite ends of the semi-trailers, side by side to the end semi-trailers. Some of the military personnel were arranged on the open military trucks, while others sat on top of the end semi-trailers. Samuel and Jonathon took positions on one of the semi-trailers. Sheila and Professor Seronen sat on top of the middle semi-trailer. The expedition teams were very organised and had set themselves up in their positions very quickly. They didn't have long before both groups of cars would arrive. Luckily, the helicopters had given them advanced warnings.

When everyone was in position, Captain Groswell consulted with his second in command. After a short discussion Captain Groswell then spoke on a megaphone.

"We are facing a large host," he said. "Probably there will be more cars attacking us than we have ammunition to stun them. We need to choose our targets carefully. The small cars will not be able to damage our tanks. So we must target the large vehicles, the trucks. We will need to be patient. If we take out their large vehicles, then I expect the cars will retreat, in time."

The army of cars coming up the rear, arrived first. They parked just outside of the stun cannon range and waited. When Captain Groswell held up his binoculars to view them, he could see that his helicopter pilot was correct. At first, he saw the clouds of dust that the cars had raised. There were hundreds of cars. The small cars were at the front of the host, while the four -wheel drives and an assortment of trucks, including some mining trucks, were at the back. The army was not like most car tribes. There was an assortment of makes and models. There were large sedans and small hatchbacks. One thing they did have in common was that they were all young cars.

Captain Groswell gave the order to Copter One to start taking out the large vehicles from the air. However, it wasn't long before the army of cars ahead of them arrived and parked outside of stun cannon range. Like the cars in the rear, there was an assortment of makes and models, and they were young cars. Captain Groswell then, gave the order to Copter Two to do the same as Copter One.

When all the cars were in position, they charged. The expedition soldiers held their fire until a large vehicle was in range. But that was a long time in coming. There were so many small cars. At least the shooters in the helicopters were able to pick off some large vehicles in the rear. On both fronts, the small cars had finally reached the outer defences of the expedition. But they didn't try to ram the tanks. Instead, they drove around and around the fortified position of the expedition. Hundreds of cars did this and as they did, clouds of dust rose up. Soon there was so much dust, the soldiers could not see clearly the cars that had approached them.

Captain Groswell realised his second in command's folly. The man was incompetent, Captain Groswell thought. He could see that the large vehicles could now approach with impunity. The expedition soldiers would not be able to pick them off.

"Shoot everything at will," he ordered into the megaphone.

Shots from the cannons and rifles rang out. Many cars were stunned. But in the chaos, the attackers were able to park five flatbed tow trucks between twenty and fifty metres away from the tanks on both sides. The tow trucks lowered their trays, making ramps. The soldiers and tanks eventually stunned them, but it was too late. They were already in position. Sports cars lined up a couple of hundred metres away from the ramps and then accelerated towards them. They were doing at least a hundred kilometres per hour. When they reached the ramps, they were launched into the air. They sailed over the tanks and crashed into the semi-trailers, causing pandemonium. Soldiers were jumping down from the trailers. Samuel and Jonathon laid flat on their trailer. Sheila screamed. She looked in Samuel's direction and saw what he was doing. She laid flat on the semi-trailer as well. However, Professor Seronen panicked, jumped down from the trailer and ran into the clouds of dust.

Captain Groswell was standing on a semi-trailer. Soldiers from either side of him had been forced to abandon the trailer. He was dumbfounded by the turn of events and didn't know what he should be doing now. If only his soldiers had stunned the tow trucks before they got in position, then they wouldn't be in this situation. Just as he was thinking this, a red Chevy Corvette launched himself from one of the tow truck ramps. The car sailed through the air and hit Captain Groswell as it was coming down. Captain Groswell fell off the top of the semi-trailer and hit the ground. He did not move.

The cannons kept shooting and the soldiers who'd kept their position also kept firing. But just as they felt they were holding the defence together, more cars launched themselves off the tow truck ramps. It was clear that the medium sized cars could cause as much mayhem as a truck. It wasn't long before most of the soldiers could not hold their positions. Samuel and Jonathon tried to keep their position on the semi-trailer but two cars that had launched themselves at the same time collided with the semi-trailer, together causing it to tip over. Both Samuel and Jonathon slid off the roof and onto the ground between the tipped over trailer and the middle trailer, where Sheila was. Samuel waved to her and made hand gestures. He got her to slide from the top of her trailer and join him underneath another trailer.

Jonathon was on the ground with his spear in hand, and Samuel continued shooting from underneath the semi-trailer. But by now the large mining trucks had reached the expedition's defence. The stun cannons on the tanks were now silent as they had run out of ammunition. Samuel couldn't see any of the soldiers. The mining trucks rammed the tanks. There was no shooting anywhere. Even from the helicopters the shooters had run out of ammunition long ago.

A Holden Kingswood attacked Jonathon. He drove straight at him. Jonathon held his spear forward and drove it into the front grille of the car. The car screamed with agony, but it wasn't a mortal blow. The Kingswood reversed and prepared to attack again. Samuel wanted to shoot it, but he had run out of ammunition. Instead, he ran at the car. He jumped onto the bonnet and grabbed hold of a side mirror. The car forgot about Jonathon and twisted and turned to try and shake Samuel off the bonnet. But Samuel held the mirror tight. He reached for his car jumping mallet and used it to smash the driver side window. The car redoubled its effort to shake Samuel off, but Samuel held tight. At last came an opportunity for Samuel to slide into the driver's seat and take control of the steering wheel. He fought the car, but it drove away from the expedition compound and into the midst of the army of cars. It wasn't long before the Kingswood was surrounded.

He heard a loud voice. "Enough."

The Kingswood applied its brakes fully, and the cars parted to allow a sleek metallic silver SSC Tuatara hyper car to enter. He was low to the ground and in mint condition. There were stunning sports cars, but this was different. He was seriously built for speed. Everything about this car was low. The head of a potential driver would only be a little higher than the wheels. He had great aerodynamics, and he could go twice as fast as most sports cars. The hyper car had an impressive bearing and he seemed to have innate leadership qualities.

In a commanding and authoritative voice, he called, "Come out of the Kingswood and you won't be harmed."

Samuel could see that his position was hopeless. He was totally surrounded. But he was sceptical that the cars would not harm him. However, he had no choice. He opened the driver's door and stepped out. He felt a gentle breeze on his face. It was cool, as it was still early in the day. There was sweat rolling down his face.

Next to the hyper car was a blue Porsche. He seemed to be deep in thought. After the Porsche saw Samuel step out, he asked a mining truck quietly, "Are there any other survivors?"

"Just two," the mining truck replied.

Sheila and Jonathon both stepped away from the wrecked fortification with their hands held high. Samuel was surprised that the cars hadn't killed them all already. It seemed that a white Volvo XC90 SUV, was reading Samuel's mind.

"We should finish them now. They were going to destroy the Womb," said the Volvo.

But the blue Porsche raised himself up on his suspension and turned his wheels towards Sheila. In a matter of fact tone he said, "She is the bearer, and she needs these two hunters to survive."

This seemed to be a truth that the blue Porsche had come at only with much deep thought. *The bearer of what,* Sheila wondered. Samuel was astounded. What would cars need with an earthling woman? Jonathon read the situation and had a rueful smile.

"Hunter's seed is very potent, lass," he smirked.

Sheila understood what Jonathon was insinuating. "Don't be ridiculous," she retorted angrily.

She had forgotten that they were all in a perilous situation. She was just angry because she took precautions. That is, she took a contraceptive pill. Actually, Jonathon had also forgotten about the dire situation they were currently in. He could just see the humour of it. Being a hunter from the mountains he probably didn't see the danger that the cars posed. It isn't that they were ten metres tall. But Samuel did see the danger and he was very worried. He thought back to his intimacy with Sheila a couple of nights back. That was so recent. How did the cars know that Sheila was pregnant?

"Enough," the Tuatara hyper car ordered. His idling engine became louder, and it seemed that he was roaring. He then growled and was stern when he said, "I'm inclined to take my colleague's advice. You meant to do us great harm."

He paused because he wanted to maximise the fear that the humans would have. He then continued, "I will only let you live on one condition."

The three prisoners had nothing to say. *What could be a condition for a car to let a human live?* Samuel wondered. The silence seemed to please the hyper car. He waited a little longer before saying, "You are not to return to the Corporation. Instead, you must live in the wilderness with the hunters."

This was directed at Sheila. She was dumbfounded. How could she, she was employed by the Corporation? They had brought her out here in the first place to write about them and Plantere. She didn't mind visiting the wilderness. It was adventurous, but she couldn't imagine living in it full time. She was about to say all of this to the hyper car, but both Samuel and Jonathon gave her a stern look. Finally, in a small voice, she murmured, "Okay."

Jonathon spoke up. "Thank you for your mercy, they will come with me to live in the mountains."

Samuel looked at him in astonishment.

"What were you thinking lad?" Jonathon defended,

"That you and Sheila would live alone at your parents' house on the cliff, and raise a child there?"

"I'm not pregnant," Sheila retorted.

"Samuel, we have a tribe. There are other women and children there. You won't be alone." Jonathon implored. "It is okay, I will teach you how to hunt bears, Jumpy Benson."

He teased and slapped Samuel on the back. Jonathon was good at giving people nicknames and enjoyed giving Samuel this one. The cars seemed pleased with the arrangement that Jonathon had outlined.

The hyper car spoke again. In a reflective tone he announced, "We will now show you what you sought."

Chapter 11
The Spaceship

The spaceship was located on the plains of a box canyon with only one entrance. It was nestled at the back. From the outside it didn't look damaged. However, you could see that it had collided with the back cliff face of the canyon. The pilot must have been able to crash land it in the valley. From the look of it, there didn't seem to be any landing gear. Most starships were designed to orbit planets and have shuttle crafts to ferry passengers down to the surface. So, if one did crash on a planet, it would be impossible for it to be launched into space, even if its engines were repaired. This spaceship was large. Sheila thought it was larger than the craft that had brought her to the orbit of Plantere. It was long and rectangular. Unlike shuttle craft, there was no consideration for aerodynamics, given that the craft would only travel in space. The hull looked strong, probably made from titanium, but its colour had faded over time and was covered in dust.

Sheila, Jonathon and Samuel were riding in the white Volvo SUV. There was a convoy of ten cars including the hyper car. They drove to the front of the ship. To the front on one side, there was an entrance that was wide and high enough for a medium sized truck. There was a ramp up to the entrance. Either side of the entrance, two military jeeps were parked on guard. The convoy was allowed in.

The white Volvo SUV told his passengers that they could get out now. At first the humans were reluctant. They were overwhelmed by what they saw. It seemed that Professor Seronen was correct in his theories. But soon, they did as they were told. The hyper car seemed pleased with their demeanour.

To the left towards the front, there was a cockpit. To the right was an open plan kitchen, with a small table. This room had a large window, that would have given them a view of the space outside. But all they could see now was the cliff face of the canyon. Then at the other end, there was another entrance, the same size as the one to the ship. That led into a large room, where some vintage cars were parked. The walls had pictures of people with their cars, and the room was colourful, due to the different lights and feature walls. The assorted cars were from different eras, from the 1920s to the 2020s. They weren't living cars. They were combustion engine Earth vehicles.

"This was the Professor's collection, which he always took with him on his journeys." the hyper car said. "Through to the next room, was his library. This was where he kept his scientific journals, that he and others had authored. We will come back here, and I will show you his diary and a book we call the Bible."

The library was a large room due to the size of the entrances and exits. It didn't have paper-based books. All the books and journals were digitalised. There was a desk and a monitor. Through to the next room, there was a workshop with two car hoists and racks with tools.

"This was where the Professor worked on his cars." the hyper car said.

Then through the next entrance they were in a laboratory. This room was bigger than the workshop. It was filled with scientific equipment. There were sophisticated microscopes and test tubes. The walls were painted white, and the air was cool. Sheila looked in one corner and recognised one of the devices there.

"This is an antique," she said.

"This is where the hunters came from," the hyper car replied. "But I will let you read the diary and the Bible."

"What is it?" Samuel asked Sheila.

"It is an incubator or artificial womb," Sheila replied. She was very good at explaining technology to the lay person, as she didn't use a lot of jargon. "When people first travelled to the stars, it took decades for them to reach their destination," she continued. "So, a starship would have frozen fertilised embryos that robots would put in the incubators, once the ship had reached its destination. The robots would then raise the children on the new world. It isn't something we do now."

The incubator wasn't large, about the size of a bassinet. It was white and shaped like a capsule and had a transparent cover. Next to the incubator she saw two of the robots she was just describing. They had faces like a man and a woman, two arms and two legs. They were the same height as an average adult human. Both of them were powered down.

"Please, through here is the last room," the hyper car said.

The other entrance took them into a very large room that was empty, except for an extremely large capsule. It was large enough to contain a bus. Unlike the capsule in the previous room the transparent cover was a door that could be lowered to make a ramp. The capsule was white and a similar shape to the capsule in the other room. Sheila was stunned and asked in a soft voice, "Is this where cars come from?"

"Yes," the hyper car replied. "We are not sure, but we believe the professor may have created other wombs on the planet."

Samuel wasn't sure what to think. He had never thought about where his adversaries came from. "I have seen mining trucks that are much bigger than this capsule," he said.

"Yes," replied the hyper car. "When cars are born, they are much smaller than the adult car. We keep the young cars here until they are the same size as an adult car. Then a car from one of the tribes would come to claim them. That's probably why you have never seen a smaller infant car."

Jonathon walked over to the capsule. He looked through the transparent door and saw a litter of foetuses. They were in the shapes of cars but had no windows or tyres. Rather than being metallic, they had a grey skin.

"How long is the gestation period?" Sheila asked.

"Very quick, less than a day," the hyper car replied. "Let me take you to Professor Hiedenburg's diary."

The hyper car led them back to the library. Sheila sat down at the desk. Jonathon couldn't read and Samuel could only read a little. His father had started teaching him before he died. The user interface was quite easy to follow. Sheila wanted to see the diary first. For the benefit of her companions, she read out important entries. Professor Hiedenburg had used Federation Standard Time for his diary. There were no years or months, only a count of the number of deca-hours, since the standard had started. Sheila didn't read out all the entries just the ones she thought were important. There were entries before Standard Date 213644 but they appeared to be research notes on projects Professor Hiedenburg was studying, and they were significantly earlier than Standard Date 213644.

Standard Date: 213644

Entered orbit of Omega 24A. The main engines have stopped working completely now. Only the short- range thrusters are operational. It has been eighteen days since I first sent the distress signal. This space is quite remote so it might be sometime before it is answered. I think I will use my diary to record the progress of my emergency.

Standard Date: 213756

My supplies are running low, and my life support will soon expire. I have taken a shuttle craft to the surface of the planet. It is barren and water is scarce. But I could probably survive there. I don't have the equipment to replenish my life support systems. That was careless of me. I think I may have to crash land on the surface. If only I had an atmosphere condenser, I could do trips to and from my spacecraft to get or grow supplies on the planet. I have to think this through. Maybe I could make an atmosphere condenser.

Standard Date: 213767

This is becoming urgent now. I can't build an atmosphere condenser. Why haven't I got one? What an idiot I am. I have no choice but to land the spaceship on the surface of the planet. I probably can do it safely using the short- range thrusters. But I won't be able to take off again. There will be so much trouble to get this ship in orbit again. This is such a mess. I'm due at the Adrian Court space station.

Standard Date: 213771

I have landed the spaceship in a box canyon. This place is so barren. What am I doing here? "Never mind you just have to get on with it". Dad's favourite saying when he hit a problem while he was working on the cars. I think the problems were the highlights of his work. I checked the journals about Omega 24A. There isn't much information. But it seems that the only animal life on the planet are yellow bears. They are ten metres tall and aggressive. But they only seem to inhabit the mountains. In terms of plant life there are various types of moss and cactus type plants. And they also are found in the mountains.

Standard Date: 213784

I have set up my vegetable garden. Julia loved gardening. I remember walking through her garden with her. She enjoyed bringing people to her garden and showing them around. She was so beautiful in her garden. I loved her so much. She was warm and creative and such a talented biologist. Her garden was wonderful. Luckily, I have water mining equipment. I have that and not an atmosphere condenser. Where was my brain? "Never mind you just have to get on with it."

Standard Date: 213801

I'm bored. No one has replied to my distress signal. I'm just pondering on my life's regrets, Julia and Clare. Normally I'm busy with my work so I don't have a chance to think about them. I should have done more to make them happy, so that at least one of them would stay with me. "Never mind you just have to get on with it." I went on an expedition to the mountains. I know it was dangerous but I have nothing else to do but study this planet. The plains are completely barren. Except for the dust. It is everywhere and gets into everything. So, I need to go to the mountains to study. I did find some plant life and I took some samples to study. They have a silicon component to the genome. It is quite remarkable.

Standard Date: 213802

I should have worn a hat yesterday. My face is so red and I have this terrible sun burn. When we went to the beach at Manly, Clare used to always lecture me about applying sunscreen. I need her here to look after me. Yesterday I left early for the mountains, so the weather was cold. I didn't think about the midday sun. The length of the days varies. It seems random to me. I have to be careful I don't want to be trapped in the mountains when it gets dark. It is freezing at night.

Standard Date: 213843

This is my ninth expedition to the mountains. I do enjoy going to the mountains. Even just to escape the dust on the plains. I found a carcass of a yellow bear. Lucky for me he was dead. I took samples of its flesh. It too has a silicon component to the genome. It is so different to the life forms I have studied to date. I'm starting to get some ideas. Currently the work I have done on Synthetic DNA is pretty basic. Maybe I could improve it. I feel so much better. Now that I have something to study.

Standard Date: 213871

Passing the time by re-reading a research paper authored by Professor Brussellford's team of geneticists. It is an impressive piece of work. His team sought to find the DNA that gives individuals the paranormal abilities of telepathy and prophecy. A very difficult task, given that these traits are so rare and the people who have them can be very different. They employed the use of the latest quantum computers, and much of their work was to develop an algorithm to isolate the genes that these gifted people had that normal people did not. They asserted, for the benefit of natural selection these traits should be rare but present in the community. But it appears in this paper they were successful. I recall the reaction from conservative church groups, who said that the gift of prophecy was given by the Holy Spirit. Not by a group of genes, like eye colour. Clare was a good Catholic. I wonder what she would have thought about the paper. I know Julia would have embraced it. Anyway, the paper gives me food for thought on my studies of Synthetic DNA.

Standard Date: 213901

I'm feeling lonely. This is a hard life. Clare, why did you leave me for another man? And Julia, we could have been happy together. Why didn't you marry me? Other than studying hard, when I feel this way, I spend some time in the showroom. My cars are my companions. They were Dad's cars. We worked on them together. Getting covered in grease and solving problems. Finding parts was the hardest job. Where could you find an Autolite 4300 carburettor? There was a club for enthusiasts of combustion engine vehicles and there were trades people who could make or repair a part as long as you gave them detailed instructions. I miss you, Dad. Sometimes I take a car and make some improvements, and then return it to my showroom. It does help, but I still feel empty. What if my cars were truly alive? I know every vintage car specialist has a bond with their cars. To them the cars are alive. But what if they were really alive? They could be my companions.

Standard Date: 213955

I'm making progress on my studies of Synthetic DNA. Being alone has made it easier to conduct my research. I'm really working hard so that I don't think about my regrets. I have created the fuel ball. It is a plant that photosynthesizes to make fuel. It was a lot of work to make it be able to absorb enough water from the atmosphere. The weather here is dry. I think it has only rained once or twice since I have been here. The cars would need the fuel from the fuel balls for food. I started with this life form because it was simpler. This was a good milestone. I can start work on the cars now. I have always liked doing these projects. I remember when I was little, I melted down some lead and made moulds out of clay. I made lead badges. I had such a good childhood.

Standard Date: 214097

I have created the Synthetic DNA for a generic car. I don't know if it would grow into a car. That is my next job. I need to create a womb so the foetus can grow. I have tweaked the DNA to have a fast gestation period. Luckily, I already have an artificial womb. That is one to grow humans. Just something I collected over the years. I have that and not an atmosphere condenser. 'Never mind you just have to get on with it.' I can reverse engineer the womb and create a bigger one for cars.

Standard Date: 214142

The womb is ready. I tried out my synthetic genome. Unfortunately, the foetus died. My poor car. Clare and I were going to have children. But it never happened. I'm studying the foetus now to try and find out what the problem is.

Standard Date: 214323

Success! This was my nineth foetus. A beautiful generic car was born. My first living car. A time for celebration. I'm finally not alone. Julia liked to celebrate when she had a breakthrough in her research. When this happened, we would go out to dinner. It wasn't planned and was spontaneous. She loved to live each day as if it was totally new and unplanned. It kept me on my toes and I loved her for it. Maybe that was why she turned down my marriage proposal. She wanted life to be unpredictable. That, or she thought I would make a lousy husband.

Standard Date: 214354

The fenders and glass, have formed beautifully. I'm on the right track. It is now time to work on the details. Also, I want to add switches in the genome for the make and model of the car. There is so much work I need to do. I feel alive. This is wonderful. Maybe I will finally have children.

Standard Date: 214615

My cars are beautiful. They are intelligent and have such wonderful personalities, and they will live on long after I'm gone. But they can't maintain the womb by themselves. I guess there are the robots, but they won't last forever. I need to create an indigenous human race. I can graft elements of the yellow bear DNA to the frozen human embryos that I have. One thing I'm definitely going to do is give them protection from the sun. That sun burn that I had took ages to go away. This world is pretty harsh. I think I will need to give them enhanced agility as well. Julia had beautiful red hair. I'm going to make my humans have red hair. That would be a nice touch.

Standard Date: 215373

I have two human toddlers and two babies. As I designed, they have bright red hair, blue eyes and a healthy tan. That is what will mark out the hunters from other humans. I have made their genes dominant, so that if they mate with another human their children will always have the hunter features. The babies are keeping me and the robots busy. My cars are helping out too. This is quite a family. It is amazing that I have found happiness and contentment on such a remote and harsh planet. I was alone but now I'm not anymore.

A Distant Genesis

Standard Date: 217423

My work is nearly done. I have been writing a book for the cars so that they can understand who they are and what they need to do to survive. I will call it the Bible.

"There are many more entries," said Sheila. She scrolled to the end of the diary. "The last entry was Standard Date 225663. I guess we should look at the Bible now."

She browsed through the user interface and found the document named the Bible. Just as she did with the Diary, she only read out the sections that seemed really important.

In the beginning there were the yellow bears. Everything came from them. The creation of the cars was a labour of love. They are as intelligent as humans and should have the same rights. Cars will come in all makes and models, but they are all loved the same.

The hunters are human, but in part come from the yellow bears, the true indigenous species of the planet. Where other humans would struggle to survive, the hunters will thrive. They will be known by their distinct features and on their homeland they will be formidable. The hunters were created to take care of the cars.

The fuel balls were created to feed the cars. All cars will be able to milk them. Where other plants struggle to survive the fuel balls will thrive.

The cars will be organised in tribes having in common their make. All cars can speak the common tongue of English. But in their tribes, they will speak the language of Earth nations that manufactured their make.

There will be a nursery tribe near the Womb to take care of baby cars. When they are old enough a member from their future tribe will come and get them.

A Distant Genesis

Just as there is a queen bee of a hive of bees, the cars will have a Queen to look after the Womb. From the hunters she will come. She will be known by her spiritual gifts. She will not seek domination or the trappings of power. Instead, she will be kind and humble and unite the cars. As there are many tribal languages amongst the cars, she will be able to speak them all.

There will be some cars chosen to look after the Womb. They will be set apart by their spiritual gifts. Some may have telepathic abilities, while others the gift of prophecy. But all will have their place. As a team, together with the Queen they will defend the Womb.

"For just as the body is one and has many members, and all the members of the body, though many, are one body." 1 Corinthians, 12:12

"They will mentor a young Queen."

"Oh my god," Sheila exclaimed. "This is a distant Genesis."

Samuel was deep in thought. "I don't know if I want to hunt cars anymore," he murmured

"So, we are like the yellow bears," Jonathon exclaimed. "Distant cousins?"

"Have you seen enough?" asked the hyper car.

"There is a lot to take in," replied Sheila.

"You will need to live with the mountain hunter tribe," said the hyper car.

"Ok," Sheila replied.

"We are a long way from home," commented Jonathon.

"It is all right," the hyper car replied. "We have a map of the whole planet, with most of the Corporation main towns marked. The professor had his satellites. I can take you to your home. It won't take long."

Sheila estimated that they were probably thousands of kilometres away, and when Jonathon showed the hyper car where his tribe was on the map, this estimate was confirmed. How long was not long?

"The professor had his private quarters and a spare bedroom," said the hyper car. "Stay the night tonight and early tomorrow morning we will leave."

The white Volvo SUV came to them and opened its hatch. The humans took out their supplies that they had brought, and they were shown to their sleeping quarters. When the humans had retired to their bedrooms, the cars were outside.

The blue Porsche was parked and had his headlights dimly showing, indicating that he was meditating. But the white Volvo SUV was very concerned, so he disturbed his comrade. The hyper car was there also.

"This is quite a risk we are taking," said the white Volvo SUV.

"I know," said the hyper car.

His engine was purring softly. The blue Porsche turned off his headlights and had exited his meditation. Today he had seen a number of visions, and he was concerned about what they meant. That was why he was meditating. But he did believe that Sheila was the bearer.

"The prophecies indicate that she is the bearer. At some point, we had to show the humans the Bible. We need them," he said to his comrades.

The other cars had nothing more to say.

* * *

Early the next morning, the hyper car honked outside the bedrooms to wake the humans.

"We need to go soon so we can get to your home before dark," he announced.

When Samuel heard this, as he laid on his bed, it made him reflect on what happened yesterday. He thought he'd faced imminent death. Now he was being woken up by a car that would take him home. Out of the humans, Sheila was probably the least affected by what had happened yesterday. She was a foreigner and everything about this planet was strange.

They got themselves ready and had breakfast, but they didn't speak to each other about the Diary or the Bible. When they were ready to leave, the blue Porsche approached Sheila.

"Listen to the hunters always and they will protect you," he said.

And with that, they boarded the hyper car and were travelling. The hyper car was fast, very fast. The three travellers all had their seatbelts on, and were glad to have them. Samuel was enjoying the ride. After a while he lowered the passenger window and stuck out his arm.

"Whoooo!" he yelled.

There was quite a cloud of dust behind them. The hyper car kept to the middle of the canyon.

It was a long day, and as the hyper car had said, they were at the base of the mountains, close to the mountain tribe just before dark.

As the humans exited the car, the hyper car said, "Take care. We will contact you again soon." Then he sped off in the direction they had come.

"It isn't far, only a couple of hours. Follow me," said Jonathon.

There was a path that took them up the cliff face and into the mountains and within two hours, they had reached the tribe.

Chapter 12
The Coming of Age Ritual

Sheila was sitting in a chair made of Yellow Bear bones and hide. There were few chairs in the Tribe. Sheila earned one because of her condition. She was also in one of the few Tribe's stone huts. The hut had windows, but there was no glass in them. This morning Sheila welcomed the breeze that came through. In the mountains the breeze was never too strong and unlike the plains, it was fresh and clean, as it didn't carry a lot of dust. The hut had only one room and Sheila's chair was the only piece of furniture. The only other furnishings in the room were the yellow bear hides they slept in. There were no pictures on the walls. It was all very barren. Sheila's back hurt. Come to think of it, everything hurt. Her breasts were getting larger also. Sheila was heavily pregnant and maybe only had another month before she would give birth. Jonathon was right, the women of his tribe had been very supportive and helped her through her pregnancy. They even made extra concessions, because she was an Earthling.

She could hear Samuel practising. Jonathon had been giving him a crash course in yellow bear hunting, as the Coming-of-Age Ritual was looming. Jonathon's son, Brenton, was only twelve years old, but he was ready. Samuel was still a work in progress. Brenton had a bigger build than Samuel, even though he was still only a child. But Samuel did try hard. He really wanted to pass the Coming-of-Age Ritual, so he would be allowed to hunt with the Tribe. In fact, he felt he could not stay with them if he couldn't participate in the hunting. Jonathon was a good teacher. He was patient and reassured Samuel that he was on track. And that he did not have to worry. But at night, together in the yellow bear hides, Samuel would confide with Sheila, his worries and feelings of inadequacy.

Samuel was practising his spear manoeuvres. There were different positions depending upon what you needed to do. He was practising with a woman's spear, because he could not lift a standard one. Generally, women in the tribe do not hunt, but because at times yellow bears would approach the camp, the women needed to know how to drive them away if the men were out hunting.

The first move was the jab. The intention here was not to strike the bear but to herd it in the direction you want. Obviously for this to work, the team of hunters needed to work in unison. For a jab, you hold the spear at the end and push small thrusts. Your feet should shuffle along, making small movements. Herding a bear requires patience and discipline.

There were two attack positions. With both of these, you needed to stand and position your thrust to maximise your strength, as it takes a lot of force to pierce the hide of a bear. Your feet need to be apart and you face side on to the bear. When you hold the spear, the hands need to be apart with the front hand about three quarters down from the spearhead. There are two attack positions. The first is a straight thrust and the second is an upward thrust.

Samuel was remembering a time he'd lamented to Jonathon about his lack of strength. Jonathon had tried to console him.

"There are three things you need to hunt bears; strength, agility and team work," he had said. Jonathon put his arm on Samuel's shoulder and encouraged him. "You are quick on your feet and have a good head on your shoulders. You will do fine."

Then when he was feeling optimistic, Samuel thought, *I got through the hide that time*. He practised the positions religiously. Jonathon had told him that if you worked with a spear well, you would get the strength you needed, because you are maximising the spear's capability.

There were also exercises that you could do that would build up your strength. Some of them involved lifting rocks. Such as a bench press, triceps and bicep curl, also, squats. But Jonathon said that good meals of yellow bear flesh would also increase a hunter's strength. Over time Samuel would build up strength while he was with the Tribe.

Samuel also practised on the obstacle course which was supposed to improve agility in the mountains. There was running, climbing and throwing. In a hunt, hunters would rarely throw their spears. Only the very strongest hunters would be able to throw a spear with enough force to pierce the hide of a bear. But for agility training, the Coming-of-Age aspirants would have to demonstrate the ability to throw a spear accurately. He had yet to complete the course successfully, even though Brenton had done it easily long ago. Samuel worked hard on it. It wouldn't be through lack of practise if he wasn't able to complete it successfully during the ritual events.

Then there was the wrestling. This was also to test agility and strength. Samuel had wrestled both Jonathon and Brenton. He could sometimes beat Brenton, but he could never beat Jonathon. Even though Brenton had a bigger build, Samuel was taller. Jonathon had shown Samuel techniques to help him use his height as an advantage.

Now, Samuel was focused on his spear skills. He went over the manoeuvres repeatedly to try and build up his capability. He was used to being alone. He could spend hours working on something and not need to talk to anyone, while he was doing it. That was how he had perfected jumping cars. It would also be how he learnt how to hunt bears.

This year the Coming-of-Age ritual would be held at Jonathon's tribe. Members from four other tribes would attend. Usually that included the aspirants, parents and other close relatives. It was the most important rite of passage for boys, but it also gave members of different tribes, time to renew longstanding friendships. There were only two aspirants from Jonathon's tribe, Jonathon's son Brenton and Samuel. From the other tribes there were nine, giving a total of eleven. This would be a challenging number for hunting a bear. Normally, there would be more aspirants, perhaps fifteen.

When people arrived, Jonathon introduced them to Jumpy Benson, the famous car hunter. He said that alongside his son he would participate in the Coming-of-Age ritual. It certainly was not common for foreigners to join a mountain tribe but there were precedents. Generally, the visitors welcomed Samuel and wished him well in the ritual. Also, Sheila managed to make an appearance and was introduced as a corporation journalist who was writing a journal about Plantere. It was the responsibility of the hosts to provide yellow bear meals on the first night. Then after the ritual, it would be the aspirants themselves who provide the yellow bear. The other aspirants were as well built as Brenton, making Samuel the scrawniest. However, Samuel was the tallest. Like Samuel, they had the hunter features of tanned skin, red hair and blue eyes. Their names were Adrian, Alexander, Brian, Cameron, David, Edward,

Frederick, Gary and Henry. Like Samuel, they were usually not called by their actual name, but by a nickname. Each tribe provided a mountain master representative to form a judging panel for each ritual event.

The Coming-of-Age ritual started early in the morning. It was still cold. Samuel shivered, not only because it was cold, but also because he was nervous. The first event was the spear manoeuvres. The aspirants took their spears and stood in a row. Cameron stood next to Samuel. He faced forward, tilted his head and cracked his neck. He then turned to Samuel and pouted his lips. He was nicknamed Jester and demonstrated why this was the case by teasing Samuel, who was holding a woman's spear.

"Come here sweetheart and give me a kiss," he said. "Show me your tits."

Samuel had been the victim of Jonathon's teasing several times, so he was beginning to get used to it. Not that he enjoyed it, and he didn't possess the talent to make a cutting reply. So, on this occasion, like so many others, he said nothing and just wore it.

Each aspirant had a turn of demonstrating their manoeuvres. Samuel was in the middle of the row. He had always admired the way Brenton did his spear manoeuvres. He used very sharp definite actions, and you could see the strength in his attack positions. When Samuel saw the other aspirants, they were equally as good. After each performance the judges would raise their hands if they thought the aspirant had performed well enough. All five judges had to raise their hands for the aspirant to pass. By the time it got to Samuel, he was very nervous. But before he started, he tried to imagine that he was by himself practising the moves. That helped a little bit. He concentrated on what he needed to do and before long he was finished. The five judges raised their hands.

"That was a pretty good effort for a foreigner," said one of the judges from another tribe. "How long have you been in the tribe?"

Each day had a different length on Plantere and the mountain tribes didn't have many devices to measure time. So Samuel provided a very typical mountain tribe answer.

"Since, when my lady had conceived," he said.

Everyone turned to look at the heavily pregnant Sheila and had a very good idea of how long Samuel had been in the Tribe.

"That is impressive," the judge replied. "Good luck for the rest of the events."

Samuel felt buoyed by that encouragement. Maybe he could do this.

The second event was the wrestling. To pass the wrestling you had to defeat two other aspirants in hand-to-hand combat. In Samuel's first two bouts he fought well but was narrowly beaten by stronger competitors. Then he faced the Jester. The Jester had won all his previous bouts, so he was feeling very confident.

When he faced Samuel, he scratched his crotch and taunted him. "Come on girly, give me a hug and kiss," he sneered

Unfortunately, Samuel lost that bout. Which, given the teasing he had endured, was a bitter pill to swallow. *I have to concentrate,* Samuel scolded himself. He had still yet to win a bout, and he was running out of competitors. He had to remember Jonathon's tips on fighting heavier opponents.

His next opponent had not yet won a bout either, so Samuel thought this was his best chance. During the bout

Samuel had more confidence. Although he wasn't as strong as his opponent, he was faster. *I can jump cars,* Samuel thought, *I can beat a boy in a wrestle.* And so, he did. He had his first victory. He only needed one other.

His next opponent had had five bouts and had won them all. Once again Samuel thought, *I can jump cars, I can beat a boy in a wrestle.* During the competition his opponent, expertly did a double leg takedown. Samuel lost his feet and fell backwards. Normally, in a wrestle that move would be enough to win the bout, but Samuel went with the move and generated some extra momentum of his own. In the end, he flipped his opponent on his back. As his opponent was stunned, Samuel was able to grip him and hold him down for the count. That was his second victory. Luckily for the Ritual, all the aspirants had won at least two bouts. There was a concern that if there were less than the eleven aspirants to go on the bear hunt, the hunt could prove to be too difficult.

The final event before the hunt, was the obstacle course. It was now midday, and the weather was quite warm. The aspirants would need all their stamina to complete the course. Samuel liked some parts of the obstacle course. He was good at the climbing and balancing aspects of it, not so good on the parts that required brute strength. But he had worked on those parts. Jonathon had given him tips on how to lift the rocks on the course so that you would use the muscles in your legs, rather than just your arms or worse, your back. With the obstacle course you only needed to complete it within a set period of time. Although there were kudos in finishing first, there wasn't a requirement to finish in the top positions. The aspirants were lined up at the start.

Since Jonathon was the host mountain master, he was the one to say, "Go."

The first part of the course was a climb to the top of the mountain. Samuel was a fast runner, so he got to the base of the mountain first, and he started climbing. His strategy was to try and complete the climbing quickly so he would have time to do the heavy lifting further on in the course. He didn't know a lot about mountains but he seemed to have a natural ability when it came to climbing. It seemed easier than jumping cars.

When he reached the top, there was a very narrow path that went around the mountain. To traverse it, Samuel needed to put his back towards the cliff and shuffle sideways along the path. It was very high up, so it was wise not to look down. Samuel felt the gentle breeze on his face which gave him some relief in the heat of the day. He found this climb easy though. He didn't have a fear of heights. But he was naturally cautious. Then there was the descent.

Once at the bottom, each aspirant had their spear waiting. In this next section, Samuel had to carry his spear, run some distance, and then throw the spear and hit a target some distance away. If you missed the target, you had to fetch the spear, run back to the mark, and rethrow. Samuel was glad that the mountain masters had allowed him to use a woman's spear for this part of the course. He was barely able to lift a standard spear, let alone throw it. When he practised spear throwing, he hit the target as often as he missed, so he was very happy that now, he hit the target on his first throw.

It was the next part of the course that was most difficult for him. There were five large rocks. They had to be picked up and placed on a ledge at around head height. The mountain masters did not allow him to use women's rocks. He had to lift the same size rocks as the other aspirants. He was doing well so far on the course, so he had time to do this. The technique he had to apply was similar to a clean and jerk. He made careful measured movements. At first, he had to squat to pick up the first rock. He was able to use his legs to help lift the rock to above waist height. Then he needed to use his arms to get the rock about shoulder height. The final part was to lift the rock above his head and spread his legs to give balance. This technique maximised the use of Samuel's legs and ensured that he didn't strain his back. When he was practising, he was able to lift rocks this size. However, he could only do it once. Now, he had to do it five times. He had chosen the largest of the five rocks first. When the first rock was on the ledge Samuel had to rest. His muscles hurt. After about two or three minutes, he chose the smallest rock to lift. During the lift Samuel tried to concentrate on the technique and ignore the pain in his arms. He had small rests between each step of the technique and fortunately, he was able to get the second rock onto the ledge.

The other aspirants had now caught up with him. He knew he did not have a lot of time to finish the course. He could not afford to fail a lift. After a two-to-three-minute break, he chose the heaviest rock left. He was so close to finishing the obstacle course. He had to make this one final effort to lift these three rocks. With determination and sheer will power, he lifted two rocks on to the ledge. He only had one rock to go. There was not much time left. All the other aspirants had passed him and finished the obstacle course. So, Samuel didn't have a rest to lift the last rock. Instead, he employed his technique and grunted with determination at each step. He could not afford to drop the rock. He had to complete this lift. Then he did. Once done he sprinted to the finish line and passed it just in time. Samuel received a round of applause and pats on the back from the spectators at the finish line.

All the aspirants had passed the ritual events so far. The last event was the hunt. For the first time, aspirants were to go on a yellow bear hunt. They would need to work together to bring down a yellow bear. This was the hardest event of the ritual. But if they succeeded, they would be allowed to hunt with their tribes. Jonathon rose to speak.

"Congratulations to all the aspirants here," he said. "You have done us proud. I'm so glad to announce that every one of you will participate in the aspirants' hunt."

Everyone clapped and some people cheered.

Jonathon continued. "This hunt will begin early tomorrow morning. Before you leave on the hunt, I will give you some final instructions."

In the morning the judges would send out some scouts who would find a yellow bear for the aspirants to hunt. They would then take them to the location of a yellow bear and leave the aspirants to hunt together.

"Once you kill the bear, you must decide who will return to us to announce the kill," Jonathon continued. "That person should be the one who took the lead or delivered the critical blow. It is a mark of great honour to be chosen to announce the kill. Boys, rest well tonight and good luck for tomorrow."

The next morning, the aspirants gathered together as a scout prepared to lead them to their yellow bear. They started early as the day would be medium length. That is, neither short nor long. The judges wanted to give the aspirants a long time to complete the hunt so they wouldn't be rushed. There were polite murmurs of good morning between the boys but generally they were subdued. Except for Cameron, who was jovial and boisterous.

"Don't worry lads," he said to encourage them. "We will cut down this bear and slice its entrails into small pieces."

He went around to each aspirant and patted them on the back. When he got to Samuel he said, not unkindly,

"Show us what you've got sweetheart."

When Cameron had moved on to the next aspirant, Brenton came to Samuel and asked, "Have you ever seen a yellow bear?"

"Yes, and the encounter didn't end well," replied Samuel.

"I have once," confided Cameron. "A yellow bear came to camp. My mother helped chase it away. I was very young, and it was very frightening."

They had walked for two or three hours before the scout announced, "This is where the bear is. See, that is the entrance to its cave." And with that, he pointed to the entrance of a cave. "Happy hunting boys," he said. "I'll see you back at the Tribes."

Samuel had been paying attention to where they had been led so he could find his way back to the tribes. But he didn't expect to be chosen for that honour. He just hoped they could kill this bear. When the scout had left, the boys had gathered together around the cave entrance.

"I think it would be easier to hunt the bear out in the open, rather than in a cave," Brenton said.

"Maybe if we make a lot of noise then the bear will come out," said Cameron.

No one disagreed with any of these assertions. So they all stood at the cave entrance and started yelling.

"Come out here, Mister bear we want to play with you," Cameron yelled.

They all yelled for some time, but nothing stirred from the cave.

"Maybe the scout made a mistake. Maybe there is no bear here?" said David.

"One of us should go inside and poke the bear to wake it up," suggested Cameron

No one volunteered. There was silence among them.

Then after a while Samuel suggested, "Let us yell some more, maybe the bear needs more time to wake up."

Nobody had any objections to this suggestion, so they all started yelling again. And just when they thought the bear was not going to come, they heard something in the cave.

"Form a line," Cameron ordered.

They all stepped back from the entrance of the cave. Cameron was in the middle of the line with Samuel and Brenton at either ends.

"I'll distract the bear," Cameron announced. "Those on the end, go behind the bear so we can surround it."

Samuel nodded to Cameron. The bear came out of the cave and did not look pleased. It was a big yellow bear. He was nearly twelve metres tall. The scout had found the grandfather of all bears. Samuel noticed that this bear had a coarser fur, that was discoloured from the normal yellow. Not that Samuel was an expert. He hadn't seen many bears in his lifetime. Samuel's heart started to beat faster. The bear roared and then strode towards the boys.

"Come here Poppa Bear, I will show you my spear," Cameron yelled.

The bear then gave Cameron his full attention. Brenton and Samuel saw their opportunity and moved behind the bear. The manoeuvre worked. They had surrounded the bear. But the bear was angry and although Cameron was doing the spear jab correctly, a swat from the bear had sent him flying. The boys next to Cameron were afraid, they lowered their spears and started to step away. Samuel saw that the bear was going to finish the job on Cameron, just like the time a yellow bear finished the job on his friend Roger. Samuel remembered the attack positions for spear craft and drove the spear straight into the back of the yellow bear's leg, just above its foot. He had pierced the bear's hide. The bear screamed in agony and in rage. The bear forgot about Cameron and turned around towards Samuel.

Samuel adopted the spear jab position. "To me, to me," he shouted.

Brenton and Edward came to Samuel and formed a line. They too adopted the spear jab position. The bear swatted at them and then tried to kick them but could not find its mark. Meanwhile, behind the bear, the boys who had lost courage before now, found it again. Both Frederick and Gary carried out upward thrusts, into the bear's upper left leg. They were good thrusts, easily penetrating the bear's hide. The bear forgot about Samuel and clutched at its left leg. Brenton, Samuel and Edward saw their opportunity and carried out some attack thrusts. All three thrusts pierced the bear's hide in the right leg. The bear fell to the ground and screamed in agony. All the boys then made their attack thrusts one after another until there was no sound from the bear.

Cameron sat up dazed.

"Are you okay?" Samuel asked.

"Yeah," Cameron replied sheepishly.

"We did it," Brenton announced. "That was one big bear."

There was silence while the boys looked at their kill.

David went to the bear and said, "Thank-you, Poppa Bear for your meat. We will feed four tribes from your gift. The other boys lowered their heads in silence.

Then Edward asked, "Who should go back to tell the tribes of our kill?"

"I vote for Jumpy Benson," Cameron said. "You saved my life sweetheart."

"Jumpy Benson!" the other boys yelled.

Luckily for Samuel, he had taken notice of the directions to get to the yellow bear from the tribes' location. In about two hours, he arrived to the congratulations from all the tribes' people. He then went up to Jonathon.

"We have killed the bear," he said.

Jonathon gave him a slap on the back and said, "Good job, Jumpy."

Just as he said that, a scream came from Sheila's stone cottage. Some women jumped up and ran into the cottage. After a while, one of them came out.

"It's Sheila," she said. "She's giving birth, now."

Chapter 13
The Fall of the Mars Atmospheric Net

The freighter was waiting in orbit around Jupiter for its cargo of liquified hydrogen gas. There was a mining operation in the atmosphere of Jupiter that garnered a huge amount of hydrogen gas. There was so much more hydrogen gas mined here than was produced on Earth, with the clientele being planets in other solar systems. This gas was so much cheaper to deliver than what could be exported from Earth. The operation was so huge that there were many freighters each day to pick up the cargo.

The captain of the freighter, Jason Bourke used to be an ambitious man. But not anymore. Now he was content to wait in line at Jupiter and make a relatively short journey to Mars to deliver his cargo. It was not really a lucrative enterprise, but it was safe. There were no risks. Jason was an older man now. He had been a freighter captain for over thirty years. The men who worked on his ship had worked with him for a long time. He wasn't a natural leader, but he was consistent and fair. If you worked for him, you would get a fair pay for the work that you did. Maybe it was not especially lucrative but it was a living. Jason was a bald man who sported a stubble of facial hair. He wore a leather outfit and carried a laser pistol by his side. He was average build and did not have any remarkable features.

In the captain's chair, he waited for a communication from the mining corporation's spacecraft control station. They were responsible for managing the orbits of freighters and delivering to them the cargo from short range shuttle craft. It was a well organised operation that was safe and efficient.

"Captain Bourke, shuttle number RL983 will join your orbit in fifteen minutes. I understand that you will take delivery of five containers of liquefied hydrogen gas. I confirm that your freighter is a D Class Series 5F Amazon Transporter," came a voice from the ship's communication panel.

"Roger that," Jason replied.

Jason's freighter was not a big ship and would normally only have a crew of about three persons. It was also not a fast ship, but it was suitable for transporting large heavy cargos that were not urgently needed at the journey's destination. When looking at the front of the ship, it was shaped like a pentagon. The containers were latched onto the five sides of the ship. That is what made the ship a Series 5. It had berths for five containers. The "F" part of the Series 5F label referred to the engine type. The class of a freighter specified the container size the ship took. Amazon Transporter was the make of the ship. This ship had been with Jason for most of his thirty years as captain and he knew it well. It was safe, dependable and reliable. Also, D class freighters were the most common craft that operated from the mine. The control station staff were very familiar with them.

In about thirty minutes the shuttle craft captain reported.

"We have coupled five containers Captain Bourke," he said. "You are good to go?"

"Roger that," Jason replied.

The D Class Series 5F Amazon Transporter had a main engine that provided the thrust to take the craft to high speed. These were at the back of the craft. But to manoeuvre the craft, it relied on four thrusters to steer and orientate it.

These four thrusters had independent engines and control, so that if any one of the engines failed, there would be three others. That was a safety feature of the craft. They were located on the end of pikes that extended from four of the corners of the ship's pentagon. Jason used the thrusters to leave orbit and orientate the craft for the journey to Mars. As expected, all four of them were functioning normally and Jason was soon able to engage the main engine. The journey was expected to take about three and a half hours. Starships could go much faster than that, but there were speed limits in the Earth Solar System. In the inner solar system spanning from Jupiter to the sun, the speed limit was 150,000,000 kilometres per hour. It was a day's work to make a round trip from Mars to Jupiter, as well as picking up and dropping off cargo.

Once the main engine was engaged, he had time to think and remember. A couple of years ago in the nearby Sirius star system, he was engaged to deliver some military cargo urgently. The company that contracted him had links to organised crime. That company was called the Artemis Corporation. It was a very lucrative job, but it had its risks. To make the journey within the deadline, he had to travel through a Nebula that had not been well researched. When inside, it was very difficult to see around him. Unfortunately, his ship had collided with an unexpected object. Both luckily and unluckily the object struck the container with the military cargo. There was only one container for this job. Only one of the ship's thrusters was damaged but the container was split open and the precious cargo had drifted into space. Jason replayed that incident over and over in his mind, wondering if there was something he could have done to prevent the accident. As a result of the accident, he was in a lot of trouble with the Artemis Corporation. They demanded that he pay them for the value of the cargo and extra for the loss of reputation they suffered as a result of the cargo not being delivered.

Unfortunately, Jason was unable to make a claim on his insurance, because delivering military cargo in the Sirius system was illegal. Since then, he had been making regular payments to the Artemis Corporation. However, he regularly received threatening calls demanding that he make larger payments, that his debt to the Corporation was large and that he had an obligation to pay it off sooner rather than later. Jason had been burned from his risk taking. That sorry saga had caused Jason to think back on his life. All the risks he had taken. What did he have to show for it? Yes, he had completed successful lucrative contracts, but he had squandered his earnings on gambling, drinking and prostitutes. He never married or even had a steady girlfriend. Now he was an old man with few assets and a large debt to a dangerous corporation. This was a turning point he thought. He'd cleaned up his act. He'd stopped drinking and gambling and didn't take on risky contracts. From now on, he was going to save for his retirement. Now, until his retirement, he was going to only take safe above-board jobs, even if they were not lucrative. He was paying off his debt to the Artemis Corporation and hoped that when that was done, he would be able to put something away for his retirement.

Jason was about an hour away from Mars when an alert timer from the cockpit sounded. He needed to book a spot in a Mars orbit. He switched the communicator to call the Mars Control Station. He was answered by a young man in uniform.

"Freighter, licence number J436123456 requests permission to orbit," Jason said,

"What cargo do you have and what was your origin?" asked the man in uniform.

"I have five containers of hydrogen from Jupiter," Jason replied.

"What is your estimated time of arrival?"

"One hour," replied Jason.

A short time later the young man spoke again. "I have you booked for a 3257 orbit."

"Roger that," Jason replied.

The 3257 was the number of kilometres away from Mars. Orbits ranged from a thousand kilometres up to ten thousand kilometres.

Jason sat back in his captain's chair and sighed. He was trying not to think about his regrets. However, a short time later he received a call from Angelina, a debt collector from the Artemis Corporation. She had short dark hair and a serious no nonsense face. Her makeup was light. She exuded the persona of someone you did not trifle with. You play with her at your peril.

"Good morning, Jason," she said sternly. "I want to remind you of your outstanding debt. You were careless with your cargo, and we want to be compensated quickly."

Jason swallowed nervously but managed to reply. "Please, I'm making regular payments." He squirmed in his chair. "It is as much as I can afford," he pleaded. "I wasn't able to claim on my insurance."

"Don't give me the scammers' sob story," she said scornfully. "I'm not interested. The Artemis Corporation has been very patient with you, but enough is enough. We want to be paid, and we want to be paid now."

Jason pleaded again. "I'm doing the best I can. I will be able to pay the debt eventually."

"That is not good enough," she barked. "I think you need a warning to motivate you. You need to care about your responsibilities to us."

Then Angelina laughed. "Try your starboard thrusters, Jason," she said.

"Why?" Jason asked cautiously.

"Just do it," she replied.

Jason operated the thruster testing operation on both the starboard thrusters. They were both offline. He tried again and still the same result.

Angelina saw the concern on Jason's face. "That is just a warning to you Jason, she said. "Next time you will not be as fortunate."

Jason was worried. The thrusters were working when they left Jupiter. He tried the thruster testing operation on the port side thrusters. They too, were offline. Angelina had not yet left the communication.

"The port side thrusters don't work either," Jason shouted. "What have you done to me?"

Angelina was taken aback. It was her turn to look worried.

"That is not possible," she said, "Only the starboard thrusters were meant to be disabled." She ended the communication.

To slow a freighter from a fast cruising speed, in this case 150,000,000 kilometres an hour, the thrusters are needed to turn the ship around at 180 degrees, so then the main engine can be fired to slow down the craft. If Jason only had his port side thrusters working, he could still do this, though it would be more difficult. Even if he only had one thruster operational, he would be at least able to navigate to deep space. But with no thrusters operational there was nothing he could do. Maybe his engineer Jack, could have a look at them. He still had nearly an hour before the ship would arrive at Mars. He switched the communication panel on to speak with Jack, who he expected to be in the main engine room. No one answered. He called again. Still no answer. He checked the freighter escape pods. Normally there were three of them. But now, one was missing.

He called the Mars Control Station. The same young man answered. This was quite common at the station. Once an orbit had been booked, the station liked to keep the continuity of relationship between the freighter captain and the official who booked the orbit. Jason said,

"I have a mayday," called Jason. "All my thrusters are offline."

The young man was serious and professional. "We are tracking your trajectory, Captain."

Although Jason had directed his spacecraft to Mars from Jupiter, that did not guarantee that the craft would hit Mars if it wasn't turned away. In fact, it was more likely that the ship would miss Mars. In that case the Control Station would have to direct other ships to leave orbit to avoid any potential collisions.

"We have tracked your trajectory Captain," the young man said. "Unfortunately, you are on a collision course with Mars. Just checking for a rescue ship."

A rescue ship had the ability to couple with freighters, so that they would be able to steer the freighter off its course. However, freighters came in different shapes and sizes and a given rescue ship could not couple with all types of freighters. Recently, there was a report that there were not enough rescue ships in the area, given that Mars was a trading hub for multiple solar systems.

"No rescue ship is available. Do you have escape pods captain?" the young man asked.

"Yes, we have two," Jason replied.

"I suggest you and your crew abandon ship," the young man said. "We'll try to shoot down your ship or move it from its current trajectory."

The Mars control station had a number of craft in orbit whose job it was to shoot at meteors that would hit Mars. Sometimes, they could destroy the errant meteor or hit it well enough to change its trajectory, so it would not collide with the planet's atmospheric net.

Jason ordered his remaining crew to abandon ship. He decided to stay though. He was the one responsible for this mess, so he would see it through to the end.

There were two meteor neutraliser spacecraft that had Jason's freighter in their sites. They both made a number of shots, but none of them found their mark.

"It is going too fast. Much faster than a meteor," said the shooter of one of the craft.

They both made some more shots and one glanced off the hydrogen containers. The container was now leaking hydrogen. It changed the trajectory of the ship a little bit, but not enough for the ship to miss Mars.

In the scientific museum of New Shanghai, one of the main cities on Mars, a curator was showing a group of school children around the museum. The curator was a warm and friendly young lady who enjoyed talking with children. She took on most of the school groups. That was her favourite part of her work. She wore a smart museum uniform and had blonde hair that nearly reached her shoulders. Her makeup complemented her pretty face.

In the final part of this tour, she took the children to the top of the museum where there was an observatory. The roof was all glass so the sky could be seen. There was one telescope. It was not directed at any planets and stars but gave a view to the Mars atmospheric net.

"Who can tell me what escape velocity is?" the curator asked the children.

Four children raised their hands. The curator chose one.

"It's the minimum speed needed for an object that has no propulsion to escape the gravity of a planet," the child said.

"Well done, that is correct," the curator said. "Who can tell me the escape velocity of Earth?"

Three children put up their hands. The curator pointed to one.

"About eleven kilometres per second, Miss," was the answer.

"That is correct," replied the curator. "But for Mars, it's only five kilometres per second." She went on to say, "I'm going to tell you about atmospheric escape. One of the mechanisms is called Jean's escape. At the same temperature, heavier molecules move slower than lighter molecules. So, hydrogen moves faster than carbon dioxide. This is why the escape velocity of a planet is so important. It explains why hydrogen gas does not escape from Jupiter and why Earth has a thicker atmosphere than Mars. That is, where oxygen and nitrogen cannot escape from Earth, the way they can from Mars."

The curator was very good with children. They were all silent, enthralled by the curator's view of physics.

"Now, let us turn our attention to the Mars atmospheric net," continued the curator. We enjoy the same atmosphere here on Mars as we do on Earth. Even though if left to the natural state of things, Mars would have a much thinner atmosphere. The atmospheric net prevents gases like oxygen and nitrogen from escaping Mars. How does it do it?"

This was a rhetorical question. The curator looked around her school group to see if all the children were engaged. She was satisfied that they were, so she continued.

"It does it through the use of quantum fields. The size of each square in the net is ten metres squared, and the rope of the net provides a quantum field for the square. Are there any questions?"

One child put up his hand. "Miss, how high is the net?"

"A good question," replied the curator. "It's about one kilometre high."

Another child put up his hand. "How do spaceships go through it?"

"Another good question," replied the curator. "There are four gates that craft can go through. Only specialist shuttles can do so. Do you remember your trip from Earth? After flying from Earth, you were transferred to another craft that landed on Mars."

The children were now very interested and a number of them put up hands to ask questions. The curator pointed to one.

"What is a quantum field? Is it magnetic?" the child asked.

"There are many different types of quantum fields," the curator replied. "For the atmospheric net, we use three fields. Each one is designed to repel a single type of gas. The gases it targets are oxygen, nitrogen and carbon dioxide. The field is not magnetic. A magnetic field would have no effect, as these gases are not charged."

The question-and-answer session that both the children and curator were enjoying, was interrupted by the sight of a fireball coming from the sky. They were all silent as the fireball hit the atmospheric net.

There was a massive explosion that blew a one-kilometre hole in the Net. That did not stop the fireball. When it crashed on the surface, it created a massive crater that was over a kilometre in diameter. In the past, when the Atmospheric Net had been hit by meteors, there was little or no damage to it. When there was damage, it was repaired fairly quickly and not much of the atmosphere had escaped. But this was different. The hole in the Net now was massive. On the Net there were a series of thrusters. They kept the Net in place, one kilometre away from the surface of the planet. Normally, in the scenario where the Net is hit by a meteor, they could adjust so that no further damage would be done to the Net. But this hole was too big and the algorithms that controlled the thrusters, could not accommodate for this. The thrusters near the hole pulled too much and the Net began to tear. Before the thrusters could be controlled manually, there was a thirty- kilometre tear.

Mars had a population of one hundred and fifty million people and although the atmosphere would still be breathable for a few days, there were not enough shuttle craft available to evacuate everyone. There were a few places that had pressurization systems, but there were not enough for everyone. This was a catastrophe on an unprecedented scale.

Chapter 14
Sheila the Cavewoman

Sheila was sitting in the stone hut on a stone that Samuel had brought in. It was covered in bear skin. She had to surrender the chair once she had given birth to Christina, because other women needed it for their pregnancies. She was also meant to leave the stone hut as well, but she didn't think she would be able to sleep outside. It got very cold at nights, especially the long ones. Christina was in front of her playing with some stone shapes. She had all the features of a Plantere hunter. The red hair, tanned skinned and blue eyes that had a violet tinge at nighttime. Being a toddler, she liked to play and had begun speaking. She could speak in the common tongue and also the language of the tribe. Sheila only knew a few phrases and words of the tribal language. Christina played well with other children. The older children doted on her and called her their sister. For that, Sheila was especially grateful to Jonathon for taking her and Samuel into the tribe. Sheila hadn't expected to become a mother yet, but now she had Christina she felt incredibly blessed.

Sheila tried to fit in with the other women. When she was pregnant and new to the tribe, the other women were kind to her and took care of her. But now, they expected Sheila to fit into the tribe and do what the rest of the women did. Although Sheila only knew a few words in the tribal language, she heard the other women call her the Princess, whenever they talked about her. Sheila really did try to fit in. She went with them on all the gathering expeditions.

When Sheila had arrived on Plantere, she didn't think that anything except fuel balls grew on the planet. But she now discovered that in the mountains there were plants that grew. They were not especially lush and didn't have sweet fruits, but they did have leaves and seeds. Some of the bigger shrubs, or small trees, had wooden trunks. The wooden trunks were gnarly and the roots found cracks in between the rocks. The small trees or shrubs had a flat top to their canopy, which was at about the same height as a person. The women collected some plants with fragrant leaves for cooking in stews and they made a type of bread from the seeds. The shrubs with the wooden trunks were used for firewood. There were also patches of straw- like grass. They were used to start fires. But overall, there were not a lot of plants on Plantere. The women had to roam far and wide to find them.

They also had to find water. Generally, pools of water could only be found in caves. It didn't rain often on Plantere. During Sheila's stay with the tribe, it had only rained once and it was more of a sprinkle rather than a shower. Because of the risk of encountering a yellow bear, they only went into the caves that were near to where the tribal hunters last made their kill. What that meant was that Sheila did a lot of walking. The children always came on these expeditions, and because Christina was young, Sheila had to carry her most of the way. And then of course, Sheila had to also carry back to the camp the plants or water they'd set out to gather. It would be later in the day when they did this, so it would be warm to hot. Sheila thought, I'm Sheila the cavewoman.

Although Sheila tried to be friendly with all the other women, she was only close to Jonathon's wife, Esmeralda. Esmeralda had previously travelled with Jonathon occasionally to visit the corporations. She knew about civilised living. Sheila would try to explain to her that she hated the stone hut because it didn't have glass in the windows and didn't have any furniture. There were no pictures on the walls, nor a proper bed to sleep in. There was no toilet or even running water. She missed watching television and didn't have access to any new books. Esmeralda was understanding and she said that she was proud of Sheila for doing as well as she had.

Sheila also tried to talk to Samuel about life with the tribe. Although Samuel had confided in her that he also had some difficulties adapting, he just didn't understand Sheila's situation. Samuel had grown up in the wilderness and Sheila thought he was still a boy. But to Samuel's credit, he did talk to her about it and did listen to her issues. He just didn't have any solutions.

Sitting on her rock Shiela thought, I'm Sheila the cave woman. That is all there is to it. Outside she heard someone preparing a midday meal. I'd better go and help, Sheila thought instead of mulling over her situation. Those cars had better appreciate the promise she'd made to them.

Sheila picked up her hat and put it on. As she was doing that she thought, none of the other women wore hats and that made her sigh. She went outside and saw one of the women near the cooking fire. Her name was Rita. Like everyone else in the tribe she had the standard hunter's features. All the women in the tribe wore their hair long. She was strong for a woman, but the women in the tribe were nowhere near the same build as the men. In the tribal tongue, Sheila said the equivalent to good morning and Rita replied with the expected response.

And then in the common tongue Sheila asked, "Can I help you with anything?"

"Yes," replied Rita, "I'm making some bread."

Sheila saw a pile of bushes next to Rita. She picked one up and started taking some seeds from it.

"Do you know what we are going to gather in our afternoon expedition?" asked Sheila.

Amongst the women there was a leadership team of three older women. They decided what supplies the tribe needed and where the expeditions would go. Rita was the daughter of one of those. Rita answered.

"We are going to the nearby cave where the men killed the bear, not long after Christina could walk," she said. "There may be some blue green moss growing inside. One of the men thought he saw it."

The blue green moss had some medicinal properties. It was an anaesthetic and could be mixed with water to make a tea. The tea was effective when weak or strong. If the tea was strong, the patient went to sleep. It could also act as a local anaesthetic if applied to an open wound.

Rita continued. "The chieftainesses thought we should go before another bear settles in the cave."

"Will we bring the children?" Sheila asked.

"Yes, it is a dangerous time for us, because we killed the local bear," Rita replied. "Another will come to stake a claim for its territory. When they do that, they roam far and wide, and will want to kill us, if we are found."

Sheila had finished taking the seeds off the bushes. She watched Rita crush the seeds with a tool like a mortar and pestle. This formed a flour, which she added water to. She then kneaded the dough. Once it was ready, she put it into a pot and covered it. Firewood was scarce on Plantere. There were few trees. The only available wood came from shrubs or small trees, and they were scarce. Predominantly, fire was used for cooking, and many dishes would be cooked at the same time to make the best use of the fire. The tribe did not sit around a blazing bonfire at night time. At best, they might warm themselves around a small cooking fire. Rita put the dough away in the pot so it could be cooked together with other dishes when the tribe lit the next cooking fire.

Sheila and Christina enjoyed a lunch of bread and dried yellow bear meat. A meal that they had often. Sheila missed the meals she had on Earth or even the meals she had at corporation forts on Plantere. The buffets in the fort mess hall, presented the delights of Earth cuisine. She remembered the seafood, the salads, curries, pasta dishes and roasts. During the meal now, the women were told that they needed to bring their spears, as this expedition could be dangerous. Sheila was not very good with spears. Samuel had complained about the weight of a standard spear and had to use a ladies' spear because that was all he could lift. Sheila had trouble lifting the ladies' spear. Esmeralda had a spare spear Sheila could use and gave her some very basic training on how to do a jab, so Sheila could participate in a wall of warriors that would drive away a bear.

After lunch the women went on their expedition. The weather was warm but the cave that they wanted to go to was not far. When they got to the entrance of the cave the most senior chieftainess Sandra, told most of the women to mind the children a short distance away from the cave entrance. A small group of three women took their spears and ventured into the cave. If the moss was there, then it would be growing not too far away from the entrance. They were very quiet. If a new bear had taken up residence, then it was likely that it would be asleep. After a few minutes, one of the women returned with some moss. The Shaman confirmed that this was blue green moss. The other two women ventured further into the cave. The eyesight of Plantere hunters was very good. If there was any light at all, they could make out shapes. But deep in the cave it was pitch black. A fire torch could be lit but the resources to make one were scarce, so this was done rarely. The other two women returned from the cave, saying that they couldn't find any evidence of a new bear.

The expedition was a success. They found a good patch of blue green moss and it appeared that a new yellow bear had not yet taken residence in the cave. The women were in good spirits on the journey back to the camp. They laughed and joked together. Sheila was teased about how she held the spear while walking. Not in a nasty way, but in a good - natured friendly banter. Now, Sheila felt that she belonged, that she had been accepted.

There was some commotion back at camp. The second most senior male of the tribe had returned from a trading expedition. Normally, this would have been undertaken by Jonathon, but Jonathon had made a promise to the cars not to visit any corporations. So, this responsibility had fallen on the shoulders of Anthony. Anthony took his son on the latest expedition. When they left, they had taken some yellow bear bones to trade with corporations. Yellow bear bones were very valuable. They were sought after to make ornamental items and statues. The anatomy of yellow bears was very unusual. They weren't a purely carbon-based lifeform, so their bones were unique. The corporations had their own yellow bear hunting operations. These hunters would take the bones of a yellow bear and then leave the meat to rot. They were not like the tribes who made use of every part of the animal. The trade of yellow bear bones was very important to the tribe. They would trade bones for artificial firewood, clothes, shoes and even spears. When Jonathon did these expeditions, he sometimes would sell his services as a mountain guide. The return of hunters from a trading expedition provided a great source of interest from the tribe. It was their only way of finding out what was happening on the rest of Plantere.

There was commotion at the camp, because Anthony had some very unusual news. Anthony didn't want to share it with everyone. He wanted to have a meeting with Jonathon and the Chieftainesses first. Then they could decide on what would be told. That didn't sit well with some of the tribal members, as the secrecy just increased their curiosity. Jonathon had suggested that Sheila and Samuel should be at the meeting, as they knew about the corporations and the outside world in general. When Sheila arrived back at camp with the other women, Jonathon pulled her aside and asked her to attend the meeting.

The meeting was held in the hut that Sheila had yet to vacate. Everyone sat on the ground, except for Anthony, who sat on Sheila's rock. Anthony was middle aged but younger than Jonathon. He was bald but sported a bushy beard. Anthony, like all the men, was well built. He and Jonathon were similar in height. Once everyone was settled, he began his story.

He and his son had visited a number of forts and found that they had all been deserted. There was not a soul. The forts were all intact and did not look as if they had been attacked by cars. The mountain tribe did have a number of neighbouring forts close by. And around their area there wasn't a lot of car activity, as many of the car tribes had been overhunted. At their fifth fort visited, they found it was occupied by a handful of men in Corporation uniform. Anthony asked them what was happening. Why were all the forts deserted? Where was everybody? What Anthony discovered, he didn't really understand.

Apparently, the Martian atmospheric net had collapsed and millions of people died. Mars was an important trading hub for most solar systems. People were scared and just wanted to return to their home planets. The corporations facilitated this by providing extra shuttles. The men who Anthony was talking to, had one last shuttle. They were waiting for stragglers before making a rendezvous with the last starship orbiting Plantere.

Like Anthony, everyone except Sheila, did not know what the Martian atmospheric net was and didn't understand why everyone would have left Plantere.

"Oh my God," Sheila exclaimed. "The atmospheric net around Mars has collapsed. I have got to go home. I can't stay here."

Samuel was surprised by Sheila's reaction. "I know it is a terrible tragedy, but what is so important about Mars?"

"It's the bridge between the terra-sapiens and the stellar community," Sheila said.

"What will happen now it is gone?"

Sheila was distressed. "I fully understand now why all these forts are deserted," she said. "People need that connection to Earth."

No-one in the stone hut could comprehend what Sheila was saying. None of them knew anything about Earth. There was silence in the meeting. Samuel broke the silence.

"You belong here Sheila. Your family is here," he said. Now Samuel was distressed.

"I don't belong here Samuel," Sheila replied, "I'm an earthling who is just visiting."

Samuel was stunned. What Sheila had just said really hurt. He did not know what to say.

"What about Christina?" said Jonathon. "What about your promise to the cars?"

"Christina should stay here," replied Sheila. "I know she is important to the cars. I'm sorry about my promise. I did try."

Again, there was silence around the hut. Samuel loved Sheila and wanted her to stay. But if she was unhappy and wanted to go back to Earth, then he would help her.

"I will take you to the Fort, Sheila and make sure you are safe," he said.

Then Jonathon stood up and went over to Samuel. He put his hand on Samuel's shoulder.

"I know you mean well son," Jonathon said. "But it is too dangerous. What if you are both killed? Christina would lose two parents in one day. Also, you made a promise to the cars."

Samuel understood, now that it had been spoken. The wellbeing of Christina was the highest priority. Sheila must really be unhappy for her to leave her daughter. He knew that Sheila really loved her. Samuel was devastated that he could not make Sheila happy on Plantere.

"Anthony, when did the men at the fort say they will depart?" asked Jonathon.

"In a few days," Anthony replied. "They let us use a truck to get back here. I think if we leave now, we could make it back in time."

There wasn't much time. Anthony had just returned. Now he was about to set out again. Sheila collected her belongings. The Tribe gathered to farewell Sheila and Anthony. Each of the women hugged her and wished her all the best on her journey back to Earth. Jonathon went over to Sheila and hugged her too. Sheila then went over to Samuel and gave him a hug.

"Take care of our daughter, Samuel," she said, with tears in her eyes. "She is very special."

She tried to keep her composure as she bent down to Christina and said, "Mummy is going away sweetheart. You need to listen to Daddy, and all the mothers in the tribe."

Christina wiped a tear from Sheila's eyes and said, "I love you Mummy. I know it is hard to be an earthling here."

Finally, they were ready to leave. Samuel held Christina in his arms, as they watched Anthony and Sheila descend the cliff face down to where the truck was parked. It was late in the afternoon, but they should reach the fort before it was dark. Samuel felt the gentle breeze on his face, but didn't think anything of it. Then he thought, what did Sheila think of the breeze? He realised that there were so many things he didn't know about Sheila and what she thought. He sighed, and he and Christina did not leave until Sheila and Anthony were both in the truck and had driven off. Samuel wiped a tear from his eyes.

"Don't worry Daddy, Mummy will come back one day," said Christina.

Chapter 15
The Negotiation

Today the women went on an expedition to collect more blue green moss. They were grateful that they could get some from the entrance of a nearby cave. It had been some years since there was a bear residing in this cave. Most of the women and all of the children waited outside, while two women ventured inside. Today was going to be an average day, in terms of length. Even though it was the middle of the day it was not too hot, so the wait wasn't uncomfortable.

Christina enjoyed feeling the breeze on her face. She was six earth years old. Christina had all the hunter's features, bright red hair, blue eyes and tanned skin. She also had Sheila's pretty face and was lanky, like Samuel. Although she was still young, you could see that she would be tall like her father when she grew up. Like all the girls in the tribe, her hair was long and rested on her shoulders.

She sat on the ground with her good friend Alexander. Alexander was eight earth years old, and had the promise of being a well-built man. He was already practising for the coming-of-age ritual and loved playing with a spear. Alexander was confiding with Christina about his progress.

"Soon I should be able to use the standard spear," he said. "Jonathon, mountain master said I have a good strong thrust."

"You will be a good strong hunter, Alex," said Christina encouragingly.

"When I grow up," said Alexander, "I will be a mountain master. What do you want to be Christina, when you grow up?"

"I will be a servant," Christina said. "I brought my spear. Could you please show me again how to do a jab?"

Christina owned a children's spear. It was smaller than a women's spear. Christina didn't have a passion for spear craft, but like everything else, she worked on it diligently. She liked tasks where she had to think and use her hands at the same time. The tribal Shaman was pleased with her knowledge and application of healing. She said that Christina could grow up to be the Tribe's next healer. Christina was also a good cook. She made fragrant bread, and tasty stews. Many people complimented her dishes as they ate. Although she applied herself well in tribal tasks, she had a passion for the news that Anthony brought back from his expeditions. The forts were still deserted, but Anthony brought back news about the cars. There were more of them now and they were less hostile to Anthony.

Alexander was pleased to show Christina how to do a jab. He then gave the spear back to Christina.

"Hold on to the end of the spear," he said. "That's it. Don't make too big a movement. You want to participate in an impregnable wall of warriors."

Christina listened to what he said and shuffled along with her feet.

"Good," said Alexander. "You're moving your feet well."

Then Christina had a wicked smile, a wide smile with one side of her lips raised. She turned to Alexander and started jabbing towards him.

"Hey," Alexander complained. "What are you doing?"

Christina was still smiling. "I'm hunting a fierce yellow bear," she said as she kept doing the jab towards Alexander.

"Grr," Alexander growled. "I will swat you little girl."

He then waved his arms and swatted Christina's spear away.

Christina laughed. "You make a fierce yellow bear. I think I will run away and hide."

The women came back from the cave. They looked frightened and concerned.

"I think there is a bear in that cave now," one of them said. "I heard some noises."

"We'd better go back to the camp quickly," said Sandra. "Come along children."

When they returned to the camp, the Chieftainesses met and decided that there should always be a lookout. This was a dangerous time, they warned. When a new bear settled in a territory, they tended to roam a lot and attack anything they find that could be conceived as a threat. The women took it in turns to be the lookout and when they did, they carried a horn. Three blasts on the horn meant there was a bear approaching.

Christina was helping out with the cooking, when she heard three blasts of the horn. The women with her told her to stay where she was, before running to get their spears. The men were out on a hunting trip, so it would be up to the women to drive the bear away.

Christina saw a medium sized yellow bear on the edge of the camp. The bear was about ten metres tall. The women had lined up and formed a wall. They started doing the jab. But when they started, the bear screamed. When a bear was angry their scream was high pitched and loud. The bear made a couple of swipes towards the women. Luckily, both swipes missed their target, but the bear was still advancing and the women had to retreat. This angry bear would not be driven away.

Christina ran to the wall of women and then worked her way through the wall. She stood with her hands on her hips and made a deep guttural sound that seemed unintelligible to the women. When a bear was angry it would scream, but when they talked, they made deep harsh sounding noises. The bear stopped screaming and stood still. Christina hadn't had any experience with bears, but she could see a sadness in the bear's eyes.

How could this small human be talking to her? thought the bear.

"Mama Bear, why are you so angry?" Christina asked in the language of the yellow bear. Christina had the tone of a baby bear asking its mother a question.

"I came to visit my son and he was not there," the bear replied.

Yellow bears were solitary creatures. They rarely gathered in groups of more than two or three. Even then, they only did so to mate, or for when the mother bears visited their grownup offspring.

Christina put her hands to her sides and looked concerned. "I'm sorry for your loss Mama Bear," she replied. She closed her eyes and became very still. When she opened them, she was in a trance. In a flat tone she said, "When you were young, you had a twin sister. You loved her dearly. Then your mother sent you away and you missed your sister."

The hair of the yellow bear stood on end. She was so surprised that Christina knew this about her.

"You bore your son in your womb for many cycles," continued Christina.

In Plantere, the length of a day and night varies each day. It seems to be random, but it actually works in cycles. Each cycle was about two Earth years. The yellow bears measured time by this. For them, time moved more slowly than for humans. They lived much longer than humans and when they raised children, that took more time.

"Then you watched him grow from an infant to a fully grown bear," continued Christina. "Each day that you had with him was a blessing. He helped you to stop missing your sister." Christina's tone did not change. It was as if she was reciting something out of a book. "Nothing was like the love you had for him. You taught him everything he needed to know to be independent and had high hopes that he would be a master of a vast territory. When the day came for him to leave you, you were both proud and sad."

The demeanour of the bear softened. She was less angry now.

"As he left, you promised you would come to him to see his territory," continued Christina.

The yellow bear was sad and all she could say was, "It is what you say." She then sat down on the ground. There was a small moment of silence. The bear said sadly, "It rained on the day he left."

One thing the bears and hunters had in common was that they both believed that a rainy day was a good omen, as rainy days were very rare.

"I'm so sorry, Mama Bear," Christina replied

Then there was silence. For the humans, the silence seemed like a long time. But for a bear it wasn't. When Christina did speak again, it may have been considered hasty by the bear.

"Our men are not here. There are only women and children at this camp now," said Christina.   Now that the bear had calmed down, Christina hoped to explain the Tribe's situation. "We too bear our children and watch them grow. The women here in this line with their spears, only want to protect their children."

The bear really considered this. She rubbed her head with her left paw. Then she said, "But when your men return, they will hunt me and my offspring."

Christina was little and liked to play. But even at this young age she knew how to be serious. She was thoughtful and considered the bear's argument.

"What if we didn't?" she asked. She paused, to get the desired effect, to make the bear think. "What if we left you in peace? So, you could live and raise another bear. We would do our hunting in other territories."

The bear rubbed her head again with her left paw and thought about this.

"Okay," she said, "I don't want to kill your young. But please leave me alone."

Christina hadn't finished though.

"Mama Bear," she said. "In the entrance to your cave there is a moss that we like to collect. Could we please be allowed to collect some? Maybe only two unarmed women would enter your cave?"

Yellow bears do not smile, but Christina felt that this one had. The bear said, "Okay, little human. You are very brave for one so small. You have saved your people." The bear stood up, turned and left.

Sandra turned to Christina. "What just happened here?" she asked.

"Mama bear won't attack us," Christina replied. "Unless we hunt her and her children first."

"We will need a meeting of the Chiefs," said Sandra.

When the men returned from their hunting, Sandra told Jonathon and Anthony about the bear and what Christina had done. A meeting of the Chiefs was called a short time later. The meeting was held in the stone hut and Christina was invited to attend. The Chiefs sat her down on Sheila's rock. Being the centre of attention at the Chiefs' meeting was a serious matter and probably more so for a child of Christina's age. Christina was serious, but she wasn't scared.

Jonathon spoke up.

"Christina, I understand a yellow bear was attacking our camp and you went through the warrior's line to talk with it. Please tell us what happened in your eyes."

Jonathon was thinking that Christina may be shy because she was in the meeting of the Chiefs. But she wasn't. She spoke clearly and confidently.

"Mama Bear came to visit her son, and found that he was no longer there," she said. "She was very upset."

Everyone in the meeting was astounded. Did yellow bears have feelings like humans?

"That is why she attacked our camp," Christina continued. "I convinced her that our camp only had women and children, but she said our men may try to hunt her. I offered to her, that if she didn't attack us, we would not try to hunt her."

"What sort of little girl is this, who negotiates with bears?" said Andrea, one of the Chieftainesses.

"A very special one," Jonathon replied.

"Mama Bear will let us collect the blue green moss from the entrance to her cave, Christina added. "As long as it is done by only two unarmed women."

Jonathon laughed. "You drive a hard bargain, little one."

"How do we know if the bear will honour the deal? She may attack us anyway?" asked Sandra.

Jonathon suggested, "Let us see if the bear will attack us."

He then argued,

"If we hunted this bear, then another will come and attack us. So, we are not worse off by doing nothing. What if the bear does honour this deal? That would be very good for our camp."

Anthony said,

"Christina is a brave little girl. But is she mature enough to understand what she has done?"

Jonathon was deep in thought and was wondering what he should tell.

He was rubbing his chin and then said,

"I have not spoken much about the arrival of Sheila and Samuel. Maybe I need to say more now."

He had the attention of everyone.

"We were on a corporation expedition to find a crashed spacecraft. The cars attacked us and killed everyone, but spared Sheila, Samuel and I." he explained. "They then showed us their most sacred site."

Jonathon was choosing his words carefully. He didn't want to break his promise to the cars.

He said, "This was all done for Christina's sake. She is very special to the cars. They have a Prophecy and they believed that Sheila's daughter would be an important leader of them. I think we can trust the treaty she has made."

Jonathon told more about their expedition, but he left out the details of the Womb. There was some more discussion at the meeting, but it was decided that the Tribe would wait and see. That is, see if the bear attacks the camp again.

Chapter 16
The Detour

Sheila awoke and felt a sense of déjà vu. She was lying in a sausage shape capsule that had a glass top. It seemed that this ship was the same as the one that had brought her to Plantere. When she looked to the ceiling, she could see the same network of pipes. She looked either side and could see distorted views of the capsules next to her. As she became fully awake, she remembered that in this journey, all the capsules had occupants. She was on the last shuttle to leave Plantere. Anthony was able to get her to Fort Lyndon before the last shuttle left. And this starship left as soon as the Lyndon shuttle docked. She had only just made it in time. Before Anthony made his farewells, he loaded a map on her journal pad. It showed the location of the mountain tribe relative to Fort Lyndon. He said that if ever she should return to Plantere, she could use this map to find the Tribe. Just the same as when she travelled to Plantere, the journey had two legs. This was because Plantere was a remote world that wasn't travelled too often. It did not justify having a direct route to Earth. This ship was destined to a major hub called New Shenzhen Station. From there, she would take another ship to Earth. This first leg should have taken three and half earth years.

As Sheila was lying there, she thought about Samuel and Christina. They would be three and half years older. What would they be doing? She didn't want to feel regret at leaving them, so she thought about the new life ahead of her on Earth. She would go and visit places that she had been to when she was growing up. She remembered the Scottish Highlands. It will be good, she tried to convince herself. She would get a good job with a newspaper. Maybe she could catch up with old friends. But then she realised that they would have aged considerably, as Sheila had done a lot of long-distance space travel. Her life had changed since she left Earth. She had changed.

A steward came and helped her to sit up. He asked if she would like a drink. She remembered that the last time she was on the ship, coffee seemed to help her when she had just woken up. So, she asked for a coffee. When the steward returned with her coffee, he told her that the captain would hold a conference in the mess hall for all the passengers. This made her worry. Why would the captain need to talk to all the passengers?

"Do you have a wheel chair?" she asked.

The steward nodded and soon returned with the wheel chair. He helped Sheila into it and then wheeled her into the ship's mess hall. There were other people there, also sitting in wheel chairs. Some of the passengers knew each other and spoke uneasily to their companions.

When all the passengers were assembled, the captain stepped out to the front. He was a middle-aged man dressed in an Iowa Corporation uniform. He was tall with long blonde hair tied in a pony tail. He clipped a microphone onto the front of his uniform and began to speak.

"Everyone, please, please can I have your attention."

He waited for all to be silent and then said,

"I hope you have been able to start recovering from your long journey."

He looked around the room and felt concern for everyone there. He felt that he needed to express how unusual this journey was.

"I wish to say that these times are unprecedented. I have been a starship captain for over eighty years and have never seen anything like it. The collapse of the Mars Atmospheric Net has affected the psyche of all people very deeply. Even people who had never lived on Earth felt the disconnection from it when Mars suffered this terrible tragedy."

He could see on some of the faces of his audience that they understood and empathised with what he had just said. He took a deep breath and continued.

"I'm sorry. I have some bad news."

He paused.

"We were turned away from New Shenzhen station because of the sheer number of vessels there wanting to orbit. The only station available to us was Zigorn station."

Sheila was stunned. *Where is Zigorn station?*

The captain continued his bad news. "Because of this detour, you have all been asleep for five Earth years."

Five years? Sheila was incredulous.

"From here, there will be a ship destined for Earth. But unfortunately, it won't arrive for another two earth years. Some corporations including ours, want to collect some equipment from Omega 24A, so this ship will be returning to Omega 24A in a few hours."

Sheila felt disorientated. She should have realised that if everybody wanted to return to Earth, that there would be some delays. Other thoughts came to her. Life in the mountain tribe was hard and wasn't like anything she was used to, but her daughter was there. Her daughter would be seven years old now. No longer a toddler, but a little girl. And Samuel. She couldn't work out what she felt for Samuel. She was fond of him but when she left Plantere, she had felt that he was too young. Her thoughts were interrupted by an older woman sitting in a wheelchair next to her.

"You are that journalist who went missing, aren't you?" the older woman asked.

Sheila suddenly remembered her promise to the cars that she had broken. How did this woman recognise her? Sheila then thought that she didn't exactly have a low profile when she worked for the Corporation. She didn't know what to say, so she said nothing. The older woman had short grey hair and she was dressed in an Iowa Corporation uniform. The older woman wasn't dissuaded by the lack of an answer from Sheila.

"Never mind," the older woman continued, "it doesn't matter now. Do you know what?"

She turned in her wheelchair and leant towards Sheila in a conspiratorially way.

"I have been working for the Iowa Corporation for thirty years. Five of them on Plantere," the older woman said, "I have never been to Earth during that time."

She then, feeling incredulous, raised the tone of her voice,

"And now, suddenly I want to go to Earth. It is not just me. It is all my colleagues as well. The Corporation just stopped working and everyone was going to return to Earth."

The older woman then sighed, "I guess we are all terra-sapiens at heart."

Sheila asked, "What work did you do on Plantere?"

"I was a senior manager in the Human Resources department." the woman answered, "My name is Lydia, what is yours?"

"Jane," Sheila lied.

"Do you have family on Earth, Jane?" Lydia asked.

"Yes," said Sheila, "my parents and my sister live there."

"I have a brother there." Lydia said, "I haven't seen him for twenty years, and now I'm racing back to see him."

Lydia sighed again,

"When you think about it, it is just crazy." Then she confided, "I liked my work at the Iowa Corporation. I never ventured out of the Fort, but everything you needed was there in the Fort. My life was pretty good."

A young man sitting in a wheelchair on the other side of Lydia, overheard Lydia's conversation.

"Me too," he said, "I was a car evaluator. I would examine the condition of captured cars and give them a grade before they were transported. It was a good job."

Then Lydia sighed again and said to both of them, "Now we have two years to think about how good our lives were."

The thought of waiting in this station for two years filled Sheila with dread. Her life would be on hold. Each morning, she would wake up and think of her daughter and Samuel, wondering what they would be doing. Having nothing else to fill her life, she would sink into feelings of regret.

A steward walked past her. Sheila reached out and said, "Please Sir."

The steward turned to her.

"Could I please see the captain, sir?" Sheila asked.

The steward wheeled her into the captain's cabin.

"The captain will come and see you soon," the steward said before he left.

Sheila looked around the cabin. It was quite spacious and had a large desk in the middle. She saw pictures on the wall. They appeared to be famous locations that the captain must have visited in his work. She remembered how she had felt not having any pictures in the stone hut she lived in on Plantere. Then she sighed. Sheila had a closer look at the pictures. Three of them were from Inter Solar System Heritage Parks. Heritage Parks were protected from over development by the formidable Inter Solar System Union.

The Inter Solar System union was funded by grants made by governments on a number of Solar Systems. Not only did they manage Heritage Parks, they also championed workers' rights and environmental protection. One of the Heritage Park pictures was from a famous world, where it was covered with water. Living on the planet, was an intelligent lifeform that looked like Earth's mysterious mermaids. There were cities built beneath the sea, like the famous city of Atlantis. Also, on this world, there was a vast variety of marine life. It must have been a very memorable visit for the captain.

It wasn't long before the captain entered his cabin and asked,

"What can I do for you, Ma'am?".

Sheila queried, "You said this ship was going to return to Plantere in a few hours?"

"Yes, that is right," he said.

"Is there room for me to come?" Sheila asked.

"I thought you wanted to go to Earth?" the captain replied.

"Yes, but I've changed my mind," Sheila replied.

"Well, you are in luck ma'am, there is a berth available. We will be leaving in two hours."

Chapter 17
A Typical Day

Today was a day the Womb leadership team hosted an open session. An open session gave the opportunity to any car to raise grievances and get mediation from the leadership team. Suvy was away on an expedition to a distant tribe, so it was left to Bluey and Tuti to listen to the applicants. They held the session in front of the spaceship. Just before the open session, Tuti met with Bluey inside the spaceship. They were examining the Womb.

Tuti said, "The leak from the Womb is getting worse."

His wipers flicked nervously.

Bluey replied, "Maybe it is time to bring Christina to us."

"She is still very young," Tuti complained.

"Maybe she is old enough." Bluey suggested and he lowered his front windows.

Tuti wasn't convinced. He was afraid of all humans and had been putting off the day when Christina would be brought to the Womb. However, he admired the Blue Porsche for his trust in prophecies and the resolution to bring them to pass.

"Okay," he finally said, "I will reach out to her."

The Womb badly needed a repair, and they needed a human to help with the repairs, but Tuti didn't sound convinced. However, Bluey let it go. The hyper car was a good leader, who did listen to advice and was proficient at finding the middle path. Over time, Bluey had often asked his friend to use his telepathy to touch base with Christina. Tuti's first contact with her was when she was a toddler. So, Bluey thought that Tuti had built a rapport with the girl. Even though Tuti didn't have the same faith in the prophecies that Bluey had, Bluey knew his friend would put aside his reservations and be courteous and welcoming when he contacted Christina to ask her to come to the Womb.

After a long pause Bluey tried to comfort his friend and said,

"It will be okay. Don't worry."

Then he changed his tone to be more upbeat and added,

"Shall we go out and see what the cars have for us?"

They exited the spaceship and took their positions on a platform just outside at the front of the spaceship. Being on the platform gave them a sense of authority to all cars that came for mediation.

It was a long day and the Blue Porsche and the hyper car heard grievances from many cars and made their pronouncements. Tuti, after a while, found it tiresome. He really missed the wisdom of Suvy. One particularly irritating grievance was brought by the leaders of a Toyota and Mazda tribe. They had been organising a parade that would be attended by a large number of cars. Cars loved hosting parades and watching them. It was a favourite pastime. There was no better feeling than to drive by the honking of enraptured cars witnessing the parade. And leading the parade was a great honour, as the leader was the first car to be honked by the cars in the audience. The leaders of the two tribes were accompanied by their candidates for the lead position. For the Mazda tribe that was a red MX-5 and for the Toyota tribe, a white Landcruiser Prado. Both cars were in their prime and looked impressive.

The Leader of the Toyota tribe, a silver Toyota Crown opened the grievance,

"Our friends from the Mazda tribe with us, are organising a grand parade. We have decided to go with the arrow formation."

With the arrow formation, the cars are organised in the shape of an arrow, as seen by a bird's eye view of the cars. Typically, the most glamorous cars held positions in the arrow head and the rest followed in the arrow tail. The Toyota Crown continued,

"But we have a dispute over who will be the tip of the arrow."

The Landcruiser lifted himself on his suspension and spoke up,

"I desire a position that befits my stature."

The MX-5 also raised himself on his suspension and followed by saying,

"I'm the most qualified for the position."

This provoked the Landcruiser to repeat, "I desire a position that befits my stature."

Tuti said, "Well, whoever leads will be followed by two cars of the other tribe, and then three cars of the leader's tribe and so on and so forth."

This did not quell the dispute. The leader of the Mazda tribe, a Mazda 5 said, "Yes, we have agreed on that. It is who will be the tip of the arrow that we can't agree on."

The Landcruiser repeated again, "I desire a position that befits my stature."

The MX-5 also repeated, "I'm the most qualified for the position."

Tuti was feeling impatient. Why were these cars coming to him for such a petty grievance?

"So, have a honking roulette," he suggested.

A honking roulette is similar to the rock, paper, scissors that humans do. At the same time, each car could do from one to three honks. If one car gives two honks and the other, gives one, then the two honks car would win. If the other car does three honks, then the first car wins. If the cars do the same number of honks as each other, then they would retry the roulette. Tuti was sure that this would resolve the dispute.

But the proposal didn't satisfy the Landcruiser and he repeated yet again, "I desire a position that befits my stature."

The Toyota Crown said, "We came here for effective mediation and you suggest that we rely on a game of chance? Tell us, who should be the tip of the arrow?"

Tuti was feeling even more irritated, but he tried to remain calm as he said, "Parades are supposed to be a source of entertainment for the cars participating in them and the spectators. Something to be enjoyed."

He may as well have been talking to himself, because the four cars in front of him did not look convinced.

Then Tuti sighed and said grudgingly, "Ok, I choose the Mazda."

The Landcruiser repeated yet again, "I desire a position that befits my stature."

Then the Toyota Crown lifted himself on his suspension and said, "This is not a good adjudication. I'm not happy."

A frustrated Tuti said, "Very well, I choose the Toyota."

The Mazda 5 idled his engine more loudly and replied, "If our candidate doesn't lead the parade, I don't think we can participate in it."

This provoked the Landcruiser to lift himself on his suspension and repeat, "I desire a position that befits my stature."

This time it was Tuti's turn to idle his engine loudly.

"Honestly," he said, "Can't you all just get along?"

The Toyota Crown lifted himself on his suspension and idled his engine loudly before stating, "If a Toyota is not leading the parade, then we won't participate."

Now Tuti was missing the wisdom of Suvy, even more. He really didn't like these disputes. The angst was just increasing and there was no resolution. Tuti found himself becoming angry as he said,

"Well don't have your stupid parade. I'm done with this."

He regretted saying this as soon as it came out. The Mazda 5 kept idling his engine loudly as he replied, "We won't do this parade anymore."

"That's fine by us!" the Toyota Crown replied angrily.

The Landcruiser repeated haughtily, "I desire a position that befits my stature."

Tuti watched the four cars turn away. The Toyotas went in one direction and the Mazdas in another.

Tuti turned to Bluey and said, "I hate those cars. It is just a stupid parade. Couldn't they just get over themselves?" Then in his most whiny voice, he mocked the Landcruiser, "I desire a position that befits my stature."

Bluey laughed and replied, "A typical day at the Womb."

The hyper car announced, "Next."

And a new group of cars came before them for mediation.

Chapter 18
A Visit to the Womb

For Samuel it had been a hard day of hunting. It had been a long day and they had been walking around during the hottest part of the day. The party searched and searched but could not find a yellow bear to slay. This long hunting expedition proved to be fruitless. Everyone in the team felt disheartened. Some of the hunters grumbled that they had a bear close to camp and they should hunt her. Jonathon wasn't sympathetic to that view, even though he felt just as disheartened as everyone else. He scowled and called them blue green moss brain morons. When they got back to camp, Samuel had a quick bite to eat and collapsed into his sleeping hide. He knew that the night would be short, and he really needed a long sleep. Christina slept in a hide next to his. They both slept outside.

At dawn, Christina woke, and tried to wake her father.

"Daddy, Daddy," she implored, as she shook him.

He was not very responsive.

She shook him again and said, "Daddy, Daddy."

Eventually he turned on his back and grumbled, "What?"

"We need to go to the Womb, Daddy!" Christina implored.

"That's miles away sweetheart, go back to sleep," Samuel grumbled.

And with that he turned on his side so that his back was facing Christina. Christina shook him again,

"Tuti will take us!" she stated as if it was an obvious answer to Samuel's sleepy objection. Samuel rolled onto his back. "Tuti, Hugh," he grumbled.

"Quickly, Daddy. We have a long ride ahead of us and a big day," Christina chirped.

Samuel gave up on sleeping and stood up groggily. Christina was already dressed and had a pack with food and water. She was ready to go. Samuel relieved himself behind a rock and dressed. All the while, Christina implored him to hurry. Samuel went over to a woman who was preparing a meal nearby and told her to tell Jonathon that he would be spending the day with Christina. In his pile of belongings Samuel found his Easy Shooter stun rifle. Samuel was finally ready.

"You won't need that, Daddy," Christina scolded as she pointed to the stun rifle.

Samuel grumbled but put the rifle away.

"Okay sweetheart," he asked, "where do we meet this Tuti?"

"Don't be silly Daddy. Where he dropped you, Mummy and Uncle Jonathon off," Christina answered.

The penny dropped. Tuti must be the hyper car. Still feeling sleepy, Samuel muttered, "This way then."

He led Christina around to the plains where the hyper car was parked.

When they reached it, the hyper car said, "Hello Samuel, I hope you are well. Little Princess let me have a look at you."

Christina playfully did a turn, and the car said, "Yes. A beautiful young lady."

"And you, Tuti" replied Christina, "are much sexier than Daddy described."

The hyper car said, "We must hurry. We have a long drive and there is much to be done. Please get in."

The doors opened and Samuel and Christina climbed in. Christina was in the driver's seat and Samuel was in the front passenger seat, next to her.

Samuel remembered the first time he had ridden in the hyper car. It was pretty special. This time was no different. The car travelled twice as fast as any sports car, and Samuel didn't have to drive. He didn't have to fight to keep control. He could just sit back and enjoy the ride. After his last meeting with the hyper car, Samuel had changed his attitude towards cars. As he was growing up, he had seen them as very aggressive and hostile animals. Especially when his parents died, but at the Womb he saw a different side. They were an intelligent and sensitive race. Even though his attitude had changed a little, he still wished that Christina had allowed him to bring his stun rifle. Christina asked,

"Is this what it feels like to jump a car, Daddy?"

"No sweetheart this is a million times better. The car is driving us voluntarily. We are not fighting him," Samuel replied.

Then Samuel asked Christina,

"How did you know that the hyper car wanted to take us to the Womb?"

She answered,

"It is hard to explain Daddy. I hear things. Tuti reached out to me and I heard."

At first the ride was exhilarating, but after a while Christina was becoming bored. It was a long time to sit in one place. She had a look at Tuti's dashboard. In the middle of the steering wheel there was a big button. I wonder what this does she thought. She pressed it and to her delight Tuti honked. The next time she pressed it she held it down. Tuti did a long honk.

The hyper car complained, "Hey, what are you doing?" He then sighed. "Do you want to listen to some music?" he asked.

"What's that?" Christina asked.

"Here, listen to this. This is my favourite," the hyper car replied. Then out of his radio speaker, he played *"I'm A Believer"* by the Monkees.

"What a wonderful noise," Christina exclaimed. She was enthralled by it and when the song ended, she asked the hyper car to play it again. Which he did and then when the song ended, Christina wanted to hear it again. After the fourth time it was replayed, Christina had remembered some of the lyrics, so on the fifth time, she sang along.

"I thought love was only true in fairytales," she sang, "Meant for someone else but not for me."

Samuel didn't know much about music, but he didn't think that Christina sounded anything like the music coming out of the radio speaker. He didn't want to be mean, but she sounded terrible. He was happy that she was occupied, so he didn't say anything. Then, Samuel thought about how Christina was with the hyper car. She wasn't afraid of cars. As far as Samuel could remember, he was always terrified of them. Then Samuel remembered the stories he'd heard from some of the women in the tribe, about how Christina talked to the yellow bear. When Samuel had asked Christina about it, she played it down. She didn't want him to be concerned. But when he heard the story from other women, it made him shudder. There was one really angry bear that Christina had approached without a spear and talked to it. It made Samuel think about his mother. Maybe Christina took after her. His mother had been a very good car hunter. She wasn't afraid of cars either. His mother was much better at jumping cars than his father.

His Dad used to say, "Why jump cars when you can stun them?"

While his mother would say to him, "I can jump young sportscars. You are lucky to jump an ancient Ford Laser."

Then Samuel thought of Sheila. She was brave. Maybe Christina took after her. Although Samuel didn't know anything about Earth and had only visited corporation forts twice recently, he did understand how hard it was to live in the wilderness of Plantere. He also had lived in a house when he was very young. He remembered his mother saying a number of times,

"Sammy, we are so lucky to live in a house that Daddy built for us."

When Samuel had first met Sheila, he was just infatuated by her beauty. Then as he lived with her, he grew to love her bravery. Samuel missed her terribly. He sighed. The one thing all the women in his life had in common, was that they were all fearless.

After a few hours, the hyper car reached their destination. The car drove up the ramp of the spaceship and let them off in the room with the open plan kitchen.

The hyper car said, "I'm sorry we only have the preserved food ration packs that Professor Heidenburg had left over."

The technology behind preserving food improved markedly when people started travelling to the stars. These food packs were hundreds of years old.

"You can find them in the cupboard over there." the hyper car continued.

Samuel opened the cupboard door and selected two ration packs.

"There is a food re-hydrator in the corner," the hyper car instructed.

Samuel had never seen one of these devices before and didn't know how to operate it. The hyper car gave him meticulous step by step instructions. Eventually, there were two hot and fragrant meals. One of them was Spaghetti Bolognese and the other was a beef casserole with rice. Christina chose the Spaghetti Bolognese, because she thought that sucking up the noodles would be fun. She was right. She twirled her noodles in the sauce and then picked one to suck up. The most enjoyable part was when a noodle was nearly consumed. It would flick sauce everywhere as it waved about around Christina's face. Samuel stoically ate his casserole while Christina had her fun.

The hyper car waited for them to finish their meals before bringing in a white Volvo XC90 SUV and Blue Porsche. Samuel recognised them from when he was last here. Suvy saw that Samuel was tense, but Christina seemed relaxed and untroubled.

With a smile Christina said, "Suvy, you are so big and strong. I know you could drive in the mountains." Her smile became wicked as she said to Bluey, "Bluey, you are pretty sexy too. But I think Tuti is more so."

Suvy saw that Christina was precocious. Maybe that is a good thing. She would need to break down the barriers between cars and humans. But her behaviour wasn't contrived or political. She was natural.

Bluey said, "It is nice to finally meet you Little Princess. We have been waiting a long time."

Suvy said, "I'm glad you could come from your mountain home to help us, Little Princess."

The hyper car looked intent and began talking business.

"Little Princess, I need you to help me make some repairs to the Womb,"he said seriously.

Christina nodded obediently.

"I wasn't going to bring you here yet because you are still young. But we have identified a malfunction, and we need your help!" said the hyper car.

The car led them to the room with the Womb. Next to the Womb was a monitor and in front of the monitor was something that looked like a treadmill. It was wide and long enough to fit a large car. Samuel was intrigued by the device.

"This is how we can access the library. We can move this all over the ship."

The hyper car drove onto to the treadmill and started driving and steering. On the monitor you could see he was navigating the library book selection to a manual for the Womb.

"Come," the hyper car said, "there is a tool kit in the laboratory." The hyper car drove off the treadmill and led them back to the laboratory. "In this cupboard," he said.

Samuel opened a cupboard door and saw a metallic box. He took it and followed the hyper car back to the Womb.

"Little Princess, I need you to do the repairs. Can you do it?" the hyper car asked.

Christina answered, "Yes Tuti, I can."

"Christina, the Womb is leaking fluid, and the problem has been getting worse over time," the hyper car explained.

The hyper car sounded worried. For some time, he had wanted to fix the problem.

"Up until now, we have been topping up the fluid more often than we would like. I believe the cause of the problem is a worn seal."

The technology behind the Womb was formidable. The hyper car spent some time giving Christina an overview on how the Womb worked. He tried not to give Christina too much information, so she would not be overwhelmed. Normally, maintaining equipment this sophisticated, would take an apprentice a number of years to become proficient. They would also have the benefit of being able to watch or be physically guided when being a taught a particular task. But Christina did have one asset. She could <u>see</u> the images that the hyper car had brought up in his mind.

Their first task was to power down the Womb, so they could start work. This was quite a complicated task. The cars had never done it before and the hyper car was relying on a manual that Professor Heidenburg had written hundreds of years ago. But the hyper car had been studying it for a long time and had a very good understanding of it. They were methodical and careful, taking each step with precision. When the Womb had been successfully powered down, they could start to fix the problem that the hyper car had diagnosed.

Now the hyper car's diagnosis was his best guess. To be sure, the Womb had to be partially disassembled and Christina would have to take a look. In the tool kit there were many different sets of tools. Some of them were needed to disassemble the Womb to such a point that they could see where the problem was. And the tools needed weren't just screwdrivers and spanners. Some were quite complicated to use and the hyper car had to teach Christina how they worked. One tool was a magnetic disrupter. It is used to take off a plate that is held in place by magnetism. As the name suggests, it interrupts the magnetic field holding the plate so the plate could be removed. It had to be applied to each of the corners on the plate, before the plate could be removed.

After the disassembly was completed, Christina could see four seals. She looked at them and tried to put the image in her mind and send it to the hyper car. The hyper car said,

"Good. I can see it. But you will need to take each one out to see if any are worn."

After some instruction, Christina was able to remove one of the seals. She rotated it and put the image in her mind. The hyper car said,

"No. I think that one is okay."

Christina suggested, "Maybe we should replace them all anyway."

The hyper car replied,

"Normally, I would agree with you, but we have a limited supply of spare parts."

Bluey came into the room and said,

"I'm sorry to disturb you, but the leaders of the Mazda and Toyota tribes have come back again to get mediation on who will lead their parade. They have decided to proceed with it."

The hyper car said,

"There is no open session today. Tell them to come back when there is one."

Bluey replied, "I tried but they were very insistent."

"Very well," replied the hyper car, "but they will have to wait until we have finished the repairs."

In a small voice Christina asked, "Is there anything I could do?"

"No, it is okay Little Princess. It is just about some stupid parade. They can't decide on who will lead it." the hyper car replied.

Bluey suggested, "Perhaps she could help. Maybe she could adjudicate?"

The hyper car was going to let Suvy handle it, but then he sighed and said, "Very well, she couldn't make the situation any worse."

Bluey left the room, and the hyper car and Christina continued with their repairs. Christina removed the remaining seals and showed the hyper car through her mind. The third seal was worn, so Christina replaced that one.

The hyper car said, "Well, we will have to see if that fixes the problem."

Carefully, under instruction, Christina reassembled the Womb and they then powered it up. The hyper car viewed the diagnostics for the Womb.

"It will take us a while to see if what we did fixes the problem, but for now everything looks good," the hyper car said.

For now, they had just needed to fix one problem and luckily, the problem was not too serious.

Samuel had been watching with interest as the hyper car and Christina worked. He was surprised at how quiet they were. But after a while he thought he needed to stretch his legs. So, he walked outside, planning to go for a walk around the outside of the spaceship. After he exited the spaceship, he turned left. He thought that he wasn't going to go far. As he was walking, he encountered an old white Honda Civic. The car was just in front of him. He could tell the car was old because of the amount of dust on its body and the windows were broken. The car also had dents on the front fender on the passenger side and dents in the driver's door. Samuel changed his direction in an attempt to avoid the car, but the car yelled, "Hey there."

Samuel was going to ignore it and keep walking in his new direction, but the car yelled, "Yes, you, hey there."

The car lowered what he had left of his windows and stretched his antenna up. He also lowered himself on his suspension.

Samuel stopped and wondered what the car wanted of him. Did the car want to run him over? Though he thought that seemed unlikely. He walked over to the car.

The car said, "So, you are one of the humans that came to help us fix the Womb?"

Samuel replied, "My daughter is with the hypercar now, fixing the Womb."

The car volunteered, "I'm so old now that I was told that I should join a geriatric tribe. I used to be on the leadership team. But I wanted to stay around the young cars. Where do you live?"

Samuel replied, "I live with a mountain tribe and we hunt yellow bears."

The car then said, "My name is Rory what is yours?"

Samuel replied, "Samuel."

The car groaned, "I feel dry and sore in my engine. It hurts. He then lowered his antenna, turned his front two wheels, and asked Samuel, "Could you please have a look under my bonnet. I think it maybe a rocket cover gasket leak."

Samuel didn't think that that was a good idea. He knew nothing about a car's anatomy. The last thing he wanted to do was to poke around the insides of some strange car.

He was about to say so, but the car opened his driver's side door and said, "The latch for the bonnet is under the steering wheel near the door."

Samuel checked under the steering wheel near the driver's side door and sure enough he found the latch. He lifted it and the bonnet popped open.

The car purred, "Thank you so much for looking."

Samuel went around to the front of the car and lifted the bonnet. He didn't know what he should be looking for.

The car asked, "Can you see oil running down the side of the engine?"

Yes, Samuel could see that. He confirmed that he could see oil on the engine. The car then gave him instructions on how to find the dip stick. When Samuel found it and pulled it out, the car told him to go inside the spaceship and get a cloth to wipe it. Samuel found a cloth, wiped the dip stick and then reinserted it in the car, before pulling it out once more. The car told him how to read the oil level on the dip stick.

Samuel said, "It looks like your oil level is low."

The car said, "I need a top up of oil. It is not going to fix my problem, but at least it should take away my dryness."

Normally, a car gets its oil from a fuel ball. The liquid in a fuel ball, has fuel, oil and radiator fluid. When a car drinks from a fuel ball, the car separates these fluids internally and applies them to the relevant parts of its anatomy. The problem for Rory was that he needed a top up of oil only. He didn't need fuel or radiator fluid.

The car said, "We have some oil that was separated from fuel ball liquid inside the spaceship."

The car then gave directions to Samuel on where to find it. Samuel didn't want to disturb the hypercar, or Christina, so he wanted to be clear on where he needed to go. The car couldn't go with him because his bonnet was up. Samuel was able to find the oil in the spaceship and returned to Rory. Samuel was looking over the insides of the car as it described to him where the location of the oil cap was. Samuel was feeling uncomfortable from looking at and playing with the car's anatomy. It was an intimacy he wasn't prepared for. He found the oil cap and was able to twist it off. Samuel then poured the oil in.

The car said, "Oh, that feels better. Thank you."

His windows remained down and he was still low on his suspension.

Samuel was feeling awkward but managed to mumble, "You're welcome."

After a pause where both Samuel and Rory didn't know what to say, Samuel said, "I'd better go back inside and see how the Womb repairs are going."

Rory felt the intimacy as well and was very grateful for Samuel's help. He responded, "Of course. Thank you for the oil top up."

Samuel went inside the spaceship and found that the hypercar and Christina were still quietly working on the Womb. Samuel watched and waited.

When the Womb had been powered up, he walked over to the Womb and asked how it went. Christina said that they would have to wait and see.

The hyper car asked Samuel, "Do you know how to read?"

Samuel replied, "A little. My father taught me a bit before he died."

The hyper car said, "Christina needs to learn how to read. I will give you a reading panel and load up some teaching material. It is solar powered, so she can stay with the Tribe."

The hyper car was pleased with the repairs and was upbeat as he addressed Christina

"Now the repairs are done, let us go and adjudicate this parade."

They went outside and positioned themselves on the platform at the front of the spaceship. The same four cars from the last open session were there. That is, the Toyota Crown and the Landcruiser Prado from the Toyota tribe and the Mazda 5 and MX-5, from the Mazda tribe.

The hyper car announced, "Princess Christina will hear your grievance and will adjudicate."

The Toyota Crown complained, "A human cannot adjudicate parade matters. She is utterly incompetent."

The hyper car idled his engine loudly and then announced, "Princess Christina will hear your grievance, or you can go away and sort it out yourselves."

"Very well," the Toyota Crown grumbled. "We need adjudication on who will be the tip of the arrow."

"The tip of the arrow?" Christina asked.

"I told you so. She cannot adjudicate," the Toyota Crown addressed the hyper car.

The hyper car revved his engine in anger and the Toyota Crown backed down.

The Toyota Crown then explained to Christina, "The arrow formation is a typical formation for a parade. The worthiest cars are in the arrowhead and the others follow in the tail. One car is chosen to be the first car or the tip of the arrow. That car is the worthiest. We need you to decide which car will have this position. Is it the Landcruiser Prado or the MX-5?"

"I see." replied Christina and continued with, "The MX-5 is sleek and low down. He has beautiful round curves. His headlights are subtle and shaped exquisitely. I love the shape of his front grille. Along with the headlights, it gives the car a beautiful and elegant face. A fine specimen of a sports car, while the Landcruiser Prado has an impressive and sturdy suspension and is a solid car. His tyres give him a strong stature. He has a no-nonsense bumper and being high up shows that he is a very formidable car. Like the MX-5, he also has beautiful curves. Both cars are worthy for different reasons."

Christina paused and then mused, "hmmm. Let me see."

The four cars waited expectantly for her decision. Christina saw that they were and paused some more. She wanted to build up the suspense.

Eventually she continued,

"I have a thought. Is there any reason why the tip of the arrow could not be two cars? With both the Landcruiser and MX-5 leading the parade, I'm sure this parade would be an extravaganza."

The four cars didn't say anything for a while. Then the Landcruiser Prado said in a small voice, "I guess that could work."

The MX-5 then spoke, "It is okay by me."

The hyper car was pleased. He announced,

"Then it is decided. Both cars will be the tip of the arrow."

The Toyota Crown and the Mazda 5 both thanked Christina for her adjudication and the four cars left together, discussing excitedly about their grand parade. After they had left Christina had a sly smile and turned to the hyper car.

"Those cars were impressive but I would prefer Bluey and you to lead the parade. That would make it a true extravaganza."

The hyper car was very pleased with how the Womb repairs had gone and Christina's adjudication. He felt that a large weight on his bonnet had been lifted.

"Well done Little Princess," he encouraged, "you have done well today. Come with me, I want to show you something."

Then he said to Samuel, "You too, come!"

Both Samuel and Christina got into the hyper car and he drove them from the spaceship and into a box valley they had never been to before.

"We are here!" the hyper car announced.

When Samuel and Christina got out of the hyper car, they could see infant cars at various stages of development. The older ones had started to grow their metallic panels and glass in their windows, windscreen and headlights, while the very youngest were blind and had a leathery skin. All the cars had developed wheels and tyres. When a car is very young the colour of their skin is a deep brown. They only start to develop their own colouring when the metallic panels grow. The infant cars stopped what they were doing and drove over to Christina. Even the very youngest did this, which was surprising, because they were blind. Christina was surrounded by infant cars. They were all making beeping sounds. The beeping of the older cars was quite loud, while the very youngest had soft high pitch beeps. They were all covered in dust. Christina patted all the cars around her. They were soft to touch and Christina found that her hands were covered in dust, after she had patted them. She then went up to one of the very youngest cars. She gave him a hug, and said,

"My beautiful children!"

Chapter 19
The Mighty Truck Demands an Audience

Tuti was on the treadmill in front of the monitor for the Womb. He was running some more diagnostic tests on the repair he and Christina had made a few days ago, to fix a fluid leak. When he'd run them yesterday and the day before, they showed that there were no problems. Hopefully, today will be the same he thought. Tuti was alone in the spaceship. Bluey had gone to his favourite canyon to meditate and Suvy went to visit the infant cars.

Tuti's mind wandered to a conversation he'd had with Bluey a number of days before he drove Christina and Samuel here. He had said,

"Bluey, the Womb has a leak. We need to fix it urgently!"

He was clearly very worried and after some hesitance he had continued,

"We may have to bring in Christina!"

At the time of the conversation, Tuti had doubts about Christina and the whole Queen of the Cars Prophecy. He was afraid of humans and felt even more fearful bringing them to the Womb. Bluey had replied,

"Okay, then let us bring her in."

Tuti's window wipers moved quickly as he had confessed,

"Bluey, I'm afraid. Should we be bringing humans here?"

Bluey too, had a similar fear, but he trusted in the Prophecies completely. He rooted his whole being in the Diary and the Bible. In a matter of fact tone he'd replied,

"You said we needed to fix the Womb."

"I know," Tuti replied.

Bluey had wound down his windows and said,

"My friend, we need to trust in the Prophecies. It will be okay."

With that, Tuti had reached out to Christina telepathically and brought her and her father to the spaceship. When he had met Christina face to face, he liked her despite his fears. Christina was lovely he thought. She was kind, gentle and funny. Her first instinct was to love the cars. His friend and colleague had been right. They needed to trust in the Prophecies.

Now, Tuti was continuing his diagnostic tests, when he was interrupted by a visitor. It was in the middle of the day and it was a long day. So, it was very warm and there didn't appear to be any breeze. Cars felt the heat, but it didn't bother them. Even when their metallic bodies were very hot to touch. The visitor was a grey Land Rover Defender. He was quite a big car and could look menacing. Tuti was startled and his antenna shot up.

"Who are you and why are you here?" Tuti interrogated.

The other car didn't answer straight away.

"You are in a sacred place and you have not been invited." Tuti remonstrated.

The Land Rover wasn't troubled by the rebuke and said,

"The Mighty Truck demands an audience!"

Tuti was very annoyed and replied,

"We have an open session every ten days. He can bring his grievance then."

The Land Rover wasn't pleased with the answer. He lifted himself on his suspension and demanded,

"Truck has come a long way and you will see him now!"

Tuti hadn't had any dealings with Truck before. He only knew about Truck through his reputation, that Truck wasn't someone you crossed.

"Very well," Tuti answered, "I will need to find my colleagues."

Tuti then drove out of the spaceship with the Land Rover behind him. As he did, he saw there was a large host of cars parked outside. There were at least five hundred cars! He could see the heat shimmering off their metallic bodies. They were parked in a formation. There was a pathway that was about three cars wide and the cars were parked either side. Sports Cars lined the edges of the pathway. The sports cars were of different colours, makes and models. They were not ordered in any particular way. The pathway was about one hundred metres long and at the other end, Tuti could see that Truck was parked with Land Rovers on either side of him.

The Land Rovers were big vehicles, but Truck dwarfed them. He towered above his following. The pathway that Truck's followers made, gave the impression that Truck was royalty. Tuti could see that Truck was very effective in portraying a powerful leadership image. Obviously, Truck had put in a lot of effort in crafting the Stage for this meeting. Whatever Truck's agenda was, it was clearly very important to Truck.

Tuti summoned a white Nissan Pulsar from the Womb community and asked him to fetch Bluey and Suvy, urgently. When the Nissan Pulsar had left, Tuti stayed where he was. Tuti could see that his visitor had returned to Truck and given him Tuti's answer. Tuti didn't want to face Truck alone. The leadership team needed to present a united face. Tuti could see that Truck was not going to move and had not ordered any of his cars to do anything either. It seemed that Truck was willing to wait for the rest of the leadership team.

When the Nissan Pulsar returned with Bluey and Suvy, Suvy asked,

"What's going on?"

Tuti answered, "Truck wants to meet with us. I don't know why!"

The three of them drove up the pathway. As they did, all the cars in the host flickered their headlights. They drove apprehensively, as they were feeling intimidated and Tuti had the impression that was the plan. When they were about ten metres away from Truck, the pathway behind them closed in. They were surrounded by Truck's cars! Truck lifted, then dropped his back tray and all the cars made a long honk. The noise was deafening. They only stopped when Truck lifted his back tray again. Tuti tried not to sound intimidated and was the first to speak.

"What is this about Truck?"

The Land Rover to the right of Truck ordered,

"You will address our leader as Mighty Truck".

Tuti did not reply. He was clearly very annoyed and didn't appreciate being bullied. Truck lifted himself on his suspension. He then raised and dropped his back tray before saying in an accusing tone,

"It has come to my attention that you have brought humans to our most sacred site!"

So, this is what this visit is about, thought Tuti. Tuti was very annoyed about how Truck was treating them, but he understood Truck's sentiment. Before he had met Christina, he'd had reservations about the Queen of the Cars prophecy. He kept silent and it was his friend and colleague who spoke. Bluey said reverently,

"Mighty Truck, we do everything according to the Law."

"What law?" Truck barked.

"The law in the Diary and Bible," Bluey said patiently.

"The humans are vermin," Truck seethed, "They should be exterminated."

Truck lifted and dropped his back tray in obvious anger. He continued,

"Not invited to the Womb?"

Bluey wanted to help Truck understand. He was sure that once he did, Truck's concerns would be placated. He said, "Come with me to the spaceship and I will show you the Diary and the Bible. Then you will understand."

Truck was furious. "You mock me," he yelled.

He then honked his very powerful horn. Truck was too big to enter the spaceship and anyway, he couldn't read. Bluey had miscalculated. Truck then continued to pursue his accusation,

"You didn't just do this once. You have invited the humans twice."

Suvy realised the offense and said, "My friend didn't mean to offend you, Mighty Truck."

Suvy lowered his windows and continued. "Perhaps this unimportant showing of scriptures could be delegated to a car of your choosing."

Suvy was trying his best to be diplomatic and accommodating. Not many cars can read. There were some in the Womb community who could though. There was a Blue Holden Commodore in Truck's host who could read. He used to live in the Womb community, but had felt very strongly about how the cars were oppressed, so he chose to join Truck's following. The Commodore knew how to read, but had not yet seen the Diary or Bible. Truck knew him and instructed the Land Rover on his left- hand side to find him.

Very soon the blue Commodore was before him. Truck ordered,

"You are to go with the Blue Porsche and look at this Diary and Bible."

Bluey knew the blue Commodore and was happy to show him the books. The pathway behind Bluey opened up so they could enter the spaceship. After an hour, Bluey and the blue Commodore returned.

Truck asked, "Well, what did you find?"

The blue Commodore lowered himself on his suspension and his window wipers were moving very quickly. He was clearly frightened. He answered in a small voice,

"The scriptures talk about a Queen of the Cars. She is human."

Bluey added, "It was she who visited the Womb, Mighty Truck."

Bluey could see that Truck was troubled, so he continued, "The Womb had a fluid leak and she helped fix it."

Truck hated humans with a passion, but he did respect the scriptures. Probably more so, because he couldn't read. There was a kind of magic in the squiggles on a computer screen that could tell a story. Truck was not one to be on the back foot though. The scriptures didn't persuade him, but they did trouble him.

Truck warned the leadership team, "I will be watching you." He flickered his giant headlights. "You'd better mind your step. I could easily have you replaced."

Tuti thought, *Truck didn't have the authority to do that.* The Leadership Team was recruited by those who had been part of the Team before. Cars outside of the Leadership

Team had no say. Truck and the two Land Rovers either side of him, turned around and drove off. The rest of the host then followed.

When they had gone and only the Leadership Team remained, Suvy asked, "How did Truck know about both visits from the humans?"

Tuti answered, "Maybe we have spies."

There was silence amongst them. They were all deeply troubled. Truck had a big army. They didn't want to have a war against him. Cars shouldn't be fighting cars.

Eventually Tuti said, "I guess we will need to mind our step."

With that, the Leadership turned around and continued with their daily activities.

Chapter 20
Going Home

It had been two Earth years since Samuel and Christina had been to the Womb. And now both of them were riding in the hypercar once more. Christina and the hypercar were talking happily about the cars and the Womb.

But Samuel was quiet. He was deep in thought and was troubled. This was not a good idea, he thought. Despite missing Sheila, he was happy having Christina and living with the mountain tribe. He enjoyed the hunting and then the banter when returning to the camp site. Samuel felt he really belonged.

Anyway, Christina had been talking to her friend Alexander. His grandparents lived in another mountain tribe and they came to visit. Alexander and his granddad would spend hours practising spear manoeuvres. Alexander loved to show his granddad his prowess with a spear. His grandfather was very impressed and gave him a present. It was a standard size spear.

"You are ready for a man's spear now," his grandfather told him and then ruffled Alexander's hair with his hand.

He often did that to Alexander's hair. Alexander was overwhelmed with pride. His grandfather also had funny hunting stories to tell him. Once, on a hunt, one of his team had made a new spear. He'd spent nearly all his money on the parts for the spear and had to wait a long time for his tribe's trader to return from the corporation fort with the parts. And then he had to painstakingly assemble it. When he was finished, he was so pleased with his new spear. He showed everyone in the tribe. Anyway, he went on a hunt with his brand, new spear. The hunters found a bear and started to hunt it. The team member with his new spear stabbed the bear in the foot, and then tried to pull his spear out. But he couldn't. The spear was stuck. Unfortunately for the hunters, the bear found a gap in the hunter's circle and escaped. Much to the horror of the team member with the new spear! Alexander's Granddad told, as he was laughing,

"The man was running after the bear, yelling, 'My spear, my spear. Come back with my spear."

Alexander adored his grandfather. Christina was happy for Alexander, but she was sad for herself. She never knew her grandparents. She approached her father.

"Daddy," she said, "Did you know Mummy's parents?"

"I'm sorry Sweetheart," Samuel replied, "they lived on Earth, where Mummy came from."

Christina knew that Samuel's parents were dead. She said, "I wish I knew something about my grandparents."

Samuel didn't know what to say, but he wanted to console his daughter. He eventually said, "The only thing left about them was their house."

Samuel immediately regretted saying this. Christina jumped on it just as quickly.

"Can we go and visit it, Daddy?" she asked excitedly.

When Samuel didn't reply she begged, "Please....".

"I don't think it is a good idea Sweetheart," Samuel replied.

"Please... Daddy," Christina implored.

In the end, Samuel acquiesced. Samuel knew the way to his parents' house from the remains of Fort Chrisholm and the hypercar knew the way to Fort Chrisholm from the Mountain Tribe location. Samuel was disturbed from his thoughts when they reached the remains of Fort Chrisholm. The hypercar needed directions from him. The memories flooded to him as he gave directions.

Eventually, they reached the base of the valley beneath the house. On the mountain side, there was a single ledge. It protruded out from the side of mountain about halfway up. The house was made from the same materials as the Corporation forts. That is, panels made from recycled building waste. The colour of the panels was a similar red to the red dust on the plains. The house wasn't large. It was single storey and the ledge it was on wasn't large. But compared to most ledges on the mountains of Plantere, it was a good size. The roof was flat, but angled down slightly, with solar panels on top. At the lowest part of the roof, there was a gutter and then a pipe that led into a rainwater tank. So that in the unusual event of rain, the water would be captured. There was a metal staircase that led from the valley floor up to the front door of the house. The stairs rose in alternate diagonals.

"I will wait here for you," the hypercar said, "take as long as you need."

Samuel and Christina climbed the stairs. As Samuel climbed, he felt the breeze on his face. On the mountains and even part way up, it felt fresher than it did on the plains. When they reached the door, Samuel was surprised there wasn't any dust. This was in contrast to the ruins of Fort Chrisholm, which had a thick cover of red dust. Samuel opened the door. They walked into a room that was an open plan kitchen and living room. There was a table and chairs. This was where he and his parents had spent most of their time. It was easily the biggest room of the house. There were two doors on the other side that led to two bedrooms. The living room was plain but comfortable. There were no ornaments or pictures on the wall. The table and chairs were the same as those in the mess hall of a fort. There was no other furniture in the living room. The kitchen was basic. It had a bench with one hotplate and a sink with one tap.

Samuel watched Christina as she walked around the room and explored. She played with the tap on the sink and turned on the hotplate. She pulled out a chair and sat down. Samuel did also. He watched her as she looked around the room. She pointed to one of the doors on the other side and asked, "What's in there, Daddy?"

"My parent's room," Samuel replied, "I never went there."

"Can I go in there, Daddy?"

"Yes, you can," replied Samuel.

Samuel stood up, walked to the door and opened it for Christina. The room had a double bed and two bedside tables. The bed was covered with a single blanket. There weren't any sheets. Samuel watched Christina as she went over to the bed and touched the blanket. It was the same as the blankets that the soldiers had in the barracks of the Fort. She then opened one of the drawers of a bedside table. In it was a reading panel, much like the ones Tuti had given her at the Womb.

"Look at this Daddy," Christina said.

"I didn't know it was there." Samuel replied.

"Can I read it Daddy?" Christina asked.

Since the visit to the Womb, Samuel had been teaching Christina how to read. He wasn't that proficient himself, so that often they were learning together. The reading panels that the hypercar had given her were very good, and she benefited a lot from them. The reading panel that Christina found here, was also solar powered, like the ones from the Hypercar. She moved it over to Samuel, so he could see and switched it on. It read:

A Distant Genesis

The journal of Michael Benson

My Alcoholics Anonymous meeting told me I have to keep a journal. How long do I need to do this? I asked. They said I would know when I can stop. What does that mean? So here I'm writing something on my panel. Damn stupid idea. I don't know what to write.

It has been five days since I have written in my journal. It was recommended that I write something every day, but it isn't mandatory. They said I should have a separate paragraph for each entry. We can read our journal out to the group at the meetings. But I don't think I would want to. I haven't had a drink over the last five days. I'm bored. I need to get a job and work. I have always worked.

I had some job interviews today for shuttlecraft pilot positions. I think they went well. The employers were happy with my experience and my good friends gave me some references. Karen would say fingers crossed. I haven't had a drink since I started with Alcoholics Anonymous. Maybe things are looking up for me.

All my job applications were rejected. When I asked why, most of the interviewers said that was confidential. One, however said that my record at Mars Star Fleet was unsatisfactory. I visited the Marilon Park Zoo. Karen and I liked going there as it is the biggest zoo on Mars. It not only had animals from Earth, but ones from other worlds as well. When our baby was going to be born, I was going to sign him up as a member of the zoo. And we would visit regularly as he grew up. Karen loved animals. I don't know why I went there. It just made me feel sad.

I still haven't got a job. I think I have to give up on shuttlecraft pilot positions. I just need to do anything. I'm so bored. I need to escape my thoughts and memories. I remember when Mum first took me sky diving. I was a little scared. But as she strapped my wings to my arms and back, she said soothing things. "Just open your wings son and you will glide like a bird." It was quite a popular sport on Mars. All my friends had done it. So, I put away my fears and jumped out of the shuttlecraft. I stretched out my wings and I flew like a bird. I loved it. That was why I went on to become an instructor. Memories. At least I still haven't had a drink.

I caught up with some friends from Mars Star Fleet. We had a drink. I said no to having a beer. But they pleaded with me. Just have one they said. I did have one drink. And then another, and another again, until I was drunk. My friends were nice to me though. They said that my shuttlecraft accident wasn't my fault and that I shouldn't have been dishonourably discharged from Mars Star Fleet. I know differently though. I was drunk. That was why I crashed my shuttlecraft.

At my Alcoholics Anonymous meeting I confessed to having a drink. The leader said I should talk about Karen. That it would help me. I told them we met at Mars Star Fleet. She was a logistics officer. At Mars Star Fleet she was well liked. She was warm and vivacious. I couldn't believe my luck when she agreed to go out with me on a date. We got married and Karen was expecting a baby.

I still haven't got a job. My friends from Mars Star Fleet invited me to go drinking again. I got drunk.

I have been drinking every day. Far too much. I still haven't got a job. I have to get out of here. This is toxic.

There is a job on Omega 24A. It is a world in a distant solar system. The position is for a contract car hunter, with the Iowa Corporation. No experience is necessary. Maybe that is what I need. I have to get away from Mars.

I got the job. They were happy that I had some basic training at Mars Star Fleet. That I could handle a rifle. They didn't want any references and they didn't do a background check with Mars Star Fleet. I leave tomorrow.

I haven't written in this journal for years. But it has felt like only a few days. I'm in Fort Chrisholm on Omega24A. My boss is Corizon. He seems rather young to be a boss. But I like him. He is good. This planet is pretty barren though. I saw it out the window of my shuttlecraft. I don't know how anything could live out there.

I met the other new recruits. There are five of us. They seem pretty rough. We will be in the same team. The guy leading us looks like he has spent a lot of time here. His face is lined with wrinkles and he doesn't say much. We have to call him Sergeant Joe. But his real name is Joe Falkner. Corizon said we should bond and have a drink together. That is the last thing I want to do. That was why I left Mars- to escape from having drinks. When Corizon asked me what drink I wanted I told him sparkling water. He asked if I was sure and I said yes. He was okay with it though. One of the new recruits Adrian, laughed at me and said that we have a teetotaller in the team. He looked rougher than the other new recruits. He was covered in tattoos and wore an earring in his left ear.

Being contractors we had to buy our own equipment. Or if we don't have the money, we can pay for it with the delivery of our first cars. I don't know much about stun pulse rifles, so I went with Brett's recommendation. He was the one in charge of all the weapons. I have some money, so I bought the rifle straight out. I got an Easy-Shooter

L8100 with thirty rounds. It came with a sight and silencer. Apparently, it is accurate to 800 metres. After we bought our rifles, we were given some training. They told us things about cars. I have never seen a car before. Apparently, the stun works best if you aim for the engine of the car. I got my uniform also. We were told that we needed to wear our hats all the time.

Tomorrow we will leave the fort and go out to hunt cars. We met this strange lady. She looks out of this world. She has long bright red hair and her skin seems tanned. Her eyes are the strangest blue I have ever seen. She was wearing a bizarre leather outfit. The stitching looked really weird. Corizon introduced her as Angela, and he gave her the title of corporation consultant. Apparently, she is going to show us where the cars are that we are going to hunt.

We left the fort today in a vehicle that looks like the ones we are going to hunt. We were sitting in the open. It was okay while we were driving, but when we stopped, there was so much red dust. We travelled all day and stopped near this field of big balls. They were about a metre in diameter and were transparent. I remember in the training they gave us about fuel balls and how the cars feed from them. Just before nighttime I saw my first dusk spectra. There were so many colours. Karen would have loved this. We all sat together around a solar heater. The heater would be charged during the day and then it could be used at nighttime. But Angela didn't sit with us. Adrian said that she didn't sit with us because she thinks that she is too good for us. He is a moron. If he is right though, she has a good reason for thinking that. The position of contract car hunter doesn't exactly attract the cream of society. A couple of my teammates had spent time in prison.

We waited all day near this fuel ball field. Still, no cars came. At lunch time Angela still didn't sit with us. I thought I would try having a conversation with her. I went over to her and showed her my stun rifle. I asked her what she thought of it. It was a coward's weapon she said. If you want to hunt cars you jump them and use one of these. She showed me a mallet. It was slightly bigger than a normal carpentry hammer, and it had a square head. For the first time I noticed she didn't have a rifle. She only had a pistol. At night time when Angela didn't sit with us Adrian and two of his friends walked over to her and said that the redhead thought she was better than everyone else. He got aggressive with her. I looked over towards Sergeant Joe. He didn't do anything. So, I stood between Adrian and Angela and told him to leave her alone. She is just trying to earn a living like the rest of us.

Today the cars came. There were many of them. Sergeant Joe said there were many more than in a tribe. They were all shapes and sizes. Clouds of red dust rose behind them. I couldn't count how many there were. And they looked fierce. We were sitting in the truck shooting at them. I thought I was a good shot, but this was hard. There were a number of cars that reached us and they rammed the truck. The truck tipped over and I fell to the ground. I thought I was going to die. And then Angela pulled up in this flashy car. It was sleek and low to the ground. The car looked fast. She opened the passenger door and yelled, jump in. So, I did. She put her foot down on the accelerator and the car sped off. Other cars chased us but we were too fast for them. We left them behind. I asked Angela why she had saved me. She said because I stuck up for her. I wasn't like all the others. What happened there I asked. She replied that the cars were very clever. This sort of thing happens. Then I asked her where we were going. She said, to her home.

We drove all night and most of the next day. Every so often, Angela would use her pistol to re-stun the car. We arrived at her home. We were at the base of a mountain. The mountain had a series of ledges going up the side. Between each ledge the cliffs were steep. As the ledges were very flat that gave the side of the mountain the look that there were giant steps reaching up to the top. There were housing structures on the first two levels, with ladders reaching up to them. They were made out of bits of car bodies strapped together. The people there all looked like Angela and they all wore the same bizarre outfits. When we got out of the car a man approached us. His name was Max and he was the tribe's chief. He asked Angela why she brought a redskin here. She said that I had stuck up for her and that I was a good guy. I was given a place to sleep on the second level. The structure I was in was like a tent. but was built out of different types of car boots and bonnets. Karen, what would you have thought of this? My dear Karen. I killed her and my unborn child. She had only agreed to do the skydiving because I pushed her into it. On Mars I was the certified skydiving instructor. It was my responsibility to make sure her wings were fastened securely. She had no certification. When Karen tried to open her wings, one of the wings fell off. She spiralled down to the ground to her death. She trusted me and I sent her to her death.

Today, Angela showed me around and introduced me to other people in her tribe. They all looked like Angela. Angela's sister, Carol was doing some sewing. Apparently, they make their clothes out of the upholstery of car seats. Angela's clothes were made out of leather, but there were other types of clothes. Some were made out of cloth or vinyl. Because Angela was a very talented car jumper, she was able to jump sports cars. And they usually had leather seats. Angela asked me if I would like to go hunting with her tribe. I said sure. I went to get my stun rifle and Angela said to leave it, as she would show me how to hunt cars properly.

When we left, there were about fifteen of us. There were more people in her tribe, but for this hunt there were just the fifteen of us. We walked all day. Eventually we reached a fuel ball field. We walked a bit further where the valley became narrower. Ahead of us was a tribe of cars. The hunters formed a line with a distance of three metres between each person. I was told to stand near the cliff face and watch.

The cars were about a hundred metres ahead of us. But they didn't charge us. Instead, a green sports car came to the front. He was low to the ground and his engine protruded in front of him where there would normally be a bonnet. Carol said to Angela that the car wanted a duel. Angela said that she would get this. Everyone else joined me near the cliff face. Angela stood with her hands on her hips.

She yelled out to the car. "Come on sporty show us what you've got." The car charged her. It roared down the plain. Angela waited until the car had nearly reached her and then deftly jumped aside as the car came close. She turned around and the car charged again. And once again she deftly jumped aside as the car reached her. She repeated this a number of times. The car honked loudly and lifted itself on his suspension. This time when it charged, Angela made her move. She jumped on the car's bonnet and grabbed the driver's side outside mirror. Within an instant she had smashed the driver's side windows and slid into the driver's seat. This lady was amazing. She was totally wild and sexy in her skintight leather outfit. She stunned the car with her pistol and drove up to her sister. She told her that she would sell this car to the corporations. She needed the money. The other hunters made the line again. But the cars didn't charge. They turned around and left. In the evening, Angela came to me and offered to teach me how to jump cars. I was lost in her eyes. When it was dark they had a beautiful fluorescent violet appearance.

We went hunting again today. This time all the cars did charge and everyone jumped a car. Angela chose a small white sedan that had broken windows. When she drove it up to me, she said my training could begin now. She had me drive slowly up to her and demonstrated the moves to jump a car. It was then my turn. I thought I was quite a sporty person, but this was hard. We practised all day. Angela was very patient with me. I couldn't do it though. It was too hard. I was sore at the end of the day.

I overheard a conversation between Carol and Angela. Carol was saying that Angela should be thinking seriously about finding a match. Carol had agreed to marry the eldest son of the current chief. Who was Angela going to marry? She came from a family with a high pedigree of car jumping, so she should marry well. Why was Angela wasting time with a redskin? Carol left Angela in tears. Angela was so fearless I couldn't imagine her crying.

We tried the training again today. Angela was very patient with me. But even at a slow speed I couldn't do all the moves. I would jump on the bonnet of the car and fall off before I could grab the outside mirror. At the end of the day, I was hurting all over. Some of her fellow hunters laughed at the redskin trying to jump a car. I asked Angela why everyone called me the redskin. It was because if I left my hat off in a couple of hours my skin would go bright red with a sun burn.

Today at slow speed I did it. I jumped the car. I grabbed hold of the mirror and was able to slide into the driver's seat. The car was old, so the windows were already broken.

I haven't written in my journal for some time now. I have been busy with my training. Angela said I was ready for my coming-of-age duel. Usually when a teenager has been trained, they have to duel with a car before they can join the tribe to hunt cars. It is some sort of rite of passage. Angela said I was ready. So, I went with the hunters. When the cars charged, I would be standing next to Angela. If the car that is charging her was suitable, she would step aside and let me jump it. We did this today, but the car that was charging Angela was a Holden Kingswood. She said it was too big. Angela has been teaching me about the makes and models of cars. I'm beginning to know about the types of cars.

Today when we were hunting, an older Holden Astra was charging Angela. She stepped away and told me it was my turn. The car was fast. It felt that it was faster than anything I had done in training. But when I jumped on the bonnet, I grabbed hold of the mirror. The car was older so it wasn't too difficult to break the driver's side window. I slid into the driver's seat and had to wrestle the car for control. For the coming-of-age duel I was not allowed to stun the car. I had to drive it until it died. When I got out of the dead car Angela came up to me looking very coy. She touched my chest and said that I was a man now. That night there was a celebration. Never before had a redskin passed the coming-of-age duel. They had a drink that was fermented from the fuel ball liquid. There were cups that were passed around. Everyone drank and everyone was happy. When the cup was passed to me, I tried some and immediately tasted the alcohol in it. I said to Angela that I could not drink it. Everyone was suddenly silent. Max came up to me and said that if I wanted to be part of the tribe I must drink. I told Angela that I was an alcoholic. She asked me what that was. I said that if I drank alcohol, I would not be able to stop myself. I would become sick. When it was clear that I wasn't going to drink Max said I had to leave the tribe next morning. Angela said to me that she loved me and wanted to leave with me. I told her I loved her too. That I had some money and could build us a house to live in.

Today Angela told her sister Carol that she was going to leave with me. Carol was upset but eventually said to keep in contact and she would visit us. We left and eventually we jumped a car and drove to Fort Chrisholm. I talked to Corizon and told him of my plans to build a house. He said we could stay at the fort instead. But I said it wouldn't be fair to Angela. He showed us some maps and we found a suitable site for our house.

I haven't written in my journal for some time. We have been busy. The house has been built. Both Angela and I work as a team, as corporation consultants. We mentor new teams of contract car hunters. I also do some shuttlecraft piloting. Carol has come to visit us a few times. She gives us news about the tribe. I know Angela misses them. But I think she is happy with our life.

Little Samuel was born. I took Angela to Fort Chrisholm when she was in labour. The Alcoholics Anonymous team leader had said I would know when I could stop writing in my journal. I think that time is now. I have had a second chance at life and I'm very happy. The ghost of Karen is still with me. But I think I have moved on.

End of Journal

Christina looked up and said,
"Daddy this is really precious. Can I keep it?"
"Yes, you can," Samuel replied, "I'm glad we came."

Chapter 21
Sheila Returns

They reached the top of the ridge and Sheila could see the tribal camp. She turned to David and asked,

"Thank you so much for getting me here, David. Do you want to join me and have a meal with the tribe before you go back?"

"No, I had better get back. The shuttle will be waiting for me," he replied.

Sheila gave him a hug and thanked him once more. The other passengers on the starship from Zigorn station worked for the Elipse corporation. They were going back to Plantere to retrieve some valuable equipment that was left behind. When they'd heard that Sheila needed to go to Fort Lyndon, they had offered to take the shuttle there first. Sheila explained that she needed to go to the mountains, and David Sullivan, a corporation lieutenant, gallantly offered to take her there. She did warn David that the journey may be dangerous, as there was quite a bit of travel required on the plains. There may be tribes of cars about. But that didn't dissuade him. He said that he had been on many expeditions on Plantere and that he would get Sheila to the mountain tribe safely.

When they landed at Fort Lyndon the fort was deserted, but its walls had not been breached from attacking cars. Sheila was surprised at how the Fort looked. All the buildings were still standing, but their walls and roofs were covered in red dust. Even on the roads she could see a covering of red dust. It really did look like a ghost town. She had to remind herself that she had been away for a number of years and during that time nobody had visited this fort. The fact that the Fort's outside walls had not been breached, gave her some confidence that maybe their journey would be uneventful.

Sheila felt a cool breeze on her face. It was still late morning of a long day and the breeze felt cooler than normal. She looked up to the sky and saw some clouds. They weren't thick black ones like those she grew up with in Scotland. They were soft white clouds and there were patches of blue sky. There were a few military vehicles in the Fort compound. They chose one that was not too big, but looked solid. Luckily, they did not encounter any cars on their journey and they had made good time to their destination. Sheila watched as David walked back down to the vehicle and she hoped that he had the same good luck going back as they had coming here. Sheila noticed the breeze again. It felt almost moist. She looked to the sky again and the clouds were thicker.

Sheila turned and walked up to the camp. There was a woman preparing some bread dough for cooking. Sheila recognised her as Frieda.

"Hello Frieda, how are you?" she said.

Frieda turned to her and said, "I didn't think you would ever come back."

This took Sheila by surprise. Until she reminded herself that for her, she had been here just a few days ago, while to everyone else it had been years. Maybe Samuel and Christina have lived their lives and moved on from the time Sheila was among them. Maybe Samuel had a new woman and she might have been a better mother to Christina. So much could have happened over the years.

"Do you know if Samuel is about?" Sheila asked.

"The men are still hunting," Frieda replied, "but your daughter is up at the house over there."

Frieda pointed to a house further up the hill than the stone hut that Sheila knew. The house that Frieda pointed to was built from the same type of panels that were used in the buildings at corporation forts. With some trepidation she walked up to the house. Her daughter would no longer be a toddler, but a teenager. The house had a door and glass windows. Sheila knocked on the door. A tall lanky girl opened the door. She had all the hunter features and also a pretty face. When Christina saw that it was Sheila at the door she exclaimed,

"Welcome home Mummy. I trust you had an uneventful journey home?"

Tears welled up in Sheila's eyes.

"Look at you!" she exclaimed, "You are a beautiful young lady."

Christina went up to her mother and gave her hug.

"I'm so glad you came back Mummy," she said.

"I'm so sorry Christina."

Sheila wept.

"It is okay, Mummy," Christina comforted. "You grew up in cities, living a civilised life. There was an expectation that you would have an important career."

Christina stroked Sheila's back and then continued,

"Of course, you were adventurous, but you could not live a tribal life forever. I understand and I love you."

Sheila cried some more. Her daughter was now all grown up. She was beautiful.

After a while she asked, "How is your father?"

"He is good Mummy. He is a very capable bear hunter now. But he missed you terribly. He built this house just in case you came back."

Now Sheila asked, "I thought the tribe could not build in the mountains, because a yellow bear could attack the camp?"

"We have a treaty with the local yellow bear," Christina explained, before sitting down on a chair next to Sheila.

"If we don't hunt her or her young, she won't attack our camp. As you know, bears are very territorial, so another bear won't trespass," Christina added.

Sheila looked around the room. All the windows had glass and the walls had pictures of beautiful places on Earth. They were of the Grand Canyon in the United States of America, the Eiffel tower in France, Ayers rock in Australia and the Great Wall in China. The floor was tiled in the same way as that in a fort mess hall. There was a kitchenette in the corner and a dining table with chairs they were sitting on now. This was wonderful and extraordinary Sheila thought. She shed some more tears.

"Did Samuel build all this?" Sheila asked.

"Yes," Christina answered, "but he had help from the Tribe."

Christina laughed and then continued,

"When Samuel first suggested it to Jonathon, Jonathon said that he would make Jumpy, chief of the Lonely-Hearts club."

Sheila's heart was thumping. Had Samuel found another woman? It was as if Christina had read Sheila's thoughts when she continued, "Jonathon tried to persuade Samuel that you returned to Earth and were not coming back. He offered to help find Samuel another woman from one of the other tribes."

Sheila wouldn't blame Samuel if he had found another woman. She had been away a long time.

"But Daddy didn't want another woman," Christina explained, "He wanted you."

Christina adored her father, because of his love and devotion to her mother.

"Anyway, despite the teasing, the Tribe did help Daddy build this house," Christina continued. "They found all the building materials at Fort Lyndon and used one of the military trucks to bring them here. Let me show you the bedroom."

Christina led Sheila into the bedroom. There were two beds, a double and a single. Samuel slept in the double bed, while Christina slept in the single. There was a desk and a chair in one corner.

"Through that door is the toilet, Mummy," Christina said.

The technology for portable toilets used in remote locations was very good. The waste was dealt with efficiently so the toilet wouldn't smell. When Sheila turned to the desk, Christina said,

"Daddy has been teaching me how to read. Tuti said that I needed to learn."

"Who is Tuti, Christina?" Sheila asked.

"He is one of the cars' leaders and is my mentor," Christina replied.

They went back into the dining room. Sheila noticed a sword hanging horizontally on one wall. She also noticed that the colour of the wall was blue, while the other walls were light grey. With wall panels, you could get different inner wall colours. So, it would have been possible for Samuel to find a panel with an inner wall coloured blue, rather than having to paint one himself. She recognised it was Sergeant Blackmore's sword. The one Samuel had used to stab the yellow bear in the foot. The bear that had killed Roger. Christina saw Sheila looking at it.

"Yes. Daddy went back to the location where he'd left the sword, so he could retrieve it."

Sheila reached out and touched it. Christina watched Sheila intently and said,

"I sometimes see Daddy practise with it. He is able to wield it now."

Sheila remembered the brave young man who had faced the yellow bear by himself, so that   he could protect her.

"He told me the story of him stabbing a bear in the foot because he had trouble lifting the sword."

Then Christina laughed again and said,

"Jonathon sees him practising with the sword and teases Daddy mercilessly. Jumpy the dragon slayer, he would say. Daddy now replies, 'Dare me and I will go out by myself and slay a bear with this sword'. Jonathon just laughs."

The front door opened and standing in the doorway was Samuel. He was not the lanky youth that Sheila remembered. He was bigger in stature and was very muscular. The mountain tribal life has had its effect. Sheila and Christina stood up. Both of them didn't know how Samuel would react. Sheila felt nervous and unsure. Even though she felt that she'd left only a few days ago, in reality here, it was years ago. So much could have changed. Samuel saw Sheila and didn't say a word. He just walked over to her and gave her a hug. He stroked her back and there were tears in his eyes. Eventually, he ended the embrace. He looked into her eyes and saw that she hadn't changed. He may have but she was still the same.

Sheila stepped back and said, "Look at you Samuel, you have filled out nicely."

On the roof they could hear a pitter-patter. It wasn't really loud, but it was noticeable.

Christina announced, "A very auspicious day Mummy and Daddy," as she opened the front door.

They could all see raindrops landing on the ground outside.

Chapter 22
The Queen of the Cars

The hyper car was driving Christina, Samuel, Sheila and Jonathon to Professor Heidenburg's spaceship. They left early in the morning. Today was going to be a short day, so it would be dark when they arrive. Tomorrow will be the coronation. A week ago, Christina told her parents that she was going to be crowned as Queen of the Cars and that from then on, she would live in Professor Heidenburg's spaceship. Sheila was very concerned as Christina was only fifteen earth years old. Christina tried to reassure her that she would be looked after by Tuti and the rest of the cars in the leadership team. Samuel was suspicious of the cars, so he wasn't persuaded by the argument. Christina also promised that Samuel and Sheila could visit her regularly. In the end, her parents accepted it, because they remembered the car's prophecy and the honour they were given when the cars showed them the Womb. The reason for this and being spared, was that one day Christina would be Queen of the cars. In fact, Sheila was impressed that Christina knew her purpose and had gained a single-minded determination from a very young age, to one day be the Queen of the Cars.

When they arrived at the spaceship, they left the hyper car and were greeted by the white Volvo XC90 SUV and blue Porsche.

"Mummy and Uncle Jonathon," Christina introduced, "this is Suvy and Bluey."

"We have met before," Jonathon said, "when you were still in your Mummy's tummy."

The blue Porsche greeted them,

"Welcome all, it is good to see you again. I trust you had a good journey."

He had his windows down.

"This is the day that we have been looking forward to for a long time. Even before we showed you the Womb,"

he continued in an ethereal tone. But then he seemed to be coming out of a trance and became welcoming.

"We are so pleased that you could share it with us. Please come inside and have something to eat. After that I will tell you what will happen tomorrow."

Sheila had brought some food for the journey. She was worried that Christina would deplete the preserved food on the spaceship too quickly. They had a meal of dried bear meat and bread. Pretty much, a standard meal. After the meal, the blue Porsche explained that many cars would attend the coronation. It would be held in a wide valley not far from here. At first there would be a parade, followed by a ceremony. At the ceremony there would be places for the three humans.

After Bluey had finished talking about the coronation, the humans were all ready for bed, except Samuel who wouldn't mind having a walk and visit his friend Rory.

He asked Bluey, "Do you know where Rory is?"

Bluey gestured, "I think he's around the corner, just outside the spaceship."

Samuel left the spaceship and turned left. He walked around the outside of the spaceship and sure enough, he found Rory.

"Hello Rory, how are you?" Samuel asked.

Rory was surprised and pleased that Samuel had sought him out. He replied,

"I'm well thank you. It's been a long time."

Samuel asked, "How are you feeling? Do you feel dry and sore?"

Rory responded, "Oh yes I think I do a bit."

Samuel said, "It's okay. I'll go and get some oil for you."

Rory replied, "Thanks."

Samuel went back into the spaceship, found some oil and brought it out to Rory. Samuel remembered how to open the bonnet. He went over to Rory's driver's side and opened the door. Underneath the steering wheel, he found the latch for the bonnet. He pulled it and the bonnet popped open. Samuel then went around to the front of Rory and lifted the bonnet up. He remembered where the oil cap was, so he knew where to pour the oil. Samuel was feeling like a real expert in car anatomy and with confidence, he unscrewed the cap for the oil, on the top of the engine and then poured the oil in. Rory exclaimed,

"Ah, that feels so good. Ah yes, I was feeling very dry."

Samuel asked, "Are you coming to the coronation tomorrow?"

Rory replied, "I wouldn't miss it for the world. It's going to be a very special day for your daughter."

Samuel agreed with that. He and Rory had a little bit more of a chat. Samuel asked Rory about whether he was still happy living near the spaceship rather than going to a geriatric tribe. Rory replied that he was very happy where he was and that sometimes he visits the infant cars in the Box Valley. He always enjoys that, and it makes him feel young again.

Early the next morning Christina was standing on a flatbed tow truck at the end of the parade. In the distance, she could see that there were many cars parked either side of the road set aside for the parade. As usual, she could feel a gentle breeze on her and she could see some clouds of dust down the route of the parade. The mountain life was definitely cleaner and fresher. She would miss that. The purpose of the parade was to show all the cars that their queen represented all of them and that she regarded all cars equally. The Bible did not describe any parade or ceremony for the queen. It was organised by the leadership team. They were concerned that many cars were very suspicious of humans. Probably with good cause, as the corporations had enslaved so many cars. But even so, the Queen of the Cars had to be a human. That was in the Bible.

The parade began. It was led by cars representing different eras. They were in pairs, presenting cars of different decades. In the first pair there was a 1920 Rolls Royce Phantom Limousine and a 1926 Packard Twin 6 Roadster. They, like all the cars in the parade, were young cars, in mint condition. Both these cars were shiny black with spoked wheels and bug- eyed headlights. In the next pair, there was a 1930 Cadillac 16 and a 1938 Buick Y Job. The Cadillac looked much the same as the 1920 cars in the parade, while the Buick had a humped bonnet. The headlights fitted in the body of the car and the tyres weren't spoked. Then followed pairs representing decades, 1940s, 1950s up to the 2020s. That is, up to when the last combustion engine vehicles were designed. After the decades, the different makes of cars were represented in pairs on the parade. Makes such as Alfa Romeo, Audi, BMW, Datsun, Ford, Holden, Honda, Hyundai, Mazda, Nissan and Rolls Royce. Following the makes there were pairs of cars that were different types. Types such as sedan, hatchback, convertible, utility, different types of trucks and sports car. Following them was Christina standing on the tray of a green flatbed tow truck. As the parade progressed, Christina could see rows of cars on either side, parked so they could witness the spectacle.

Samuel, Sheila and Jonathon were standing on the tray of a white flatbed tow truck, which was parked at the end of the parade route. The parade route followed a circle at the end, so that everyone at the end of the route could see the full parade. Samuel's parents had an appreciation of cars. They didn't just have a shrewd economic outlook, where you weigh the cost of a stun round against your prospective target. His parents instilled in Samuel that it was good to be knowledgeable about cars and have a passion for them. Even though they did hunt them. After Samuel's parents died, he just had an enormous fear and distrust of them, but over the years this had been tempered. And now, partly because of Christina and also, because he was safe in the mountain tribe, he began to have a curiosity and wonder about the cars. So now, Samuel was thoroughly enjoying the parade. His favourite car makes were Italian. He especially liked the red Alfa Romeo 4C. But he was also in awe of the mining trucks. They were so big and powerful.

For Sheila, twentieth and twenty-first century combustion engine vehicles were entirely foreign to her, before she arrived in Plantere the first time. The vehicles that transported people around modern-day Earth were very different. Part of being a journalist, Sheila loved history. So, the favourite part of the parade for her was the first part, where cars of different eras drove by. She loved seeing the evolution of design through the different eras. From spoked wheels and bug-eyed headlights, to humped bonnets. From iconic body designs of the Volkswagen Beetle and Kombi Van, to the soft curves of more aerodynamic vehicles.

Jonathon grew up in the mountains and it wasn't until he was much older and a mountain master, that he ventured out on the plains. He had a healthy caution when it came to cars. He wasn't terrified of them, but he always tried to avoid them in his travels. Jonathon was very practical. When he helped Samuel bring the building panels and fixtures from the abandoned Fort Lyndon, he appreciated the truck-like vehicle they used. So, in terms of the living cars, he liked the working vehicles the best, such as the utilities, tow trucks, small and big trucks.

When the parade had ended, Christina's tow truck faced the row of parked cars that were the leadership team. The hyper car was the one conducting the ceremony. Now, the cars had a special ability. They could transmit what they were saying through their antennae, while other cars could hear the transmission, also through their antennae. For the benefit of the humans and cars close by, the hyper car spoke, but for all the cars present, he also transmitted. He announced,

"Today is a day we have been waiting for, for a long time."

The hyper car's antenna was up and his engine idled loudly.

"Our Maker planned for this day from the very beginning."

The hyper car was reverent.

"He had a vision of a queen to serve us. A queen who loves us, comforts us and looks after our young and also helps us maintain the Womb."

Then his tone became warmer and more familiar.

"I have known Princess Christina since she was very young. She is a remarkable young lady and has many qualities."

To the hyper car, it wasn't just about prophecy or words in the Bible. He adored Christina. If cars could have human children, then he would see Christina as a daughter.

He continued,

"Princess Christina loves us. She feels with us and applies her talents to benefit us. Together we will welcome her to our family as our Queen."

The hyper car then addressed Christina, who was standing on the tow truck in front of him.

"Christina, do you pledge to serve us, live with us, to rule with compassion and love, for the benefit of all cars?"

Christina replied, "I do."

There was exuberant honking from all the cars present. At the sound, Christina turned around, blew kisses and waved at the cars. The sound of cars honking filled the air and continued for some time.

Then, Christina's tow truck turned around to face the majority of all the cars. The leaders of each tribe, drove up to Christina to pledge their allegiance.

They each announced, "We pledge our tribe's allegiance to you, my queen."

It seemed that all the tribes were represented at this coronation. However, there was one notable absence. The freedom fighter, the mighty Truck, did not attend. Each time a leader pledged their allegiance to Christina she responded with,

"I pledge to support and serve your tribe."

After all the leaders had pledged their allegiance to their new Queen, there was a collective honking from the sea of cars. After some time, it abated. The ceremony had been a success. It appeared that at least among the cars present, they were enthusiastic about their new Queen. Now that the ceremony was over, the cars dispersed and the different tribes returned to their homes.

This ceremony was the first of its kind. Very rarely do cars of different tribes ever gather together. The armies of the great freedom fighter Truck were a notable exception. Never before, had cars accepted a human leader. The leadership team had planned each element of the coronation and instructed Christina on what she needed to do and state. It had not been a long or involved ceremony. Quite simple and straightforward. This was because the leadership team hadn't had any experience in running ceremonies, but also because they only had one goal in mind. That is, for all the car tribes to accept Christina as their Queen.

For Christina, it highlighted the weight of responsibility she faced. She felt somewhat overwhelmed by the presence of so many cars. Before, she had only corresponded with the leadership team and visited the baby cars. Now she had to look out for every tribe. But she trusted the leadership team and especially Tuti. They would guide her and they wouldn't let her go astray.

Sheila, Samuel and Jonathon stayed another night at the spaceship. They would return home early next morning. Christina was grateful for the extra time she could spend with her parents and Jonathon. She knew that being Queen of the Cars was her destiny, but she would miss just being a little girl in the mountain tribe. After dinner, she and Sheila went for a walk. It was nearly dark and the dusk spectrum was showing. Sheila looked up at it and said,

"When I see this, there are so many colours that remind me of Earth."

She held Christina's hand.

"It makes me think that maybe Earth is not so far away."

Christina looked up at it and responded,

"The colours remind me of the colours of the cars. Until I saw the diversity of them, some colours were completely foreign to me."

She turned to Sheila and said, "But the spectrum appears the same here as it does in the mountains. It must mean that home isn't far away."

Next morning, the hyper car was about to return Sheila, Samuel and Jonathon back to their home. There were tears in Sheila's eyes as she said farewell to Christina.

She said, "Take care, my daughter."

Sheila stroked Christina's hair. Christina was so young to be leaving home, and although she was mature for her age, Sheila was still concerned. Samuel was going to miss her terribly. For many years Christina had been his family, when Sheila was not there. Now, he didn't know what to say. So, he just went over and hugged her. Christina tried to reassure them,

"It is okay Mummy and Daddy you can come and visit me anytime."

She went over to Samuel and Sheila in turn and touched their shoulders.

"Also, I will come and visit you."

Eventually, they completed their farewells and the hyper car returned Sheila and Samuel home.

Chapter 23
The Roundup

Colonel Benjamin Jefferson was the go-to man for difficult and urgent projects. He had worked on many different worlds and his work was his life. He didn't have a family and worked long hours. In fact, he'd never married and was nearing retirement age. But he wasn't looking forward to retirement. He had wisps of grey hair that tried to cover his bald head. But other than that, there was nothing about him that seemed elderly. He was very fit and alert.

As he surveyed the plains of Plantere from his helicopter, he wanted to confirm that his meticulous planning was still on track. Ever since the Mars catastrophe the export of cars from Plantere had dried up. As the mining operations on other worlds were beginning to ramp up again, there was an urgent demand for living cars to work in the mines. However, most of the corporations were still only in "the planning phases" of returning to Plantere and resuming normal operations. Benjamin's task was to fulfil a large order of cars urgently with minimal setup.

The Colonel had a reputation of advocating and delivering on ambitious plans. This plan was no different. The Colonel, as usual consulted widely with a large range of experts, from car anatomy professors, space shuttle and helicopter pilots, to contract car hunters and heavy artillery officers. He held meetings with them and asked penetrating questions. He thought through a number of scenarios and possible events, before finally crafting his plan.

A few days ago, his team had finished establishing the sites needed for this project. The accuracy of the designation of locations was critical to the success of the operation, as there was a sizeable investment made by the Clements Corporation. One of the sites was the landing pad for the freight shuttle craft that would transport the captured cars. The landing pad was located in a very wide valley and wasn't fortified. It was vulnerable to attack, but the Colonel gambled that the cars would not be aware of, or be troubled by its presence, as it had been a long time since they had been hunted. However, it was still important that the operations would be started and concluded in a relatively short space of time.

Only a few minutes ago, the pilot of a scouting helicopter had contacted him.

"Colonel, Sir," a voice on the communicator said, "There is a herd of cars at the fuel plantation. Should we initiate the combat operations sir?"

The fuel ball plantation was important to the Colonel's plan. He needed to guarantee that there would be a tribe of cars at any given location within a short period time. He was pleased with this start. It was still early in the day, so they had plenty of time. His answer to the pilot of the scouting helicopter was "Yes." That prompted him to check the readiness of all the teams. Finally, he instructed his pilot to take him to the fuel ball plantation.

A Hyundai tribe of one hundred and fifty cars, were feeding there. It was a good size tribe. At this height there were no clouds of dust and the car tribe didn't seem to notice the helicopters. But the Colonel knew that when the helicopters flew lower, clouds of dust would be raised. There were five helicopters armed with missile launchers that held four missiles. The helicopters also had lasers but none of them had stun weapons. The Colonel watched the helicopters make a formation and when they were ready, he ordered them to attack. The helicopters flew low and targeted old or small cars with their missiles.

The soldiers who manned the missile launchers had telescopic sights so they could see their targets very clearly. They looked for cars with broken windows or windscreens to be targets. Also, the computers on each missile had an algorithm to track a twentieth century vehicle, that the missile was locked onto before it was fired. Because of this, even though the target could be moving at speed, the missiles were still deadly accurate.

This innovation was one that the Colonel was very proud of. To have ambitious plans you had to have detailed and creative planning. As the Colonel wanted to maximise the profits of this operation, he ordered old and small cars to be targeted for missiles. Next to a yellow Elantra, an elderly small i30 Hatch was hit by a missile. The i30 exploded and became a ball of flames. The yellow Elantra screamed in terror and sounded his horn in a long wail. Five cars were destroyed, and the attack caused the other cars to panic and flee. The clouds of dust that the helicopters raised, also added to the panic of the cars. Some of the cars honked in terror, while others flickered their headlights. This attack had taken the cars by complete surprise, and they were all terrified.

The Colonel didn't know a lot about cars, but he could see that they were terrified and stressed.

"Good," he thought, "they will do what I want."

Because of the helicopter formation and luckily for the Colonel, the cars drove in the direction he'd planned. But because of the panic, there were a couple of cars that didn't. One of the pilots called, "Colonel, a couple of the cars went in the wrong direction."

The Colonel cracked his knuckles. "Stupid machines," he thought.

"Forget them," the Colonel ordered, "Focus on the herd."

To keep the cars moving and in the correct direction, the helicopters used their lasers. The lasers were not strong enough to destroy or severely damage a car, but they did hurt them. The helicopters flew at low altitude and targeted the boots or hatches of the trailing cars. The orders for the teams in the helicopters were to only use the missiles if the cars dramatically changed their direction. Also, they were to use lasers as much as possible. This was successful while they were rounding up the cars along the wide valley.

However, they came to a point where they needed to turn the cars from the wide valley they were in, into the entrance of a much narrower valley. To do this, two of the helicopters flew to the front of the oncoming cars and fired a missile each. An older metallic maroon Kona medium-sized SUV and a middle-aged green i30 small medium sedan exploded and burst into flames. The effect of the attack was enhanced by the clouds of dust that the attacking helicopters raised. The cars at the front were in shock and immediately applied their brakes. They also honked in terror. The cars at the front were already terrified and this latest attack compounded their fear. There were two helicopters behind the tribe. The teams in those helicopters were concerned that the cars might double back and ignore the pain of being hit with laser bolts. So, they too, fired missiles. An elderly grey Kona SUV and a young white i30 sedan exploded and burst into flames. To help force the cars into the narrow valley there was one other helicopter that flew on the left of the stampeding cars, to block the cars from travelling to the left, instead of turning right, in order to drive them into the entrance of the narrow valley. It too, fired a missile. An elderly silver Elantra medium sedan was hit and exploded into flames. There was more honking in terror and some cars increased the frequency of their headlight flickering. After these attacks, most of the cars turned right and went into the entrance of this narrower valley.

However, this was the home of the Hyundai tribe, so they knew the landscape. Three of the tribal chiefs realised that they were being forced into a narrow valley that had no exit. They understood that they were in great peril.

They honked their horns in a long blast and yelled, "To us! to us!"

Then they drove straight ahead where the front two helicopters had flown. About fifteen cars followed them. They ignored the threat of the missiles, because they knew they would be doomed if they entered the narrow valley. The Colonel feared that the entire herd would turn from their path and escape.

He cracked his knuckles again and thought, *obstinate animals*. He ordered coldly, "Take out the leaders."

The two helicopters targeted the leading cars who were the chiefs of the tribe. Three missiles were fired. The chiefs, an elegant black Tucson large SUV, a stylish red Santa Fe large SUV and a young green Veloster sedan, were all hit by missiles. They all exploded and burst into flames. The fifteen cars that were following them were terrified, but stayed their course.

"Honestly," the Colonel thought, "just go right."

As if he was telling the cars what they must do.

He then sighed before ordering, "Forget them. Concentrate on the rest of the herd."

So, the fifteen cars escaped. The main body of the tribe kept driving down the narrow valley until they reached the end.

I have you now, the Colonel thought.

Now the Colonel had arranged for stun cannons to be set up along the ridges of the valley, and also eight tanks with stun cannons were parked on the sides of the valley. As the cars drove through, they formed a front behind the cars.

The Colonel clapped his hands and thought, *Got you.*

When the cars had reached the end of the valley, the Colonel ordered the soldiers manning the stun cannons and tanks to fire at will. The cars had no chance of escape. When cars saw that their colleagues were stunned, they tried to double back and go the way they had come in. They were panicked and sensed their doom. There was forlorn honking and flickering of headlights. The Colonel was pleased with what he saw. The eight tanks stunned the cars leading the retreat, halting their progress. All the while, the stun cannons on the ridges were taking out cars at a tremendous rate. It didn't take long, before all the cars had been stunned. The plan so far was successful, but the Colonel was focused now on the delivery of the cars.

He ordered some drivers to go to the cars immediately. The drivers were selected from the ranks of professional car hunters. This task was as important as the rest of the operation. They were to drive the stunned cars to the landing pad, where there would be a freight shuttle craft waiting. This part of the operation had to be done quickly before the cars woke up. A freight shuttle craft could hold twenty cars. The Colonel had acquired the services of four. As each craft was filled and moved off, another would be there to land and take its place. The first two craft had to make two trips, so the operation to unload them and return to Plantere had to be done quickly. The drivers all had stun pistols, so if the cars woke up, they could stun them again. It was early in the afternoon before they were finished. At the end of the operation, they had captured one hundred and eighteen cars. It was enough to fulfil the order, so the Colonel was satisfied with the results.

Chapter 24
The Resolution

The Queen and the leadership team hosted an open session every ten days. It gave any car the opportunity to raise their grievances and have mediation from the leadership team. Christina always attended, but generally she deferred judgement to the leadership team. They had been running these sessions long before Christina had been born. Suvy, was particularly good at suggesting compromises and making wise judgements. His opinion was sought after by the other team members. The sessions were hosted out the front of the spaceship and were open to every car. They began their meetings in the middle of the morning to give them plenty of time.

Generally, before the session was opened, Christina and the leadership team would meet to discuss private matters. The day had started to warm up. Christina had raised the issue of performing regular services to the Womb, as she had read in the Manual that this is recommended. Tuti agreed, that it would be optimal, but they needed to source a regular supply of spare parts. The cars didn't trade and they didn't have funds to buy spare parts from the humans on other worlds. It was determined that Christina would talk to Jonathon about the issue. He might have suggestions.

Bluey raised the concern that the freedom fighter Truck, had declared himself, the King of the cars. Before the exodus of the corporations, he was instrumental in taking the fight to them. He had inspired many cars to follow him and join his army. It was expected that once the corporations had left, his following would dissipate and there would not be a need for Truck to lead. But instead, Truck consolidated his grip on power. Bluey noticed that there were less cars attending the open sessions. He also added, that Truck had not attended Christina's coronation, and although the turnout was good, there were some cars that had stayed away. Christina said that as long as Truck didn't interfere with the guardianship of the Womb, he could be King. She said, once the young cars had grown up and joined a tribe, they were under the leadership of that tribe.

"We might offer the services of mediation, but generally the tribes rule themselves. If they want to submit themselves to a king, then that is up to them," she announced.

The rest of the team were not so sure. There was no resolution on what should be done. With that, the private meeting was closed and the open session started. The chiefs of two tribes brought their dispute to the session. The tribes were of Ford and Kia. There were two chiefs from the Ford tribe. They were a red Ford Mustang convertible and a green Ford Falcon XR8 sedan. These cars were in their prime and commanded a substantial presence. There were three chiefs from the Kia tribe. They were a black Carnival SUV, a metallic grey Sorento hatch and a blue Seltos sedan. They too were in their prime.

The Ford convertible spoke with an effort to be calm,

"Thank you, lords for hearing our concerns."

But his anger overwhelmed him. His engine idled more loudly before he blurted out, "Our tribes are on the verge of war, because the Kia tribe grazes on our fuel ball plantation in the Horton Gorge, which is our territory."

He was interrupted by the Carnival SUV who also failed to be calm, despite his effort,

"The Horton Gorge is our territory."

At that, the Ford chiefs all honked their horns in anger. This provoked the Kia chiefs to do the same. The territories of the tribes that lived near the Womb, were established a long time ago. It was believed that some of them may have been defined by Professor Heidenburg. But as tribes had moved further away from the Womb, the territories were negotiated by the tribes themselves. With these two tribes, they lived close to the Womb, so it was likely that there would be a record of the boundaries between the tribes.

"Enough." Tuti ordered, "Bluey, could you please access the archives and see if the boundaries have been recorded."

Bluey drove into the spaceship.

"Now," Tuti said sternly.

"Your tribes are neighbours. You need to be friendly with one another."

Tuti then idled his engine loudly before he preached,

"Err on the side of generosity and you will all lead happier lives."

The chiefs fell silent. It wasn't long before Bluey returned.

"The boundary goes through Horton Gorge." Bluey reported. "Probably originally, the fuel ball plantation would have been on one side of the boundary," Bluey explained.

He lowered his passenger windows in an effort to persuade the chiefs to be calm and conciliatory. He continued, "But now it has appeared to have grown, so that it spreads across the boundary."

Tuti asked, "Suvy, what do you recommend?"

Suvy thought for a while and then replied, "The fuel ball plantation exists on both sides of the border, so it belongs to both tribes."

Suvy then moved his side mirrors. He had something profound and wise to say. He added, "I suggest you take it in turns to feed from it. Each tribe will have ten days to visit the plantation before it is the other tribe's turn. When it is your turn, do not overfeed."

Then it was his turn to preach. "As the hyper car said. Err on the side of generosity."

None of the chiefs seemed happy about this outcome. That was probably a sign that it was a good compromise. However, the chiefs did leave peacefully, and it was hoped that there would not be a war between the two tribes.

The next supplicants were seventeen Hyundai cars. They had a spokesman who was a white Tucson medium SUV. He said,

"I have grave tidings my lords."

The SUV didn't know how to start telling his story, so there was a pause before he continued,

"We are all from the Hyundai tribe that live in the Kansas canyons," another pause,

"As we were feeding at a fuel plantation, we were attacked by helicopters. I think they were sent by the corporations!"

Even though he was stationary, he turned his front wheels. He was clearly stressed. He continued, "There were helicopters behind us and helicopters in front of us. They flew low and fired missiles at us. None of the missiles missed. Every time a missile hit a car, the car would explode and burst into flames. It was terrifying."

He raised his antennae, and it seemed hard for him to speak. He tried to gather his thoughts calmly as he knew that it was important to sound competent in front of the Womb leadership team.

After he had gathered himself, he continued. "Looking back at it now, I think they fired on us, simply to drive us to a specific location. Most of the tribe were forced into a narrow box canyon."

He was then forlorn, "Only the cars here escaped."

He then thought about his heroes. He would forever be grateful for their sacrifice. He reminisced, "Our chiefs bravely drove towards the helicopters at the front. Even though they knew they could be destroyed. They sensed that the tribe was being herded into a trap, so they wanted to find a way to escape. They gave their lives to secure our freedom."

He looked around at his comrades. There was now a special bond between them. They had gone together and had driven towards the helicopters, even though the helicopters had destroyed their chiefs. He told,

"When the fifteen of us saw our chiefs being destroyed, we took courage from their bravery. All of us drove where our chiefs led, and by luck we escaped."

He then sadly explained, "We took refuge with the nearby Holden tribe. The next day, a few of us went back to the fuel ball plantation to search for the rest of the tribe. There was no life there, only the smouldering shells of burnt- out cars. It was very traumatic "We also went to the narrow valley where most of the tribe went. And even there we could only find the burnt-out shells of the cars that had been destroyed. There was no sign of our tribe. I think they were all captured and taken away."

He then remembered his chiefs fondly, before saying, "The chiefs were right. The humans, with their missiles forced us into a trap."

He didn't know what the survivors should do now. That was why they had come to the Womb leadership team. He added sadly, "There are too few of us now to form a tribe and we don't feel safe living in our homeland anymore."

Christina's eyes were filled with tears.

"My poor cars," she wept.

The hyper car spoke. "We can find you another Hyundai tribe you can join. Hopefully you will feel safe there and be able to make a fresh start."

"Thank you, sir," replied the Tucson SUV.

Christina wiped some tears from her eyes and then said sympathetically, "You have lived with your tribe your whole life and have known peace."

She wanted to console the surviving cars. She wanted them to know that she tried to understand their pain. It was the least she could do. She continued. "Your mentors and friends were there. The tribe gave you great joy and happiness, and then one day it was taken away cruelly."

She had tears that had now turned into anger. "In a terrible act of violence, you were repressed. Where before you lived with contentment, now you live in fear."

Her anger subsided. There was now only regret.

"I'm so sorry for the cars that were lost and for the cars that remain." Christina cried some more.

The Tucson SUV said quietly to Christina, "Eomma gamsahabnida."

In the tribal language this meant, "Thank you Mother."

And with that the seventeen cars left the session.

There was silence among the leadership team and the queen, until finally through some tears Christina again said sadly, "My poor cars."

Despite the weather becoming warm, Christina felt cold. She shivered.

"Gentle Queen," Bluey said, "We may have had a reprieve in these last few years, but unfortunately, to be hunted is our lot."

Then there was more silence. With tears abated and with cold determination, Christina announced,

"This will not stand." She then paused and was thoughtful. "Have the corporations returned to their forts?" she asked.

"We send scouts out fairly regularly, as you know," the hyper car replied. "But maybe now we should send them out more often."

Then Bluey added, "Except for Central Spaceport, I don't think the humans have returned to their forts. But maybe that will change soon."

In the same cold determined tone, Christina replied, "We must raise a large army and go to Central Spaceport." She was thoughtful again for a moment, then she announced, "This army won't just have cars. There will be hunters and yellow bears as well."

Christina then raised her voice and increased her determination.

"The indigenous population of Plantere must rise together and claim our lands. We are not fodder for foreigners to exploit. Let us go forth and send them back to where they came from."

Nothing like this had ever been said before. Certainly, the freedom fighter Truck, in his speeches, implored his followers to throw off the yoke of their oppressors. But no one had ever suggested that yellow bears, hunters and cars should unite.

Suvy was concerned and said, "It is the humans that hunt us and what do we know of yellow bears?"

However, Bluey had a slightly different perspective.

"In the Prophecies." he said. Bluey loved to talk about the Prophecies. "It is said that the Queen of the Cars will take us down a path we would not normally tread."

Tuti, was not convinced about Christina's plan. But he was conciliatory and said, "Christina grew up knowing about yellow bears and lived with humans who didn't hunt cars."

Suvy honked his horn as a sign that he understood the point being made. It could be said, that the Leadership Team in general were troubled by Christina's plan. But they loved their Queen and knew that she was very special. So maybe they should support this ambitious plan. Professor Heidenburg's Bible said nothing about cars being hunted and what should be done. It was clear that the cars needed to find their own way through this. Perhaps their Queen is right. For now, they will accept her plan. And see what happens.

Chapter 25
The Application

Sheila was waiting patiently in a hologram room at Fort Lyndon. The official she was scheduled to meet virtually was running late. Sheila didn't mind though because she was feeling nervous. Also, she was enjoying the air conditioning. It was the middle of the day, and it was very warm outside. Sometimes she wondered what she was doing here, and whether it was wise to have this meeting.

Two weeks ago, when Christina had returned, it had been so good to see her. She seemed well and appeared to be happy living with the cars. But Christina had told a tragic story about the disappearance of a tribe of cars. She told how she wanted to meet with Jonathon, to get support and participation from the mountain hunters for her plan to raise an army. She planned to visit Mama bear, because she wanted the yellow bears to also join her army. It was this plan of Christina's, to have a combined indigenous life form army, that had got Sheila thinking. There were other worlds that had similar issues, of foreigners exploiting the indigenous population. Sheila had then told Christina,

"I have an idea. I know I broke my promise, but do you think you could ask a car to take me to Fort Lyndon?"

Christina reached out and touched Sheila's arm. She replied,

"Don't be concerned about your promise Mummy. I explained to Tuti that you are an Earthling and you felt homesick. Also, I emphasised that you didn't tell anyone about the Womb." She smiled reassuringly and said, "Of course I can ask for a car to take you. But wouldn't you want Daddy to come with you also?"

"No darling, I need to use some of the equipment there and do a lot of writing. He would be bored," Sheila replied.

At this stage Sheila didn't know if she would proceed with her idea, and she didn't want to talk about it yet. That was why she wanted to go alone. To do some investigation and come up with a plan. Luckily, there was a Holden tribe nearby and she had a ride in a Kingswood.

When she arrived at the Fort, she found that the service door was still unlocked from her previous visit to Plantere. The Fort was still deserted. She remembered that her friend David was able to switch on the power to the Fort. He wanted to be able to communicate with the orbiting mothership. The Fort had extensive solar panels and battery storage. That was her first task. She retraced the steps David had taken, and then after some time she was able to switch the power on. The other thing she needed to do, was to find out if there was any preserved food. She went to the kitchen and found that there was a lot of rotting food. It wasn't a pleasant search, but eventually she did find a cupboard with some preserved food.

Satisfied with her progress so far, she went to the library and used a communication panel to bring up the site for the Inter Solar System union. The information there was quite extensive. So, it took a while before she found what she was looking for, the chapter on World Heritage Park status. She looked at the benefits section, which included, being posted on tourism marketing platforms and grants from the Inter Solar System union. The one she was most interested in, was that corporations would need a permit to do business on a Heritage Park world. Convinced that this idea was worth pursuing, she searched for the application process for Heritage Park status.

She downloaded the application form. It had a hundred and thirty- six pages. Then she read the sections on how to apply. There was a plethora of tips, what not to do and encouragement, that she waded through. Since Sheila hadn't known how long she would be at the Fort when she'd organised the lift with Christina, it was arranged that the Kingswood would return to the Fort the next day. However, when she met the Kingswood just outside the Fort, she told him that she would have to stay at least a week.

This application process was going to be a big task. The library at the Fort had some useful information about Plantere, such as geography, weather patterns, day lengths, known locations of car tribes and yellow bears. Sheila also had her journal. She wished she had access to Professor Heidenburg's diary and the Bible. At times she wondered whether she should return home and contact Christina to get more information. But then she wondered what would Christina think about this application to become an Inter - Solar System Heritage Park? What would the cars think? Obviously at some point she would have to broach the subject with them. But she didn't want to do it yet. The application might be unsuccessful. There was no point in raising hopes prematurely, she justified to herself.

Providing the information that the application form required was difficult. But what proved to be more difficult was to work out what information could be provided and what should remain hidden. The weight of the promise she'd made to the cars, the one she had broken, was hard to bear. Especially while she was trying to fill out this application form. She did make compromises, but she rationalised that it was for the greater good. Then at times she wondered if she was doing the right thing, making this application at all.

She worked diligently every day, putting in long hours. It was a mammoth task. However, despite her doubts and worries she completed the application form. It took her over a week. As she submitted it, she worried about whether she had betrayed the cars by providing too much information and then she also worried that the application would be unsuccessful, if she didn't provide enough information.

She looked at the site and it said that if it was decided to progress the application to the next phase, she would be notified within a few days. So, when the Kingswood returned to the Fort, she said she would have to stay at least another week. Sheila passed the time by browsing through information kept in the library. She didn't know how long she should wait for a reply. Maybe she wouldn't hear anything for months. But she took what was said on the site to heart and decided she should wait a few days.

And sure enough, she did get a reply to say that her application had progressed to the next phase. She had been given an appointment to meet with an official. They recommended that it should be done in a hologram room, if it was possible. Luckily for Sheila, Fort Lyndon did have a hologram room. She knew that most forts did not have one. Although it was only a recommendation, Sheila was grateful that she did have access to a hologram room. It should make the meeting more intimate, as it would seem as if they were both in the same room. Eventually, Sheila received a signal to say that the official was ready for the meeting, so she activated the hologram room.

The official was a small middle-aged woman who sported a pair of spectacles. She wore a long brown skirt with a matching jacket. The outfit was loose fitting and conservative. She also wore a white blouse that was buttoned up to her neck. Her brown hair was tied back into a bun. Sheila thought that the Official reminded her of her headmistress at school.

The Official didn't say anything and was browsing on the panel in front of her. Sheila guessed the woman was arranging the one hundred -and thirty-six pages application form. If they were going to go through the application form in detail, this was going to be a very long meeting.

Sheila broke the ice.

"Hello my name is Sheila McSporran," she said. "I would like to thank you for meeting with me today."

"Don't thank me, this is my job," the Official replied curtly. "You can call me Dr Stockholm."

After some more time preparing the panel in front of her Dr Stockholm was ready.

"Now, I understand that you are seeking Heritage Park status for Omega 24A?" she said.

"Yes, Doctor," Sheila replied politely.

"Why do you want Heritage Part status for Omega 24A?" the doctor asked.

"The main reason," Sheila replied, "is to stop the corporations from exploiting the indigenous population."

"Isn't Omega 24A a desolate wasteland?" the Doctor countered.

"Surely the corporations can eke out a living there, if that is what they desire?"

Dr Stockholm wasn't finished. "You must understand that the Inter Solar System Union isn't against private enterprise."

Sheila was put off balance and wasn't able to articulate as well as she would like. "But the corporations are enslaving the cars," she said.

"Hmm," the doctor mused. "You are listed as missing, presumed dead. But you are here and very much alive." The Doctor looked down her nose over her spectacles. "I can only conclude that you are a person of dubious character," she added in a disapproving tone.

This was not going well, Sheila thought. *How could she say that she was just trying to keep a promise to the cars?* This meeting was proving to be much more difficult than filling out the application form. Sheila didn't know what to say, so she said nothing. This could be a really short meeting.

"You mention a number of times in your application form, something about a sacred site for the cars?" the Doctor continued, flipping through the screen on her panel. "What's at this sacred site?" she asked pointedly.

Sheila really didn't know what to say.

"Well?" the Doctor asked impatiently.

"It's secret," Sheila mumbled.

The Doctor continued her questions.

"You said that the cars were intelligent life forms. How do you know that? They could just be machines with artificial intelligence."

Sheila felt that she was in a court of law and was being interrogated by a hostile lawyer. Then she remembered her history lessons from school. In particular, the Artificial Intelligence war.

It occurred in the late twenty-first and early twenty-second centuries. The factions fought over self-awareness of machines. The pro- life form faction had feared that self-aware machines would seek to dominate humans. It was a particularly nasty war that shaped how people viewed machines, even now. Eventually the pro- life form faction won even though they were out gunned and had less access to technology. It was a remarkable victory. At the end of the war a self-awareness Accord was signed. It was a complex document that ensured only living beings could be allowed to be self-aware. It became a legal and moral requirement.

That didn't mean people stopped using Artificial Intelligence. It was advanced and as useful as ever. Especially with space travel. Probably the car's Womb used it as well. Sheila remembered her teacher asking the class what self-awareness in life forms was. A tricky question. One student suggested it was the idea of something thinking, "I am." Another said that it was a being who was conscious of itself. Then Sheila suddenly thought, what if this official decided that cars were self-aware machines with artificial intelligence? Instead of Heritage Park status, the Inter Solar System Union would send part of their considerable military force to exterminate a dangerous pest. The corporations would then be in trouble for exporting self-aware machines. Sheila became extremely worried and concerned.

"Professor Seronen studied them for some time. He said they were asexual life forms," she said.

"This professor Seronen is also missing, presumed dead," the Doctor countered scornfully. "Like you, maybe he is lurking about somewhere?"

Sheila really did feel off balance and uncomfortable. All she could do was be truthful but not reveal too many secrets.

"Unfortunately," she replied, "he died."

"There are some quite considerable gaps in your account on the application form," accused the Doctor.

Sheila didn't know what to say, but she eventually mumbled, "Some things, are confidential."

"Did you read our privacy statement on the site?" the Doctor asked. She looked down her nose again and continued. "The information provided on application forms is kept within the Union in the strictest confidence." And then as if she had been offended in some way she stated, "We are not some fly-by-night Company. We are the Inter Solar System Union."

Then she softened her tone.

"All employees are professional and ethical in their conduct," she added in a softer tone. "If you want this application to succeed, you need to be open and transparent with me."

Sheila felt persuaded by this. After all she was an Earthling and journalist who had encountered bureaucratic organisations like this in the past. They can be maddening to deal with, but they also follow their own rules religiously. Sheila took a deep breath and thought, *another time I will break my promise.* "I know the cars are life forms because I have seen the mechanical Womb in which they were born," she said.

The Doctor raised her eyebrows and looked startled at this. Sheila was pleased with the reaction so she continued.

"I went with a corporation expedition to look for professor Hiedenburg's spaceship," she said. "The cars attacked us but spared three of us from the expedition. They showed us the Womb, but we had to promise not to return to the corporations or tell anyone about the spaceship."

The Doctor sat back in her chair and looked thoughtful. Sheila had the impression that she had just made an impact.

"Are the cars aggressive?" the Doctor asked.

"It is a harsh world," Sheila replied. "But the cars have endured many years of being captured and enslaved by the corporations."

From the look the Doctor gave her, Sheila felt that she understood and appreciated the suffering of those who were exploited.

"Out of an entire expedition, why did the cars spare you?" the Doctor asked.

"I was pregnant with my daughter," Sheila replied. "She is now Queen of the Cars.".

"Where have you been living?" the Doctor asked. It was clear that she was now very curious.

"I've been living with my daughter's father with a mountain tribe. He is a yellow bear hunter."

Doctor Stockholm asked many more questions, and the interview continued for a long time. Sheila didn't notice the time. In a way she felt better after opening up about her life on Plantere. And for a short time, she didn't feel bad about betraying the promise she had made to the cars. At the end of the interview the doctor announced, "This application can now proceed to the next phase. You are in luck. I'm close by."

She packed up her panel and other belongings and as she was doing so, said, "I should be at Omega 24A in two weeks. I have the location of Fort Lyndon, so I can meet with you there." Then she added pointedly, "I trust that I can meet these cars and visit their Womb."

"Yes," Sheila replied. "I will take you there."

"Very good," the Doctor said. "I will be at Fort Lyndon in the morning."

With that, the interview ended. Sheila sat in the hologram room for a while. She felt cool and noticed that she wasn't sweating. Sheila thought that, ultimately, the interview had gone well. The application would proceed to the next phase. She should be pleased. But she had this nagging thought.

"What have I done?" she asked herself.

Chapter 26
Meeting with the Bears

Christina considered Mama Bear to be a friend. After making the treaty with Mama Bear, Christina visited her regularly and they would talk for some time. But Christina knew that what she was going to ask of her at this meeting, was going to be challenging. Christina always visited Mama Bear alone, as the bear was very reclusive and didn't want to face too many people, or even too many bears for that matter. This was a common trait among yellow bears. Actually, compared to other bears, Mama Bear was outgoing. Mama Bear loved her friendship with Christina. It helped her not to think about her twin sister or son. Christina could see that Mama Bear was melancholy; that she was so outgoing compared with other bears, but still so reclusive, which presented a massive hurdle to what Christina wanted to ask.

When Christina reached the entrance to Mama Bear's cave, she called out. This is what Mama Bear preferred, rather than be surprised by an unexpected visitor. Christina knew it might be some time before Mama Bear would answer. One of the reasons their friendship flourished was that Christina learnt about and adapted to the culture of yellow bears. When Christina made mistakes and was made aware of them, she quickly adjusted her behaviour for next time. After a number of visits, Mama Bear started to really enjoy them and she began to like Christina. After an hour at the entrance to the cave, Christina still hadn't received a reply. It was warm outside, and Christina was tempted to go into the cave, just a short distance, to be in some shade. But out of respect to her friend, she decided not to. It was possible that Mama Bear was out foraging. Yellow bears do go out but they spend most of their time in caves, so Christina still thought that Mama Bear was probably at home. Christina understood that time moved slowly for bears. They have long lives and generally are not very active.

After an hour and half, Christina heard a greeting from Mama Bear and ventured into the cave. Since Christina had become Queen of the Cars she hadn't visited Mama Bear for a long time. But to Mama Bear that last visit seemed recent. Mama Bear enjoyed finding out what Christina and her family were doing, as it seemed to her that they crammed so many activities into a short space of time. So, when Christina and Mama Bear were face to face and were both sitting down, Mama Bear asked, "Little One, what have you been doing?"

Christina told Mama Bear about her now being the Queen of the Cars and the changes to her life because of that. Christina didn't apologise for not visiting earlier because she knew, for Mama Bear the time between visits was not long. After Christina spoke about her life, she ventured to speak about the car tribe that had been captured.

"Mama Bear," she said. "A most appalling thing has happened. An entire tribe of cars, over one hundred souls, were captured and enslaved by a corporation."

Christina's voice wavered. It was hard to speak the language of the bears at the best of times. Now Christina still felt a depth of emotion and grief. Mama bear picked up on it though and listened attentively.

"We thought the corporations had left us," Christina continued. "But it now appears that they are coming back."

Because the cars lived on the plains, Mama Bear didn't know much about them. She only knew what Christina had told her. To the bears, the entire time of the cars' existence had happened in a blink of an eye. But Mama Bear did remember her own loss and could empathise with Christina over the loss of her cars.

"I'm sorry for your loss Little One," Mama Bear replied,

Christina took a deep breath and then pressed on. "I'm going to raise an army to take to Central Spaceport. It would have cars, hunters and if you will help me, yellow bears."

Mama Bear was taken aback by this bold request and her fur stood on end. Over her body the yellow fur became prickly. The request had surprised her and quite frankly, made her feel stressed. She sighed. Her little friend just didn't understand so she explained.

"Little One, we are solitary creatures, that like to live alone in our mountains."

Christina nodded. She did understand. Mama Bear sensing that she did, continued.

"We have our simple routines and our lives are peaceful. I don't think we can participate in an army."

"I'm sorry Mama Bear for the enormity of my request," Christina replied. "I know it is not your way. I don't want to burden you." Christina knew this was difficult, but she was desperate, so she continued to plead. "But my situation is dire. The future of my cars is at stake. The corporations are relentless, and they do not care what harm they cause."

Mama Bear was quiet for some time. Christina knew that when Mama Bear was confronted with something difficult or complex, she did not reply straight away. Mama Bear was very thoughtful and rubbed her head with her left paw. She took her time to process her thoughts and would be quiet for a long time.

After a half an hour she spoke quietly. "What would you have me do, Little One?"

Once again, Christina took another deep breath and then said, "I need to meet with a large number of bears and try to persuade them to join my army."

"How many bears do you need to meet, Little One?" Mama Bear asked. "Two, three or is it five?"

"Over twenty," Christina replied.

Once again Mama Bear's fur stood on end and was again quiet for a long time. Christina waited patiently. Eventually Mama Bear spoke again.

"Little One, meetings of that size are extremely rare. It has probably been hundreds of years since the last one." She felt the need to repeat herself and said, "We are solitary creatures and we don't like large gatherings." She then sighed before adding, "Also, even if we did have this meeting, I don't think any bears would join your army."

"I'm sorry Mama Bear, you are probably right, but I need to try," Christina replied. There were tears in her eyes.

Mama bear looked kindly at her friend. ""You are my dear friend Little One, so I will arrange this meeting for you," she promised.

Christina was so grateful. "Thank you so much Mama Bear," she said. Then, Christina quipped, "Maybe you will meet your boyfriend there."

When a communication is needed to reach a large number of bears, which was extremely rare, the way the bears would do it, was this:

Mama Bear would visit three bears and deliver her message to them. Then each of those three bears would visit three of their friends, or family and deliver the message, and they would do likewise.

In the end, Mama Bear's message reached thirty-five bears. She had arranged the meeting to be held in an ancient meeting cave. That cave was very large and formed a big part of yellow bear folklore. It had been used before for large meetings. Christina had to promise that none of the mountain hunters would try to hunt the bears that were attending the meeting. Not that the hunters would be silly enough to try and hunt thirty-five bears at once.

Jonathon and Samuel were worried for Christina's safety, when she told them about the meeting. They both insisted that they should come along. Christina thought that was rather silly. What would two hunters be able to do to thirty-five full grown yellow bears? But to allay their concerns, she agreed.

The three humans travelled with Mama Bear to the meeting cave. Mama Bear's message had conveyed that the meeting was urgent, so surprisingly, the meeting occurred only after two weeks since the message was sent. Christina was sincerely grateful to Mama Bear. Time was of the essence and Christina knew that bears do things slowly.

When they reached the entrance to the cave, the humans followed the lead of Mama Bear. She called out at the entrance and waited for a response before they entered the cave. The response came quite quickly, as the meeting was an expected event. They followed the tunnel, and it took them deeper into the cave. The air grew cooler as they continued. The humans hadn't brought any torches. Instead, they kept close to Mama Bear. Yellow bears have very good senses when in a cave. Eventually, the tunnel opened out into a massive cavern. There was a hole in the ceiling and sunlight came through. The humans could see the rays of light that made the cavern fully visible.

Christina could see there were at least twenty bears. The bears were sitting down on the ground. They did not sit together. Instead, there was a considerable social distance between each bear. *That was probably why the meeting was called to be held here,* Christina thought. Most of the bears were the same size as Mama Bear, but there were a couple that were between two and three metres taller. Then there were a couple of bears that were smaller and looked younger. Christina though, didn't have any idea of how old the bears were, except that the two smaller bears had probably only recently left their mother. In terms of seniority, as far as Christina understood, there was none. Because yellow bears were solitary creatures and didn't live in tribes, there were no chiefs. Mama Bear told Christina that not all the bears had arrived yet, and that they may have to wait awhile. While they were waiting, Christina noticed that the bears didn't make conversation with one another. They all sat in silence.

Over time, other bears arrived and when the last expected bear was present, Mama Bear spoke. What Samuel heard was a deep rumbling sound coming from the bear's mouth. Then he heard Christina making the same sound. It was like the sound of rumbling stones during an earthquake. Samuel was in awe of his daughter, as she was able to make the same sound as the bears, but he had no idea what was being said.

Mama Bear introduced Christina to the other bears. "Have peaceful sleeps, and may your caves be quiet." This was a formal greeting that the bears used. When bears had a meeting, it was always a very formal event. "This is my human friend." Mama Bear continued. "Her name is Little One."

Christina looked around the cavern after this was said, but she couldn't see any reaction from the bears.

Mama Bear continued, "She asked me to send the message out for this meeting today. Little One has a request for you. I will let her speak."

Christina began with, "Have peaceful sleeps, and may your caves be quiet."

The bears were astounded. None of them had ever heard a human speak their language. There were a few of them that had never seen a human before. Christina waited a while before saying anything more. She understood that the bears may be surprised to hear a human make the standard bear greeting. They needed time to come to terms with their surprise and be ready to hear more. It was half an hour before Christina spoke again. And even then, she worried that she might be considered too hasty.

Almost as if she was in a trance Christina spoke.

"Yellow bears are the only ancient race of Plantere. They have been here since time began and will be here when time ends."

Christina looked around the cavern. Not for affirmation because Christina knew that what she was saying was simply the truth.

"The time that humans have been on Plantere is merely a blip in history," she continued. "Probably everyone here can remember a time when there were no humans, and that memory wouldn't be felt as distant."

A number of bears nodded in agreement.

"As bears only like to live in the mountains, maybe none of you know about the cars," continued Christina. "They too have been only recent additions to Plantere. And they only live on the plains."

Christina stopped there and waited. She knew that she had given a lot of information. The bears were silent. After another half an hour she spoke again.

"There are two types of humans," she said. "Ones who are born and always live here. Then there are those who are visitors from the stars. You see my kin here. They came from Plantere. See their red hair, tanned skin and blue eyes. They are the hunters of Plantere."

Many of the bears were intrigued. Of the bears that had seen humans before, they thought that all humans looked the same. Once again Christina stopped and waited. She had a grave look and was serious when she spoke again,

"Some of the humans from the stars have ill intent towards all who live on Plantere." Now there was anger in her voice. "They capture and enslave the cars, who are my children. They use helicopters to hunt bears. They do not respect the bears, as the hunters of Plantere do. Instead of taking a bear and using the whole flesh, fur and bones for their needs, these evil humans slaughter many bears, just for their bones and making money."

Once again Christina stopped and waited. She was still angry. But she knew that she had to make her argument calmly if she was to have any chance of recruiting any bears. She took another deep breath and continued.

"Just recently, some humans from the stars, killed a number of cars and enslaved the rest of an entire tribe," she said. Her attempt at being calm ended. She now spoke with full emotion. "It broke my heart. We have to stop these humans from coming here and doing harm to the indigenous populations of Plantere." Then Christina calmed down before closing with a plea. "That is why I'm here talking to you. I want you to join my army."

Christina had discussed her speech with Mama Bear before the meeting. Obviously there needed to be some explanation, but Mama Bear resolutely advocated getting to the point as quickly as possible. The bears didn't enjoy being in meetings and even Christina's brief explanations still took a lot of time. The yellow bears didn't have tribes, groups or committees. It would not be the case of them holding a vote and then if there was a majority they would all go. Each bear would simply decide for themselves if they would go or not. A bear would not tell another bear what to do. After Christina made her request, she waited for a reaction from her audience. A tall bear spoke first.

"You were right to say, Little One, that the time humans have been on Plantere is merely a blip in history. I'm sure they will be gone in another blip. Why should we concern ourselves?"

Another bear spoke.

"I lost two of my children in one day, due to an attack from flying humans. That memory will be with me longer than a blip in history."

"Where will this army go?" asked yet another bear. "I'm afraid to go to the plains. There are no caves there and we are exposed in the open."

Christina waited for more bears to speak but none did. She waited a bit longer and then answered.

"The army will travel on the plains. But if you come with us, you will be amongst friends. The humans from the stars will never go away. Only if we force them will they go."

No other bears spoke. Mama Bear waited for another half an hour and then asked, "Little One, do you have anything more to add?"

Christina replied that she didn't. Mama Bear announced, "When the time comes for the army to be assembled, I will send a message, for bears to meet at my cave. Please think carefully over this request and make your decision to come or stay when you get my message."

There were grunts of approval made by a number of the bears. Then the meeting was over. As silently as they came, the bears left for their homes. When all bears had left, Christina thanked Mama Bear for her leadership and assistance.

"We will see how many bears will join your army," replied Mama Bear.

Chapter 27
The Grand Tour

Christina and the hyper car were waiting outside the gate to Fort Lyndon. They had been travelling all day and were happy to arrive before dusk. Sheila and the Inter Solar System Union official were inside waiting for them. When Sheila had first broached the subject of the Heritage Park application with Christina, Christina was livid. Her mother had made a promise to the cars to keep the existence of the Womb secret. Now it seems she was telling random people about it. But when Sheila explained the benefits of having Heritage Park status to Christina, Christina came around. Her mother did have the interests of the cars at heart. Although Christina could see the benefits of telling the union official about the Womb, she was not confident about convincing the cars that it was a good idea. Christina called a meeting with the leadership team soon after she had spoken with her mother.

The three cars and Christina met at the entrance to the spaceship.

"Christina, why did you call this meeting?" asked Tuti.

Christina was apprehensive. She didn't know how to ask the cars about giving a human from the stars a tour of the Womb. Even telling them that her mother had spoken about the Womb was difficult. Christina took a deep breath and decided to start with the benefits.

"I spoke with my mother," she said, "and she said there is an organisation called the Inter Solar System and that they could stop the corporations from enslaving cars."

"That is good news, I guess," Tuti said guardedly.

The cars were silent. They were waiting for Christina to explain what this meeting was about.

So, Christina explained.

"My mother has made an application for Heritage Park Status to the Inter Solar System Union," she said.

The cars didn't understand.

Christina then blurted, "An official from the union wants to see the Womb."

Tuti honked with anger, "Your mother spoke about the Womb?"

"She was trying to help," Christina pleaded. "This union could really help us."

"She was not to tell humans about the Womb," Tuti replied angrily.

Suvy was more pragmatic. "Do you think that your mother feels that they could trust this official?" he asked.

Bluey was normally calm and centred, but now he interjected before Christina could answer. "Sheila is a person of dubious character, so why should we trust her opinion now?"

This was not going well, Christina thought. But she felt she needed to defend her mother.

"My mother left the mountain tribe because she was homesick and wanted to return to Earth," she said. "She didn't speak about the Womb to anyone else."

Tuti had calmed down. "So can we trust this official?" he asked.

"My mother didn't think the official was very friendly, but she did trust her," Christina replied.

The cars flickered their headlights because they were dismayed and undecided.

Christina felt a little more confident. "You have shown the Womb to humans before," she pointed out. She put on her wicked smile and then continued. "And now you have me."

"Yes, we listened to the Prophecy and showed your mother the Womb," Bluey said.

Tuti continued. "And now we have the Queen of the Cars." He lowered his windows and said, "We are eternally grateful."

"Maybe, this time it would work out for the best as well?" Christina suggested.

The cars weren't convinced and mumbled amongst themselves in dissatisfaction.

"I think it would be a good idea to show this official around," said Christina. "Not to just show her the Womb."

Tuti's window wipers were moving. "You are our Queen, and we trust your judgement," he said reluctantly. "Maybe it would take an official from the stars to rid them of the humans," he added thoughtfully.

With a lack of enthusiasm, the cars agreed to give this official a grand tour.

So here they were now at the gates of Fort Lyndon. They had expected that the official arrived earlier that day. So, they had spent the night here to give the official a tour and show her the Womb. Sheila opened the gates and when Christina climbed out of the hyper car, Sheila met her daughter and gave her a hug. Dr Stockholm was standing just behind Sheila. She was dressed in a light brown uniform that had the logo of the Inter Solar System Union on the shirt. The uniform was of cotton trousers and a long sleeve shirt. Doctor Stockholm also wore sturdy shoes and a wide brim hat. She of course, still sported her spectacles and had her brown hair in a bun. When Sheila had greeted Doctor Stockholm in the morning as she disembarked from the shuttle, Sheila commented that Doctor Stockholm's outfit was very suitable. Doctor Stockholm had replied that it was the required attire for work on location.

Sheila then introduced Dr Stockholm to the Hyper car and Christina.

"This is the lead car, and this is my daughter, Christina, the Queen of the cars."

Then Sheila introduced the official to her daughter and the hyper car.

"This is Dr Stockholm, an important official at the Inter Solar System Union and who is currently evaluating our application for Heritage Park status."

"Thank you for coming. You must have come a long way to see us. We hope to show you a bit about us," Christina said warmly.

"It is my job," said Dr Stockholm curtly in an official manner, but then her tone softened a little. "But I look forward to seeing what you will show me."

Sheila had organised rooms for Christina and Doctor Stockholm and also prepared a meal for them from the preserved food stores in the Fort. They ate outside, so the hyper car would not be left out. Sheila had set up tables and chairs out the front of the mess hall. The sun was beginning to set, so the heat of day was waning, and it was quite pleasant sitting outside. During the dinner, Dr Stockholm bombarded the hyper car with questions, such as, "If you run over a sharp rock do you feel pain on your tyres?

"If you break or crack your windows, do they grow back?"

The hyper car patiently answered the questions.

"I would feel the stone, but it wouldn't be painful" and "When a car is young, the damaged glass does grow back, but when a car becomes old, the windows don't grow back anymore."

Sheila was pleased with how this visit had begun and was grateful to the hyper car for his forbearance. The day ended well, when the dusk spectra appeared in the sky. Dr Stockholm confided that she had seen this phenomenon on other worlds she had visited. But nevertheless, she did enjoy the spectacle.

Luckily, the next day was going to be a long day, as the journey back to the spaceship would take all of it. Dr Stockholm sat in the front seat of the hyper car, while Christina and Sheila sat in the back. To entertain Dr Stockholm during the drive, the hyper car played some music on his radio. So, as they sped along, he played *"Take On Me"* from A-ha. This was a favourite song of the hyper car. It made him want to drive faster.

Dr Stockholm noted, "Ah classical music."

Another favourite song of the hyper car was *"Poker Face"* from Lady Gaga, as well as *"I'm a Believer"* from Smash Mouth. These two songs also made the hyper car want to drive faster and because these were his favourites, he played them more than once. Generally, when the hyper car had passengers, he wouldn't play his songs, because he felt embarrassed. Except of course, when Christina was the sole passenger. She would sing along or try to. Christina persuaded him to play his music this time, because she believed the official might like it. Except for the one comment Dr Stockholm made, she didn't make any others. At one stage Dr Stockholm did ask if the passenger windows could be wound down. The hyper car then wound down the passenger window. Sheila was impressed by how well the hyper car was looking after their guest. Dr Stockholm didn't say a lot, but Sheila gained the impression that she was enjoying the drive.

As they drew closer to the Spaceship, there were cars lined up either side of their route. The cars from different tribes mingled together. The younger cars were parked on the front rows, either side. It was an impressive sight to see all the different cars together. Trucks, sportscars, cars of old heritage, and others were next to each other. As the hyper car drove past, the cars on either side honked their horns and flashed their headlights.

They arrived at the spaceship with some daylight hours to spare, so Christina thought it might be a good time to show Dr Stockholm the Womb. The hyper car drove up the ramp and then through to the room with the Womb. In there, his occupants got out. Dr Stockholm quietly walked over to the Womb, taking care with her steps. Christina could see a litter of embryos partly formed in the Womb. She estimated that they were about halfway through the gestation period. Sheila saw it as well and was pleased. One of the main doubts Dr Stockholm had about the cars, was whether or not they were lifeforms. She thought they could just be robots with artificial intelligence. Doctor Stockholm walked over to the Womb and touched the glass. She said nothing, but Sheila thought she looked as if she was in awe of what she had just seen. Before dinner, Sheila showed Dr Stockholm Professor Heidenburg's diary and the Bible. After Dr Stockholm had seen them.

"The Womb is very precious to the cars. They never show it to humans," said Sheila. She wanted to explain more so she continued. "Before the cars showed me the Womb, they made me promise that I wouldn't tell anyone about it."

She had Dr Stockholm's attention. Finally, she emphasised, "For the cars to show you the Womb, the Diary and Bible, they demonstrated an enormous leap of trust."

Dr Stockholm reaffirmed the confidentiality of Heritage Park status applications.

While Sheila was showing Doctor Stockholm the Diary and the Bible, Christina prepared dinner. When they were driving earlier, Christina had asked Dr Stockholm what food she liked to eat. Dr Stockholm had said 'anything that was not too spicy', so Christina prepared spaghetti Bolognese from her preserved food stores.

During dinner, Dr Stockholm didn't speak much about what she had seen. Sheila had the impression that she was keeping her cards close to her chest. So, Christina took the opportunity to explain what they were going to do tomorrow. They were going to visit a fuel ball plantation and then visit the Valley of Infant Cars. It was going to be a short day, so that was all Christina had planned for it. On the following day, Tuti would take them to Sheila's mountain-tribe, where she would introduce Dr Stockholm to the tribal hunters. They would then go and visit Mama Bear. Sheila asked Dr Stockholm if there was anything else she would like to see. Doctor Stockholm replied that what they had planned was enough.

The next day when they were at the fuel ball plantation, Christina explained that the fuel balls provided food for the cars. The hyper car demonstrated how a car feeds from a fuel ball, extending a hose from his side and piercing the skin of the fuel ball. Sheila was hoping that this demonstration and the Womb would convince Dr Stockholm that cars were lifeforms. Their next destination was the Valley of the Infant

Cars. That too, thought Sheila should persuade Dr Stockholm that the cars were life forms.

When they arrived, Christina was swarmed by the infant cars as she left the hyper car. Speaking in their tribal languages, she greeted each car as best she could. She signalled Sheila to bring Dr Stockholm over to meet them. Sheila felt that the Doctor was exhibiting a mixture of apprehension and curiosity, so she coaxed her to follow.

"It is okay Dr Stockholm," Sheila said. "Christina is their Queen and mother."

Eventually Dr Stockholm was standing next to Christina, surrounded by adoring infants. Christina picked out a very young Volkswagen Beetle. He hadn't started getting his colour yet and had a leathery skin instead of a metallic body.

"It is okay Dr Stockholm," Christina said. "You can pat him."

Dr Stockholm followed Christina's lead and started stroking the little car. Sheila noticed that she was smiling warmly. Maybe her harsh official exterior had melted a little. Perhaps this, rather than the visit to the Womb, would be the highlight of the tour for her.

The next day the hyper car took them to Sheila's mountain-tribe. It was a long drive, so all the passengers were tired when they reached their destination. They still had to walk up the mountain trail to reach the camp of the tribe. Sheila had been worried. Would their guest not like the red dust on the plains? Maybe she would enjoy the mountains better? Sheila took them to her house. Jonathon and Samuel were waiting there.

She introduced them. "Doctor Stockholm, this is Jonathon, mountain master, a tribal leader, and this is Christina's father, Samuel."

"Nice to meet you," Doctor Stockholm replied.

Sheila prepared a meal of dried yellow bear meat. During dinner, Doctor Stockholm noticed Samuel's sword on the wall and asked Sheila about it.

Samuel was pleased that she had and said, "This is the famous sword of Sergeant Blackmore."

Normally, Samuel was quiet and reluctant to speak, but when the topic of the sword was raised, he became more animated.

"After dinner, I can show you some of my moves with the sword," he suggested.

"He is our resident dragon slayer," Jonathon teased.

Doctor Stockholm asked over dinner, "Is this meat from yellow bears?"

"Yes, it is," Jonathon replied. "As you can see Dr Stockholm, we are fierce bear hunters." He then pointed to Christina and teased, "But this one here prefers to talk to them instead."

The jest went over Dr Stockholm's head. She only replied, "Mmm, this is good."

Sheila had prepared a bed for Doctor Stockholm and because they had had a long day they went to bed soon after dinner.

On the last day of the tour, Jonathon showed Dr Stockholm around the camp. Luckily, they had killed a yellow bear recently, so he was able to show Dr Stockholm all processes the tribe did to skin, debone and harvest the meat from the yellow bear kill. After that, Christina took her to visit Mama Bear. *Maybe that could have been better organised,* thought Sheila. Christina took Dr Stockholm to the entrance of Mama Bear's cave. She called out to Mama Bear and waited for her reply. She explained to Dr Stockholm that bears were solitary creatures and didn't like surprise visits. It took a couple of hours before Mama Bear replied. When Christina took Dr Stockholm into the cave and into the part where Mama Bear slept, they saw her. Mama Bear stood up and then sat down. A sign that she was no threat to the visitor.

"Thank you Mama Bear for allowing me to bring you a visitor," Christina said.

Doctor Stockholm looked amazed as she saw Christina talking to the bear.

"This lady may help us stop the corporations from exploiting the indigenous population," Christina continued.

Mama Bear had said that she understood. Christina and Doctor Stockholm didn't stay long. Christina didn't want to impose too long on her friend. After a brief conversation together, they thanked Mama Bear and both left the cave.

Christina was hopeful that the tour they had arranged was good enough to sway Dr Stockholm. But Dr Stockholm didn't make known her feelings of how the application for Heritage Park Status was going. At worst, Christina was hoping the doctor would not tell the corporations about what she had seen. Christina took the doctor back to the tribal camp and then Sheila took her back to Fort Lyndon via the Kingswood that had taken her there before. The shuttle landed and before Doctor Stockholm boarded, she said to Sheila that there were further stages in the application before they would attain Heritage Park status. However, she would keep in contact with Sheila and update her on the progress of the application.

Chapter 28
A Strong United Force

The leadership team were all concerned for Christina's safety as they made preparations to meet the freedom fighter, Truck.

After an open session when only the Leadership team and Christina were present, Christina said, "We need to make preparations to meet Truck."

She had broached this topic before, and the Leadership team had found excuses to put it off. Excuses like, "It's a long way and we need to watch the Womb." All three cars were turning their wheels and they said nothing.

Christina was not dissuaded. "There are many cars that follow Truck," she continued. "We need him in our army."

Suvy lowered his suspension and said, "Christina, you don't understand. Truck has an extreme hatred of humans and we believe that he would not respect you as Queen of the Cars." He sounded defeated.

Christina smirked.

"So, I'm going to sit on a throne, holding a gold sceptre and make Truck bow down before me?" Then she looked serious and determined. "I don't want Truck's respect," she said firmly. "I want his army so we can free all the cars."

Tuti could see that Christina was determined. He also remembered that he'd said he would help Christina raise her army. His engine idled more loudly and he said, "If you are determined to meet Truck, then we need to bring a strong contingent of cars for protection."

How many cars would be needed for a strong contingent? Christina asked herself. She wasn't a bully or a strong person. She liked to get her own way through persistence and gentle persuasion. Finally, she said, "If we bring a large number of cars, it will only aggravate any tensions between us and Truck."

All the cars were flickering their headlights. Christina understood that they were frightened for her.

"If the entire leadership team came with me, Truck would respect you as Keepers-of-the-Womb, even if he did not respect me," she suggested.

Suvy understood Christina's proposition and thought it was possible she was correct, but also thought it was risky. What if Truck did turn on them and killed them? Then there would be no one left to protect the Womb.

"Tuti and I will come with you," he said.

Bluey raised his antenna in query.

"If we don't come back, then we need one of us to look after the Womb," Tuti explained. His engine idled loudly again as he added, "Rover will come with us also."

Rover was a quiet car, but exuded an air of strength. He had acted as a bodyguard to the leadership team on a number of occasions. He was a large four-wheel drive with a metallic copper colour. Christina had known him also and was glad that he was coming along. Though she thought that if the meeting went badly, he would not be able to protect them from Truck's army.

Tuti read Christina's mind. "Truck respects strength," he said. "Having Rover with us will improve our standing with him."

Everyone agreed that anything that could improve Truck's demeanour would be a good idea.

Truck had his throne at the back of a box Valley, not far from the Womb. It still took them all day to reach it, as Suvy could only drive a fraction of the speed that Tuti could. On the way, they passed tribes who were loyal to Truck. So Tuti took the opportunity to greet some tribal members and ask some questions. Some cars were fervent supporters of Truck and advised that it was Truck that drove the corporations away. There were others that had some respect for him as a freedom fighter, but felt he went too far by declaring himself King of the cars. With regards to Christina, most of the cars had either attended her coronation or heard stories about it. So, they understood her role in protecting and maintaining the Womb.

The day was neither short nor long. They had reached the entrance of the valley with a couple of daylight hours to spare. At the entrance to the Valley, there were five large four-wheel drives, who were the guards. They were of different makes and models.

A white Ford Ranger spoke.

"Who are you and what is your business?"

"We are the keepers of the Womb seeking an audience with the mighty Truck," Tuti replied.

"He is King Truck," the Ford Ranger scolded. "Wait here."

Then, the four-wheel drive turned and drove down the Valley. The other guards blocked their path but didn't say anything. Christina and her companions didn't speak either, even to each other. They waited patiently. It had been a long drive to get there, and Christina was tired. She climbed out of Tuti to wait, as the day had started to cool down. It was about an hour and half before the Ford Ranger returned.

"King Truck will see you now," he announced, "Follow me."

As they drove down the Valley, about halfway there, sports cars were parked on either side. They were very impressive cars, who were handpicked by Truck from various tribes to perform this important role of providing an impressive entrance to Truck's throne area. Tuti had known about it from the recollections of other cars who were his friends and had visited Truck. He didn't say anything about it to Christina and Suvy. The sports cars were of different colours, makes and models. They were not ordered in any particular way. Tuti was most impressed by a yellow Lamborghini Huracan and an orange McLaren 720S. That was, until he saw a small Vespa that was black with painted flames. This car had a massive V8 engine that protruded above the bonnet. When they had reached the end of the Valley, they could see a large mining truck parked on top of two Ford F550 flatbed tow trucks. They were both white. On the right-hand side of Truck was a yellow Porsche.

When they were close enough, Christina climbed out of Tuti.

"Why did you bring a human to my sacred Throne Valley?" Truck asked. "Humans are enemies of the cars."

Rover drove up protectively next to Christina, on her other side.

Tuti replied, "She is Queen of the Cars."

"Bah." Truck honked.

Christina spoke gently as if in a trance. "The humans killed your only friend, Three Wheels, when they raided your tribe," she said.

Truck began to raise his back tray.

Christina continued. "As a result, you charged the humans during the raid bravely, but were captured by the Corporation and held in a pen at a fort."

Truck lowered his back tray. He was distressed, but he didn't interrupt Christina.

She continued again. "All the cars around you were afraid of their fate. There were rumours of the suffering the cars endured when they were sent to toxic mines on distant planets in the stars." Then Christina was in awe of Truck as she said, "Your encouragement gave them strength and you took an opportunity to escape from those terrible holding pens."

Christina had an admiring tone as she complimented Truck. "You led a brave troupe of cars and escaped the clutches of the ruthless corporations," she said. "Your actions have inspired many cars who hope for freedom."

"How do you know about Three Wheels?" Truck replied angrily. "He was weak.".

"I find it endearing that you were friends with a disabled car that everyone else had rejected," Christina replied warmly.

As his name described, Three Wheels only had three wheels. Both he and Truck were treated as outcasts by their tribe. Truck, because he was seen as big and stupid, and Three Wheels because he was a disabled freak. They had been close friends and Truck was deeply affected by his friend's death.

"What would you know?" Truck said angrily. "You are just a stupid little human girl." He turned to Tuti. "How does this human know about my history and what would she know about the aspirations of the cars?" he snapped.

Tuti replied mildly, "She is the Queen of the Cars."

Truck leant towards the car on the right to whisper something. The righthand tow truck wheezed under the extra weight. Christina was concerned.

"Are you okay? Is he too heavy?" she asked with concern

"I'm happy to serve my king," the tow truck replied.

"How dare you, human," Truck said angrily.

This wasn't going well, Christina thought. *Maybe it would be better if I didn't speak.*

Tuti spoke up. "She didn't mean offence to you. She is concerned about the well- being of all the cars."

"Why are you here?" Truck demanded.

In a serious tone, Suvy said, "The corporations have come back. We learnt that they enslaved an entire tribe, after destroying a number of cars from that tribe."

Christina sensed that Truck too was concerned by the loss.

"We are raising an army to drive to Central Spaceport," Suvy continued. "We need to act now or the corporations will return and enslave us as they did before."

Truck was deep in thought. For now, he had forgotten about Christina, and was pondering a new battle.

"You are right," Truck replied eventually. "We should have taken the war to Central Spaceport long ago."

Christina thought that maybe she should tell Truck the army would also have yellow bears and hunters. But then she thought the better of it and remained silent. Suvy was doing a good job. If Christina spoke it would only inflame tensions.

Suvy continued. "We need a strong, united force if we want to drive lasting change."

Truck's mood improved. He liked to talk about fighting the corporations. "The defences of Central spaceport are formidable," he said.

"That is why we need your help," Suvy replied.

"Very well," Truck replied. "We will join your army on one condition. All the cars I bring will remain under my command."

"Understood," Suvy replied. "We look forward to benefitting from your vast battle experience."

Truck seemed pleased with the compliment. After they discussed the meeting time that the armies would meet and the location, Truck summoned a blue Ford Escape.

"Take my guests to my fuel ball plantation," he ordered, "so they can fill up before their long journey home."

And just before they left, Truck farewelled his new battle companions. "Onwards friends to victory over the Corporation scum," he proclaimed.

Tuti felt relieved when they had left. Suvy had done a really good job. The meeting went better than he'd thought it would. They had Truck's army and Christina was still alive.

Chapter 29
Amongst Predators

The hypercar really didn't think this was a good idea. Even Christina's father thought that this was a bad idea. He understood Christina's desire to raise an army that included representatives from the whole indigenous population of Plantere. But, reaching out to the car hunters was dangerous. Even Christina's father said it would be very unlikely for any car hunters to join her army.

The hypercar sighed. He had stupidly said that he would be able to find the location of the car hunters, because the mountain described in Christina's grandfather's journal was very distinctive. And yes, he was able to find the location through his network of car chiefs. Christina said that any car that takes her to the car hunters could drop her off early and she could walk the rest of the way. But the hypercar was adamant that he would not leave her to walk. He would take Christina all the way, even though he would be amongst predators.

When Christina first suggested to her father that she and the hyper car would go alone to the car hunters he was very worried. And probably with good reason. He insisted that if they were going, he would come too. The hypercar was parked with Christina at the normal rendezvous point for the mountain tribe. They didn't have to wait long before they saw Samuel coming down the mountain. He had brought Sergeant Blackmore's sword.

"I brought the sword just in case of any trouble," he announced when he reached them.

The hypercar thought that although Samuel was probably proficient with the sword, it would be unlikely that he would be able to overpower the whole tribe. But maybe

Christina's Father's words would highlight to her the gravity of the situation.

They chose a long day to travel. They would be travelling all day and would have to spend the night camped out. They should arrive at the car hunters' location during the next day. In the evening Christina and Samuel stretched out in the hypercar to sleep.

"Do you know anyone from the car hunter's tribe Samuel?" The hypercar asked.

"Only my Auntie Carol," Samuel replied. "She used to visit us occasionally."

The next morning, they left early. The hypercar was feeling worried.

He asked Christina, "What were you planning to say when we get there?"

"That I'm raising an army to drive out the corporations from Plantere, and could they please join us?" Christina replied.

"They make money selling cars to the corporations," said Samuel.

Nobody else said anything for a while.

By the middle of the day, they had reached the camp of the car hunters. As the hypercar approached the camp, he could see the ledges on the mountain. He saw that on the ledges there were structures made out of parts of cars. He saw bonnets, boots and fenders of different types of cars strapped together to make tent-like accommodation. Many cars would have died for their making. The hypercar felt sad and afraid. He parked just below the first ledge of the mountain.

The hunters stopped what they were doing and congregated around the hypercar. All of them had the typical hunter's features of red hair, tanned skin and blue eyes, with a violet tinge at night. When the hypercar saw them, he recognised where their clothes came from. Some people were wearing leather, others cloth upholstery and some vinyl. The clothes all came from seats from captured cars. The hypercar felt even more afraid and sad.

Christina and Samuel climbed out of the hypercar.

One woman hunter said, "What a fine catch you have there, little girl."

Another said, "I can sew you a fine suit out of the leather seats from this little beauty."

Other hunters stroked the hypercar and admired him, until a man said, "The windows aren't broken. How did you catch him?"

"Maybe she used the weapon of the redskins," said another.

The group then looked disapproving, as they realised that neither Christina nor Samuel were redskins, so they shouldn't be using stun rifles.

Christina was offended and haughtily said, "He isn't my catch. He is my companion."

"That's precious," said the first woman.

Everyone laughed. Another man said, "If he is not your catch little girl, maybe I should make him mine."

Christina was angry. She had also seen the structures and clothing. "You will not," she exclaimed and then paused before announcing, "I am the Queen of the Cars."

Everyone laughed again. The hypercar thought that the crowd looked menacing. Obviously, he was not alone. Samuel pulled out his sword from the sheath behind him and stood in front of Christina holding the sword in a defensive position to protect her.

A man with a stern look stepped out of the crowd. Like everybody else in the crowd he had hunters' features. He was quite tall compared to others in his tribe. He also had a beard that had streaks of grey, as he was middle aged. Next to him stood a proud woman who also stepped out of the crowd.

"I am the Chief here." said the man. "Why are you here?"

"I am raising an army to drive out the corporations," Christina replied.

The chief asked, "What do you want from us?"

"I want you to join," Christina said.

Everyone laughed.

"Nobody here will join your army little girl. I suggest you leave before we take your car," the chief said.

Then the proud woman next to the chief spoke. "Samuel? Is that you?" she said in surprise.

"Auntie Carol?" replied Samuel, astonished.

The hypercar saw that the woman had some grey hairs amongst her head of red hair. But other than that, she didn't look old. She had a commanding bearing and stature. The hypercar guessed that she had a leadership role in the tribe. Maybe not the same as the chief, but still very senior.

When Christina turned towards her, she had a vision. Without thinking and in almost a trance Christina said, "You saw your sister's death and it has haunted you ever since."

Auntie Carol was stunned. How did this girl know this? Samuel didn't see it, so how could she know? Her eyes were wide in surprise. Auntie Carol didn't really understand why, but she felt that she needed to tell the story. Normally, she felt that she didn't need to explain herself to anyone. That was how the hypercar interpreted it.

"Angela, Michael and little Samuel were with me. We were going to a car hunter's meeting," she said. Her voice stammered a little. "We had stunned a small car earlier and were driving it to the meeting. Michael had insisted we use his stun rifle to pick off a car rather than try to jump cars in their tribes, because there were only three of us."

She had a worried look as she said this, as she was afraid of disapproval. She crossed her arms. But then she thought *I'm the chief's wife,* uncrossed her arms and stood tall.

Then she continued. "Anyway, we encountered an Audi tribe. We knew our car wouldn't be able to outrun them, so we got out of the car and formed a line. Michael told Samuel to run up the mountain and wait there until we fetched him."

There were tears in Auntie Carol's eyes. She paused as she recalled what had happened. Then she said, "We were lucky, we thought. The chief of the Audi tribe wanted to challenge one of us in a duel. The car was a white Audi TT sportscar. Angela said that she had this. So, Michael and I stood aside."

Everyone in the tribe was silent. The older members knew Angela and knew that she was a very formidable car jumper. Most of them did not know the full story. Only that Angela had an accident while jumping a car.

Auntie Carol continued. "Angela let the car charge multiple times, and the car became frustrated and angry because he couldn't hit her. The car honked loudly and lifted himself on his suspension. She had this, I thought." Auntie Carol wiped her eyes. She said, "The car charged once more. Angela jumped on the bonnet and grabbed the driver's side mirror. It broke. The car must have been older than she thought. When the mirror broke, Angela fell off the car and the back wheels ran over her legs."

Samuel listened intensely. He had never known any of this. Auntie Carol paused and stammered, "Michael was devastated. Before I could do anything, he ran to Angela and continued the duel with the car. Michael had passed his coming-of-age. That was a big achievement for a redskin. But he didn't have the talent to challenge a sports car in a duel. The sports car ran him down."

It was now Samuel's time to cry. Tears welled in his eyes. He couldn't help himself.

Auntie Carol continued. "I jumped the car on the passenger side and was able to escape, because this car was so much faster than the others."

Then Auntie Carol went to Samuel and touched his arm and said, "I'm so sorry I didn't come back for you Samuel."

Samuel said stoically, "It is alright. We all have to make our own way."

Still in a trance-like state, Christina looked at her father and said, "You waited in the mountains until it was nearly dark. Then you came back down to the plains and saw your parent's bodies."

She went to him and gave him a hug. Auntie Carol was still in tears and repeated, "I'm so sorry Samuel." She said it again and again. She was really remorseful. Eventually she stopped and asked, "Samuel, will you join this girl's army?"

"Christina is my daughter," Samuel replied. "She has mountain hunters, yellow bears and most of the cars in her army. I will march with her also."

"My grandniece," Auntie Carol exclaimed.

Samuel lowered his sword. Auntie Carol went over to Christina and gave her hug. Then she stepped back.

"Look at you," she said. "Samuel has a fine young lady." She turned to Samuel and exclaimed, "And Samuel, how did you get so big?" Then she added, "Please forgive us, we are not good with strangers. Stay with us, please."

The hypercar really didn't feel comfortable. The last thing he wanted to do was stay around a place with so many parts of dead cars. Luckily Christina was sensitive to his feelings.

She said, "I'm sorry we can't Auntie Carol. But come with us. My parents live with a mountain tribe. When you are ready to return, Tuti and I can bring you back."

Auntie Carol smiled. "Ok, I think I will," she said. Then she yelled out, "Steven, Katrina where are you?"

A slim young man and woman came out of the crowd.

"This is my nephew Samuel and his daughter," said Auntie Carol. "I'm going with them to their mountain tribe. Samuel and Christina, this is my son and daughter, Steven and Katrina."

For a while Auntie Carol had forgotten that she was the chief's wife. She was just so happy to see Samuel and his daughter. She was relaxed and content.

On the drive back to the mountain tribe, Christina sat in the back with Auntie Carol. They seemed to have a lot to talk about. The hypercar sensed that Christina was really happy. To find a long-lost relative was really special to her. Then when the hypercar was waiting at the rendezvous point for the mountain tribe, he knew that Christina was absolutely beaming when she introduced Auntie Carol to her mother.

In the end, there was some success in Christina's recruitment efforts for her army. Auntie Carol had said that she and her son and daughter would join the army. And she said she may even be able to persuade others in her tribe to join. This was a big thing for her to say. Because she was the wife of the chief, it was her responsibility to follow his lead, not to oppose it.

Chapter 30
The Mustering

Christina decided to go with the mining trucks to pick up the bears. The plan was for a group of mining trucks and other cars to rendezvous with the yellow bears in a valley that was close to the cave where Christina had met with the bears. Also, at that meeting place there would be a number of mountain hunters. Christina was expecting over two hundred mountain hunters. She had organised seventy-two cars to transport them. Once they had picked up bears and hunters they would meet the rest of the army in a large valley at about ninety kilometres west of Central spaceport. Auntie Carol was bringing eight other car hunters, and they were going directly to Central Spaceport.

As part of her contingent, there were a number of cars included that would act as scouts. The intelligence that Christina had though, suggested the corporations had not yet begun to return to the forts and had at this stage only populated Central Spaceport. There were also cars that belonged to tribes that lived in the area of the rendezvous point and others who lived near Central spaceport. Christina had a detailed map of the route they needed to take on her communication panel. This was going to be a long journey. If she was in the hyper car, then it would only take the best part of a day. But the mining trucks were a lot slower, so she expected that the journey would take eight to ten days. One problem she had was determining how many mining trucks to bring, because she didn't know how many bears would decide to come and whether a mining truck could hold more than one bear in their tray. She wished that she was better organised. Maybe she could have asked Mama Bear to try out riding on a mining truck beforehand. And maybe she should have arranged with her to send a message to the other bears to ask them their intentions. In the end she decided to bring twenty-one mining trucks. She thought she should over cater.

Yes, the meeting included thirty-five bears, but Christina had estimated hopefully that ten bears would join her army. Another issue she had was how to feed her army. There was no problem with the cars, as they could feed upon the fuel ball plantations along the way. They would just have to manage the feeding as there would be many thousands of cars. The hunters would bring their own food of dried yellow bear meat. Christina was worried about that, as the hunters would be standing side by side with the bears in her army. She had asked Jonathon to tell the hunters to be discreet with the handling of their food. Yellow bears never carried their food. They would instead, graze on what was around them. So, Christina had asked the hunters to harvest plants and moss, for the bears. It was a huge undertaking as yellow bears did eat a lot. Sheila was in charge of organising the women in different tribes to collect the food for the bears and then to organise the men to pack it all.

When her contingent reached the rendezvous point, Christina could see some hunters and bears on the mountain ridge. They had been waiting for her to arrive. Once they saw Christina's cars, they descended down the mountain. The hunters let the bears go first. Christina counted twenty bears. That was amazing. She was surprised that so many had volunteered to come. None of the bears looked comfortable descending into the valley. When they arrived, Christina could see that some of them were shaking.

Christina waited for the last bear to reach the valley before she spoke to them.

"Thank you so much for coming with me."

The hunters only heard a deep rumbling sound from Christina, but the bears were listening.

Christina continued. "I know that being in a valley is incredibly uncomfortable for you."

Christina sounded very sympathetic. In the language of the bears, she was able to express her depth of feeling which was quite impressive.

"And you will need to ride in the back of mining trucks for a number of days, an experience you have never had before." Christina paused here, so the bears could process what she had just said. After a short silence, Christina spoke again. "Also, I understand that spending time with humans that hunt you will be challenging. Please come to me directly or ask Mama Bear, if there is anything I can do to make this journey easier."

Christina then turned towards Mama Bear to ask after her welfare and thanked her again for making this possible. When the hunters had descended, Christina hugged her parents and Jonathon. Jonathon had brought his bear hunting spear, which Christina wasn't pleased about. Samuel had left his Easy Shooter stun rifle at home and instead, brought Sergeant Blackmore's sword. *I guess there could be a battle Christina* then thought. Perhaps the men did need to bring weapons. Then she spoke to all of the hunters.

"Thank you so much for coming with me. And thank you for providing the food for the yellow bears."

Christina looked around at the faces of the hunters. They all looked very serious and apprehensive. She continued. "We are going a long way from home and I know that you will be travelling with companions that you would not be used to. Please come to me directly or ask Jonathon if there is anything I can do to make this journey easier."

A mining truck could carry a medium build yellow bear without discomfort to both the truck and the bear. Christina was relieved. She was also relieved that she had brought twenty-one trucks. *All is well that ends well,* she thought. She had got away with being disorganised this time. There were enough cars to take all the hunters too. When everyone was in a car or on a truck, they left.

The journey was uneventful, until just before nightfall. It wasn't a long day, so the weather was mild and not too warm. The cars could drive through the night, but the humans and bears needed rest. Yellow bears sleep a lot, and they had been unable to sleep when travelling in the back of a mining truck. So Christina ordered the contingent to stop and set up camp. She chose a site where there was a fuel ball plantation. When they were unloading, Mama Bear approached Christina.

"Little One," she said. When she knew that she had Christina's attention she sat down and started her request. "My brothers and sisters aren't comfortable sleeping out in the open on a plain. They need a nice reclusive cave to feel safe."

Christina thought, *of course!* She should have thought of that. However, it was nearly dark so there wasn't anything Christina could do about it now.

"I'm so sorry Mama Bear," she said. "I should have thought about that." She paused and thought for a bit, and then suggested, "The trucks and cars could park in a formation that would give the bears cavities to sleep in."

Mama Bear didn't look convinced.

"Let's try this out for tonight and if it doesn't suit, we could stop earlier tomorrow, so that the bears could find a cave in the mountains," suggested Christina.

Not that Christina was pleased with that option though, as it would make a long journey even longer. The next morning Christina asked Mama Bear about how well the bears had slept.

"Little One," she said, "the parked cars helped, but most bears had trouble sleeping."

Christina looked disappointed, so Mama Bear suggested that they try this again tonight, as today was going to be a short day. Then maybe tomorrow, they could find a cave, as it would be a longer day, and the following night would be long as well.

The camp broke early so they could cover as much distance as possible that day. Scouts that were sent out the previous day met with the contingent part way through the day. They reported that there was no activity in any of the forts. So once again, the travelling during the day was uneventful. The bears did sleep better that night, but in the morning, they were all looking forward to sleeping in a cave that night.

This time Christina did stop to make camp earlier, so the bears could look for a cave in the nearby mountains. She wanted to go with them and thought it was a good idea to bring Jonathon and her dad as well. She met them and explained.

"Daddy, Jonathon," she said. "The bears want to find a cave to sleep in tonight."

They both knew that they had stopped earlier today, so the bears could do that.

"I think it may be a good idea if we come with them," Christina continued.

Jonathon was not convinced. "Christina, any cave that they may find probably already has a yellow bear inhabitant who won't be pleased that twenty bears have invaded his territory."

"I know. You are right," Christina pleaded. "But this journey is hard on the bears."

"Okay, then we will come with you," Jonathon replied.

They went with the bears to the mountains. They climbed up the ridge into the mountains. None of the bears knew this area, but they all had the ability to find a cave. Christina never understood how they could do that. When she had ever asked Mama Bear about it, Mama Bear just shrugged and said she didn't know. It wasn't long until they found an entrance to a cave. Mama Bear called out and they all waited. Even though they didn't hear a reply immediately, they still waited. Just when Christina thought the cave was uninhabited, a yellow bear replied from the cave.

Mama Bear took charge and said, "I apologise for the intrusion and the trespass." She waited to hear what the response would be. She didn't hear anything, so she continued. "There are twenty of us. Could we please sleep in the cave for just one night?"

For a while, the occupant didn't reply. He was probably taken aback by the request and may have been frightened. When he did reply, he announced that he would meet them at the entrance of the cave. The yellow bear living in the cave was an older bear. When he came out, his fur stood on end. As with most older bears, his coat was frayed and he had some grey hairs. He had been living by himself for a long time. He was not only surprised to see twenty bears on his doorstep, but there were three humans as well. He was stressed, but he made an effort to not let it affect his behaviour.

"Papa Bear, you have been living in peace for a long time," said Christina. "I apologise for disturbing you."

Christina noticed a deep sadness in this bear. She really did feel bad that there were so many of them at his cave entrance. "None of us wish you any harm," she continued. "We are on a long journey and need a place to sleep for tonight."

If the yellow bear was surprised at seeing humans with twenty yellow bears, he was even more surprised to hear one of the humans talk to him. He hesitated and he didn't know what to do.

Mama Bear took the opportunity to speak. "Can I please tell you, our story? Everyone else will wait outside and if you want us to leave, we will."

The older bear acquiesced, so Christina, Jonathon, Samuel and nineteen yellow bears stayed outside to wait. Christina feared that it may be a long wait. Their story was a very long one for a yellow bear to digest. The other yellow bears didn't appear to be worried though, so Christina saw that as a good sign.

It was dark before Mama Bear returned. She said that the older bear would allow us to sleep in his cave tonight. Mama Bear organised the group to sleep close together, as far as possible from the older bear. That included the humans as well. The other bears didn't mind though. They were just grateful to be able to sleep in a cave tonight. Christina took the opportunity to express her gratitude to them for coming on this journey. Most of the time Jonathon and Samuel didn't know what was going on. Christina had to give them frequent updates.

The next morning the twenty yellow bears were refreshed and ready to proceed on their journey. It had been a long night, and it was exactly what they'd needed. The older bear whose cave they were staying in, was in a deep conversation with Mama Bear. He looked much more relaxed. Christina thought that maybe he was relieved the night was over and his visitors were leaving. She left the cave and went outside. There was a cool breeze on her cheeks. She realised that she missed being in the mountains, as she looked around her. The breeze felt different up here, cleaner and fresher.

After some time, Mama Bear came to Christina outside and said, "Our host has a request."

Christina was intrigued. Then she thought that the request would be that they leave immediately. Mama Bear said, "He wants to join your army."

This time it was Christina's turn to be surprised. Apparently, the older bear had a daughter. The last time she visited, she had complained about noisy helicopters in her territory. After that he didn't hear from his daughter for a long time. So, he went to visit her. He found her dead body in the mountains and he knew she wasn't killed by the mountain hunters, because she was left with just her bones missing. The mountain hunters always used the whole bear. *Mama Bear would have been a sympathetic listener to the older bear's tale*, Christina thought. Maybe he would have been by himself for all these years since his visit to his daughter's cave. Even yellow bears needed others to talk to when they are grieving. Maybe it was good that they had visited him. Anyway, Christina was grateful that he was joining her army. Then she thought it was lucky that she had brought twenty-one mining trucks.

Chapter 31
The Gathering

Christina's army was gathered just outside the Stun Cannon range of Central Spaceport. Central Spaceport was a formidable installation. It was located in the middle of a wide valley and was spread out across the plains. Not only did it have a large number of buildings, it had an extensive range of car pens. They were used to hold captured cars before they were transported away. It also had three landing ports for space shuttles. Central Spaceport was defended by three high walls that surrounded the town with stun cannons mounted on each. The walls formed inner and outer squares and facing each direction, there were five stun cannons on each wall. That is, there were sixty stun cannons in total. Each wall had a platform near the top for soldiers to stand on. On the inner wall, there were four missile launchers. One for each side of the square. Just outside the outermost wall was a row of used car tyres.

Christina thought it had been a significant achievement to assemble such a large army of cars, bears and hunters. She looked over the plain and she marvelled at the size of her indigenous army. So many makeshift soldiers who risked everything to help with her plan. Christina was extremely grateful. She would try to lead them responsibly and with care. Christina's contingent of cars was four thousand while Truck brought three thousand. They now had to decide how to proceed from here.

The War Council consisted of Christina and the Womb leadership team, Truck, Mama Bear and Jonathon. They stood or parked around in a circle in an area just behind the army. It was mid-morning of a long day, so it had started to get warm. During their meeting Truck was advocating strategies for attack.

He lifted himself on his suspension and spoke.

"We should concentrate all our forces to the front of the Spaceport, so we will only have to defeat fifteen stun cannons," he said.

Christina noticed the sweat on her face and was silent. She had wanted to raise an army as a show of strength. She hadn't contemplated fighting a war. When no one replied to his suggestion, Truck was worried.

"We should prepare to attack immediately," he said.

Christina had a lot of respect for the fighting abilities and bravery of Truck, and she had raised an army. She could hardly blame Truck for wanting to use this army to wage war against the Spaceport.

"Truck, you are a brave and competent warrior," she said. "We are lucky to have you with us." Christina was earnest about that, but she had a feeling that they should wait. "I know you are keen to attack," she continued. "That is why you are here. But I think for now we should wait."

"Wait for what?" Truck bellowed and he lifted and dropped his back tray.

"Wait for a response from the spaceport," Christina replied.

"I know what their response will be," Truck roared. "They want to capture and enslave us. We must fight and rid ourselves of these vermin."

"We may not need to fight, if the Spaceport surrenders or makes concessions first," said the hypercar.

Truck turned to Christina. "Queen of the cars, Bah!" he said mockingly. "You are no queen. You are just a scared little girl." Then he lifted himself on his formidable suspension and announced, "I will take my army and attack. If you have any spine, you will join me."

And with that, Truck left the War Council, which now needed to decide what they wanted to do. One of Truck's conditions for joining this army was that he remained in charge of his contingent. This had been agreed. But the authority of the rest of the army belonged to the War Council.

"I have travelled to many forts, but none of them were as well defended as this one," said Jonathon.

Jonathon had never fought in a battle before, but he could be brave. You needed to be brave to hunt bears. However, he appreciated how difficult it would be to overrun this fort. Christina explained just what had happened to Mama Bear, who didn't have anything to say. This whole situation was very foreign to her. Christina felt for her friend. She was worried for the bears if they did indeed need to attack. There was some silence in the War Council.

Christina broke it by saying, "Truck is a warrior and he is very brave. But I think we should wait."

There was no dissent. The rest of the War Council supported Christina's position and decided not to join Truck's attack.

Auntie Carol, Sheila and Samuel waited together with the rest of the hunters near the front of the gathering. They could see a large number of cars breaking away from the main army and making a formation.

"I wonder what is happening?" Sheila asked. "It looks like those cars are going to attack. But no one has told us to prepare for battle."

"I have never seen so many cars together," said Auntie Carol.

Samuel didn't say anything. It was going to be a hot day. He was breathing deeply and was preparing himself for battle. He had never fought in a battle before but had thought that maybe he would be brave. He had tried to persuade Sheila not to fight, but she said she needed to support their daughter. Sheila looked towards the spaceport and saw three helicopters flying towards them. They had speakers attached to the front of them.

When they reached the cars, a huge voice bellowed, "You are illegally gathered here. Disperse now or we will be forced to take action."

They repeated this a number of times as they flew around Christina's army.

When Truck heard the speakers on the helicopters, he thought that this is the response they had been waiting for. He summoned his deputy, Captain Land Rover.

"Organise the attack as we planned." Truck said. "I will speak to the cars before we charge."

He waited for his deputy to arrange all the cars, before he went to the front of them.

"Today, will be the day of our final victory over the humans," Truck announced. "We will send the last remnants of this scum back to the stars and away from our home." He had venom and intent in his voice. He now encouraged his army further. "Take courage my friends, he shouted. We have fought before together and have vanquished our enemies. We will do it again today."

The cars in his army honked their horns and they chanted, "Truck, Truck, Truck."

The noise was deafening, and Truck was pleased. *This will be the last attack*, he thought. *Today will be the day of final victory.* He waited for the chanting to stop and then moved to one side. He saw that his army was ready.

"Attack!" he yelled.

At the front of his army were the small and old cars. He was using his tried-and- true strategy of sending his weakest cars first to absorb the fire of the stun cannons and allow for the entire army to get close to the fort. Some of the small cars were Holden Astras, Ford Lasers, Fiat 500s, Volkswagen Beetles. The old cars were varied in size. But even the big ones were slow. Truck took his position with the heavier vehicles, and they followed the sports cars.

When the front line charged, initially they were only in range of the stun cannons. They were still too far away from the spaceport to be in range of the soldiers standing on the platform. The small and old cars were brave. As they drove, they raised clouds of red dust. They drove as fast as they could and they kept on driving, even when they saw their companions stunned. Truck could see the clouds of dust they stirred as they charged, and he was pleased. However, the impact on the charging cars from fifteen stun cannons was severe. The pulses from the cannon fire reverberated across the plains. The stun cannon fire was relentless. So many cars were stunned. They had never before charged this number of stun cannons.

Truck thought as he watched the attack that his army had not gained any ground. *Maybe the larger cars will have more success.* However, at this stage nearly all the small and old cars had been stunned. The larger cars had bigger engines and included sedans such as Ford Falcons, Holden Kingswoods, Holden Commodores, Honda Accords and

Mazda 5s. These cars could reach higher speeds, so Truck was hopeful they would make some progress. The large cars roared down the plains, and like the small and old cars they drove as fast as they could. They too raised clouds of dust. Even though they had seen their smaller and older comrades being stunned, they bravely made their assault. The stun cannons fired continually at them. The cannon fire continued to be relentless.

However, the missile launchers had not been used. Maybe the humans thought that they could beat the attack with stun weapons alone. *That would be to their folly,* thought Truck. He also thought with determination, *we will prevail.* So many of the larger cars had been stunned but they still made some progress. Truck acknowledged to himself that the large cars had driven bravely and had made as much progress as they could. He was hopeful that the next wave of cars would be able to take his army to the outer walls. The larger cars made enough ground to be in range of the soldiers with stun rifles.

There were about fifty soldiers standing on the outermost wall platform and they were armed with the most sophisticated Easy Shooter stun rifles. The soldiers didn't use silencers on their stun rifles so, as they shot, the cars could hear popping sounds. The shots from the stun rifles had a devastating impact on the charging larger cars. The rifles were semi-automatic and were deadly accurate. Very soon, most of the larger cars had been stunned. Truck was hopeful though that they would reach a point where they would be inside the stun cannon shadow. That is, stun cannons cannot shoot at anything that is very near to them.

But the problem for Truck in this attack was that there were stun cannons on the two inner walls, so the shadow would be narrower.

The sports cars made their attack. They were led by Famous 46, Wildcat and Greeney. Now the soldiers on the wall were all Corporation employees. They didn't get a commission on any cars captured as a result of their shooting. So, they shot at any car and had as their primary objective the defence of the spaceport. Also, they had an extensive storage of ammunition. At Central Spaceport they would never run out of ammunition. The sports cars were very fast and it looked to Truck that they would reach the outermost wall. They too, drove bravely as their powerful engines roared, even when they saw their companions next to them get stunned. Sports cars were always seen by other cars as great heroes and an inspiration to all cars. Perhaps today they would carry the day, Truck thought. Let the humans on the wall hear the engines of the sportscars and be afraid.

Truck and the other heavy vehicles were nearing the outer wall. The trucks and Land Rovers with bull bars would be able to ram the wall and bring it down. By the time the heavy vehicles had reached the outer wall, nearly all the sports cars had been stunned. The heavy vehicles were the only cars left in this attack. They rammed the outer wall. The soldiers on the platform retreated as they knew their wall would soon be brought down. There were at least fifty soldiers ready on the next wall. The heavy vehicles breached the outer wall, but the breach was narrow, so the vehicles could only trickle into the area between the second and outer walls. The soldiers were able stun the vehicles easily as they entered the area. Truck was determined. This was his battle to win. He rammed the outer wall to try and make the breach wider. He reversed and rammed over and over again. After each time he honked loudly.

Eventually, he brought a large section of the wall down. He thought, *this human scum will not prevail*. But when he had made the breach wider, he was in the line of fire of the soldiers on the second wall. A number of soldiers fired at point blank range. Truck was a formidable car. A single stun round would not bring him down. Perhaps not even five or six stun rounds. But this time Truck took over twenty rounds. Enough to stun him.

Chapter 32
Hosting the Inter Solar System Union

When David Kessler woke, he knew that today would be a difficult day. Yesterday, he had reports of a convoy of cars, yellow bears and hunters making their way to Central Spaceport. Also, today he was hosting a meeting between the Inter Solar System Union and the corporation heads. No one knew what the meeting would be about, but he was expected to attend. David wished that he knew what it was about. He really didn't like surprises. David was the Marshal of Central Spaceport. Central Spaceport was a combined facility and was not run by any of the corporations that had a presence on Plantere. An independent organisation was engaged to manage the security of the spaceport.

This organisation was called Stellar Security and David had been employed as the Marshal for three Plantere years. He had been with Stellar Security since he left the police force on a space station, twenty years ago. He was still a young man, perhaps thirty-five Earth years, as he had made some long-distance space travel. He was medium height with a slim build. He had a full head of short black hair and he was clean shaven. His features were unremarkable, except for a scar above his left eyebrow. As did all soldiers working at Central spaceport, he wore a grey uniform with the Stellar Security logo on his chest. The uniform also included a wide brimmed hat, but David wasn't wearing it today, because he would remain indoors.

Even when all the corporations had abandoned Plantere, Stellar Security had maintained a garrison at the spaceport. Luckily, David had thought, that extra soldiers had arrived only a few days ago, as it was expected that the corporations would resume operations soon.

Since David had to attend the meeting with the Inter Solar System Union, he delegated the defence of the spaceport to his deputy Kevin Baker. He met with Kevin in his office. David leant forward and made eye contact with Kevin.

"Can you please give me an update?" David asked.

"Yes, some of the cars have left the main army and appear to be making an attacking formation. I believe that the freedom fighter Truck, is leading them," Kevin replied.

"Have you sent the helicopters with speakers, demanding that they disperse?"

"Yes, Sir," Kevin replied.

"How many of the cars do you think will attack us?" David asked.

"About half of them," Kevin replied.

"I know that is a lot of cars," David said, "but I think we should be able to keep them out."

David was worried about the number of cars attacking, but was sensitive to political machinations and he wanted his deputy to understand them as well.

He maintained eye contact and continued.

"We are hosting the Inter Solar System Union today and they are sensitive to violence. So can you please only use stun weapons to keep the cars out."

This was a difficult position to take, as the defence of the fort was paramount. But David didn't know why the Inter Solar System Union had called this meeting and that made him worried.

"Yes Sir," Kevin replied.

"If there are any important developments please come and get me from my meeting." David said.

"Do you know what this meeting is about Sir?" Kevin asked.

"No, I don't," David replied.

The meeting with the Inter Solar System Union would be held in the main conference room at the spaceport. It was a state-of-the-art hologram meeting room, that was designed to accommodate multiple inhouse and remote attendees. Essentially, there were hologram chairs, where images of remote attendees would be shown. The chairs were placed around a large oval shaped table with a marble top and metallic legs. The meeting room was rectangular with a large cylindrical platform at the front. This was used to show three-dimensional video recordings. David understood that two of the corporation representatives would be attending remotely. Apparently, the Inter Solar System Union had requested that the corporations send very senior managers and that if at all possible have them attend in person.

The Corporation attendees arrived first. They talked amongst themselves. The main topic of conversation was whether anyone knew what this meeting was about. Because they were hosting a meeting with the Inter Solar System Union spaceport, catering was engaged to provide refreshments. David ordered a cappuccino and nibbled on a croissant. He didn't enjoy them though, as he was worried about what this meeting was about. David really didn't like surprises.

Doctor Stockholm arrived fifteen minutes late. She went to the front of the meeting room and sat down. She didn't apologise for being late or make any pleasantries to the other attendees. Instead, she began formally.

"The reason why I called this meeting, is that there has been an application for Heritage Park status for Omega 24A," she said.

She was very business-like and indifferent to the fact that the news might be a shock to the Corporation attendees. And it was a surprise to all the other meeting attendees as well. No one looked as if they were happy with the prospect of Heritage Park status.

"One of the phases of the application process is to consult other stakeholders," Doctor Stockholm continued.

Not all the corporation attendees knew a lot about Heritage Park status, but the member for the Attacca Corporation did. His employer was expelled from another world that had been granted Heritage Park status, even though they had made multiple representations against it. It was a difficult and challenging exercise. The member's name was Paul Shipperd and he was quite young to be in senior management. He was tall, with blonde hair and blue eyes. In the Corporation, he was seen as a go-getter.

"This is totally unnecessary," said Shipperd. "There is nothing of heritage value on Omega 24A. It is a desolate wasteland." His tone was dismissive. "If we can find profit here, then that should be encouraged."

The other corporation attendees gave their support.

"Hear, hear," they said.

"What about the cars?" Doctor Stockholm asked.

"They are just machines," the member for the Epsilon Corporation answered. His name was Jack Rogers and he was an older man, nearing retirement age. He was of medium build and had grey hair. He sported a goatee beard. He had been sent to this meeting, because the more important managers were busy on other matters.

"Very intelligent ones, it would seem," Doctor Stockholm quipped. "They don't seem to be happy with the operations of your corporations," she continued.

"Nonsense," said the member of the Iowa Corporation, Jacob French. "They are ambivalent to our operations."

Jacob was a balding middle-aged man and was very fit. He just happened to be in the area when the meeting was called, so he had volunteered.

"So that is why you build very secure forts to keep them out?" Doctor Stockholm observed.

"They are savages," a remote attendee answered.

The management of the Horizon Corporation were very worried when they'd found out that the Inter Solar System Union had called a meeting on Omega 24A. They did have other managers in the area but felt that they needed someone with experience in dealing with the Union to attend the meeting. Colin Brannot was the one who qualified, so he had attended remotely.

"Are they machines or savages? Which is it?" Doctor Stockholm asked pointedly. She was beginning to enjoy the meeting, as she liked the adversarial tone it was taking. Colonel Jefferson represented the Clements Corporation. He was the same Colonel Jefferson who organised the mission to capture a tribe of cars. The Clements Corporation was very pleased with his operation and promoted him to head of operations on Omega 24A. But the Colonel hadn't had experience with the Inter Solar System Union, and didn't appreciate the power they could wield.

"I don't have time for this. I have missions to organise," he said dismissively.

There was a knock on the meeting room door. *Oh no,* David thought, *what now?*

Kevin was at the door. *Something bad has happened* David thought. He was already feeling very stressed. He stood up and apologised.

"I'm sorry, there is an operational issue I need to deal with," he said.

"There was an attack," Kevin announced. "The cars broke through the first outer wall, but we have subdued them now."

Kevin sounded relieved, but David could tell there must have been some anxious moments. David had hoped that his instruction to only stun cars would not jeopardise the defence of the fort. It appeared that it was okay. But only just. He ran his hand through his hair.

"All the cars that attacked have been stunned," Kevin said. "But I didn't think it was safe to go out and retrieve them, because there still is a large army out there."

Kevin was a professional and was rightly risk adverse. However, he was happy to announce, "We did capture some of the heavy vehicles and we have the freedom fighter, Truck."

Jacob French stood up and leant forward over the table towards Doctor Stockholm. He went on the attack.

"Who made this application for Heritage Park status?" he demanded. "We have heard rumours about a journalist we hired, Sheila McSporran."

Jacob stared at Doctor Stockholm and observed her carefully to see if she reacted when hearing the name. But her face revealed nothing, and she didn't seem perturbed by Jacob's aggressive behaviour.

"She was missing presumed dead, but she could be actually living in the wilderness of Omega24A," Jacob continued. Then with distaste he added, "If she is still alive, we see her as a person of dubious character."

Doctor Stockholm replied with her stock standard statement on privacy. "The details of a Heritage Park application are confidential. I would invite you all to read our privacy statement on the Inter Solar System Union site." She wanted to get this meeting back on track so she added, "Your job here at this meeting is, if you are opposed to the Heritage Park status, then provide me with compelling reasons why it should not go ahead."

"Very well," Paul Shipperd said. He stroked his chin and continued. "We provide employment opportunities to the local human population. That is, the hunters."

"Hunting cars?" Doctor Stockholm asked.

Jacob leant back in his chair and held out his arms in an open gesture. "The cars are merely animals," he said firmly. "Everyone on the Planet sees the benefits of our operations here." Then with a friendly persuasive voice he stated, "You should ignore the scurrilous individual who made this heritage park status application."

Doctor Stockholm ignored that last statement. "So, you are saying the cars are not intelligent?" she asked, as she looked down her nose over her spectacles. When Jacob didn't reply she said, "I understood that their value in the mines where they are sent to work, was their intelligence."

There was some silence in the meeting. Doctor Stockholm continued.

"Let us explore the assertion that everyone on the planet sees the benefits of corporation operations," she said.

Doctor Stockholm was beginning to make her case. And

she really was enjoying this meeting. Step by step she would craft an argument.

"From our contacts here, we learnt of an army that was making its way to this very spaceport," she said. "So I instructed a helicopter pilot to do some surveillance."

David Kessler thought, *oh no the union knows about the car attack*. Luckily, they hadn't used any live ammunition. But this meeting is about Heritage Park status. *This is bad,* he thought.

"Let us look on the hologram platform to see just what the pilot saw," Doctor Stockholm invited. She swung around on her chair and started the recording. The helicopter had flown around the perimeters of the army, filming as it went. The cars were at the front, while the yellow bears and hunters were at the rear. The yellow bears and hunters were sitting down, and the cars didn't have any particular formation. It seemed to those in the room that the army was just waiting.

"Hmm there it is, the army. Yes, there are a lot of cars, probably thousands." Doctor Stockholm was playful when she described what was on the screen. "And look, there are some hunters. I can also see yellow bears." She touched her chin and added, "I thought they only lived in the mountains and never ventured onto the plains." Then she suddenly changed her tone and became forceful. "But here they are in this vast army preparing to attack us."

No one in the meeting said anything. The film showed that when the helicopter made another pass, a large number of cars, perhaps nearly half that were there, left the main group and organised themselves for attack. The cars lined up to form a front and were grouped, with the small and old cars at the front, followed by large cars, followed by sports cars and then the heavier vehicles.

Today was full of unwelcome surprises David Kessler thought. He also thought he needed to say something to allay the fears of the meeting attendees. "We repulsed an attack by the cars and captured Truck the freedom fighter," he said. "Please don't be concerned about your safety here."

"Truck the freedom fighter?" Doctor Stockholm asked. "What an apt name for what we have here." Then she turned to David Kessler. "Yes, I have the battle recorded." she said seriously. Then in a lighter tone she continued. "But before we view it, I would like to thank Marshal David Kessler and his team for keeping us safe while we have our meeting."

Doctor Stockholm wasn't one for pleasantries. She had thanked David to make a point. David was also aware of this but he didn't feel thanked. Doctor Stockholm then played the recording of the battle. It was brutal. Wave after wave of attacking cars were stunned, but the cars had gradually made ground to the outer wall. Then when the heavier vehicles were knocking down the outer wall, the helicopter stayed in position. The recording finished with Truck widening the breach and being stunned by multiple rounds.

After the recording had finished, Doctor Stockholm said forcefully, "The cars breached the outer wall of the most impregnable fort on the planet." Then she added thoughtfully, "Car hunting is a risky business."

Colonel Jefferson cracked his knuckles and said firmly, "That is why the Union should leave it to the professionals."

Doctor Stockholm smiled and replied, "That is the trick, isn't it?" She stood up and then leant forward on the table towards all the attendees and looked around. Eventually, she stared at the Colonel, looking down her nose over her spectacles and said, "That is what will be decided."

Chapter 33
The Conclusion

Christina was deep in thought. She lamented the defeat of Truck's attack. They had come so close to victory. Maybe if she had joined his attack with the cars loyal to her, they might have prevailed? What should she do now? She was no General. Could she lead her army in battle? She had no strategy. Tuti, Suvy and Bluey were with her at the front of the army. They were not in range of the stun cannons.

"We need a meeting with the War Council," Christina said.

She really did need some advice on how to proceed. But even though she valued the opinions of the Womb leadership team, Jonathon and even Mama bear, she knew that none of them had ever fought in a battle. Although she didn't really like Truck, she missed him now. Just as she had this thought, overhead, she could see a helicopter flying towards them. Undoubtably, to broadcast a message demanding that they disperse, or maybe to gloat over their victory over Truck's attack.

She was then surprised, when she saw the helicopter land in front of them. The wind from the rotor, caused her to cover her face, because of the cloud of dust it raised. She couldn't see who was in the helicopter. Eventually the rotor spin slowed, and the dust cloud cleared. Christina was even more surprised when she saw Doctor Stockholm disembark from the helicopter. Doctor Stockholm seemed unperturbed by the noise of the helicopter. Christina thought that Doctor Stockholm probably rides in helicopters often.

Over the noise of the helicopter Doctor Stockholm asked loudly, "Is Sheila McSporran about?"

Tuti answered with equal loudness, "She is probably with the hunters. I will fetch her."

The helicopter pilot turned off the engine. A short time later Tuti returned with Sheila and Samuel. Sheila wasn't expecting a visit from Doctor Stockholm so, like Christina she was surprised.

"What is this about?" Sheila asked.

"Your application for Heritage Park status has been approved," Doctor Stockholm announced.

Christina was stunned. "What does this mean?" she asked.

Sheila was beaming when she answered. "The corporations will no longer be able to hunt cars."

This was such good news. Sheila felt vindicated for all her efforts to apply for Heritage Park status.

"That is correct," Doctor Stockholm confirmed.

Christina was still stunned, but her next instinct was to affirm that all her cars were okay. She was their motherly Queen. "What will happen to Truck and the other captured vehicles?" she asked.

"They have been released," Doctor Stockholm replied. "We need to meet to discuss what will happen now," she continued. She directed this to Sheila, as she was the one who had made the Heritage Park Status application. Doctor Stockholm's demeanour had changed. She now saw Plantere as part of the Union family, instead of an aspirant. As a result, she was softer and warm.

"My colleague Trevor Baker, will be able to help you," she added. "The full resources of the Union will now be at your disposal." Doctor Stockholm really was very welcoming and wanted the transition to being a Heritage Park to be as smooth as possible. "Gather together a leadership team who will liaise with the Union over Heritage Park matters," she continued. "We will meet with you tomorrow in the grounds of Central Spaceport."

And with that, Doctor Stockholm boarded the helicopter and left.

Christina summoned Truck to meet her at the location of the army. Truck was deflated after his defeat, but relieved to be released. He was covered in dust and seemed to be very tired. Truck believed it was Christina who had ordered his release, so that was why he answered her summons.

When he arrived, Christina said, "I hope you have fully recovered?"

Truck indicated that he was okay, but he was very quiet.

"You should have waited with us rather than lead your own attack," she said. "Three-thousand, of my children were stunned in battle," Christina said sternly.

Christina actually didn't blame Truck for wanting to attack. He was a General and a freedom fighter. That is who he was, but Christina really didn't like the way he'd parked on top of two tow trucks when she visited him before, so she continued her reproach.

"You represent cars who want freedom from oppression, who just want to live their lives freely and without fear," she said. She wanted to acknowledge Truck's role and also affirm his position amongst the cars as a brave freedom fighter. "You have a heavy responsibility, and you need to advocate for the least of the cars." Christina continued.

Truck was deep in thought. His defeat weighed heavily on him and he was contrite, which was very unusual. Showing this to a human was significant. And maybe it signalled that he was beginning to respect Christina's role as Queen of the cars.

He lowered himself on his suspension and replied, "Very well, I will do my best."

Christina was pleased with Truck's demeanour. Maybe she might be getting through to him that yes, he was a brave freedom fighter but that he shouldn't lord it over the cars that follow him. She continued. "I need you to attend the meeting with the Inter Solar System Union to discuss our Heritage Park status," she said. Then forcefully she added, "The cars that follow you need representation."

Truck had nothing more to say. His window wipers were moving slowly. Christina interpreted Truck's demeanour to be one of acquiescence, which she was pleased with.

The next day Christina, Sheila, Samuel, Jonathon, Auntie Carol, Tuti, Suvy, Bluey and Truck all assembled in the grounds of Central Spaceport. It was mid-morning and the weather was mild. They were outside, so that the cars could attend the meeting. Doctor Stockholm introduced her colleague Trevor Baker, who managed Heritage Parks in the area. He was a middle-aged man with short dark hair of medium build, clean shaven and dressed formally. Trevor took the group through the procedures and protocols of being a Heritage Park. They were quite involved, but Trevor assured the team he would be available to assist at any time.

Christina had something important to say. "We need to trade with other planets." She was worried that now the corporations were gone, Plantere wouldn't have access to products they need. She continued. "There are specialised parts for the Womb that we need. I want to be able to regularly service the Womb, but I haven't been able to do so because we don't have the spare parts."

Auntie Carol added her lament. "My tribe are car hunters and we used to sell cars to the corporations, so that we could have goods from other worlds."

"Of course you can trade with other systems," Doctor Stockholm replied warmly. "The difference is now you can do so on your terms."

Christina was deep in thought and said, almost to herself, "What do we have to trade?"

Trevor had heard this question many times from new Heritage Parks, so he gave his standard answer.

"One feature that Heritage Parks have in common, is that they attract a lot of tourism," he said. "There are many folks out there who have retired and travel vast distances to the next tourism destination."

"If you give them the same tour you gave me, I'm sure Omega 24A will become a popular tourism destination," Doctor Stockholm added warmly.

"What about us?" Auntie Carol asked.

Jonathon spoke up. "I saw Jumpy Benson do his jumping thing with the cars," he said. "It was pretty entertaining to watch. Maybe the tourists would enjoy it also."

The cars in the meeting were silent on this. Maybe they didn't like being jumped. But after some shared glances between the cars of the Womb leadership team, Suvy spoke up.

"I guess if the cars had the passenger windows wound down, then maybe it would be okay to jump cars," he said.

After the meeting, they farewelled Doctor Stockholm and Trevor Baker as they left in their shuttle. They would keep in touch. It was now time for Christina's army to return home. She was grateful to all who had joined her army. She understood how difficult it had been for the yellow bears to travel on the plains. She appreciated that for the hunters, it was difficult, because they were facing other humans. Then she thought about her brave cars. They had to face their enslavers. Many had fought in a battle.

As they began their journey back home, she had tears in her eyes. Not tears of sadness, but tears of relief. Tears of happiness and tears of deep emotion. Three large sedans volunteered to take Auntie Carol's car hunters home. Auntie Carol gave Christina and Samuel a hug before they left.

"Don't be strangers," she said to them. "Please come and visit me anytime."

Both Christina and Samuel were so glad to have an extended family. And yes, they would visit Auntie Carol as often as they could.

The remaining contingent would take longer for the homeward journey, so that the yellow bears could sleep in caves every night. The yellow bears were taken back to their rendezvous destination. Christina thanked them all once more.

Mama Bear said, "Little One, this journey is one we will always remember. Thank you for including us."

Mama Bear joined the other bears as she wanted to spend time with them. In fact, unusually the other bears felt the same. The experience had been so profound, that they needed some company for a while. For Mama Bear, her life was changed so much since her meeting with a little human girl who could speak the language of the bears. A change for the better Mama Bear thought. Once the bears had been dropped off, Christina, Sheila, Samuel, Jonathon, Tuti, Bluey and Suvy drove back to the base of the mountains, near Jonathon's mountain tribe.

As they got out of the cars, Sheila asked Christina, "What will you do now, Sweetheart?"

"We believe Professor Heidenburg constructed other wombs, so we thought we could search for them," Christina replied.

This would be a new venture for Christina. She was Queen of the Cars, so she would do everything she could to protect and maintain the Womb, or wombs, if they found more. She loved the cars, and the Womb leadership team was as much family to her as the mountain tribe. That was who she was, and she had known it since she was a child.

Samuel and Sheila waited at the bottom of the mountain ridge and watched as Christina and the cars left. Sheila thought back to when she first arrived on Plantere. It was so harsh and desolate. A place that was difficult to survive in. She would never have thought that she would meet a scrawny, shy young man and have a beautiful daughter with him. Now Plantere was her home. She loved how Samuel had built a house for her.

She smiled to herself and said to Samuel, "Come on Darling, let's go home."

Samuel didn't say anything but put his arms around Sheila and gave her a hug. Before he had met this beautiful woman, his life was a struggle of survival. Now they had a family and a home to go to. Samuel would forever be grateful.

Jonathon broke the silence and said, "Come on love birds, let's go. I'm hungry."

Doctor Stockholm was in her mother ship. She had a journey to her next Heritage Park applicant. This one was further away. It would take a couple of months to reach. There was a community of Psionics who lived in a world where it rained every day. Apparently, they had amazing powers. The community was led by a powerful Necromancer. But the community was persecuted by people in the neighbouring worlds. As Doctor Stockholm read the brief again, she sighed. It was a never-ending task. There were so many wondrous worlds out in space. Before her ship left, she took the time to look at Omega 24A. The planet filled her window. It was a yellow world with thick red veins. As her mother ship moved away from the planet, it became smaller and the red veins became thinner. So, it looked like an ancient pottery piece whose glaze was cracked with age. And then, as the mothership moved further away, the planet looked like a smooth yellow billiard ball orbiting one of the largest red suns in the galaxy. It was the only planet in the Solar System.

The spaceship left the Solar System light years away from Earth and hundreds of years into the future.